THE FANTASTICAL MYSTERY OF RITTERHOUSE FAY

ISBN 978-91-979188-6-2

Cover design by Leif Sodergren

LEMONGULCHBOOKS
www.lemongulchbooks.com

To the memory of
my wonderful, pioneering
grandmother, Vera,
also known as Ma.

*

To the memory of
my other, poetical, grandmother, Bessie May.

*

Yet again,
to the memory of the
magnificent Betty Marsden,
actress extraordinaire,
comic genius, humanist, muse
and dearest of friends.

*

And, as usual, for Keif,
he knows why.

Also by
Donovan O'Malley

LEMON GULCH
New Edition of the Comic Cult Classic.

A darkly comic moral tale -- 12-year-old over-grown precocious misfit Danny narrates his surprising adventures in his search for acceptance in "a uncaring world".

THE IMPORTANCE OF HAVING SPUNK

A lesbian couple's comic pursuit of the perfect donor in the Scandinavian wilderness -- a Comic Novel with a twist to the battle of the sexes, and a nod to Oscar Wilde.

THE JIMMY JONES SKANDAL

The five-year-old with a forty-year-old mistress.
A humorous bedtime story for grown-ups.
Illustrated by the author

SKANDALEN OM JIMMY JONES

Translated to Swedish
by Leif Södergren

OUR YANK

A Comic Novel -- an American student comes of age in Oxford during the Cuban Missile Crisis of 1962

Coming soon:

LOVING WILLY
AND OTHER STORIES

LEMONGULCHBOOKS
www.lemongulchbooks.com

THE FANTASTICAL MYSTERY OF
RITTERHOUSE FAY

BY
DONOVAN O'MALLEY

A NOVEL IN
FOUR PARTS

It is with fire that blacksmiths iron subdue

Unto fair form, the image of their thought:

Nor without fire has any artist wrought

Gold to its utmost purity of hue.

Nay, nor unmatched phoenix lives anew

Unless she burn.

Michelangelo

prosopopoeia:

n...the personification of an abstract thing. [Latin from Greek prosopopoiia; prosopon 'person' + poieo 'make']

PART ONE

1

Never start a novel on the same day you quit smoking. Just ask fifty-four-year-old Rita as she slumps wearily over her typewriter loathing her hair, loathing the magenta pimple at the very tip of her nose, loathing the shiny bottom on her jodhpurs, loathing starting a novel on the very same day she has quit smoking. But most of all loathing being *fifty-four* and, by her lights, nearly invisible.

Teetering here at the very threshold of invisibility and God knows what else, she sucks noisily on her long ivory but empty cigarette holder, thinks: I'm a sodding mess, and reads the first and only line of her first novel-to-be:

> Desiree Doolittle had attempted suicide exactly fifty times, once for each year of her meaningless little life.

Rita sighs and types: *She was a sodding mess.*

*

"He'll smile soon," whispers Fay; her cupid's bow lips glistening, her cheeks roses in high summer. She's in the first seat behind his glass partition, can see his curious eyes in his rear view mirror. The handsome young bus driver seems about to turn and smile.

"Hugs and kisses are just around the corner!" sighs Fay.

She is on a London bus, m'dears, doesn't know quite how she got here but here she is. Ritterhouse Fay, the very personification of love, longing for a hug, pining for a kiss as she purses those cupid's bow lips, flirts outrageously. But the young driver does not turn his head, does not smile. Fay frowns and instantly loses interest.

Fie, Fay! Love is not love that alters where it alteration finds! But then, this is only an exercise; practice for the ordeal to come. You, my dear, are on Square One of a mini-saga of love applied and love denied. A *game*. For what is love, caring and cruel, but a game?

Fay smooths a bit of soot from her frayed black skirt, murmurs

"Soot? Where could *soot* have come from? A fire?"

She pats the keys in her paper carry-bag, they jingle. Comforted, she exults -- in a very special way. A way that I have taught her.

"Who *are* you?!" cries Fay.

I hold my so-called *tongue*.

"I'm going home," she whispers. "Home to my comfy little nest. Home is where the heart is!"

Keep that thought, Fay. Then imagine a dark closet, chock-a-block with tumbled stacks of yellowing newspapers, five full to bursting, red plastic carry-bags and other acutely flammable debris. Amongst these disintegrating broadsheets, these tattered tabloids, lurks a wholly stunning carpet. Ach! See it glimmer, see it pulse! Hear it rejoice for conquests yet to be! For it is the shape, m'dear, of things to come.

Our mystery begins.

Ninety-nine-year-old Mrs Taylor -- she of the flat above Rita-writer, she of that dark, chock-a-block closet, thumps her way across Rita's ceiling.

"Must the bleeding woman gouge her heels into my bleeding ceiling every bleeding step she takes?" mutters Rita not realizing that Taylor's cane, not her heels, is the culprit.

Mrs Taylor, a red plastic carry-bag in her hand, a cluster of inconsistent thoughts clattering in her head, drops into a cushioned, carved oak chair, hangs her cane and the carry-bag on its arm. On a table before her is a gigantic pile of old postcards and a magnifying glass; beside her, a small rubbish bin. She snatches up the magnifying glass, grabs a hand-tinted postcard of a towering sequoia tree with a shiny 1930's roadster protruding from its massive, tunnelled-through trunk. She squints at the postcard's crudely drawn signature: a heart with an arrow. Clucking, she kisses it and stuffs it into the red carry-bag then plucks another card from the pile, glances at it and without reading it drops it into the rubbish bin. Both cards are in the same handwriting so why does she kiss one, m'dears, and chuck the other? Don't ask. She wouldn't tell you even if she could remember. Sometimes she can't remember. This morning she can. But don't ask. She won't tell you. It's none of your goddamned business!

Bottles clatter from the hall just outside her door.

"Mrs Taylor, milkman."

Taylor freezes, holds her breath, listens.

"Mrs Taylor?"

Taylor is motionless till she hears the retreating footsteps of the milkman down the stairs. She opens the door and as quickly as her arthritic old wrists will permit snatches up a pint of milk and a half of cream. A bill flutters from the bottles. She ignores it and slams back into her flat just as the door opposite opens.

Hugh appears. He's twenty-six, a lithe, wavy haired lad, newly awake and robustly erect under tight, blue briefs. He yawns, grabs his two pints, shuts his door softly.

On the sofa-bed of his tiny flat lies a sleeping figure buried under bedclothes. Modestly tucking in his taut crotch, the barefoot Hugh pads into his kitchen, takes a whistling teakettle from the cooker, makes two cups of instant coffee. He douses each with milk, sets them on a wooden tray and returns to the sofa bed where he sits and plants a steaming coffee into a hand that shoots out from the bedclothes. The cup disappears for an instant then reappears, is set on the sofa table. The hand creeps into Hugh's briefs, clutches his stubborn erection. He laughs, gives the hand a playful smack. "Don't you *wish*!"

Gets a mite intimate here. Not everybody's cuppa. We'll move on – but gimme just a *min* -- alrighty?

Fay steps off the bus into the wind. Her eyes are unaccustomed to this merciless assault of gasses and glare. She brings her fist to each eye in turn, wipes, grimaces, ponders -- her fate? No m'dears, that's *my* terrain, thank you very much indeed.

But must she change here, to another bus?

"I'm certain I've been here before," muses Fay, sooty finger to cupid's bow lips. "Bus or Tube? Tube or bus?"

A million experiences are crammed into her head (mea culpa) and have crowded out the minutia that most people, mired in commonplace, do by rote. So what is it with Fay? Is this gal simply nuts?

"Who said that?!"

Fay spins round. People rush by. "Who said that?!" she cries, "Who?!"

Rita-writer rereads her precious, now altered, two sentences:

> Desiree Doolittle had attempted suicide exactly four times. Once for each ten years of her meaningless life...

"Too old. The pathetic cow is still too old," sighs Rita. But suddenly inspired, she types furiously, using *all* her fingers just as she has been taught at that excellent evening typing class where *novels* are feverishly encouraged. A terrible thumping erupts from above.

"Quiet down there!" shouts Taylor through the paper-thin floor.

Rita stops typing. The thumps cease. She growls, rips the page from her typewriter, crumples it, tosses it away. Perishing for a cigarette, poor thing, she continues to type.

People are crashing into Fay. So many people! Are these swarming people after her cardboard suitcase? Her handbag? Her battered carry-bag? "These are mine! Mine!" she cries and clutches them closer.

Flowers! She must buy flowers!

She pauses before a street vendor. Why must she buy flowers? "Do I like flowers? I once *loved* flowers, adored them! When I was a florist. But I can't afford them now."

The street vendor overhears, takes pity, hands this shabby, almost pretty, nay, almost *beautiful*, creature a tiny wilting bouquet with his compliments (it probably fell off the back of a lorry – *looks* like it, says me). Fay curtsies, murmurs "Mummy loves flowers. I must send Mummy a card and a posie, tell her precisely where I am."

But Mummy already *knows* where you are, dearie.

The street vendor turns away to help a customer. Fay pouts, speaks to the back of his head, "Honestly, I would send a card if I had her address. In any case, I won't write till I have good news -- *and* Mummy's address, of course. I seem to have misplaced it. But I can always write to someone in authority. They'll have dear Mummy's address. You can always count on someone in authority."

Huh?!

"Abdullah will help me! He's such a sweet old man. "Salaam-a-lay-kum, Abdullah!"

Fay trips happily down the street, grins as this sweet old man smiles in her head. Who needs rude, uncaring bus drivers, or fickle flower vendors, or swarms of pushy people when sweet old men can be so easily summoned up -- and right smack in the middle of ones own head!

The crowd surges by her, whirl-pooling down the steps into the Underground -- The Tube. "What a funny little name!" she giggles, "The Tube. The tubey-tube-tube!"

She hugs her belongings to her, careful not to further bruise the fragile bouquet. Wind whips her shabby black skirt against her legs. "I have superb legs!"

She squints down at them (cinders are flying!), "Where did I get such really superb legs?"

Don't you remember, Fay? Don't you remember *anything*? Ach. Bear with me, m'dears. We've a seriously succulent saga on our salver. Plus daring deeds to do.

"Shut up!" cries Fay, "Shut up, you alliterative monster, whoever you are!"

This outburst prompts several scurrying persons to turn abruptly and collide with one another. "What fools these mortals be!" cries Fay, calling the kettle black. She turns to seek further transport. That's precisely how it came to her, so peculiarly put: to *seek further transport*. She'd much rather fly, of course. Now where did *that* come from?

Forty-year-old Nelly, lavender safari shirt tucked into orange corduroy trousers (a safari shirt tucked *into*?), sits alert on her sofa drinking the last of her morning coffee. She listens without emotion to Rita's typing directly across the hall and Mrs Taylor's thumping from the floor above. She's seen Rita glaring in the street and knows her name from the call box and the mail table -- mostly bills, no personal mail at all. Well, hardly ever.

Nelly is no snoop, m'dears.

Rita, thinks Nelly, is not necessarily unfriendly -- must have a lot on her mind and simply *appears* to glare. People are like that especially when they've got a lot on their minds.

That's right, good-natured Nelly. That's right, m'dear.

Nelly has only lately begun to nod at Rita and has never set eyes on the shrieking Mrs Taylor. For Nelly has lived here at Number 13 only a month and, though a naturally friendly woman, she is too shy to initiate even casual contact, especially with people who glare and people who shriek.

"Quiet down there!" screams Taylor through the floor at Rita.

Nelly hardly notices -- she has a lot on her mind as well. For example, Bill, who two floors above, now starts down the stairs.

Nelly gulps her coffee, fastens her magenta duffel with its yellow, fake deer-horn buttons, grabs some books and waits just behind her door, a spider in her web, although she would prefer not to put it that way.

Bill reaches the landing and begins the last descent. Nelly forces a happy smile on her face. She's terrified! As breezily as she can, she enters the hallway. But Bill doesn't appear, has forgotten something and returned up the stairs. Nelly jumps back into her wily web behind her door and crouches. Rita's typing continues.

"Quiet down there!" shrieks Taylor.

Bill's footsteps again! Nelly rushes into the hall, locks her door and without turning drops her keys directly in his path. It isn't Bill! It's Hugh who bends to retrieve the keys, Hugh who hands them back to her and who with a courteous smile is on his way. There's no time to drop the keys again -- Bill has rocketed by directly behind Hugh and is already out the door. He hasn't even seen her! He must have something really serious on his mind. His divorce? Is he divorcing his wife? Is he married? Nelly hurries down the steps and joins Bill and Hugh at the bus stop. So many people, thinks Nelly, have so much on their minds.

Especially *these* days, my dears.

At her window Rita scowls and sucks irritably at her empty cigarette holder. Who are these three persons who have just exited this house and now stand waiting for the 7.55 Red Arrow? One must know about people to write about them. Why do they not speak to her? Because she never speaks to them? They aren't at all friendly. Is she? Why has her acting career collapsed? Is it her temper? Is it her cognac? Or is it simply a dearth of good roles for impossibly difficult, frequently tipsy, fifty-four-year-old-semi-visibles in jodhpurs? Too late for revelation, Rita. Give it a rest, dearie. Get back to your novel, you churlish old baggage. But she won't. She frowns down at the three of them there on the street waiting for their bus. Who is the other man? The one that poor dishevelled cow can't keep her eyes off? Is he new here too? What do I care? I'm writing a novel certain to be made into a film in which I shall take the leading role. At fifty? thinks Rita (54, dearie!). Get real, darling! You, a thirty-year-old? No. But how about:

Desiree Doolitle had attempted suicide twice.
Once when she was twenty and once again,
on her thirty-seventh birthday, yesterday. And
she looks a sodding mess!

"These *Tube* people, sitting opposite, are staring at me," whispers Fay. "I will disembark at the next stop. Take a bus from there. I cannot bear these unpleasant people just now. Not with this... soot on my skirt. Not with this fire in my mind. But my destination comforts me. Home is where the heart is."

That's right, Fay. Keep those bleeding home fires burning (I chuckle appropriately).

Fay wishes this faint laughter in her head would fuck off -- the comments too, these altogether inappropriate comments. They're so unlike her.

Still waiting at 8.15 for their 7.55 Red Arrow, Bill and Hugh nod indifferently at one another. Neither speaks; Hugh, because he feels the silent Bill prefers it and Bill, because he's got a lot on his mind -- Nelly is correct -- ever since he moved here three weeks before.

Nelly has only begun taking this earlier bus because Bill takes it. She has never encountered Hugh except on the street or stair but unlike glaring Rita he's always nodded and she has always nodded back. Now, though she nods, she doesn't speak to Hugh because Bill might think she fancies Hugh and not him. Gosh! It's so complex!

A pity *you* aren't, dear Nelly. But you do have your points. I'm beginning to like you. It's crucial, darling, that I do.

Nelly wonders if Bill is gay, hopes not, just this once. Because she needs, at forty, more than a confidante; is just the tiniest bit wary of lending, yet again, her firm, broad shoulder to cry on. True romance would be so much nicer. With a sickening jolt she suspects that her lavender safari shirt (tucked *in*) and orange trousers are a disaster. Gosh! She'd only meant to appear appropriate – I mean, she does teach pottery classes. She pulls her magenta duffel closer and feels extremely, what is that posh word that makes bad taste sound exotic? A student in her pottery class used it. Dishabille? Dishevel? It's disha-something.

"Sweet Jesus!" mutters the recently observant Rita from her

window, "Somebody give that rag-bag a mirror!"

The Red Arrow arrives, disgorging a noisy crowd of office workers. Nelly, Hugh and Bill climb on. Rita watches the bus disappear in the morning traffic. Who are these three people? Why has she never met them? "They've just walked out my front door not ten feet from where I stand," murmurs Rita, "One must know people to write novels about them."

"Wait!" screams Fay, at a departing bus as it moves on leaving her in a choking cloud of exhaust. She'll catch the next one. But she's getting closer. Closer to home? *Home*, Fay? Pardon me while I laugh. Oh I'm not nice, I admit it. Who says I've got to be nice, m'dears? Who says I've got to be anything? Though, of course, I am *everything*. Ask Fay. On second thoughts, don't.

Taylor waters a window box of geraniums. She pulls a face at the office building opposite. It has stolen her morning sun. Damn it to Hell! Must Progress always be disfiguring? She'd fought that office building tooth and nail -- when she'd had teeth -- and what a bite she could deliver! She and her litigious mind had held up construction for a month and when they finally built it she had even contemplated burning it down, had tried black witchery, a few accoutrements of which -- including a tiny thatched shrine -- lie hidden even now at the back of her hall closet beside *a rolled-up, extraordinarily beautiful rug* (mark this again, m'dears) and great stacks of very, very old (*tinder dry*! – mark that as well) newspapers. Plus five crammed full, red plastic carry bags. Crammed full of precisely what, you may ask? Be patient, poppets. Yes, the closet in question is indeed that chock-a-block one, and its portentous potpourri, for reasons of our own, requires reprise.

Taylor, fraught, had abandoned her witch's spells when that unfortunate window washer fell two stories and was seriously injured while squeegeeing beneath her stony witchlike gaze and her shrill incantations. That was many years ago, wasn't it, Mrs Taylor? Since then you've learned to take this Venerable Art more seriously. Quite seriously. Though it comes and goes, doesn't it, love? -- comes and goes like ducks on a dirty great pond.

Taylor's gnarled old wrist suddenly goes limp. Her watering can is thrust askew and a torrent springs over the edge of the flower box, cascading against Rita's window below. Rita leaps back. It isn't the first time nor will it be the last. But mordant Rita, unfazed, sucking at her empty cigarette holder is thinking hard about something else: With a face-lift she can be thirty...seven? No, ducky, still too old to be Desiree. Rita shudders, considers a cognac -- not quite yet, what's the time anyway?

Too soon old, Rita, too late, smart. A woman over thirty is of questionable interest. A woman over forty is ectoplasm and over fifty-five completely invisible.

A bit too Sci-Fi, love -- not the stuff of movie dreams. And your *own* theory, darling, so don't go blaming *me*.

Sod this man's world, thinks dying-for-a-cigarette Rita. But she must be literarily practical. The Desiree of a successful novel must be no older than thirty -- thirty at the very outside though she may look a sodding mess.

Another bus pulls up. Another crowd is disgorged for that office building opposite. They disperse and here standing alone on the pavement is a waif of a woman in a full, black, sooty skirt. She has a cheap, cardboard suitcase in one hand, a paper carry-bag on one arm, a drawstring handbag over that arm and a forlorn little bouquet of flowers in her hand. She is about thirty -- thirty at the very outside -- and she looks a sodding mess.

2

"What's her game?!" is Rita's first reaction to this woman who pauses beneath her window and to whom she has taken an instant dislike -- though she has no idea why (and I ain't tellin'). Is it the soot on the woman's skirt?

My dears, be assured this will all come back to haunt Rita again and again. If only she had known then, known for certain, known what Fay was about and acted upon it. Tripped her on the stairs and frightened her away, dropped a flower pot on her head, cut her lying throat! Anything. Anything! Before it was too late.

But, my jodhpured, aging scribe, interference with Destiny can... bugger! Let's get on with it.

Taylor too, from her flower box, watering-can limply clutched, sees Fay who now has one magnificent leg up on her cheap suitcase studying a map she has taken from that tattered paper carry-bag. Her pause has become, *through no fault of her own*, a pose.

"Pass on witch," mutters Taylor, as it takes one to know one, "pass on, witchy-witch-witch."

For Fay is dressed entirely in black and the wind whips her full skirt about those excellent legs in a peculiarly disturbing and witchlike way, a way only too familiar to old Mrs Taylor. When she remembers.

Here at her flower box the strangest feelings come wafting up from Fay to Taylor. Taylor shudders. Something is wrong. Very. Or right. Very right. Perhaps *Mr* Taylor -- Oscar -- for all his shortcomings, knew precisely what he was talking about? (I'll vouch for that) Then, alas! At the delicious edge of comprehension, this thought is lost. As it always so frustratingly is.

Boil! Boil! Trouble and toil, my little chickens!

"Hush!" clucks Fay and checks the house number and reconsults her tattered map. "Yes, oh yes! This is Number 13. This is home!"

Fay looks up, sees Rita and Mrs Taylor peering at her from their respective windows, one above the other. The middle-aged woman with the impossibly long cigarette holder is very attractive, thinks Fay. But obviously flamboyant. I've had enough flamboyance, thinks Fay, to last a lifetime.

Whose lifetime, love?

"What? What was that?" mutters Fay and shoots a singularly captivating smile at each window. Singularly uncaptivated, both women turn quickly away. Nonsmoking Rita because nicotine abstinence makes her churlish, nonagenarian Taylor because it takes one to know one. And the postman only nods perfunctorily as he passes.

Poor Fay. Undaunted, with her suitcase and her handbag and her large paper carry-bag and her little bouquet, Fay ascends the entrance steps, and at least one square on our board game, to the house of Rita and Mrs Taylor and Nelly and Bill and Hugh. It is a smaller house than she'd anticipated for Pimlico, only three floors, and two of its natives are not friendly and the postman is a cold fish. Never mind. Fay never receives mail.

We saw to that.

"What?" asks Fay, who stands for a moment, tangling in the wind, searching for my whisper's source.

Or sorcer*ess*, m'dears!

At the top of the steps Fay sets down her suitcase and her little bouquet and sticks her nose close to the brass bell plate. She squints and carefully reads the names in the slots and repeats each aloud.

Flat 1 Rita Lambert
Flat 2 Nelly Wilkinson
Flat 3 Mrs O. Taylor
Flat 4 Hugh Woods
Flat 5 William Hope-Jones
Flat 6...

"What nice names!" cries Fay who is certain she will soon win over those two window-gazing recalcitrants. "Everybody needs friends. The world turns on friendship. On love! My goodness! Yes! Yes! Yes!"

And other things, darling. As you well know. Or, in any case, *I* well know.

But Fay simply will not contemplate these other things. Not now. She also detests this mysterious prompting that began quite recently. Only this morning in fact, on that empty bus. Though she cannot at the moment precisely recall anything prior to this morning. She also firmly wishes the subject of *other things*, whatever that irritating voice meant, had not been brought up -- against her will, brought up. "Things?" she murmurs, "Other things? What other things? I know of nothing."

This, I must admit, planted thought, this 'nothing', clangs like an alarm bell through her head. "How can I know nothing?"

Easily, dear.

"What?" says Fay. What was that?"

Oh, my. Ach.

Fay must soon write to someone in authority and solve this maddening matter once and for all. These ridiculous words and ideas that clatter about in her head! "My goodness! It isn't that difficult, writing to someone in authority. There's E-mail. Oh yes!" says Fay, "I know all about E-mail. And I'll have it!"

You won't, love. Not if I have anything to do with it. And I do.

Fay taps her forehead several times. I mercifully allow the buzzing to stop. "Ah," she sighs, "That's better."

She's done far too much today, has poor Fay. She needs rest. Soon. Soon.

"Soon," she whispers, "Yes, soon. I shall lay my head upon my very own plumped pillows on my very own beddy-bye. The Fay needs rest. Soon. Soon."

She scans the bell plate again, polishes it with the corner of her tatty cardigan. Flat six is empty. She sits on her suitcase and takes a scrap of cardboard and a tiny pair of scissors from her carry-bag. Holding the cardboard against the empty slot, she trims it to size. On this newly cut card, with a much chewed biro, she prints neatly: 'RITTERHOUSE, FAY'. She slips the card into the sixth slot, stands back and admires it then gathers up her handbag and her paper carry-bag and her suitcase and her little bouquet and skips, yes, skips into the house! "My house!" cries Fay, "My own house, at last!"

Calm down, ducky, you're only one amongst five. Though things must change. All in good time. And for good reason.

In the hall Fay pauses at a table scattered with the morning post. Her imagination leaps with the beauty of belonging. Belonging *somewhere*. "I know this place! I am at home! There's no place like home!"

Copy that! No place like home. And positively no place so bright as Fay's frivolously fancied future.

"What is so frivolous about my future?" asks Fay of the first fleeting shadow to pass her way. This shadowy something, however, pauses, puzzled to be questioned so early in the game, then passes on. As bade, of course, by me.

Fay, meanwhile, is attracted to the pile on the post table, carefully notes both senders and addressees, and repeats the names to herself as she had the names in the bell plate slots. "My friends," she murmurs to herself, "Surely my friends-to-be."

Her finger darts to an over-mascara-ed eye, wipes away a muddy yet completely sincere and *surprisingly* difficult to produce tear on its wispy way to a wide grin.

Rita senses the passage of Fay outside her door, wonders why Fay pauses, wonders where she is going. That suitcase – Sweet Jesus! Is she a new tenant?

Grist for your mill, dearie.

"Grist for my mill," says Rita, as though it were an original thought. Bless her, bundled in her aging naïveté. And bless you, too, m'dears. Bless us all! We'll need it.

Taylor shudders, holds her breath as Fay ascends to Taylor's floor. That peculiar feeling -- much closer. Taylor's heart bumps. Fay moves on, thank God! up the stairs. Taylor sighs. People are pests. Let 'em send postcards if they must. But let 'em stay away. Like Oscar and his tortoise-shell spectacles and his over-tinted, over-stuffed sequoia! "Yes! Stay the hell away! You hear me, Oscar? Do you hear me Oscar Taylor?! Stay the hell away!"

You'll regret that remark, old thing. *Very* old thing.

This shifty stranger in swirly black, thinks Taylor, let her disappear at once! Why does old Mrs Taylor feel this way? Oh yes. It takes one to know one. One what? Taylor pauses, almost remembers, enjoys a blessed moment of quasi clarity, chuckles to herself.

This is all partly your fault, old woman. In a way -- though I am the valid villain.

Fay climbs to the top floor, pauses puffing and fumbling in her carry-bag before flat six on the worn though thoroughly welcoming, and it must be admitted, rather over-excited hall carpeting. She finds a key and thrusts it into the keyhole. It won't turn -- finds another key, the door sighs, tries – this key won't turn either. Fay begins to cry tearlessly (sorry about that, m'dears), pokes deep, finds another key, turns it, the keyhole accepts it with a smile that only I, at the moment (for your enjoyment), care to note. The door swings open.

If one listens closely there is laughter to be heard. No one is about so where is it sodding coming from? From on high? From inside Fay's finely sculpted skull?! From me? Take yer choice, m'dears. Certainly Fay doesn't know. Nor should she -- or the jig is up.

Sobbing now easily produced tears of joy, Fay grabs up her handbag, her suitcase, her paper carry-bag and that pathetic little bouquet. She rushes into the flat, slams the door behind her.

Her mind is awash in happiness. She'll have what she never had. Friendship! Intimate conversation! Tolerance! Kindness! "Oh, Mummy," whispers Fay, prostrate on her newest friend, a bare and severely stained though amiable mattress, "Oh, Mummy, me so happy me want to cry!"

"Quiet up there!" shrieks Taylor.

"What?" murmurs Fay into that dank, though attentive mattress, "What did you say?"

Were her new neighbours already welcoming her? "What?" peeps the exhausted Fay again and again till she sleeps and her daydreams become nightmares of half remembered pursuits and captures and endless reprises of said; nightmares always fashioned from the same recipe. Nightmares that embrace fires, wind, high-pressured hoses spurting torrents of rib-cracking water; a great deal of soot -- and those endless pursuits and captures. Who are the pursuers and who the pursued, she is not certain.

Lie there, Fay. Dream your desperate dreams, twist, turn, burn, writhe on that wretched bed and amuse us for a time. Alrighty, dear?

"What?", mumbles Fay awakening. "What did you say and who are you?"

Only laughter.

"Who's laughing?" peeps Fay, "Who?"

But laughter can lull. Mine can. And Fay is soon asleep again.

This morning's excitement, this black clad, sobbing stranger, has tired Taylor. Her irritable cane thumps diminish, stop. Her tousled, white head flung back, her lips making delightful little flapping sounds, she sleeps, plunging into a dream about that oddly familiar witch-woman in the swirling skirt in the whirling wind. Cane snugly hooked by the red plastic bag on her chair-back, she snores into her quivering though crucial postcard mountain.

Rita's novel has taken right off (naïve creature)! Her eyes glow with What Might Be as she dances into the kitchen to rescue whistling kettle from cooker. Pirouetting, she fills an intricate coffee device from several small packets of exotic blends, mixes them carefully with a tiny spoon, pours in the boiling water. Humming merrily, she watches the fragrant coffee trickle through.

Rita's happy. Why not? Perhaps her literary efforts can lead to something -- not peter out like every other project she's attempted since she gave up on acting, or rather, acting gave up on her.

"Golly, I feel odd. And I don't *even* know why," whispers Fay as she lies on her bare-mattressed bed, the only furniture in this tiny, one room flat. She watches a ray of weak morning sun struggle across the worn linoleum floor. Her forlorn little bouquet, stuck in a jam jar, is on the sill of the only window in the darkish room. "Such a tiny window. Maybe that is why I feel odd," whispers Fay.

I doubt it, darling.

"I am sick to death of tiny windows," she sighs, "Tiny windows that lead to nowhere."

You are going *somewhere,* aren't you, my dear? From square to square with every roll of our allegorical dice, right round our board, our little *jeu de la vie*.

"What?" asks Fay, wiping the sleep from her eyes, "I don't speak French."

Nor do I, darling. Isn't it obvious?

Fay ignores me, glances anxiously round, pulls herself up with a tiny grunt, smooths her rumpled, mouse-coloured cardigan and wanders barefoot to the bathroom. She examines her face in the basin mirror. She isn't pretty. Was once (she is certain). Not any more, at the moment, anyhow. Not sure why. She studies her mauve eyes, red nose, flaming cheeks, her... Ach! Her mousy hair! She can scarcely see where her mousy hair leaves off and her mousy cardigan begins. "I am clay," she murmurs, "Hair, flesh, cardigan, feet and all. Where has my brief happiness gone?"

A question, my dear, that begs, in many a life, an answer.

"Why," continues Fay, "has the thrill of this unfamiliar privacy so suddenly evaporated?"

Curiously put, ducky. But understandably so in the circumstances. And *such* circumstances.

Fay ruffles her hair with both hands, violently musses it, begins to cry again and, crying, runs her finger over the porcelain top of the WC. Dust! Germs! Grime! Enemies all!

Ach, m'dears, unhygienic toilet seats are a sin against Nature.

Still crying, Fay springs from the bathroom, throws herself at her suitcase, snatches out a threadbare tea towel. "If I cannot be happy I shall at least be tidy!"

Still crying, she rushes back, falls to her knees and thoroughly dusts the outer parts of the WC, taking particular pains with the toilet seat which she polishes to a high gloss. Still crying, she hitches up her skirt -- she wears no panties today -- squats on the now shiny toilet seat and pees. Oh, how she pees! She wipes her eyes on her sleeve and cries some more, pees some more. Cries and pees. It is delicious.

She suddenly hears snoring and fainter still, typing. The snoring comes from directly below her feet, at the front of the house. It must be that nasty old lady who frowned at her, frowned at dear little Fay, and abruptly left her window this morning.

The typing, however, is from the ground floor though she can't tell from which side of the house. She listens, relaxes. Rested, her hearing is phenomenal. She can hear the tread of small creatures from great distances. Perhaps not an ant, but certainly a salamander through stillest water. "Honestly I can," she whispers, "My hearing is acute."

You don't have to convince *me,* ducky.

As a child, Fay had amazed her sister with her keen sense of smell, her extraordinary eyesight, her acute hearing. Later, she had amazed her sister's woman friend whom she, Fay, didn't trust. It was her sister's friend's shoes -- big, masculine shoes (like mine) -- that Fay couldn't abide. She remembers them perfectly, lit by flames. Now everyone wears shoes like that -- though not necessarily lit by flames, not necessarily planted menacingly on crumbly blocks of mossy stone. Not necessarily silhouetted against a grey and roiling El Greco sky.

The typing continues. Fay squats on the toilet listening. Like a small radar antenna her head oscillates slowly from side to side. She will soon pinpoint the typing's source. Her hearing is phenomenal.

That is why she can hear me. When I wish.

3

Rita hasn't felt so good in months. She believes in herself again. She has a Future (who hasn't?). She stops typing, sips coffee from a fine, china cup, stuffs a cigarette into her ivory holder, lights it and puffs perilously though happily. Sod nicotine stains. Sod lung cancer. Her eyes gleam as she peruses the nearly full first page of her novel-to-be (such naïve but not *completely* displaced, confidence!).

Rita grins into the mirror beside her writing table and likes what she sees. Her unrouged cheeks pulse with pink life. Her hair does not offend. That odious pimple has popped, subsided. Ecstasy. Is it the cigarette? She takes a deep, satisfying puff and exhales. Partly. Is it the coffee?

But wait! Is it *magic*? Mais oui, darling! Certainement!

Rita picks up her fine china cup and is about to take another fragrant sip when a sharp pounding at her door nearly startles her out of her jodhpurs. Her fine cup topples to its saucer and this morning's most irritable Rita returns.

"Bloody Hell!" she screams. The pounding at her door continues, "Bloody, sodding Hell!"

She hears moaning. Moaning?! Then more pounding, more moaning! Rita marches to her door, flings it open. Here is that bizarre woman, her mussed mousy hair a wreath of writhing snakes, her lipstick smeared, her garish mascara awash.

Fay sobs, moans, sways in the door, pausing before this next square, is just able to utter through her tears "I'm your new neighbour!"

Enter The Ritterhouse Fay!

Choking back great gusts of flamboyant misery, Fay leaps unbidden into Rita's flat, ostentatiously wipes her eyes with a damp and tattered hanky, whinges "May I sit down?!"

"Do!"

Fay drops into Rita's sofa, and Rita, catching her breath, says "What in God's name is it, then?!"

"What is what?" asks Fay, wondering why such obvious misery should be so summarily, so heartlessly, questioned.

Ach, Rita! Give her pain at least a moment of its own!

"Huh?" says Fay, eyes darting above, below, beside, for this sweet source of succour, "What did you say?!"

Rita's numerous bracelets jangle as her arms fly akimbo. She fixes her fierce eyes on Fay. "What the hell do you want?!"

"I've no sugar," squeaks Fay.

"No sugar?"

"No sugar. No coffee. No clothes. No furniture."

Fay again appears close to tears but Rita isn't buying. Is silent. She can only stare at this -- what is she, *what*?

Then from Rita: "Desiree Doolittle was not only discontent. She was mad as a hatter!"

"Sorry?" peeps Fay.

"How old are you?" Rita fairly spits the words.

"Golly," Fay brushes away salty traces (echtes salz, m'dears) of earlier tears, "One never asks a girl her age."

"How old are you?" repeats this Rita of stone.

"Twenty-one. Just."

"My arse!" spits Rita, "You're thirty if you're a day. I can give you a cup of coffee but you'll have to go elsewhere for the clothes and the furniture."

"Coffee would be simply lovely."

Fay sinks further into Rita's tastefully worn sofa, emits a tiny, pleased grunt. Far nicer, this, than her stained, bare mattress. Nicer than...anywhere she has *ever* been. She screws up her painted cupid's bow in a small, contented grin, opens and closes her fingers, like cat's claws, into tastefully faded cretonne. Seems not to notice Rita's rude demeanour.

But I do. *I* do, m'dears.

Rita winces (as though she's heard me), about-faces, marches to the kitchen, reaches for her special coffee but changes her mind and snatches up a jar of ancient, partially congealed, Instant.

Alone, Fay shoots from the sofa and begins a thorough snoop. "What superb objects! Superb objects everywhere," she whispers. Her eyes light lovingly upon silver and enamel vases, aged but very, *very* fine rugs (*you'll* have a rug one day soon, Fay. A rug that'll knock your socks off), and two silver-framed miniatures and several superbly mounted theatrical posters. "Ach!" Cries Fay (how very like Mummy), "Oh my!"

Yes. The lack of lovely objects, yes! That is what makes Fay cry. The simple lack -- can a lack be simple? -- The lack of anything. Would that she had lovely objects, superb objects, to give to all her friends. There would be many. Many, many friends is her immediate goal. She has so much love to give as well (Believe her!). So *incredibly* much! (and mind the italics, darlings).

She will start right here, right now, at Number 13. She will instantly befriend them all and, one day soon, sit them all, every man Jack/Jill of them, in a loving circle on soft cushions, preferably tasteful cretonne cushions exactly like Rita's, and give them all lovely gifts, costly gifts! Every single one of them! "Every man jack!" squeaks Fay, "and Jill"! and idly runs her finger through the dust on the mantel. She inches open a bureau drawer and peeks inside -- nothing of note -- nudges it shut, studies some framed photos on the mantel, inspects pictures on the walls then stops short at the typewriter. "Oh! You're a writer too!" cries Fay, deeply pleased, because she was one -- a writer -- in a fuzzy past that, like almost everything else lately, darn it, escapes her for the moment.

But how like Taylor.

"What?" says Fay, "What was that?"

"Yes," says Rita from the kitchen, pleased in spite of herself, "I'm attempting it. Writing."

"I heard your typing, adds Fay, "I imagine everyone in this house can hear your typing. It does make a racket."

Darlings, you can't blame Fay, though diplomat she's not. She's only telling the truth as she experiences it.

Experience.

Fay waits for an answer. None comes. "Your typing drew me down," she adds, "The walls are paper."

So the walls, it seems, like the floors, are also paper. How convenient to our task, our ultimate purpose.

"The walls are paper," repeats Fay, knowing nothing of 'task', nothing of 'ultimate purpose'. Yet.

Rita ignores her -- checks the flame under the kettle, finds a loaf of bread, sets it on the bread board, reconsiders, puts the bread back in its box.

That was mean of you, Rita. There are remedies for this sort of meanness. We needn't help you with your novel, ducky. Mind, Rita, mind.

"Have you sold your writings?" asks Fay -- stressing the plural -- as Rita returns.

"No."

"Then you're not really a writer, are you?"

Fay grins instantly, attempts to neutralize Rita's dark look. "I mean," she stammers, "not exactly yet."

"No," replies Rita, darker still, "Not exactly yet."

"But you must..." continues Fay, her eyes now riveted on Rita's richly coloured, ostensibly expensive (though *smallish*) Persian rug, "...but you must know a great deal about valuable antique floor coverings."

"Yes, I do. I do know a very great deal about valuable antique floor coverings," replies Rita, too irritated to be flattered, but warmed the tiniest bit that her extensive university study on this very subject has resulted in a compliment – even from this queer bird who has just a moment ago abruptly alighted in her very private life.

Life, as we know, dear Rita, private or not, is simply something that happens while one is waiting for something yummy. An apt, though well-worn homily appropriate to your own experience, love. 'Cause you've been waiting, a wrinkle a day *at least* (your mirror is my witness), for something to happen. You've been waiting for what seems an eternity. Ach! Believe me, it is not an eternity, darling, not by a long chalk.

Their coffee drunk in great haste, Fay casts those sharp eyes longingly into the kitchen from whence it came. Kitchens have always had deep significance for Fay. She could have dreamed whole days away in a kitchen, any kitchen -- if Mummy (or Granny) had allowed it. If --

"You've got some very exclusive coffee blends I see," says Fay, rising and shaking away sad -- they must have been, why else should she shake them away? -- sad memories of the past, "I'd loved to have sampled an exclusive brand."

Understandable, pet. You're an exclusive brand yourself.

"They're ancient. I wouldn't give them to a *dog*," replies Rita before Fay can react to that buzzy voice that seems to come from just under her left foot. (Mind, Fay, don't tread on me!)

Fay turns sharply from the kitchen, wiggles this left foot for at least thirty seconds under Rita's watchful, perplexed, and irritated gaze, then roves about peering intently at every thing in her path as though she intended to pocket it there on the spot, or play with it like a cat and consume it later at leisure.

"Objects! Things!" Fay giggles happily to Rita, "Wonderful things! Your charming abode is all so, so domestic, so personal and comforting, so..."

"Do sit down," hisses Rita through fine, straight teeth that are, every single one of them, and happily at fifty-four, her very own.

We can simply *never* overestimate the importance, m'dears, of sound chewing equipment of the ur-variety.

"But I adore exploring new abodes," pouts Fay. Her hands dangle at either side, playing kittenishly in that frayed, black skirt. "Do you weally mind?" she asks, now the curious child.

"Yeth. I weally mind very much indeed. I'm a pwivate perthon," mimics Rita, who'd never met a child she didn't loathe.

Fay is hurt, shows it, sits, composes herself, gazes earnestly at Rita and just, somehow, manages in a squeaky little voice:

"My house...burned down."

"To the vewy gwound?" asks Rita and strikes a match, applies it to a newly inserted king-size cigarette in her queenly holder.

Here is Rita, cruel again, unyielding. She can't help it. This *woman* is -- Rita feels that shudder rising from the soles of her feet, pausing in her jodhpured thighs, proceeding to her chest where it tightens into a nasty premonition; the same sort of feeling Taylor felt. Of course Rita has no idea what Taylor felt or feels as Rita has never actually spoken to the old woman.

But I have. Chronically! To my cost! And, ultimately (love that word), to hers.

"Yes," moans Fay valiantly fighting new tears, "Burnt to the ground. I don't even have a kettle."

The wall behind Fay is alight with blue flame as Rita, blind, of course, to this ravishing spectacle, suddenly says -- very contrary to her nature -- "That, I can give you."

Rita takes a hugely satisfying drag on her cigarette, strides, exhaling, to the kitchen, returns immediately with a dusty, greasy kettle she thrusts at Fay.

"Oh, I couldn't."

"Oh, puh-leeeze take it."

Why can't she feel sorry for this wretched tear-drenched woman?

I ain't sayin'.

Fay whips the kettle from Rita's hand and tucks it firmly on the floor behind one leg so it cannot escape and somehow wriggle its way back to Rita's cupboard.

"My sister's name was Jane," says Fay from nowhere, "She lived with an older woman who wore tweeds and brogues and kept hounds. And snuffed her."

Rita, drily: "Set the dogs on her, did she?"

"When they opened her at the autopsy her lungs were like burnt sponges. She smoked, you see, like you do."

Fay earnestly hopes Rita will stop smoking immediately. It could injure her health. Rita could expire before Fay has a chance to gift her. "She's on my gift-list," whispers Fay to a cretonne cushion and checks Rita's expression, goes on, "Jane's murderer said to me one day, told me straight out: I have every intention of murdering your sister."

"I told her she had better not," continues Fay, "as I was prepared to immediately contact someone in authority. I meant it!"

I do mean it! cries Fay to herself. I would have! If only...

God! Will this creature never leave?! thinks Rita.

"Glory!" cries Fay and jumps up, thrusts her hand before her, vigorously shakes Rita's unextended fist.

"You don't even know my name! I am Ritterhouse, Fay!"

"Rita..."

"Lambert! I memorized the bell buttons outside. I have a photographic memory."

We have a photographic memory. Though it's *not* what it seems.

"Right. Now if you don't mind, Ritterhouse..."

Rita moves quickly around Fay who immediately snatches up her kettle from behind her own magnificent legs and skips (though she does not know it) into another square on our board game de la vie (I've given up counting them pesky squares, m'dears, but I'm certain there will be an adequate supply – Destiny takes its own time no matter in whose so-called *hands* it lies).

Rita opens her door, slides quickly behind Fay and backs her out much as Fay had backed Rita in. But faster. Ach, so *much* faster!

"Thanks ever so," says Fay, waving her kettle, "for this wonderful..."

"Use it in good health, ducky."

Rita closes her door before Fay has quite finished and returns to her typewriter where she sighs with relief and, with a great, rude prod from me, quickly types:

> Doolittle Desiree was totally bonkers and a
> bit of a witch. "Why else," mused the bemused
> Robertson, Janet, "would I have parted with
> an excellent second-string tea kettle?"

"Quiet down there!" shrieks Taylor from on high.

4

Fay stares blank-eyed at the door Rita has virtually slammed in her face. "Lambert Rita, dear," she whispers, pressing her face against the door, "I shall treasure this kettle. It is a gift of our budding friendship. I have, therefore, lovingly inscribed your name at the top of my gift-list."

Well-meant but don't overdo it, darling. We can take care of Rita. And will. When the time comes.

After a moment Fay turns away, holds Rita's kettle close before her eyes, examines it. "Kettles are meant to see reflections in," she murmurs and begins to polish it on the sleeve of her cardigan. "Kettles are meant to see reflections in."

Rubbing furiously, she starts up the stairs and directly into another square.

"Excuse me."

It is Hugh and he is sooooo handsome! Fay whoops, flings the kettle directly into Hugh's arms. He handily catches it.

"Sorry!" says Hugh.

"Oh!" cries Fay, "you frightened me out of my wits!"

"Sorry."

Fay is blocking his descent, rolling his handsome smile and lithe form round and round in her addled head: He will be my first really *good* friend. He is not so problematical as Rita.

Fay is no fool. She knows deep in her -- whatever -- what Rita's about. I saw to that when I arranged their, well, *clash*. (Take in those italics, m'dears. They often denote more than dramatic effect. Though not *necessarily*.)

Hugh offers the kettle. Fay curtsies low – a difficult feat mid-staircase -- and accepts it with a shy smile.

"I wonder if you have a minute?" she asks, dimpling a dimple she hadn't realized she'd got -- this is all so *new* to her.

"I'm only here because I forgot something. It's my lunch hour," replies Hugh. He is suddenly overcome with guilt and has no idea why.

But I do.

"It's my cooker," moans Fay, "The gas is off. I can't get it on."

Hugh squats before the ancient cooker in Fay's tiny kitchen.

Fay, rapt, watches him. What a friendly, sweet man. Handy in the kitchen too. It is good to have a man around the house again.

Dear Fay, when have you ever had a man around the house?

"What?" Fay is about to ask, "What was that?" but Hugh rises and it skips her mind as she smiles full at him -- he will be her first new *real* friend and who knows...

Hugh twists on a burner. The gas hisses to life.

"Have you got a match?"

She shakes her head. "I haven't got anything." Then, forehead knitted, eyes liquid: "My house burned down."

Hugh twists off the burner. "Be careful when you light this. There could be air in the line. You could have a little explosion."

"Explosion?!"

Fay slumps against the wall, her mind aflame. She slides to the floor and sobs.

Hugh is stricken, looks about the grim, bare flat. "I'm so sorry."

"Th-Thanks," manages Fay, small flames crackling round mutilated memory.

"Really. I am sorry. About your house."

"Th-Thanks," manages Fay through a shoulder-shaking sob. She makes no attempt to rise from the floor.

Hugh pats her awkwardly on her shoulder. "I'll be late back to work. I really must go."

"Then you really must go."

Fay's sobs diminish quickly to sniffles. Hugh extends a hand and hoists her up. She is lighter -- incredibly lighter -- than he'd anticipated and he sees grime under her fingernails. Or is it soot from a burning house?

"Use my flat today," he says as he's jabbed up his arse by an abandoned fly-swatter that darts handily out from beneath a pile of old newspapers to do (oh so subliminally) our bidding.

Hugh offers his key to Fay, "There's plenty of food in the fridge."

"I haven't eaten for days! I'm starving!" she cries. "Oh but I couldn't! I'll be all right, honestly I will."

She means it. She doesn't wish to impose upon anyone. Her intentions are -- "Hush!" she whispers to me, and aims a heroic smile full at Hugh, "It's just these... these first few days..."

Still proffering the key, Hugh says "Please take it. It would make me very, very happy."

"Vewy, vewy happy?"

Pardon her baby-talk, m'dears, but Fay is younger and/or older than you might think and she'd simply adore making Hugh vewy, vewy happy. It is a first important step towards enduring friendship. "Would it really make you happy?"

"Yes it would." (That fly-swatter again. Incidentally, it's got a lovely, cloisonné handle compliments of someone's mischief and I'm not saying whose -- even if I *knew*.)

Poor Hugh is still not certain what's just happened. He's not generally so free and easy with his key. Particularly with indigent strangers. Although there *are* exceptions to that rule, m'dears. When *we* make them.

"What will *you* do for a key?" asks Fay snatching the key and pocketing it in her mousy cardigan's tattered pocket.

"I always carry two."

"I don't deserve this," says Fay, meaning every word, "You are too kind, sir!"

Hugh blushes, flicks a fetching curl from his forehead, turns to leave. "I'm flat four."

"I know!" she calls after him, "Oh, Honey, I *know*!"

5

Now pay attention:

Hugh is scarcely out of the house when Fay marches into his flat. A sixth sense draws her directly to the tiny fridge – Golly! Has she been here before?!

She empties the fridge's contents onto a small kitchen table; three eggs, a fat triangle of cheese, a pint and a half of milk, a slab of bacon, a small but expensive cut of meat, two tomatoes, a celery and a lettuce.

She adjusts the gas cooker to high, quickly locates a frying pan, slaps in the meat, slams it on the burner and watches the flames lick at the edges of the pan. She can't take her eyes off flames. Flames frighten, fascinate (as well they should!). Her hands tremble, her house burns down before her eyes. "Fire follows Fay!" she screams and the whole kitchen seems alight with it.

Crying, she tears her eyes from the flaming burner, breaks great chunks of cheese from the slab and stuffs them into her mouth. Chewing and crying, she finds a large wooden bowl, dismantles the head of lettuce with a sharp blow of her tiny, perfect fist, throws in whole tomatoes and ragged, hastily chopped chunks of celery. Drowning everything in vinegar and olive oil, she makes herself a crazy salad.

Impatient for the meat, she hacks off a blood-red corner and crams it between teeth that have already begun to chew. Bliss-Bliss-Bliss!

Everything stops dead! Fay panics, looks about. What to drink?! "I hate milk!" she cries with more emphasis than I'd deem appropriate. "With anything," she continues, "but bread and butter -- or toast -- or custard tarts!"

She ransacks the upper cupboards, falls to her knees and ransacks the lower cupboards. "Ah! Vino!"

She uncorks the bottle and cuts her little finger on the cork-screw -- not badly, just a scratch, just enough to bleed. "Oh! I've hurt myself! Boo-hoo!"

The room tilts (Yes, m'dears, actually tilts) which further alarms Fay. She turns down the fire on the steak and finds the bathroom and wraps her bleeding finger in great wads of toilet tissue. "Mummy, Mummy! I've hurt myself! Boo-hoo! Boo-hoo!"

The room tilts back. Fay cries "Glory!" and stumbles into yet another metaphorical square. She steadies herself with an arm to the wall.

The fun begins, m'dears.

"What?!" cries Fay, "Who are you?!"

But mum's the word – or should that be Mummy's the word?

Wounded Fay is not to be deterred. Not finding a bandage in the cabinet, she pulls out a drawer and discovers a stack of men's muscle magazines. Flipping through one, she peruses its abundant array of biceps, triceps, abs, glowing pectorals and prominent, tightly bound crotches. She laughs gaily, drops the magazine on the floor. She must buy, when she's flush, many, many such magazines for Hugh, her handsome young benefactor. "He's a such good friend! My best friend by far! Rita can't hold a candle to him!"

Nor should you, my little pyromaniac.

In another drawer Fay finds gauze and tape, binds her little finger in enough gauze to swaddle an infant and rushes back to the kitchen. She turns up the fire under her steak and there she waits, her nose turning in the air, savouring the splendid aromas of her luncheon-to-be; the most sumptuous meal she's had in -- a year? Two years? Four?! Has she ever had such a meal?

"Have I ever had such a meal?!" she exclaims, prompted by you know who, who replies cryptically: What goes round, ducks, comes round.

She tucks into said repast, further exults: "Have I ever had anything so completely sumptuous?! Have I ever savoured more splendid aromas? Have I ever tasted such a...such a crazy salad?!"

Draw your own conclusions, Fay. One day you shall know who you really are. But pass on, there's a love, another square awaits your *magical* presence.

Mrs Taylor awakens to twilight and the staccato of Rita's typewriter and gives the floor a sharp thump. Then lifts herself from her chair, clatters across her cavernous living room to light an ornate paraffin lamp with a long wooden match she takes from a box beside it (Mark this, m'dears).

Lamp in hand…(she detests electric light, too revealing, could add at least ten years to her circa-one-hundred so she consumes electricity only in bedroom and bathroom. My parenthetical phrases, m'dears, seem to expand with each passing page!) …so as said, lamp in hand, Taylor thumps to the kitchen, spreads a slice of bread with marmite and makes a horrifying face as she washes it down with milk.

"One day," she growls, hobbling back towards her postcards chair, "one day..." and yawns, "one day..." and sits with a resounding plop, turning her head to stare idly out the window. Fading sunlight forces itself through window glass that might be cleaner and bounces from her one rheumy eye to the other.

Old Mrs Taylor seems momentarily to have forgotten Fay who, even now, sways, clenched knuckles white, mumbling as in a dream, directly over Taylor's head in her, Fay's, spare -- save a bed -- little flat. But Taylor will remember. One day soon she will remember, to her cost, something. Then she'll forget it again. It's all plotted out, m'dears. For now. Be patient.

Don't even try to *guess* who I am.

Rita, muse-abandoned but hopeful, slouches by the window (Posture, ducky. If you'd stand up straight you could ditch a decade from that sagging silhouette). But there she slouches, puffing at her long-holdered cigarette, irritably watching this evening's monoxidic homebound traffic. She drops herself on the sofa, grabs a book from the coffee table, tries to read. Can't. "Buggery!"

She closes her eyes, listens to the buzz of traffic and the lately only intermittent buzz of the inchoate novel in her head.

A bus pulls up. Very separately, Hugh and Bill disembark from the Red Arrow. They nod to one another as they cross the street and climb the welcoming but sadly ignored steps of Number 13. Mrs Taylor munches bread and marmite and peers down at them. Hugh sees her, waves. Taylor frowns and departs muttering "cheeky!"

Another bus arrives not long after. Nelly disembarks.

Terrible dresser, thinks Fay from her window one floor above Taylor, two above Rita. Poor Nelly carries herself so awkwardly. More of a lumber than a walk. That hair. "I could do wonders with that tangled mop. I could be infinitely helpful," murmurs Fay, positively swamped with a longing to serve, to do the needful for a fellow human being.

Don't be presumptuous, sugar.

Hugh enters his flat, goes to the kitchen: Lettuce lines the narrow galley floor amidst a damp rubble of smashed tomatoes, bits of cheese rind and egg shells. The cooker is a pool of congealed grease, the sink a chaos of dishes and burnt-crusted pots and pans.

You must learn, Hugh, your husky buttocks clenched, to stand clear of ostensibly abandoned, cloisonnéd fly-swatters. Here's what a magical jab up the arse got you!

Hugh is dismayed at his rubbished kitchen and if he'd listened carefully he might have heard that odd laughter that often erupts in or around Fay. But he'd have to listen very carefully as she's on the next floor just now (and already in the next square!). Poor Fay, poor Ritterhouse Fay. An open book only to me.

The knit-snooded, pillow-buttressed Mrs Taylor reclines tucked up in her ornate iron bed sipping a steaming cup of Bovril. She studies a postcard, drops it into that red plastic carry-bag which now hangs from her bedpost. Incidentally, remember those several more identical, stuffed-full, red plastic carry-bags in her closet (you shall be periodically reminded, m'dears, of these. They are essential). Said red plastic bags lie nestled beside that rolled up, *simply splendid rug* (Does it shine? Does it glitter? Does it sigh? Does it move? Does it beckon? Yes, indeed! When it takes a mind to). Ach! And that small shrine lies so cosily adjacent. But old Mrs Taylor has forgotten the shrine, along with almost everything else in her dimming, drifting world. Everything except that damned dairy. For the moment.

From overhead come muffled sobs. Taylor's eyes narrow. She snatches her cane from the bed-rail, nearly tumbles out. Steadying herself, she climbs onto a low footstool and tilts her ear towards the ceiling and listens. That woman who gave her such a start this morning! That witch is crying! They do that sometimes. Witches. When they're sad. Witches get sad just like anybody else. Sadder. It takes one to know one. Taylor knows -- when she remembers.

Swaying dangerously on the low footstool, her flannel nightie flaring in a draft, old Mrs Taylor thumps her cane smartly on the ceiling and shouts. "Quiet up there!"

The crying instantly stops. Taylor clutches her cane in both hands, wonders what the hell she's doing up here on this perilous footstool, and painstakingly lets herself down. She hangs the cane on the bed rail beside that red carry-bag of postcards, climbs back into bed and adjusts her snood. Painfully -- her arthritis is playing up -- she switches off the bed lamp and is soon asleep.

Hugh drowses off. He couldn't face that debris in his kitchen. He will tidy up tomorrow. What a bizarre woman. A bit mad? He slips into a dream, is pursued by a creature in black, is not sure if it's Fay. It probably is. But then again it could just be *all* women (pompous bastard!). With, of course, the notable exception of Jenny.

As usual, Nelly is dreaming of Bill. He is asking her if she is forty years old.

And Bill sleeps, earlier than usual, the Evening Standard across his chest. He's had a lot on his mind but he's not dreaming and he wouldn't be dreaming of Nelly even if he were. He hasn't really met her yet -- though he does faintly remember a not unpleasant though awkward rainbow noted from a corner of his eye whilst waiting for the Red Arrow that morning.

In the wee hours Rita dreams she glares into a mirror and sees absolutely nothing. Being fifty-four, she should, according to her theory, see ectoplasm glaring back. Total invisibility doesn't come until fifty-five. She does not like this dream, panics, struggles, wakes violently, reaches for her cognac. No sleep again tonight. But she's got Monsieur Courvoisier for company. And he's a smoothie.

Fay's eyes are fixed on her cracked ceiling studying fantastical patterns that shift and seem to sigh longingly – so like herself. She's flat on that bare mattress. A shabby black (and sooty) coat, she's got no bedclothes, covers her. She tosses the coat aside, rises and takes her forlorn little bouquet-in-a-jam-jar to the kitchen, freshens its water. "Little bouquets need fresh water like the dickens," she murmurs. She wishes she had a window box to air it in -- *plants need air.* She returns, drops herself on that stained (though friendly) mattress and begins to whimper. But softly, so that old hag below won't shriek at her. "Why am I weeping? From loneliness? No. From happiness! Me so happy me want to cry," lisps Fay through a sob and, at last, comfortably managed tears.

Morning light filters fuzzily in through Fay's single, sooty window (soot's *everywhere,* darlings).

So you weep from happiness, Fay? We'll see.

"Who is this unseen intruder?" asks Fay, "Who are you, unseen intruder? What the dickens are you saying to me?"

Mind your own bees-wax, lovey. Who of us has a right to foreknowledge? That comes, in due course, with wisdom. Depending on who you are. Or, let's face it, lovey, on who you *think* you are.

6

Nelly, in her scruffy, magenta duffel, drooping with sleep, drinks tea. She often varies it, alternating so she won't become set-in-her-ways, between a morning tea and a morning coffee (I wasn't inconsistent with her characterization, m'dears – so *don't* find fault with me! It could be dangereux.). Besides, Nelly, unlike Fay, does precisely (she assumes, like all of us) as she wishes. So she sips her morning tea from a large, ceramic mug she has made herself. She is pleased with the mug and studies its coppery glaze for a moment then checks her watch, listening for Bill on the stairs. She becomes again the Nelly-spider lurking in her web. She laughs. It doesn't help at all. She *despises* -- a strong word for dear Nelly -- being a spider, would rather be its *pretty* prey.

Fat chance, love. Though I *could* pin a ribbon in your hair and photograph you through a brick wall, post it on the Net and who knows what tomorrow might bring?

Rita is content for the moment. She luxuriates in a wondrously pink bubble bath. Bottles of fine scent line the so charmingly retro black and white tiled walls of her bathroom. She hums, visions of full visibility through Literature dancing in her head.

Mrs Taylor, in a heavy, faded bathrobe, washes her face with good, strong soap, splashes her grey felt slippers where they've been splashed countless times before and gleefully recalls her morning exchange with the milkman. A knock at her door! Taylor freezes. Another knock! -- but the milkman has much earlier come and gone! She creeps to the door, presses her ear against it. Another knock! Her head snaps back.

"The milk money was in the bottle yesterday!" snarls Taylor through the closed door.

Outside, Fay grins appealingly, rehearsing her/our menu of smiles.

"That's a fact!" shouts Taylor, "If somebody stole it that is your affair not mine! I am legally within my rights! Mr Taylor is a barrister and he knows the facts of this matter!"

Why, you trusting old darling.

Facts! Flood 'em with facts! Taylor is exceptionally clear-headed this morning when it comes to *facts* (ho-ho!).

"Mrs Taylor?" chirps Fay.

Taylor is about to say "Since when do ladies deliver milk?" but says nothing. Fay says "I'm your new neighbour. I live directly above you."

Taylor, tight-lipped, listens.

"I live in the flat above you!"

"You have already delivered the milk today! Is this event to be construed as harassment?!"

"I am your new neighbour. I live in the flat above you!"

Taylor pauses. That odd feeling lurches through her.

"You the one who blubbed all night?"

"I wish to talk to you, dear," says Fay in a reasonable yet door-penetrating voice.

"I don't talk to no bawl-babies!"

But that Feeling suddenly evaporates. "Do you type?" asks Taylor.

"No, I do not."

"I told you I paid for the milk yesterday. The money was in the bottle and that's a fact."

The walls of Taylor's sitting room suffuse with a comforting mauve. If she'd had a certain rug under them the soles of her feet might have been lovingly massaged.

"I am positive you paid for the milk yesterday,"

"You are?!"

Taylor edges open the chained door.

"Yes, Mrs Taylor, I truly am."

Taylor warms. Partly because Fay's smile is simply luminous, partly because her, Taylor's, walls have suddenly suffused with mauve, partly because Fay's voice is soothing and familiar in an odd...faraway... but mainly because Fay sees milk money where no milk money is.

"What d'you want then?" barks Taylor.

"Just a social visit," chirps Fay.

Taylor unhooks her door chain, sticks her head out, scowls in either direction and with the crook of her cane snatches Fay in by her elbow, latches the door and leads her into the huge sitting room.

Taylor is not sure why she allows Fay into her inner sanctum. No one but a plumber and an especially privileged grocery delivery boy -- now married with offspring -- have been allowed in for sixty years -- ever since she arrived in London from the good old U.S. of A to be assistant buyer for a long since defunct clothing establishment.

So why, ponders Taylor, is this blubbing, whining woman standing here? Why have I let her in? Is she is a potential ally against that money-grubbing milkman and his dastardly dairy?

Fay drops herself with an unpleasant jolt onto an unexpectedly hard chair as Taylor resumes her place at the postcard table. "What a lovely, large room, Mrs Taylor!"

"Biggest room in the house -- how did you know I paid my milk bill?"

Taylor's eyes are slits.

"Because," lies Fay, shocked at the unkempt appearance of this wrinkled old crone, "I saw the money in your milk bottle this morning."

Fay must, she instantly decides, assist this ancient, decrepit, *needy*, woman even if it means a dangerous descent into mendacity -- that what-a-tangled-web-we-weave-when etc pitfall. Though honesty really is the best policy Fay will be friends whatever the cost. She is (bless her), at the service of the desperately deprived and downtrodden. Ask her, m'dears!

Taylor, in spite of her earlier premonitions, is pleased.

You poor old dear! Enchanted so easily?

"What's your name?" says Taylor.

"Fay. I was named after..."

"Pretty name, Fay. Suits you."

"I was named after..."

"How long you lived here?"

"Since yesterday."

"Which flat?"

"Directly above you."

"You're the one who blubs, ain't you? Poor Mr LaFarge snuffed it, has he?"

"The former tenant?"

"Kicked the bucket, has he?"

"*I* don't know."

"He ain't still there, is he? You ain't livin' in sin?"

Taylor cackles lasciviously.

"No, Mrs Taylor. There's just little me and my house burned down."

"Your house did what?"

Fay mists over, but manages, as Taylor's walls are lapped with suitably illustrative, hopefully harmless flames: "My house burned down. That is why I am here."

Oh, Fay. If you only knew why you were here. But it would be unsporting of me to tell you just now. Plus would considerably diminish my pleasure, indeed, the assorted pleasures of all attendant at our gamy game table. Is that not correct, m'dears? (Don't be rude!)

Fay pauses, heart pounding, looks about, certain she sees amongst these licking flames, a curious indigo shadow where a shadow ought not to be. Are there specific places where shadows reside? She catches her breath.

She almost sees me -- when I choose.

She relaxes for the briefest of moments. Until her smooth brow knits and she repeats: "My house burned down."

"Is that a fact?" replies Taylor.

"Yes and no. It wasn't exactly a house."

Taylor's eyes flash. "What was it then? Just the facts, dearie."

"A flat."

Fay brushes at a glistening eye, grins bravely, turns away. "Why must I feel so deeply," she whispers, "Why must I constantly feel so bloody deeply?"

For someone so singularly shallow?

"Huh?" asks Fay of a sylph flashing by.

"Burned down, did it?" barks Taylor, "Sorry to hear it."

"I lost my cat too."

How she had loved that *cat*!

"Never cared for cats," says Taylor.

"She was black as sin."

How apt, lovey.

"Cats piddle on carpets."

Not *that* carpet, lovey! And you know the one I mean. Or do you? You vague old darling.

"Still," says Taylor, "Sorry to hear it. Musta been a shock."

"I had him for five years, eight months and seventeen days. I've still not recovered."

"You look all right to me, dearie."

Fay brightens, she will win over this churlish old hag (my words not Fay's).

Fay springs up, skips to the centre of the room, twirls. "Your sitting room is palatial!"

"Grandest room in the whole damned house."

Taylor kisses a card, drops it in the red carry-bag.

"Why did you kiss that postcard, Mrs Taylor?"

"That's for me to know and you to find out," barks Taylor, instantly sorry, as research should never, never be encouraged in witches.

Fay sets down a large, intricately painted and surely valuable vase she has been studying, moves on to that ornate old paraffin lamp by the closet door, picks it up with both hands. Muscles she never knew she had, flex. She considers the lamp for a moment then opens and peeks through the closet door. Taylor watches Fay's every gesture, smiles and nods to herself, whispers "Yes, Oscar. Yes."

"What would you say," asks Fay, setting down the paraffin lamp with an unbecoming grunt -- is it burning her fingers? It's not even alight! "What would you say if I marched right into your kitchen and made us both a perfectly lovely breakfast?"

"Only a witch could make a lovely breakfast in that kitchen and that's a fact. But march right on in, dearie."

"Truer words," mumbles Fay when she sees the shabbily austere state of Taylor's kitchen, "were never..."

But the rest of this homily escapes her.

And only *I* know why.

Fay winces, swallows a bite of marmite and bread. Why are the women in this house so ill-mannered and mean? thinks Fay. Rita (Fay's got *her* number regardless of the gift of that kettle -- perhaps because of it) and this old fright, who hunches over her hideously soiled tablecloth. Why are they so discourteous? I'm only being friendly.

Which is true. Up to a point, isn't it, Fay? Now get hopping! Squares await, Ritterhouse.

Fay frowns, thinks of how wonderful this first meeting with a potential friend could have been, debates summarily removing Taylor from her gift-list and daubs another piece of bread with marmite. She takes a bite, frowns again, this time at Mrs Taylor, who swipes her frayed sleeve at her dribbling mouth and hisses, "I'm going to pay my milk bill tomorrow, dearie, you just keep your eyes open."

"Of course, Mummy," murmurs Fay into her heavily creamed coffee, "I'll tell Mr milkman you paid your bill because, like this morning, I will see the money on the bottle."

"You do that and you and me will get along just fine."

"I also saw," says Fay, reaching across the table and dabbing with a soggy serviette at Taylor's bristly chin, "a gorgeous carpet all rolled up in your hall closet. Golly! What a waste to keep such a yummy carpet all rolled up in a dark and musty old closet."

Taylor's eyes glitter then narrow, the fuzz lifts -- sweet clarity! "Then take it, take it!"

"Oh, I couldn't. It looks so valuable."

Really, how can she relieve a helpless old lady who eerily resembles her dear mother -- much aged, of course – relieve this doddering old hag of a -- well, rather special -- carpet? But then… (my words, m'dears, the 'but then')...(*and* the 'doddering')…(and, of course, the 'hag').

"Then don't take it," barks Taylor.

"I shouldn't but I shall. You are really too generous, Mrs Taylor."

Fay, if you only knew how generous.

And how nécessaire to our task.

"What task?"

"Put it on your floor," says Taylor, "It'll muffle your blubbing and I can get me some sleep. You'll keep the whole house awake with your blubbing if you're not careful. Not that it makes any difference around here. Nobody says a bleedin' word to nobody around here and that's just fine."

Fay peruses Taylor's food-encrusted old cardigan. "We really must take care of ourselves, mustn't we? Our bodies are temples, aren't they?"

Fay feels she can be *infinitely* helpful to this vulnerable old woman, can (what is that phrase? Ach! Ja! Can *make a difference*.) First thing though is to get Taylor out of that filthy cardy and have it laundered. Fay scribbles a notation in the dark place, deep in her well-shaped skull, that she assumes is private. But we know better don't we? Our eye is on that sparrow, ain't it? Any old sparrow.

Gnarled Mrs Taylor will become Fay's mission in life -- one of many. Mrs Taylor's place in Fay's so-called heart, at least carpet-wise, is now secure. Gaily, with this fulfilling thought in mind, Fay skips into the kitchen, oblivious to the thundering applause of the walls, floors and ceilings of grateful Number 13 and its architect – me. Or moi, if you prefer, m'dears. Or even, in a pinch, 'Ich'. I'm versatile, darlings, in *every* bleedin' way.

"Quiet," whispers my innocent accomplice, "You're confusing

the crone and what was that 'task' you spoke of?"

None of your beeswax, lovey.

Fay shrugs and pours more grainy coffee for Taylor who takes a swallow and chokes. Fay watches her curiously. Fay must be realistic -- simultaneously sympathetic and realistic, for the old woman's time is exceedingly nigh. But oh my goodness! What if Mrs Taylor expires before Fay has shifted that splendid carpet to her shabby little aerie upstairs? The thought chills. To calm herself, Fay imagines the carpet safe in her flat and herself upon it puffing a water pipe, cross-legged like a gauze-pantalooned houri in a Grand Wazir's palace.

Similar to mine, m'dears. (I jest)

Mrs Taylor continues to choke as Fay reflects on Taylor's projected funeral service. She, Fay, will be the chief mourner, glamorous in haute couture that she soon will purchase. Mauves and deep purples and, of course, purest cerulean blue. Fabrics of shattering perfection, all accessories in black. Such ensembles could shake the very heavens let alone little Pimlico! She holds these irreverent thoughts unwillingly. My whisper has put them there -- *my* voice. Fay is really not like that at all. She's an angel, m'dears, a bloody angel. And I am not as nice as I may seem. But then, neither are you.

Fay rises suddenly and claps Taylor on her back. Taylor stops choking and Fay hands her the marmite stained serviette into which Taylor spits then hands back. Fay has nothing but kind thoughts for this dear, semi-familiar old woman. She knows she has. She feels she has. She *must* have. If only that whisper would stop suggesting otherwise. If only that whisper would fuck off!

Fay and Mrs Taylor gaze at one another across the spotted tablecloth. Two sphinxes. Each with secrets of harrowing import. If only they could remember them.

7

Fay arranges her -- Mrs Taylor's -- new carpet on the floor of her tiny flat. Thank goodness old Taylor had not expired in her choking fit -- at that age anything is possible. Fay has such fulfilling plans for her though Taylor would not part with that despicable old cardigan when Fay had so kindly offered to launder it. Fay earnestly wishes to ease this old lady's increasingly perilous journey through life. Fay's plans include gifts of all descriptions and price ranges. She will ponder their infinite diversity tonight, or first chance she gets. How lovely to give gifts. How doubly-lovely to receive them!

Fay's one room had contained only a bare-mattressed bed. Now, this wondrous carpet with its close-clipped pile of outlandish colour, indescribable colour. It glimmers and glows. Phantoms of extreme ecstasy play through its nap. If, my dears, you look close enough. If, my dears, your vision is not obstructed by some perfectly useless, mythical soul.

This magnificent floor covering is the finest thing Fay has ever owned. Is it? She casts back: Cold, worn linoleum for her tiny childish feet. No carpets at home. There was a carpet once. In someone's house. She did not like that person. She does not remember why. That person loathed her. It was the person with *the shoes*. Nothing's changed. How old was she then? Can't remember. Who could harm a helpless child? Who?!

Don't ask.

Fay rises from her knees, stands away, admires her magical carpet. Still admiring, she backs into her tiny kitchen, twirls, pours boiling water from Rita's kettle into a cup she has pilfered from Hugh, over Hugh's purloined instant coffee. She adds milk (from Hugh) and, from her cardigan pocket, a handful of sugar cubes spirited away right from under that sour Rita's snooty nose. Perfect. This is what life ought to be. Sharing with generous (and some not so generous) others. Making love to them through their domestic accoutrements and/or major appliances. Wouldn't she open her own refrigerated larder (and heart!) to the temporarily needy? Well. If she had a larder (or a heart, sugar?). But soon. If. No. It's a promise! She'll work it out. "I'll work it out!" she cries at the multi-cracked ceiling which offers only a laboured grin in return. Yes. She'll work it out. She's done it before, hasn't she? She's a good girl, she is. An exemplary person. She *will* do good. Will find and give love. Especially, *find*. If only...

How like so *many* of us, m'dears.

But, thinking back, Fay suddenly encounters a blank wall. A wall alight with flames. Can think no further, whispers "What the dickens! Am I an amnesiac? And if I am – golly!"

So she sips from this nicest of Hugh's cups. Why the nicest? Now! It all comes back! Her house burned down, that's why! And her childhood hangs about her neck like a stinking, burning tyre, that's why!

Darling Fay, I couldn't have put it better myself.

Come to think of it, I just have.

Fay squats dead-eyed, cross-legged and barefoot on Mrs Taylor's carpet, still houri-like though minus gauze pantaloons, minus water-pipe. She dabs her mouth with one of Mrs Taylor's frayed cloth serviettes, sips Hugh's coffee -- heated in Rita's kettle, sweetened with Rita's sugar -- from Hugh's nicest cup. All talismans. Never underestimate the value of a talisman.

I taught her that.

Why shouldn't she enjoy her newfound booty? Her bleedin' house burned down, didn't it?!

Rationalisation, m'dears, is the balm of monstrosity and can lead *anywhere*. Specially when I'm doin' the leadin'. So follow your leader.

Fay goes to her window, her only window, sips coffee from Hugh's cup and looks out over the evening traffic. Directly below her, Mrs Taylor, on her cane by her geraniums in her window, in the blotting shadow of the building opposite, curses the loss of her sunsets.

Rita is at her window too, puffing away in a cloudy renaissance of cigarette bliss, one blue-veined (but otherwise *extraordinarily* smooth and graceful) hand plucking lazily at a damp fold of jodhpurs caught in the cleavage of her chair-flattened bottom.

A bus pulls up. Nelly leaps off. Mrs Taylor and Rita and The Ritterhouse Fay watch clumsy Nelly clomp up the steps of their house. Taylor, because she is ever-suspicious (when she has the energy, m'dears); Rita, because writers of novels need material (grist for that proverbial mill); Fay, because she is simply ravenous and could do a lot with Nelly's tangled mop of hair. "I know I could! I'd *love* to try! She'd be my friend for life!"

Whose life?

Fay's eyes shine with projected munificence. The future sprawls before her in all its compassionate splendour. "I shall do unto others!" cries Fay in a fit of fond feelings, "I shall do unto others..." she breaks off.

Golly! She's forgotten the rest.

Well. We'll see, won't we? She will certainly *do* unto others. But it will all be, *mark my words,* for their own good. We must take that on faith, m'dears. Which, of course, is how one must take *everything* on this bleedin', blood spattered sphere of ours. Sorry, of *yours*.

"What?" says Fay, "Who? Who is there?"

8

"I shouldn't have said 'burned down'. It didn't actually 'burn down'. It was a flat. It 'burned' up. V"

"You mean," replies Nelly helpfully, proffering a plate of home-baked cookies, "it was gutted. When it's a flat fire they generally say 'gutted', don't they?"

Nelly articulates 'gutted' with gusto, causing Fay to knit her forehead and look away uncomfortably and work especially hard at producing another tear – for emphasis, m'dears.

Nelly leans back. Her large healthy breasts shift with an audible thump. "I'm so glad you fell over just outside my door," says Nelly guilelessly and with a sincerity even Fay might find difficult to duplicate. "Poor Fay. It *is* 'Fay'?"

"Ritterhouse, Fay, at yer service," replies Fay, blinking away a tardy tear that to Fay's chagrin escapes near-sighted Nelly's notice. "I was named after Fay Wray, that poor woman who played the hapless heroine in King Kong."

"King which?" asks Nelly good-naturedly.

"You know," says Fay, 'King Kong'. That old horror film they're always showing on the telly. Mummy was a telly addict. I am named after that poor woman who is abducted by a gargantuan ape."

"Gosh. How awful," splutters Nelly, munching -- grateful for company, any company -- a mouthful of cookie.

"It seemed," says Fay, "to set the tone of things. For my life. My luck hasn't changed."

But it's about to, ducky.

Fay looks anxiously about for the source of this saucy retort. Is it, too, couched in indigo? Was that it, by the kitchen door an instant ago? But she sees no fleeting shadow, wonders if Nelly, too, has heard my remark.

"Cookie, love?" says Nelly. "Mother always called them cookies, not biscuits. She was American."

Fay scoops up another handful of what-ever-they-are (depending, apparently on ones nation of origin!), drops three in her cardigan pocket. "I lost," says Fay, straining to squeeze out one more tear, "everything."

"I baked them myself," says Nelly as Fay's two arduously

wrought tears slide lip-ward, unseen.

Is she blind?! screams Fay in her head. How can we be friends if she is not more observant?! "They're yummy," says Fay aloud, smothering the scream, "Do you keep a diary?"

"Once. For a week. When I was in love."

Nelly leans back, sighs with pleasure at the very thought of love, takes another bite of 'cookie'.

"I kept a diary," says Fay, "right up to the night of the fire. One page for every single day of my life."

Yeah. Sure, you did, sugar.

Fay crams in a whole cookie, munches noisily -- she may as well! Nelly seems to have no manners at all! Does Fay really need a friend with no manners at all? "Go away," says Fay to these bitchy thoughts for which, she is certain, she is not at all responsible.

Roger to that.

"Roger to that," whispers Fay towards my whisper.

"What, love?" says Nelly.

"From the age of seven," replies Fay, spraying crumbs and reaching for another cookie, "I'd written volumes in my diary. Nothing was too trivial to be included. Because what can be trivial about a human life?"

The facts, Fay, just the facts, please.

"It all went up in flames. The complete story of my life. In sizzling flames."

Fay pauses mistily. "When my flat burned down."

"Up," corrects Nelly and offers another cookie which Fay accepts and shamelessly pockets. "Or was gutted. Say 'gutted'. Your flat was 'gutted'," says the kindly Nelly, attempting against occasionally insurmountable odds to be logical. "I do pity you, love."

Fay is soothed by Nelly's concern, says "I'll survive," and smiles helplessly.

They sip and munch and look awfully thoughtful.

"Lovely cookies, an absolutely unsurpassed treat" says Fay. She grins and pockets at least three more, "I was starving, a mere shadow of myself."

You can say that again, peaches.

"I don't cook much else," replies Nelly, "I tend to eat out. What's the point of cooking only for ones self?"

"Oh, Nelly! One must cherish ones self. What else have we but our bodies? They are our sacred temples, Our shrines. Cook delicious, nutritious meals for yourself. You won't regret it."

Nelly lifts an ample breast with one hand and pulls at her tightly belted waist with the other. "I eat too much already."

Fay eyes Nelly's ripe midriff, winces, says "Apparently."

Though Fay had really meant to say: 'Not at all, Nelly, darling, you haven't a trace of a weight problem.' For flattery is the true way to lasting friendship, and friends, as ever, are on her wish-list.

Two lists, m'dears. Wish *and* Gift. Good girls always have at least two lists in their hope chest.

Did I just hear myself say *Hope Chest*?! Did I just hear myself say *Good Girls*?! Sometimes I feel so, so... oh, fuck it.

Fay *will* have friends. As many as possible. As soon as possible. She herself will be the dearest friend any of these friendship-paupered prospects will ever know. She'll see to that.

So will I, m'dears.

Fay ignores me, sticks out her empty coffee cup. Nelly tops it and laughs generously at Fay's frank reference (it seems *so* long ago!) to her midriff.

A bus stops, idles noisily as passengers depart. Nelly's ears prick up. Bill gets off the bus. Fay sees him through the window, says "What about the other people in this house?"

The front door opens, closes.

"Oh gosh!" gasps Nelly, recognizing Bill's footsteps on the stairs. "It's him! He must have worked late."

"What about," asks Fay -- she's nonchalant -- "the fellow at the top, opposite me?"

"Bill! That's him who just came in!"

Nelly's eyes gleam. So do Fay's. Though in not quite the same way. I could be such a good friend to Bill, thinks Fay. And he to me. Just till I'm on my feet again.

Or on your back, harlot!

"Please!" gasps Fay.

"I call him Bill," says Nelly, with a tiny, peculiar glance at Fay, "to myself. He's divorced I think. I saw some letters from his ex-wife on the post table the other day. Of course the letters could be from his mother or sister and he could be unmarried. Gosh! I hope he is. Unmarried or divorced. Preferably never married. Gosh! how I fancy him. But he won't look at me."

Nelly closes her eyes, listens as Bill's footsteps grow fainter up the stairs.

"Perhaps he's gay like Hugh in four," says Fay.

"Oh, I wouldn't know. We're all very private here so it wouldn't make much difference in any case. But I don't think so. Bill's not masculine enough to be gay. All the gay blokes I know are weight-lifters. Gosh! I doubt Bill could lift a bowling ball."

Fay watches Nelly carefully. She reminds Fay of her sister. The ungainly one my Fay tirelessly alleges was murdered.

"He's dying to be mothered," says Nelly and sighs and washes down a cookie with coffee. "I hope those letters were from his mum."

Rita's typewriter starts up.

"What about that *person* across the hall from you? The odd, churlish woman in those scruffy, shiny-bottomed jodhpurs."

Fay does not conceal her distaste for Rita, who had closed friendship's door as surely as she had closed her own in Fay's face. Worse, had refused to take seriously our poor little Fay's conflagration. My God! A fire is a fire is a fire! Rita should have one of her own. Perhaps one day she will.

Count on it, Rita.

"That odd, churlish one," repeats Fay, "who types. What about her?"

Nelly, still thinking of Bill, tries hard to concentrate on Fay's question. Rita is not odd to Nelly, churlish perhaps, but not odd. No one is odd to Nelly. They're simply people. "She types a lot. At least lately," says Nelly.

"She's an unemployed actress and her name is Rita and she is attempting to become a professional writer. I met her yesterday."

"You do work fast!"

Fay bridles. "What do you mean by that?"

"Oh nothing, love. I believe 'Rita' and I have said two words to one another in the month I've lived here. 'Good' and 'Morning'!"

Nelly laughs a big, hearty laugh, Fay does her a world of good! It's lovely to talk to someone of an evening. "Of course, Rita and I have nodded to each other at the grocer's but we've not really spoken. I never thought it odd until just now. Until you asked. I mean we really are private people."

"And perhaps just a bit lonely?"

Like you, ducky?

Fay's eyelids flutter. She considers – though she doesn't know it – stepping into the next square of our game, decides – though she doesn't know it – not to, reaches for another cookie instead, ignores me so I hiss: finish the goddamned cookies and let's get on with it!

and I give her a firm pinch on her shapely botty and am rewarded with a tiny 'ouch' as Fay dutifully lunges into our next square.

"Lonely?" Nelly ponders for an instant. "I...err have my friends and I imagine they have theirs. I mean they get letters. Mrs Taylor, the lady upstairs who's begun thumping on the floor since..."

"Rita."

"...since Rita began typing, gets postcards and sometimes they're signed with hearts and arrows."

"You read their mail, do you?" asks Fay, knowing *everything*, fair or foul, can be crucial in the pursuit of hugs and kisses or even a sweet smile.

Or a soothing shag.

"Of course I don't read their mail," says Nelly, colouring slightly, "but postcards are public property, aren't they?"

"I'll remember that."

Let's not be sarcastic, dear.

"What?" says Fay.

"Have a cookie," says Nelly.

This is where *I* came in!

Mrs Taylor lights her paraffin lamp, looks into her closet, wonders where that fine carpet has gone, remembers, shudders, "The witch took it. The blubbing witch. Suits her."

Only too well, ducky.

Taylor smiles. All is going precisely as Oscar Taylor planned. Though her closet does seem a bit...a bit what? Ah. A bit dimmer somehow. No *enlightened* rug, m'dears, companion to those tinder-dry newspapers, those stuffed to bursting red plastic carry-bags. Now she'll certainly need that paraffin lamp with her if she requires something from the closet. But the dear old thing'll never go there again. I've seen to that.

Bill fries sausages and eggs. Bill has sausages and eggs for breakfast lunch and dinner. He knows there is a new tenant across the hall. She'd peeped through her door at him this morning as he left for work. He wonders what she's like. He's not avid, just wonders for a moment. He's got a lot on his mind.

"How about tonight?!" cries Nelly with surprising vitality -- that reading lamp (though she seldom reads!) directly beside her has just gone all soft cerulean blue and a touch influential.

"I'd love to but...since the...fire," says Fay, "I'm strapped."

"My treat!"

Instantly: "I'd love to, Nelly! I'd absolutely love to!"

"I will treat you to dinner and a film. It's not every day a new friend's flat is gutted!"

Fay throws herself against the couch, arches her back and weeps raucous tears of joy. How abundant is this early harvest of friendship! Perhaps not a fine, glimmering carpet alive with a rainbow of ecstatic phantoms but rich indeed. Good intentions always triumph!

"Oh, God! Fay, love," says Nelly, gripping the sobbing Fay's shaking shoulder, "I'm sorry! Gosh! Me and my big mouth!"

Nelly takes Fay's hand. "It was you, wasn't it? Crying last night?"

The house knew. All Pimlico might have known if I hadn't quietened down my darling prosopopoeia.

9

"For a start," says Nelly, who has always known that true generosity means giving up something one would achingly miss, "can you use this?"

"Oh, Nelly, no!" cries Fay, running her fingers over the smooth, honey-coloured, carved chest of drawers.

"But," adds Nelly, "we've got a problem. How the heck do we shift this monster?"

Fay caresses her new furniture. "Him's no monster," she whispers, "Him's lovely. Him makes me so happy me want to cry."

Fay rests her chin on the bureau's gleaming, decoratively carved top, beams at Nelly. Nelly, enchanted, beams right back. So does that bureau. In its way, m'dears, *in its way.*

Bill chomps the last bite of his sausage and egg, downs it with a swallow of light ale. He sighs, takes his dish and bottle to his tiny kitchen and sets them in the sink, sighs again. Goes to his bed, drops himself on it, picks up his evening paper but closes his eyes. He thinks of his helpless young son, his ex-wife, his parlous economy -- but he *is* up for promotion. He belches, sighs yet again.

How do people end up in these excruciating situations? By chance? Or execrable planning? It's beyond *me,* m'dears. And I'm beyond Pluto.

"The men could shift it," says Fay. "Maybe Bill would look at you if you asked for help. People are always generous when one is desperate. We'll be desperate. It never fails."

Fay beams again at Nelly. Nelly, poor cow, again beams back. What babe-in-the-woods-Nelly doesn't know about people would fill several thick volumes that Nelly would never read anyway.

"Bill will be forced to look at me, will he?" asks Nelly.

"Ummm!" chirps Fay.

Nelly, stricken, says: "But will he like what he sees?"

Rita, before her bathroom mirror, snaps shut the last large pink plastic curler into her greying locks.

Honestly, m'dears, why *does* she bother? Beauty comes from within. Whoops!

She takes up a snifter of brandy from her toilet seat and sips and says to her reflection: "Suicidal, semi-bonkers Doolittle Desiree was dangerously discontent and would stop at *nothing* to achieve errrr...contentment."

Rita giggles as she unknowingly hits the nail on the head.

Fay dances about Nelly like a boxer, jabbing here, poking there, hitching Nelly's elastic-waisted skirt higher (Nelly's legs aren't *that* bad), pulling her neckline lower and tighter against those big healthy breasts -- moving that hair-mop about. "Got a brush? Genuine bristles?"

"I'll see what I can do."

"Me so happy!" peeps Fay as she follows Nelly to a dresser where Nelly chuckles with delight and slides out a messy drawer. Fay peers with great interest into the drawer. Nelly finds a brush (genuine bristles!), hands it to Fay and Fay says "You'll have to sit down. You're unusually tall."

Nelly sits, hunches before her dressing table. "I know," she says, knowing only too well. But isn't it marvellous to have a friend to so ingenuously acknowledge her height?

Well, darling. Yes and no.

Fay brushes away at Nelly's beautifully abundant red mop. Oh how Fay enjoys grooming her new, hopelessly dowdy friend. And those sarcastic whispers -- hallelujah! Those fretful, cruel whispers are momentarily mute. "What a day this had been! What a fine mood I'm in!" says Fay, "It's almost like having a friend!"

What would *you* know about friends?

"What?" says Fay, "What was that?"

Mrs Taylor is asleep in her chair. Postcards lay scattered from her lap to the floor beside her. A smaller pile of cards has, glacier-like, calved from the main postcard mountain and slides towards the edge of the large table. Several cards are already fluttering through the air to various points on the worn carpet, the carpet that might long ago have been replaced with the fine carpet she had stored in her closet until this very morning -- beside the little thatched shrine. That splendid carpet that has flown in the arms of the black-skirted sobbing witch. The witch who will lie about dairy money if need be. This is precisely what Mrs Taylor is dreaming as her cascading postcards flutter to the floor, like card-tricks gone rogue.

The house itself, Number 13, every anxious living brick from bottom to top, side to side, is hushed, yea *flushed* with expectation awaiting the next throw of our mysterious dice. But I shall pause now for a sippa. I, like Rita, favour a first-class cognac now and again.

There, m'dears! Refreshed! On to oblivion!

Nelly sits obediently at her dresser. "Oh Fay. I couldn't seduce a moose. I'm nine feet tall. Wouldn't it be easier to pay a removals man to shift your chest of drawers?"

"Glory in your height. My dear sister did, God rest her."

Nelly looks that sad question at Fay. Fay nods, "She was murdered by an older woman who wore tweeds and brogues, kept hounds and shouted oaths."

"Oh God!"

"Her corpse was hung in a tree for the blue tits to peck at!"

"Oh my God!"

Hugh and his handsome friend sit at coffee over Hugh's kitchen table gazing deeply, gravely, into each other's eyes.

"Well?" says Hugh.

Hugh's handsome friend loosens his colourful Liberty's tie and takes a swallow of coffee, simultaneously moving his knee firmly against Hugh's.

"You've got lovely breasts, love, but they sag, they go flippy-flop. Your titties must thrust upward! Towards the heavens from whence all succour proceeds (don't you wish). Your titties must titillate! What you need is a good, stiff support bra."

"A support bra with these melons? I only want to talk to Bill not lodge him against a wall."

Rita is on her third or is it her fourth cognac? Never mind. She opens another pack of cigarettes, loads her holder, lights and puffs. She remembers things -- doesn't wish to remember these particular things -- because they include Ian. Long, oh so long ago lost Ian. She thinks so often, too often, of Ian. She stops. Thinks of something else. Thinks of her beloved evening French classes she gave up so she could *write*. Thinks of Fay. Sweet Jesus! Why does she keep coming back to Fay? Her novel, of course, m'dears. Fay is grist for its tiny (so far) mill. And who, by the way, are these people who live in this house? Novel writing has opened Ms Pandora's box. But really now, who is this strange woman who makes her so uneasy? This crafty sneak on the top floor? Rita can see everything in Fay's eyes.

Think again, novice author. Fay's eyes are opaque. I saw to that. You only think you penetrate their mauve mystery.

Rita pours her fourth or is it her fifth cognac? But who's counting?

No one, dear. *Absolutely no one.*

Life is nasty, boo-hoo and short, ain't it?

"These were my mother's."

Nelly dangles a pair of ankle-strapped, clear plastic, extremely high-heeled shoes with tiny clusters of plastic sunflowers at their open toes. Rather large shoes too, m'dears, for huge feet. As opposed to *my* so-called *feet* which are so tiny, darlings, that Marcel, a fervently French, acquaintance once remarked that my feet must surely, to inhibit their growth, have been bound at birth, in the ancient Chinese fashion. "Your petite feet," he once assured me, "are nearly as small as were the Dowager Empress of China's." "Ach, More so, Marcel!" I replied. Nice man. He occasionally slips a French letter through my slot. Or did. Memories, sigh I! Toujour l'amour cry I! Have I mentioned that I was reared in Calais -- not *brought-up,* darlings, *reared.* Hence my curiously persistent attention to the French language. But, upon subsequent rumination, I must admit I deeply resented the '*nearly* as small as the Dowager Empress of China's feet'. I am second to no one, m'dears! For I, I, I, I have sunk more ships than Helen launched!

But I digress. I do digress. I do, indeed, digress.

10

"She called them her 'fuck-me' shoes," says Nelly, "She was killed falling off them."

"What a dreadful thing to say about Mummy, Nelly. We must cherish our mothers," says Fay.

"But Mum *was* killed falling off them," insists Nelly, "She tripped and fell into the street and was..." Nelly's voice crumples but continues. "...and was struck by a bus. Daddy tried to save her but he was run over too. I was twelve."

"Where's the bra?" asks Fay, one might say, callously though this was anything but our Fay's intention. She is simply engrossed in recreating this poor, now it seems, motherless-fatherless Nelly -- though losing *both* parents does seems like carelessness. And she, Fay, has always, at least as far back as I allow her to remember (which ain't *that* far), assumed she had a monopoly on tragedy.

Fay does, however, manage to squeeze out: "How sad," and thrusts Nelly's lipstick at her. "Thick. Accentuate your upper lip. You've a good upper lip. Men go crackers over a good upper lip. Make it pout. Drives them randy. I speak from experience."

You can say that again, slag.

Bill and Hugh struggle up the staircase with Nelly's chest of drawers. Fay follows, accompanied by Nelly, large and miserable and wobbling on those impossibly high heels. Nelly's bra-bound breasts, jammed into her radically lowered peasant blouse, thrust comically up and out. Her hair, which could have used a simple wash and fluff, is pulled tight up, tied with curlicued red wrapping ribbon, and piled on top of her head adding several completely redundant inches to her height. She is heavily lipsticked, rouged, purple-eye-shadowed and mercilessly powdered. What a large, trusting woman she is; her heart of gold begging to be snatched. And so I did, m'dears. With apologies yet again to our dear Oscar Fingal O'Flahertie Wills Wilde: The one thing I cannot resist is temptation.

Fay glances over her shoulder at lumbering Nelly then up the stairs at labouring Bill and Hugh and is pleased for Nelly. She'll guide her to romantic fruition, realize for Nelly her fondest dreams!

"Oh me so happy!" cries Fay.

Moi aussi! Je suis très amusé! I'll check this out later. Me French primer has just plummeted into a chasm -- a *chasm*, darlings?!

As they reach Fay's door on the third floor, Fay motions covertly to Nelly who, as arranged, poor good cow, rushes around the two men, opens the door and smiles what can only be, amidst her absurd kit, the ravaged smile of a duped freak. Bill gapes at her. Is she some over-ripe lap-dancer?! Poor Nelly, crushed by Bill's incredulity, seeks succour from Fay. But Fay, nipping at their heels, has followed Bill, Hugh, and her new chest of drawers right into her flat.

Nelly dares not continue, starts briskly down the stairs. On the first landing, Mrs Taylor, drawn by the ruckus and swaying on her cane, peers sleepily out through her chained door. "Strumpet!" she hisses, "Tart!"

Swaying on her treacherous heels, Nelly teeters down the remaining stairs. The poor thing hooks a heel in the frayed carpet on the very last stair and plummets with a great crash against Rita's door which Rita, a further brandy on in a bathrobe and pink-curlers, throws open. Rita's "What the sodding fuck?!" and Mrs Taylor's "Quiet down there!" echo simultaneously as Nelly flops backward, on the threshold and rests neatly between Rita's slippered feet.

"And your name is?" slurs Rita.

Nelly takes scowling Rita's proffered hand as Rita attempts to pull her up but misjudges Nelly's considerable weight, slips, falls to the floor beside her and they lie firmly wedged together in the doorway.

Honestly, m'dears! It's a three-ring circus!

"Awfully Sorry," says Nelly as her sense of humour overcomes her embarrassment and she squeals with laughter. She struggles to her knees then to her feet and teetering on her deceased Mum's fuck-me shoes offers the floored Rita a hand which Rita gladly accepts and between guffaws says: "Lambert, Rita."

"Wilkinson, Nelly."

With ballast to spare Nelly easily pulls Rita to her feet but soon begins again to teeter. Rita chokes with laughter, manages to steady Nelly and simply can't remember when she's had such a good laugh. "Join me for a drinkie?"

"Love to," replies Nelly.

Fay, from the first landing, stares achingly down the staircase at Rita's closing door then starts up the stairs muttering -- as she'd had every intention of being a good girl tonight -- "Damnation" until she meets Hugh at the first landing.

"Thanks so much, Hughie, you are a darling. And a super-shifter!"

"Feel free," he says, "With my key, I mean. Until you're more settled."

Never underestimate the persistent power of a cloisonnéd arse-poking fly-swatter, m'dears.

With a nod towards her flat Hugh says "It's a bit grim up there. Nice rug though. Very nice."

If he only knew how nice.

"Yes, isn't it nice? A gift."

"Nice gift!"

"I will feel free with your key, Hughie. If you really don't mind. But I do feel guilty about your kitchen. It's this finger," Fay sticks her bandaged finger in Hugh's face, "I think it'll need stitches."

"You'd better see to that."

Hugh moves past her down the stairs, "It could go septic. Goodnight."

"Your friend, Hughie," calls Fay, "I hope we haven't inconvenienced him."

"Oh, he left some time ago."

"A friend in need..."

But Hugh has vanished into his flat.

"...is a friend indeed," finishes Fay with a broad grin towards an even broader grin loitering in the still air several inches above the banister (You figure that one out, m'dears).

Thundering "Well done!" Fay scurries by my little anomaly to intercept Bill before he can close his door.

"Pretty bare in here," says Bill, "Furniture not come?"

"My house burned down."

Darling, that's so obvious. But do go on. Who knows where it might, with my help, lead.

Fay is encouraged by my whisper. She leans languidly against the stair rail, arches her back to accentuate her fine, firm breasts and flings her hand -- further defining her perfectly pulchritudinous profile -- over her shoulder towards her door. "What you see in there is the sum total of my earthly estate," sighs Fay, "One bed, here when I came, one chest of drawers courtesy of the somewhat bizarre Nelly, one rug and a kettle."

I, an inveterate shit-stirrer, naughtily injected *the somewhat bizarre.*

Fay laughs a brittle little laugh, "Behold, my dowry."

"He mentioned it. What's-his-name," says Bill, "The fire. Bad luck."

"Yes," replies Fay levering out her chest to accentuate her now hardening bra-less nipples.

I am merciless!

"Yes. Very bad luck. It never rains but it pours."

And you, my incendiary little bird, had better stay out of that rain. Though you will, in the not far future allow yourself, to the further detriment of your ill-realized abilities, to be soaked in a deluge. Apres moi, of course!

Fay shoots another bright, heroic smile at Bill. She knows *she* would be on 24 hour dedicated duty if it meant pleasing, or easing the psychological burden of some newly beloved. She has every intention of doing just that. And soon.

Please, Fay. Not too soon.

Fay casts her eyes about. "What did you say?"

"Nothing," says Bill.

"Not you, love," murmurs Fay.

"Well," says Bill, puzzled as he shyly attempts to ignore Fay's renewed, nippled exertions, "Well. Hope you'll make out all right."

"Bill? It is Bill, is it not?"

"Yes."

"Bill. Could you -- I feel awful -- you've already been so helpful. But could you move my carpet just a smidgin?"

Fay flashes Bill a glance unequivocal even to a man with a lot on his mind. They enter her flat and Fay crosses to the other side of Mrs Taylor's fine carpet, gestures. "If we could just move it from here...to...here? I'd be so grateful, Billy."

Cheeky!

"Bill."

"Yes... Bill."

Fay watches the room change, cued by Mrs Taylor's curious carpet as Bill turns away to slide Nelly's chest of drawers off its edge -- change from cold and loveless grey to warm and loving pinkish orange, glimmering here and there with tiny staccato surges of delight, desire, and longing.

Some carpet, eh? Some room!

As 'Billy' labours for her alone, Fay quickly unbuttons the top four buttons of her blouse, reveals a willing wedge of cleavage. Going to her knees to straighten the carpet's fringe she presents this cleavage in a series of flattering angles to the now extremely observant Bill as she moves along the carpet's edge. He says:

"Will this do? Where do you want it?"

"Just there!"

Fay rises and, floats gracefully off the carpet as Bill tugs it a bit to the left.

"Stop! Just there! Lovely!" cries Fay.

"What's your situation?" asks Bill.

Fay is instantly on her knees again apparently straightening more carpet fringe (There is *such* a lot). "What do you mean?"

"Single? Married? Divorced?" replies Bill. Then more pointedly, gazing down at those shapely breasts. "Alive?" Then yet more pointedly: "Kicking?"

Fay burbles a tinkling laugh. "Alive," she giggles, "Alive *and* kicking!"

The carpet rejoices, its titillating task partially completed.

Ensconced somewhat sloppily (to be brutally frank) on her cretonne sofa, Rita, now ever on the lookout for mill-grist, smiles and attempts with no success to focus her eyes. "In that case, I'll come."

"Friday then," says Nelly, "Six? I'll tell Fay. Poor little thing, and I'll speak to the men tomorrow. I couldn't face them again tonight. Not dressed like this. I knew I looked ridiculous in this unbelievable bra -- I grew out of it years ago -- and these heels. But Fay would have been so hurt if I'd... God knows I don't know how to dress but..."

"You were duped, darling."

My very words! But is this so surprising?

"She's confused. She's doing her best."

"Yes. Her *very* best."

"It won't be a whole evening," says Nelly failing to note Rita's irony as the only thing Nelly knows about irony is that it applies to retro spiral staircases and Victorian bridges. "Just a little welcome before everyone does what they usually do on Fridays.

That's what *she* thinks.

Nelly rises. "Well. Goodnight then. Fay and I are off to the pictures."

"I've enjoyed this," says Rita swaying only slightly as she leads

Nelly to the door.

"So have I. Gosh, I've been here a month and we've never spoken."

"We'll make up for it."

Rita fuzzily wonders if they will. Wonders if after her cognac glow evaporates she will want to but hopes she will. She is taken with Nelly and might even have been cordial without the brandy. Odd how Ritterhouse arrived when she did. Odd how her presence is inadvertently bringing people together.

Inadvertently, Rita? Mind those squares, love! They're everywhere! Really! I thought you were a writer! Focus those saggy eyes!

Fay wiggles on her knees, crossing at least two squares towards Bill, propelled along by a tiny but insistent forward ripple in the grinning, glinting carpet. Her intentions are clear. "My house burned down, Billy..."

She unbuttons the top button of the astonished Bill's fly, pulls his zipper down, down, down. Reaches into the heat. "...so I've only got a bed."

Ach! The pause that enmeshes.

And don't blame Fay. I had a so-called *hand* in this.

11

Nelly trembles with happy thoughts of comradeship. She's in sensible shoes and clothes, makeup scrubbed away -- every bit. She climbs the stairs to Fay's flat, knocks. "Fay? Fay? It's Nelly, love."

No answer. Nelly turns, sees that Bill's door, just opposite, is open. She peeks in. "Fay? Fay, love?"

No Fay. No Bill. Nelly cannot, of course, see the jagged orange glow (flame-like, m'dears) licking beneath the under edge of Fay's door, nor can she see indigo shadows escaping like forlorn spirits at its top hinge. She obviously does not note the slight, sudden tilt of the hall because it just as suddenly tilts right back.

How unobservant we are, m'dears, of all that proceeds around us. Merry molecules, darlings, about their delightful duties. And much more. Oh, so much more. What a mad alternative universe!

Nelly taps on Fay's door again, hears a whisper, says "Fay?"

A muffled scuffle. Nelly, dear Nelly, naive as she is, realizes what's happening -- she's read a couple of novels. But gosh! she's glad she's got on sensible shoes as she's weak in her knees and her heart flutters in her throat. Oh. Nothing serious – she's disappointed but not grief-stricken. Is she jealous? She has no right to be. She's never even properly met the man. It's all rather funny. A joke. On her. Nelly is a good sport. Why shouldn't poor Fay have her fun? Her house burned down.

And if you looked more carefully, love, you could, like Hugh, see the soot under Fay's nails, and a puff of soot even now, spurting from what might at one time have been, by the side of the door, a mouse-hole (or the beginnings of one – specificity is a given with us whatcha-macallums).

Nelly descends the stairs, grateful for her sensible shoes and her loving though deceased family and, not least, for her little annuity. Money is important – though she has never thought about it so much as recently. But it's easy to say you don't care about money if you've got it. Nelly, thankful she's got it, at least a very little bit of it, disappears into her flat with much sympathy for Fay who hasn't any -- even a very little bit.

Yet.

In his bathroom Bill wipes Fay's lipstick from his mouth with a long strip of toilet paper. He washes his face and hands thoroughly, dries them and frowns into his basin mirror. He had a lot on his mind before. Now he's got a lot more.

Oh where have you been, Billy-boy, silly boy? Oh where have you been, silly Billy?

Time for a nip, darlings. Bear with me whilst I slurp. Ach. Hit the spot. Let us now, with alacrity, proceed. We women must do what we women must do.

A moment later Fay rushes from her door. Her clothes are askew, her lipstick smeared. She claws her fingers through her hair, m'dears, whips it into a frenzy and descends the stairs by two's, pounds with both fists until Nelly opens her door.

"Oh Nelly," sobs Fay, "it was awful! He covered my mouth when you knocked! I thought I would suffocate! But I got away! Though simply stupefied with fear, I got away!"

Do you really believe that, Fay? Of course she does!

"Please! Please, stop!" cries Fay at me as the hallway shifts from cerulean to pink and back to cerulean and the hall carpet sends tiny fearful tuftlets ceiling-wards. Or, if one prefers, *heaven*ward (for what it's worth).

Nelly throws her arms around Fay, leads her quickly in. Whether Fay lies or not -- and she must be lying because Bill is only a helpless, sweet, troubled man -- makes no great difference to Nelly. Nelly understands. She plants the flailing, wailing Fay gently as possible on the sofa and drops beside her, holds her tight, safe from horrors only Fay, apparently, can see. Though I too, m'dears, have glimpsed my share.

"It's my fault, I know!" wails Fay through tears now comfortably copious, "But I've been so unhappy, Nelly. I'm not myself. I didn't mean not to be a friend to you. You're my only friend, Nelly. Everyone died in the fire, Nelly (Except you, darling Fay. *Think* on it.). Everyone and everything. Nobody likes me, Nelly. Nobody loves me. Nobody wants me. Forgive me, Nelly, please. Men are brutes, Nelly. Brutes! But I didn't capitulate, Nelly. I did not capitulate!"

Fay buries her head between Nelly's breasts.

"There's a love. There, there, love, don't cry. Nelly's here," whispers kind, prematurely invisible Nelly who must now drop one of Fay's hands to wipe a tear from her own eye. An eye, incidentally, in which that mythical soul is embarrassingly visible.

But we mustn't speak of souls in our furtive Fay's presence.

"What?" whimpers Fay from the valley of warmth 'twixt Nelly's breasts, "What did you say?"

"Nothing, darling," replies Nelly.

The good Nelly yawns, opens her eyes but quickly shuts them; the morning light through her living room window, even with curtains drawn, is too bright. She stretches on her cramped sofa, reaches for her robe, remembers last night and shares a small reprise of Fay's pain. "Poor little Fay," she whispers and checks her wristwatch and jumps up.

Nelly is now fully dressed in clothes nearly as garish though miles more comfortable than last night's. Her beautifully thick red hair has received its required wash and fluff. To keep from waking Fay, she used the hair-dryer on 'low' and only half as long as she should have. (Has kindness no limits?)

Nelly gulps the last of her morning coffee, pours another and takes it into her bedroom where Fay, slowly, comfortably, is just waking in (where else, m'dears?) Nelly's comfortable bed.

"Fay, love. Coffee."

"Oh. Nelly. It's *you*!"

Who did you expect, bimbo? Godzilla?!

"What?" says Fay, "What did you say?"

"I said coffee, darling."

Nelly sticks out the cup of fragrant, steaming coffee. Fay sits up, smiles radiantly, snatches it saying "How very, very good of you."

She means it, m'dears. Have mercy and mercy will be shown thee – I mean it too.

"I'm off to work, love. Lock up when you've finished. Fix yourself a nice breakfast. There's eggs and bacon in the fridge. Don't make any plans for tomorrow night. I've got something up my sleeve."

"Oh, Nelly! What *can* it be?!" cries Fay, splattering her coffee on Nelly's fine antique patchwork quilt. "Plans-plans-plans!" chants Fay, perilously near the correct timbre of a forgotten incendiary incantation, perilously near burning the house down here and now.

"A nice little surprise," says Nelly who refuses to be upset by a quarter cup of indelible coffee on a valuable heirloom, a present from her deceased, beloved mum of the fuckable shoes.

Forbearance, m'dears. A lesson for us all. Goodness doesn't

grow on trees. Nor should it. Though *I* have plucked it more than once.

"I was a naughty girl yesterday," says Fay, "*Je* don't deserve a nice surprise."

"Shuh?"

"Sorry," says Fay, "I sporadically lapse into the exquisite French language. My mother was reared in Calais.

You bet she was, sugar! And she *loved* it!

"N'est-ce pas?" coos Fay -- who, herewith, exhausts her gallic vocabulary.

Nelly laughs and replies louder than intended, "Oui oui!"

Fay giggles and claps her hands. "Golly! You speak French too!"

"And, you," says Nelly, blushing violently and abruptly changing the subject, "you are getting a surprise tomorrow night whether you want it or not. So there!"

Nelly enjoys being firm in a good cause. She gathers up her canvas carry-all, blows a kiss to Fay and joins Hugh and Bill at the bus stop for the 7.55 Red Arrow.

Fay, in frayed cotton panties, her only pair (an oversight on my part, m'dears -- she wears them every other day) watches from Nelly's window. They're laughing out there! Nelly, of all people seems to have said something funny! Shy, slow Nelly is suddenly become a comedian. Fay is pleased for Nelly. Pleased to see that her, Fay's, assistance has borne early fruit. Nelly is so much more confident now. Tomorrow Nelly will climb a tree. Perhaps two! Fay promises herself she will be more careful in future about sleeping with -- if indeed she did sleep with (what do *you* think, m'dears?) a potential girlfriend's potential boyfriend.

You know how those things just errr...sort of happen? Through no fault of our own? Yeah, sure you do.

As Fay watches through the window, Nelly turns serious. Hugh and Bill turn serious. Both nod solemnly. Fay knows it has to do with her. Don't ask her how she knows. She couldn't tell you because she doesn't know how she knows.

But I know. The house knows. And our influence is wide. Certainly wide enough to extend a few feet to a Red Arrow bus stop.

Mrs Taylor waters her window box, the excess splashing over Rita's window below. Rita, at her window, jumps back, looks up, frowns, looks down at the bus stop, smiles. I now know one of these people. Nelly. For better or worse. I'll meet the others on Friday at six-thirty. One must know people to write about them.

Right you are, sugar. You'll soon know another one of them far better than you'd care, too. But it's 'grist for the writer's mill' as you insist upon saying so unpoetically (or is it *me*?). Or, 'mill-grist'. Is that me as well? It seems, sometimes, that everything is me.

As indeed it is.

At least so far as I am concerned. Look into your hearts, m'dears. Similarities abound. Are we so different from one another?

12

The Red Arrow arrives and Nelly, Bill and Hugh, laughing again, climb on.

"What is so funny?" murmurs Fay, still at Nelly's window. "What was so bloody funny out there? Too much confidence is worse than none at all!"

Atta girl!

Gosh! Nelly, comfortable in her bus seat beside Bill, can hardly believe what's happened. She has said something funny and Bill and Hugh laughed. She cannot remember precisely what it was. Something about her clothes last night? The crazy inappropriateness of her clothes? Oh yes: She said: 'My continuing experiment in dishevelment' -- or was it 'dishabille'? She made herself out as an eccentric dresser by design -- felt that, after last night she had nothing to lose. Bill likes her! As she spoke she felt herself (as in Rita's wretched little theory) materialise; first become ectoplasm, then, wonder of wonders, fully visible! Gosh! She's got it right. She thinks she has. Maybe she has. Dear, good Nelly. Kind Nelly. Be careful, Nelly, and good luck. You'll need it, lovey. If I have my way. And Fay, bless her, through my malfeasant guidance is learning a thing or two herself. Let us hope she is not *too* apt a pupil. Else our gamey task might be a pushover and no fun for no one -- might even self-destruct without a trace!

Somewhat later, Mrs Taylor opens her door a crack, surveys the hall, checks if it's safe to venture out. Nobody here. It's safe. She creeps, puffing, down the stairs looking this way and that, prepared for any horrifying eventuality -- she's had a few, all fortunately forgotten. Time, and I, can be kind.

Is that witch about? The witch who stole her carpet? But that was fate not theft. She chuckles and secure on her cane descends so slowly, deeply suspicious of each creaking, complaining stair. And of course oblivious to the kaleidoscope of outrageous colour playing about her knobby, cotton-stockinged knees.

Open your eyes, my darlings! Look about! There is more to see than you can safely reckon with.

At the post table Taylor snatches up a card, reads it, kisses it (don't ask why -- even though she remembers this morning she still wouldn't reveal her secret -- it's too bleedin' important).

Fay listens just inside Nelly's door. It is not enough to listen so she inches the door open, peeks at Taylor who hunches over the post table. "What a fragile old thing," whispers Fay, "What a tragically fragile old baggage. A tiny tumble down those stairs could snap her spine like a match stick. I must see that this never happens. I must take special pains with this dear, crotchety old creature. After all, every old lady has mum-potential. I need a mum. Desperately. Or perhaps a Granny. Or at least some *hair-of-hag*."

Fay gasps. "Why did I say that?! Why did I say hair-of-hag?"

Caaaareful, daaarling. When the time is ripe all shall be revealed.

Fay inches the door shut again, twirls and begins a thorough, hour-long snoop of Nelly's flat, loading her cardigan pockets with various small and practical articles. She keeps a careful tally in her head, has every intention of paying back to Nelly a hundredfold the myriad Nelly-won't-miss-'em minor items she pockets, including those voluminous but beautifully laundered, faded mauve, panties.

At the back of a disorderly drawer she finds a black silk scarf, fancies it, pockets it too. "Me love black!" lisps Fay, "Me so entirely gorgeous in black!"

Because it's your colour, darling, one of them.

"What?" says Fay, "What was that?"

The room groans as only rooms can groan, stretches, vibrates, morphs from off-white to moss-green, seems to sprout small mushrooms, each topped with a miniscule salamander, belches and returns to its former state – all in the twinkling of an eye. "Well?" says Fay, "Answer me."

But I have no intention of doing so. I will not be interrogated.

Rita types, lost in a bliss of creation and an early cognac. Why not? Mr Courvoisier never lets her down though he is an expensive date.

But an actress's sources of revenue are divers, aren't they dear?

"Divers?" asks Rita, as though she too hears me.

"Scooba divers?" laughs Rita, thankful that she had, most contrary to her nature, squirrelled away a good deal of revenue during those long ago fat-cat-role days before she tippled away her proscenium possibilities. "But divers?" murmurs Rita, "Where did *that* come from?"

Fay at last deserts Nelly's flat and halfway up the stairs realizes it's lunchtime. "My body is a temple and it is time for worship."

She commences to cross herself but I stay her hand. I will have no other gods before me!

She hurries up the now uncomplaining stairs to her own flat, rushes in and empties her bulging cardigan pockets on her bed then exits, securely re-locking her door, checking the lock again and again. Then once again. Plunder must be protected (though that glimmering carpet could bark loud as Cerberus at any intruder).

But 'plunder'? Fay wouldn't have put it that way. It's only a loan, isn't it, Fay? After all, your house burned down. Or was it 'up'? No. It was a flat. It was *gutted.* Ask Nelly.

Isn't incendiary chat amusing?

Fay clambers down the stairs, her ravenous appetite nearly overtaking her, unlocks Hugh's door, sashays right in.

My little minx has a cute way of ambulatin' that was entirely my idea.

"What?" says Fay, but drops my thought as she's fixed on food -- peculiar metabolisms require abundant fuel. Often. Sow-eeeee!

She proceeds directly to Hugh's kitchen, not seeing the completely blanketed figure sleeping in Hugh's sofa bed.

Whoa!

In the kitchen she finds some cookies in a tin on a shelf -- Nelly's were simply not enough, stuffs two in her mouth, six in her pocket, and turns on the cooker, strikes a match. The burner ignites with a small flaming explosion. She screams and falls against the kitchen sink, leans here trembling, engrossed in something flame-like that twists in her head. You'd lean there trembling too, if you were Fay. A Phoenix is a strange bird.

Fay's burning contemplations are interrupted by a heavy yawn from Hugh's living room. "My, my," says Fay, recovering, "What the dickens can that be? Me must go and see!"

She places the kettle on the cooker, shoves two more cookies into her mouth, wonders why Americans say cookies instead of biscuits, and tiptoes to the kitchen door. The concealed figure on the sofa bed turns, yawns again. Fay smiles. Mischievously? Malevolently? Even Fay doesn't know. However, her arms instinctively arch akimbo, rest there aggressively (with only minimal prompting from me). The concealed figure yawns twice more from beneath tented sheets.

Still munching cookie, Fay moves nearer this mysterious figure, bends and smiles. Spitting crumbs, she cries "Are you Hughie's boyfriend?"

The bedclothes fall away. The figure, startled, sits up, regards Fay blankly until it regains its composure then replies, "No! Are you?!"

This naked creature has pert little breasts! Two of them!

"Ritterhouse, Fay," stammers Fay, "My house burned down."

This pert-breasted young woman replies "Really? And were you in it?"

Fay backs away. Her lips tremble. A crumb tumbles from the corner of her mouth. Again she says:

"My house burned down."

For that is all she can manage.

Poor Fay. There are reasons -- reasons that beg forbearance. Reasons that -- Ach! Enough of this! Get on with it, Fay! Before I lose my patience! Pull up your socks! A new square awaits! Abandon ship!

The buzz of evening traffic permeates Fay's room. Her one room -- not counting the tiny kitchen and bath. One room. At the top. On the street. Shabby. *So* shabby (descriptive detail, m'dears, a necessary evil though it does make the time fly by).

Another day has passed, another morning, another afternoon. Fay has remained here the whole time, like a bug in, or rather on, her fine new rug; afraid if she ventures out she will meet the irate young woman she encountered in Hugh's flat the day before. She of the two pert breasts and the towering frown.

Fay exists on leftovers from her feast at Hugh's. She'd better have them now. They'll begin to rot – but it wouldn't be the first time she'd eaten decayed food (Or so it seems to Fay).

This poor creature has no idea of the scope of her latent powers. She will. If and when she does her homework. Bleeding hell! I can't manage everything at once, can I?

Nelly has appeared briefly, twice, to tell her about tonight then not again. But Nelly has a job – went off for some teaching conference somewhere -- and is also busy with tonight's surprise. Fay has heard her in the hall, just now, talking, laughing, planning for tonight!

Ah! New friends! So near! Just beyond her grimy paint-peeling door. "Me so happy! Me so happy me want to cry!" exults The Ritterhouse Fay and leaps on her bed, it's hers now, this bed. It was here when she came. "Finders-keepers-losers-weepers," chants Fay with a marvellous smile. Her scuffed leather draw-stringed bag and that cheap open suitcase beside her, she unpacks into Nelly's chest of drawers -- *Fay's* chest of drawers -- which is not so fine as it had seemed upon first inspection -- pressed wood, not carved. But "beggars-can't-be-choosers," chants she.

Fay will present Nelly -- when the time comes, of course -- with an excellent lime-wood, hand carved something-or-other. Fay can't quite remember the last page of that gift catalogue she had carried with her until its pages disintegrated and, like an ancient sepulchral bouquet, became a handful of dust. Think on it, darlings, such awaits us all. But let us into our next square *mundanely slither,* Ach! That ever-apt adverb and its virulent verb partner!

From her suitcase Fay takes a large ball of twine and four paper carry-bags, places them in the bottom of her new chest of drawers. An overripe banana moulders mashed between three wrinkled apples at a corner of the suitcase (I *always* provide a simple box-lunch, m'dears). She removes this fetid fruit cocktail, sets it on a shelf in the kitchen -- "waste-not-want-not" (more chanting). She returns to her bare mattress bed where she gathers up plunder from Nelly's and places it on a shelf in the kitchen beside pillage from Hugh's. She is appreciative, more grateful than anyone can surmise! She will thank Hugh and Nelly later too, in earthly goods as well as bubbling love. "Oh, they won't be sorry!" cries Fay, immediately adjacent to ecstasy.

Appreciate this, m'dears. Take Fay to your hearts. I have.

Fay snatches from her suitcase a large, blue velvet table cloth embellished with silver embroidered minarets and crescent-moons and covers the bare mattress. It mates magnificently with Mrs Taylor's -- Fay's! -- carpet. "They were made for one another!" cries Fay.

Don't be daft, dearie, of course they were. And *you* were made for them.

Fay's eyes dart to the side, eyebrows arched and suspicious, ears pricked towards that infernal whisper. But I am silent. So she soon forgets (Like Taylor -- is it *hereditary*?!). Some forms of lower animals, darlings, forget in a matter of seconds. Salamanders, we are told, do. And indeed I have seen it. Where *does* that leave our Ritterhouse Fay who steps back, admires her wonderful carpet, sighs with pleasure, wipes away a tear -- a real tear (it may as well be real). She is too happy for words until she begins again to remember what she'd forgotten. Mrs Taylor's voice was familiar wasn't it? Fay had heard it before in the dim...the dim *what,* dear? Never mind.

Isn't this fun?! No, m'dears, I am not sadistic. Don't you dare to think it!

13

It is twilight. The sun has prematurely disappeared behind that multi-storied palace of progress across the street as Fay pants with excitement for the evening at hand. She switches on a bare-bulbed wall lamp, squints disapprovingly into the glare. She snatches a felt-tipped marking pencil from her bag and removes the twin light bulbs from the lamp and -- mumbling something unintelligible (she never took our seminars seriously) -- pencils the bulbs blue, returns them to their sockets and switches on the lamp. The effect is negligible but pleases her. Not so harsh. She's learned a thing or three from Blanche DuBois and me. In a glare her thirty years could melt easily into a hundred? This must be avoided at all costs. At *all* costs. My charmed cheque-book, darlings, ain't infinite.

Fay carries her wilting bouquet-in-a-jam-jar from the window sill and sets it on Nelly's chest of drawers, does a wee turn in the middle of Taylor's -- Fay's! -- carpet and claps her hands. The carpet giggles surreptitiously, wiggles suggestively and just manages a tiny belch of pleasure. But it's got mischief on its mind.

"Party-time!" cries Fay, "Oh, it's nearly party time!"

Her new friends will soon press close around her, full of concern, predicts Fay, full of good intentions. Full to bursting with...with, golly! camaraderie and endless questions about her well-being: How is Mummy? How was lunch? We once owned kittens too, every man-jack (or woman-jill) of us. We understand, at the deepest level, the grief of your feline loss (the kittens, m'dears, the *kittens*! Or was it a cat?). As well as your sorrow over that sad and pesky, uncommunicative Mum, plus the loss of your singular sister, and house and/or flat etc. Do you need money? We can all of us spare a tenner now and then -- we mean, just until you get back on your feet. A fire is no picnic...etc... etc... etc...

"Oh! me so happy!" sings Fay, "Me so happy me could bust!"

*Com*bust, darling, *com*bust. Not yet. It's too early.

"You won't make me cry today!" sings Fay who flies to the kitchen on gossamer wings (metaphorically, m'dears, just now anyhow), "I'm having a party!"

From behind that little old cooker she snatches a bottle of wine, compliments of Hugh unbeknownst, opens it with a corkscrew, compliments of Nelly ditto, pours into a large glass, compliments of Hugh, adds three cubes of sugar, compliments of Rita and quaffs it amid, what amounts to, a miniature ritual built upon other peoples' possessions about whose meaning Fay is clueless. Let me just hint, however, that Nelly's place in this ceremony of found objects, is far more developed than Hugh's. Rita, at the moment, despite her late kettle and sugar cubes (eleven in number) seems a lost cause though nonetheless a challenge. But ach! The floor-boards, tittering, tingle with anticipation for the evening ahead. The celebration! Goodness! We've already seen what Fay, with a little help from her inanimate friends, can do with a cloisonné fly-swatter! The previous tenant, a certain Mr LaFarge, celebrated nothing, certainly not his own untimely demise head-in-the-oven of that tiny appliance that calls itself (out of earshot) a cooker.

Not for naught, m'dears, the Number *13*. Trite but often oh so true. Believe it. Gather your experiential advantages like cabbages on a crisp but dewy night. 'Cause you *never* know.

Fay carries the wine bottle and glass to the bathroom, twists on the bathtub tap and perches on the tub edge, pours and quaffs another glass of wine. She hurtles back to the kitchen, pours another glass, adds more sugar, quaffs. Pours yet another, hurtles to the bathroom, sets the wine glass on the tub's edge.

But ach, m'dears! Fay has an excellent body. A smallish, wasp-waist, fine, well-shaped breasts, a flat tummy and creamy, full, but not too full, thighs. Plus splendid calves. Her skin, such skin! Her body is a temple. But there is something about her face, the face she now regards in her bathroom mirror, that...

She turns sharply away from the mirror, something about her face that what? Fay, the eyes are the windows of the soul.

> I got those early evenin' blues...

> sings Fay

> Those ce-ru-le-an blues
> Ain't never been so blue
> Got those ce-ru-le-an blues

Cerulean, m'dears, the colour of clear sky? But why so blue over a clear, dark blue sky? Ah yes, Fay's ubiquitous shadows, of course,

I sit here weepin'
My tears go seepin'
Down 'tween my toes

sings Fay

But who knows?
Who knows?
Who knows?

I know, Fay. *I* know. But personally, I prefer Duke Ellington.

Fay's eyes pinwheel! "*Who* prefers Duke Ellington?!" she cries, "Who else in my squalid little bathroom prefers Duke Ellington?!"

Oh, Fay, come off it. You know who.

Fay slumps a moment, dazed. Squints, focuses, and peers again into the basin mirror. "I cannot see my soul," she murmurs. "I cannot. Do I have one? Who am I? Who was I?"

"RITTERHOUSE, FAY, 1-6-4-5-2, PRESENT AND ACCOUNTED FOR!" swells up from somewhere. She clenches her teeth, looks deeper into the mirror. Her nose touches, leaves an oily smudge. She snatches a bit of toilet tissue and scrubs at the smudge -- it's her oily skin keeps her face so young (she inaccurately surmises). She scrubs again at the mirror smudge, finds herself breathing hard for such little effort. Finds herself frightened. She was so happy a moment ago.

Naked and frightened, at her new chest of drawers, she removes a threadbare, somewhat *singed,* bath towel, throws it over her shoulders. Barefoot on her splendid carpet she digs her toes in. The carpet sighs with pleasure, allows an arpeggio of tiny orgasmic grunts to escape its silken nap.

The wine warms but the room is cold. "Brrrrr!" she whoops, and shivers. She springs to the bathtub and, careful of the wine she has set at the tub's edge, lowers herself gently into the hot water, warmer water than she is accustomed to, warmer water than was allowed where she came from. She loves it. Who wouldn't?

"Ohhhh!" she cries. "Ohhhh!" she sighs and lies back. The steaming water closes over her well-shaped breasts and flat tummy and creamy, full, but not too full, thighs. And, oh yes. Her splendid calves. And that skin. Such skin! Her body *is* a temple. A sunken cathedral.

Fay takes a long satisfying swallow of her ritual wine, sets the ritual glass carefully back on the bathtub's edge, sings:

> I got those ce-ru-le-an blues...

Using a small shampoo sample, compliments of Nelly who'll never miss it, Fay scrubs her hair vigorously, gets shampoo in her eyes, grimaces, splashes it out, sings:

> Ain't never been so blue
> Got those ce-ru-le-an blues
> I sit here weepin'
> My tears go seepin'
> Down 'tween my toes...
> But who knows?
> Who knows?
> *Who* knows?

The *shadows* know, peaches.

Fay stops singing. She's worried about her soul, that pesky soul, again. "Perhaps I should look for it in Nelly's silver flea-market mirror?" peeps Fay, wishing she had pocketed that too. She turns cosily in the unaccustomed watery warmth, "I'm certain Nelly saw souls right and left in that flea-market mirror. She is sweet and soulful and so sincere. Perhaps, in her dresser mirror, I might have seen what lies behind the misting mauve of my eyes?" bubbles Fay into the hot, nose-level water, the poetry of her/our prose waxing to new mini-heights.

A bit of scientific information: Fay's eyes, even if reflected in dear Nelly's mirror would simply remain opaque, each dotted at its centre with a microscopic black hole that, similar to its galactic counterparts, sucks everything in and allows nothing, but nothing, m'dears, out.

Rita thought she saw right into Fay's eyes, saw deceit -- more fool you, Rita. For I guarantee there is no deceit in Fay. There is nothing in Fay that *I* have not ordained. Well, *almost* nothing (Oh to see ourselves as others see us!). Fay is not familiar with the word 'deceit'. Fay, left alone is, for all intents and purposes, one of those... innocenti?

So here lies our faultless Fay on her back submerged to her

nose in the soothing hot water, hotter than was allowed (where she came from). She raises both splendid legs high into the air. Water cascades from toenails that could be cleaner. Soot? She thrusts the offending toenails into the water, hides them in soapy clouds, wishes she had a nail brush, must find one, Nelly might have one, Rita might have one. No. But Hughie might have one in his bathroom drawer of bulging muscles and frontal bustles...

Fay lies very still and frightened, whispers:

"No. No. No."

I do feel guilty. Who wouldn't whisper 'no' if their bathroom had, at the drop of a hat, cloaked itself in quivering, depressive shadows of deep purple and indigo? But never mind.

"What? whispers Fay.

Nothing, darling. Water dries the skin. God only knows what it does to potential phoenixes. However, our task lies, ever gleaming, on that hinder-most of burners, unobtrusive and unwilling to spoil my amusement at hand. But there, m'dears, decidedly there.

"What?" repeats Fay, "What was that?"

Belt up and bathe, bimbo.

14

Fay is dressed (in that familiar shabby black ensemble), stands before her basin mirror. A thousand thoughts clatter through her head. If only she could connect with them -- derive some meaning from them. "I'm in a right muddle, Mummykins." But she's never called her mum 'Mummykins'. Who the hell is 'Mummykins'?

"None of your business," says Fay, "None of your bleeding bees-wax."

Beware, Fay, I can get tough with you!

"What?!" says Fay.

Fay blinks, widens her eyes, scans the bathroom a moment then hitches up her skirt, drops herself on the toilet seat and sighs. She is exhausted and hungry -- for whatever. *Whatever* usually requires the abundant application of makeup so she trowels on an adequate amount of that dark red lipstick filched from Nelly's dresser.

I should have taught you more about cosmetology, Ritterhouse. You are not subtle.

"I was a beautician of highest calibre!" replies Fay who crams the lipstick back into her cardy pocket, pats herself dry, thoroughly, even savagely, washes her hands and marches defiantly into her bed-sitting-room where she poses at parade-rest, surveys her domain. The crescent-moons bed covering and Mrs Taylor's fine carpet lend an exotic, dreamlike air to the emptiness, the shabbiness. She sighs happily then turns and snatches a tray of watery ice cubes from the miserable little fridge. She will offer ice water in that horrid, discarded old plastic pitcher, to her loving new friends. Ice water is all she's got. Her dark red lipstick will do the rest. They will understand. People always understand. When your house burns down.

Nice schtick, Honey. But remember, you're just the piano not the music. Credit, *doll*, where credit is due, huh? Get it? Got it?! Good!

Nelly carries a large tray of sandwiches and freshly baked cookies, taps shyly at Fay's half open door, pushes it open. She is closely followed by Rita who tipsily bears a box of clinking glasses and cutlery. The women go directly to Fay's little kitchen.

"You are...too kind," manages Fay from her sweetened-wine euphoria.

"Much too," sing-songs Rita, passing.

"Leave the door open, love," calls Nelly over her shoulder, "More is on the way!"

Hugh brings a very small drop-leaf table and is accompanied by that young woman, she of the two pert breasts, who, seeing Fay, smiles a tiny smile at Hugh.

"Oh, Hughie!" cries Fay, "For me?"

Hugh nods, says "Where shall we put it?"

"Oh Hughie! You shouldn't have!"

"That's what I said," says Two-Breasts.

Hugh repeats:

"Where shall we put it?"

Fay slaps a finger to her chin and hip swung radically awry, pauses, m'dears, poses and ponders. "Oh Brave new world!" she exclaims, "that hath such people in it!" She grins at Two-Breasts as though they'd never met, skips gaily over her exquisite carpet to that one grimy window.

"Listen, kiddies! It was made for here!"

The young woman stares at Fay, fascinated by this mannered, black-skirted freak who jumps about swinging her hips and exclaiming odd things – in baby-talk to boot! Was she born yesterday?!

Not yesterday, Jenny. But you're close.

"Fay," says Hugh, nodding to Jenny as he places the table where designated, "This is Jenny."

"Hello to you," says Fay revealing nothing.

"Hi, Ritterhouse," says Jenny.

"'Fay', please," replies Fay who wonders why people insist upon calling her Ritterhouse, "Please call me Fay."

"Fay it is, Ritterhouse," says Jenny, who dislikes being rudely awakened by sneaky, gender-challenged intruders. Hugh'd better get his key back – and pronto.

Bill clumps into the room with a tiny armchair – Nelly and I convinced him. He's sweet on Nelly. Fay twirls to meet him and squeaks delightedly "It's Christmas, everyone! Christmas in October!"

Fay moves too close to Bill -- Nelly should see this but she's still in the kitchen -- and says, her hand on the chair arm:

"Whatever did I do to deserve this?"

Jenny smiles, knowing precisely what Fay's done. She'd heard the noise on the stairs two nights ago, opened the door to see the dishevelled, wild-eyed Fay fly past down the stairs, heard Bill return to his room. The walls are paper.

I've said that before -- about the paper -- and I'll say it again -- it's crucial. Paper burns so easily, m'dears. And its ashes are so fine, so wind-friendly.

Fay's glance darts to a crack in the ceiling surrounded by a curious discoloration she hadn't noticed before. "Can strange voices emanate from sinister discolorations?" she asks Jenny.

"It depends," replies Jenny with the straightest of faces.

But Fay isn't listening, she's caressing the worn but serviceable little armchair that Nelly has charmed from Bill for her, while Bill says, with a shudder, precisely as he said it two nights before: "Where do you want it?"

Fay takes Bill firmly by the elbow, leads him to the other side of her magnificent carpet. "Here, Billy," she says.

"Bill," he corrects.

"Bill," she says, "It must go here. It couldn't possibly go anywhere else. Because..."

Fay twirls, curtsies to everyone and recites:

> There is no place
> Just like this place...

She stoops (*lithely*, I must, reluctantly, add), touches her palm, without bending her knees, to the floor where the chair is to be placed. Rises, continues:

> ...Anywhere near
> This place.
> So this...

She stoops again, touches the floor.

> So this
> Must be
> The place!

And it is, darlings. Indeed it *is*.

Fay laughs merrily, looking from face to face for approval. All she's ever wanted is a hug or a kiss plus maybe a shag or three along the way – but who, I ask you, does not? Let's face it, m'dears, that's a *given*.

Weak smiles appear consecutively on Hugh and Bill while Jenny only gazes studiously at Fay, seriously wondering how she manages to move her lips through so much lipstick.

"That wasn't nice at all," thinks Fay who often hears things she oughtn't. Take it from me, darlings, it can be painful being sensitive and obtuse at the very same time. And perfectly excruciating being my darling prosopopoeia.

Bill sets the armchair where Fay has indicated, says "I need a drink."

Jenny laughs. Hugh pokes her. She laughs louder.

"Friends in need are friends indeed!" cries Fay and twirls merrily yet again.

"I'll second that!" says Jenny who does a small, dead-eyed twirl of her own to the intense displeasure of both Fay and her carpet. And me. Mind, Jenny, nasty thoughts, like nasty deeds, do not go unpunished.

Nelly enters relaxed after two sips in the kitchen -- gosh! she's just so nervous. Bill has smiled at her and she resolutely does not think he did what Fay said he did and furthermore...oh, gosh! Alcohol goes straight to her head.

Rita is beginning to wonder how she, Rita, came to be here at all. But she follows along after Nelly and is tipsy enough to be broad-minded -- for the moment. Besides, her novel proceeds apace, mill-gristed from every quarter. So she smiles too. Then, with arms about each other's waists she and Nelly make for the door and Nelly places a finger to Rita's lips as they disappear.

Fay spins from the door to face Hugh and Jenny and Bill. "Whatever can they be up to?" she cries and giggles to each in turn – literally *to each in turn*.

Honestly, Fay, if this wasn't so much fun I'd be embarrassed.

"I'm not lissssten-ning," replies Fay. "So you can just belt up!"

Who can Fay be speaking to? Someone from that crazy 'discolouration' in the ceiling? wonders Jenny.

Nelly sticks her head in, says: "We need two men," (who *doesn't* dearie? Preferably simultaneously). Hugh and Bill go out. Jenny starts to follow but Fay grabs her arm.

"Stay. Please stay!"

The room, it *will* do this, tilts, so that Jenny, if she'd wished to leave just then, couldn't -- but of course, she is not aware of this and only regards Fay icily.

"Sit down. Please," says Fay and motions to the recently arrived armchair. "I couldn't have said that yesterday, 'Sit down', I had no chair yesterday."

"Your house burned down," replies Jenny and sits.

"Yes it did. But tragedy is often a sheep in wolf's clothing."

"I wouldn't know, I've not had that many tragedies."

Careful, Jenny, it can be arranged. Fay might remember who we are and dish out a few.

Fay drops herself beside Jenny's chair on that lovely, multi-talented rug, crosses her legs Indian-style. "I've had more than my share of tragic sequences."

Tragic sequences, Fay? Where am I going wrong here? Get out your thesaurus, darling.

"But it doesn't pay to moan about misfortune, does it?" whispers Fay uncomfortably close to Jenny's ear.

"Doesn't it?"

"You are very lucky."

"How's that?"

"Hughie is a fine person. A sensitive, caring, *versatile* man."

"You're very well informed."

"I make it my business."

"I've noticed."

Jenny relaxes into the armchair that wasn't here yesterday, looks steadily at Fay, prepared not to believe anything, *anything*. But Fay continues, so seriously. So believably. And the armchair cradles Jenny and the room rocks so amiably.

"I'm much more complicated than..." Fay pauses, "than I seem."

"I do hope so."

That wasn't nice, Jenny.

"I immersed myself, Jenny, in psychology until my dear sister's demise necessitated my constant presence at Mummy's side. Sis was murdered."

Jenny is impassive -- for a moment, only a moment -- wondering again at Fay's curious use of language. Then an odd vibration begins to move through her. It's like the time a student friend attempted to hypnotize her, and Jenny's arm, having nothing to do with herself, began on command to rise and she slapped her own face then, panicked, shouted to her friend to Stop! Stop!

"What did you say, Jenny?" says Fay.

"I said nothing," but to herself: I thought it, I thought it!

"What?" says Fay.

"You're hearing things," says Jenny. Sweat beads, stings her eyes.

"Yes," says Fay, "I am hearing things."

She sweeps Jenny with a curious smile, whispers conspiratorially, "Sister Jane was murdered," then, sliding closer, "by an older woman who wore tweeds and brogues and kept hounds and shouted oaths."

Oaths, Fay? Not *incantations*?

"Mummy was destroyed."

That is what is known as a *plaint*, m'dears, or a *lament*. That sister Jane bit, or even a *leitmotiv*? Ach! I must do my own homework. In any case, leitmotivs are a valid literary tool. Particularly in a saga. Or, stretching it, *even* an opera! So no lip, please.

"In the fire?" asks Jenny, sorry the moment she's said it but she can't help herself. "Your mother was destroyed in the fire?" she adds recklessly.

Fay makes people feel sorry. Sometimes. One day she'll make Jenny feel very sorry. But all in a good cause, of course.

Which *is*...?

"She is incommunicado, Mummy," continues Fay, pointedly ignoring me though I did cause her to blink uncomfortably several times. "It has not been a picnic. Mummy is confined now. I have sent her a veritable flood of flowers and medium sized gifts. All my meagre shop-clerk's wages would allow. Nothing helped."

It never does. Pardon my cynicism but it's dark out here.

Jenny leans forward in the chair. These vibrations are stronger now. Worrying.

"Then," says Fay, her voice breaking, "with the fire, my own source of comfort and encouragement -- my daily diary entries -- went up in flames. I had kept a diary from the age of six."

Fay's hands jerk up to cover her face. The odd vibration in Jenny leaps and grows. Can she be wrong about this woman? Her mind tells her certainly not. Fay is a phony (food for thought, m'dears). But something else, something in this vibration, intimates...

"Is it possible, you may ask, to suffer so? In silence?" asks Fay.

"Apparently not," replies Jenny, attempting to free herself from these...are these *shackles* around her wrists?! Rusty *shackles*?!

Fay's face glows as though lit by a hidden spotlight. How does she *do* that? thinks Jenny.

"I must apologize for yesterday," says Fay, "I had no idea you were in Hughie's flat."

"I stay there from time to time. Hugh and I occasionally fuck one another. It's refreshing."

"I was a million miles from myself," says Fay, seeming not to have heard Jenny.

Suddenly, Jenny can't speak. Is it the wine? She and Hugh had had a bottle -- but he'd drunk the most -- before they came. Is it the wine?

No, Jenny, be assured it is not.

Jenny's odd vibration throbs anew. She smells a strong aroma too; a peculiar perfume to match this odd vibration. Where is it coming from, this perfume? From that drooping little bouquet in a jam jar? Some unseen exotic flower? Some new species?

Indeed *yes*, Jenny. Oui oui to all.

Jenny hears Fay's words, is more affected by them then she ought to be, knows it. She sits straight as possible in the little arm chair, struggles against the rusty shackles about her wrists, tries to shake off these words that keep coming at her, this scent! And smoke! She smells smoke! The woman reeks of smoke! The woman is a sorcerer! But attractive. So attractive. In her... sooty, sooty way.

"You don't believe me, do you?" asks Fay, "You've a perfect right not to. But my tragic life has made me what I am. I cannot help being what I am."

Who *can*, love?

"Perhaps I'll forget it all -- now that my diaries are burnt."

Diaries? Fay? Who the fuck do you think you are? Mr Pepys?

"Diary" corrects Fay and laughs merrily and claps her hands, startles Jenny, "It's no help having ones misfortunes at ones finger-tips, is it? Being able to summon up past agonies with the flip of a page. Perhaps I'll forget now. Everything. Now that my house has burned down."

"Yes," replies Jenny. Her tongue is not her own. The room wobbles and fades in and out. Where are the others? These shack-les at her wrists! Come back, others! Come back! Someone be real!

"...but we must be adequately insured, mustn't we?" drones Fay. "Emotionally, I mean. Against the slings and arrows of outrageous *mis*fortune?"

Fay begins to sob. How her tears flow! The floor fairly sloshes with them. "I'm afraid my defences were and are still down!" she cries and leaps up, seems somehow to pause in the air -- suspended, her full, black skirt spread and fluttering in an impossible wind. It can't be! Jenny squeals. She's dizzy! She's falling through the floor! Fay alights, bends, thrusts her tear-drenched face directly into Jenny's, looks steadily into her eyes, seems to draw her back, says:

"But I have not capitulated. I have not capitulated."

Not yet, darling. Oh fiery death where is thy sting-a-ling-a-ling?

Fay extends her hand. Jenny, swept again by this vibration, this odd perfume and, now an unearthly light, takes it. She sees soot under Fay's nails, sees flames through a window where no window is, smells smoke, feels a hot, tropical breeze on her face, senses, somewhere, a glaring red sunset. That's only me, Jenny dear. I'm sombrero-ed, pancho-ed and beached south of the border at the moment, down Meh-he-co way.

Jenny struggles to escape Fay's grasp, cries out. I abruptly shake the sand from my so-called *feet*, intervene and assure Jen it's only the wine; that she's seen nothing unusual. Which is true. By our lights, m'dears, anyhoo.

Hugh and Bill enter, each with a kitchen chair in both hands, each wondering what they're doing here. Nelly couldn't have been *that* persuasive.

Nelly enters with a small foldable table, Rita with a large, pounded-pewter tray, its perimeter peculiarly -- suspiciously -- glyph-engraved. I nearly stop Rita in her tracks but with a lightning perusal I determine said engraving is harmless. For now. For the *duration*. Where do these objects come from, m'dears? Have *you* been mischief making?

Fay drops Jenny's hand, wipes her eyes, humbly regards these welcome intruders. "Oh thank you. Thank you."

Fay beams with love and light, is certain they have been talking about her behind her back. They have, but the gossip was leavened by good Nelly, kind, innocent, Lucifer-thwarting Nelly.

Jenny stumbles towards Hugh who asks, "Had too much, love?"

"Yes," she mumbles, "Yes."

Rita laughs, sways into the kitchen and returns with several bottles of wine, slams them on the foldable table Nelly has set up. So much wine -- it just seemed to materialise, with that pewter tray, in a cupboard she'd not explored for years.

Into a more than willing bottle that has repositioned itself, unobserved, directly beneath her hand, Rita stabs a corkscrew. Ouch! Cries the bottle, beyond human understanding.

15

"If we're going to have a sodding party," yells Rita, "let's have a sodding party!"

The wine bottles and kitchen cutlery clatter in preternatural agreement and suddenly everyone is busy. Hugh and Bill self-consciously arrange the chairs, Nelly sets out food and dishes and Jenny, recovered though dazed, fetches wine glasses for Rita. Hidden spotlights seem to illuminate each over-willing worker at his/her task but it's only me, m'dears, shining with benevolence. And, of course, rearranging, sequentially, a few squares that have naughtily wandered off.

A half hour later Fay proudly holds up the fine ceramic teapot she has just received from Nelly. Bill looks on, but can't take his eyes off Nelly. He needs so much to trust again. There is something trustworthy about Nelly.

Precisely, Bill. When she's not unduly influenced by you-know-sodding-who.

I give Fay a moderate kick up the backside and she skips into a newly rearranged though somewhat confused square and thrusts the teapot at Bill, "Nelly gave this to me. She made it with her very own hands."

Bill nods, says "Nelly is a charmer, isn't she?"

I prompt Fay to say something nasty but she won't – she adores Nelly. "I won't," she mutters, searching for a complimentary remark about Nelly's skills as a potter as well as a deeply trusted friend. But Fay, distracted by me, searches in vain, is mute.

I am a harsh mistress. Or whatever.

Hugh and Jenny sprawl and speak low, on a corner of that singular carpet -- for which I have such plans -- drinking their fourth glass of wine, unaware of the flickering perimeters of their bottoms or the outlandish luminescence where this wondrous yet sneaky floor covering has lovingly smooched with their sweating palms and/or buttocks.

Rita, of course, is ahead of everyone, downs her sixth. But who's counting? I am, m'dears, from now on. Let not one sparrow plummet beyond my gleaning glare.

Fay munches a delicious cheese sandwich, sips wine and hovers at the edge of the action in an odd but happy reverie (the first of many we've arranged). She belongs at last. People care. People pay her tribute. Food. Furniture. She is adored at last. As she should be. As she has a right to be. Love is triumphant.

Fay shakes herself -- these reveries can be discomfiting, particularly when accompanied by my infernal whispers. She quaffs her wine and skips to the drinks table, snatches a new bottle -- where did they all come from? She opens it with a flourish and flits back amongst her guests refilling their glasses and laughing exuberantly; her amusement of a most interior kind.

Having refilled her own glass several times, she sashays to the centre of our now delighted carpet and announces:

"My friends. My dear, *dear* friends!"

The carpet flaps with joy. But people are *so* unobservant.

"Yes, Ritterhouse?! Yes?!" cries Rita, splashing her wine and gripping the lone window sill for support, "I hang on your painted lip!"

Jenny and Hugh titter. Nelly and Bill smile. Fay frowns.

That was cruel, Rita.

"Our special evening is marred by an absence," announces frowning Fay, hurt Fay.

She's not chopped liver, darlings!

Fay pauses, making intense eye-contact, person by person, with everyone. Jenny feels that vibration again, shivers, shakes it off.

"What's wrong?" whispers Hugh.

"Nothing," lies Jenny though she and Hugh had promised to be perfectly honest with one another, particularly after a fuck.

"Our evening is marred by the absence of Mrs Taylor," continues Fay, "She of the postcards."

"She of the thumping stick," adds Rita, splashing her wine again. The carpet flinches away, wary of spilt wine, even from the hand of a fledgling writer. Literary people can be soooo calloused!

A ripple of laughter. Everyone, at one time or another, has heard Mrs Taylor's thumping stick.

Have I said that the walls are paper? Of course I have. Question: When is a redundancy not a redundancy? I will answer with another: When it's a *crucial* leitmotiv. A signpost, if you will. Must I draw a picture?! I *have* mentioned this before, m'dears! Listen... and live.

"So Ritterhouse Fay will commandeer our dearest of nonagenarians!" cries Fay who also sways and must lean, like Rita, on something for support. She chooses the kitchen chair Bill sits in, brushing her hand against the back of -- oh it's so smooth -- his neck. He jerks his head away.

"But it's awfully late for her," replies Nelly reasonably, "Mrs Taylor is a very old woman. She must be in bed by now."

"But, dear Nelly, we are incomplete without her."

Indeed they are.

"What was that?" replies Fay, searching for me as she fondles Bill's neck. Again he jerks away. Fay acknowledges cupid's escape, removes her hand which, in any case, she needs for her next dramatic gesture.

"Our little family," she declaims, waving this hand, "lacks its prodigal daughter! Granny Taylor!"

"Oh God!" cries Rita, adopting Fay's theatrical demeanour because, after all, it is she, Rita, who is the sodding actress, "Then fetch Taylor! Pray, for chrissakes, fetch her! Let the fest-til-ities continue!"

Fay is not happy with Rita's sarcasm. Nor is she overjoyed, m'dears, with the sweet regard Bill now lavishes on the good Nelly, who, even after Fay's fervent denunciation of Bill's brutishness, seems actually to enjoy his awkward attentions. "How can I be a good and loyal friend if my excellent counsel is not embraced?" whispers Fay in her much intruded-upon inner sanctum. But she stifles her hurt, grins at everyone, turns with a flourish, sways a bit too far to one side, swings back just a wee bit too far to the other, rights herself, and lurches out the beckoning door to the cheers of the furniture.

In the hall voices call after her. No one else can hear them unless they listen very carefully; even then it's not a sure thing. But my Fay hears them. My darling Fay has always heard them. Is she mad? Well, m'dears...if she is, I'm responsible so *I* honestly wouldn't know. In any case, if she *were,* we'd all be tarred with that self-same brush.

Rita marches to the drinks table and pours herself a tenth goblet of wine.

"The woman is a pathological liar," announces Rita at centre stage on Mrs Taylor's superb carpet (which cringes -- doesn't trust negligent Rita-writer's unsteady grasp of her wineglass). "Ritterhouse is in direst need of the prodigal," giggles Rita, "I mean proverbial, Psychiatreest!"

"She says she studied psychology," says Jenny, now free of the troubling vibration. "She's says she's treating herself."

Rita rakes her eyes over Fay's new possessions.

"And very well by the looks of it!"

"Be nice, Rita," cautions the good, the kind, the tipsy Nelly.

Rita throws her hip awry à la Fay. "Oh! I quite forget myself!" she whimpers to the frightened, recoiling ceiling which realizes there's trouble ahead, "If I do not post a letter to myself every goddamned day I quite forget who the bleeding hell I am! You see, my darlings, my town burned down! Not just my house! My whole sodding town! Right to the sodding, bleeding ground!"

London's burning, Rita. London's burning around *you*, you lonely old baggage. So mind your mouth.

Rita laughs maniacally, unaware she's sowing at least an acre of dragon's teeth. Tearing at her hair, she pours from yet another over-willing bottle (Ach! Did no one see it leap into her hand?! It flipping *flew* from the kitchen!).

Jenny giggles, elbows Hugh who belches. Bill, by now as tipsy (uncharacteristically) as Rita, takes another swallow and smiles fondly at Nelly who takes another swallow and smiles fondly back.

"In it, my town," continues Rita, "were short people, tall people, thin and fat people, people with one leg, ebony pussies, three-headed calves plus a unicorn with a flower up its arse. All perished. Gone. Up the spout. All cinders and singe-ed bone. Finito, dear friends, Finito!"

We've all had nights like that, haven't we, my darlings?

Everyone is laughing, drunk. Odd that. None of them, with the notable exception of Rita, usually over-imbibes.

"Rita! for shame," cries Nelly through reluctant giggles.

"It is a private Hell when your town burns down!" shrieks Rita.

And Hell hath no fury like…

"The quality of mercy is not strained..." cries Nelly.

"It is *too*," yells Jenny, refreshingly free of vibrations.

For the moment, m'dears.

"It droppeth as the gentle rain from heaven..." tries Nelly again, plumbing half-remembered dregs of a long ago, evening drama class.

"And droppeth and droppeth and droppeth!" squeals Rita.

Everyone falls about. Though *I* am not amused.

"But her house burned down, Rita, her house burned down!" cries Nelly.

"Her flat, actually," says Rita, pouring her twelfth, from a certain fervent bottle, "My whole goddamned town burned down!"

Jenny shouts: "Her sister was murdered!"

"The murderer wore tweeds!" cries Rita.

"And brogues," says Nelly.

What is going wrong here?!

"And kept hounds!" giggles Jenny, "God! I'll pee myself!"

"Sister Jane had lungs like burnt sponges! They crumbled in your hand and wouldn't do a thing for your kitchen walls!"

That was Rita.

"Sister Jane was tall," cries Nelly, almost choking on her wine, "She had big feet! Like me!"

"She climbed trees!" shrieks Rita, clutching helplessly at her sides.

"Unlike me," cries Nelly who knows she should know better. But she's only human.

She'll pay for being human. I'll see to that, damn her! Damn them *all*!

Bill, sodden, chuckles. "Have a heart, ladies."

Good for you, Billy. But it won't do you much good.

Hugh stands, sways, says: "She cut off her finger in my flat. I have it in a jar!"

"But it grew back!" screams Jenny, "It's got a fork in it! I saw it, tonight! It grew back on!"

"Mir-rack-u-lously!" shrieks Rita.

"Like a salamander's tail!" adds Jenny, flopping back into that serviceable chair Bill brought.

"The woman is a witch!" shouts Rita.

"Have a heart, ladies," says sodden Bill blurrily recalling a brief moment of blighted bliss with the absent accused.

Nelly stops laughing, says grimly:

"She only had a bed. One bed."

Bill says "But she's alive and kicking!"

And *he* should know, m'dears!

Saintly, tipsy Nelly is angry at them all: "One bloody bed!"

"Hardly bloody, love," laughs Rita who begins to weave about the room making a comic inventory: "One bed. Granted. But now she's got...let us examine... One foldable, all-purpose table, one fine – well, adequate -- chest of drawers, solid birch though the 'carving' could be better, one period-unknown – and should remain so -- though comfy chair, assorted little chairs, one passable drop-leaf

-- maple? cherry? -- table..."

"Lowly pine, I'm afraid," slurs Hugh, "I think."

Rita bends, examines the carpet and straightens up instantly, sobered eyes wide as HC Andersen saucers. "And one...one priceless...*priceless* Persian rug!"

And she oughta know.

16

Rita steps gingerly off the now extraordinarily grateful carpet and drops awkwardly to her knees to examine it more carefully. The others slide gently off it and crouch around its fabulous, fringed and preening, perimeter. The carpet shimmers, commences to pipe a hymn to its own beauty. I hush it before anyone can hear – even if they were listening.

"Our little Fay," says Rita peering into the carpet as she ruffles the glimmering (giggling) weave, "was at one time either excessively wealthy or extremely lucky. This rug is prime, friends, prime. I'm certain! Completely certain! For God's sake, keep your wine away from it!"

All rise and, carefully clutching their wine glasses, shrink just beyond the edges of the now taciturn, though thoroughly attentive, carpet.

The door swings open, in comes Fay and on her arm, snooded, wizened, and bewitched Mrs Oscar Taylor, plus her thumping cane.

"There it is!" cackles Taylor, slamming her cane onto her musty, tinder-dry closet's erstwhile companion, "There's my carpet!"

Silence all round.

"She *gave* this to you?!" gasps Rita.

"Isn't it lovely?!" sighs Fay. "Mrs Taylor was so kind. So very, very kind."

Fay strides warily to the drinks table, pours herself a tall tumbler of wine, takes a hefty swallow. She also pours one for Taylor and leads her to the small armchair, mid miraculous carpet, sits her down and places the wine in her hand.

Everyone waits for Fay's answer. Fay sips, smiles to each in turn, always, each in turn, enjoying their lavish attention. The silence is nearly audible (except for the anxious sighing of the walls – which, annoyingly, no one hears anyway, more fool, they – if only you people would *listen*). Fay glances casually at Rita, says, "Of course she gave it to me, silly. You don't think I stole it, do you?"

"Do you realize what it's worth?" asks Rita who is certain Fay does.

Well, Rita is desperately wrong! Fay, to her cost, hasn't a scintilla of the carpet's real significance. Neither, in fact, has Rita though she fancies herself an expert.

"It's a lovely carpet," says Fay, "from a friend in need."

Fay moves close to Taylor, strokes her gently on the shoulder. Taylor shivers, stiffens, swallows her wine in one gulp, sticks out her glass to Fay who refills it. "We're bamboozling the milkman," giggles Taylor.

Rita reels back for another look at the carpet. "This is a very fine rug indeed, Mrs Taylor. Has she bewitched you?"

Of course, Taylor's bewitched, Rita! I thought you were a writer.

"Damn right it's a fine rug!" barks Taylor. Fay is refilling her glass.

"But," says Rita, righting her sway with a hand to the back of Taylor's chair, "it is worth a great deal. Are you sure you..."

"Friends in need are friends indeed!" cries Fay, lifting her glass to the others. They don't respond, are waiting for something, anything, from Mrs Taylor.

Taylor empties her second glass and thrusts it at Fay who has begun to move around the carpet's edge offering refills to her now silent guests. One by one they decline, holding their glasses away. Fay grins uncertainly, pours herself another, quaffs it. "But it is written..." she mumbles and trails off mysteriously, a continuing mystery to herself.

But oh dear! Let's face it! Who in this whirling, wacky world *isn't*?

Mrs Taylor cackles. Fay tops her glass and the old woman gulps greedily and wipes her mouth with her sleeve. "We're bamboozling the milkman! The witch looks after me milk bottles, sees when I've paid so they can't cheat me! Don't you, ducky?! Look after me milk bottles? What'd you say your name was?"

"I wonder if I might have my errr key?"

That was Hugh, "I've errr lost my spare and..."

"Of course."

Fay yanks the key from around her neck, tosses it at him.

"Thank you," says Hugh, shamefaced but adamant.

"Thank *you*," replies Fay, her face a perfect blank.

"It is late," says Nelly our peacemaker, "I'm sure we..."

"Of course," says Fay.

"You're a liar," says Rita. "You're a liar, Ritterhouse Fay."

"Of course, we are," says Fay.

"No!" says Rita, "Not *we*! You, Fay, you are the liar!"

No, Rita, 'we' is correct. And you, me middle-aged darling, are mildly mendacious yourself.

"Rita, please..." tries Nelly.

"Of course I'm a liar," says Fay. "What else should I have been? Under the circumstances."

How right you are, dear! I'm on your side on this one!

"Thank you," whispers Fay to her unseen interlocutor, "I have always depended upon the kindness of strangers."

Two on the aisle, that's me! But wait! *Stranger,* dear? *Me, a stranger*?

Fay tilts the wine bottle to her lips, swallows, wipes her mouth on her sleeve, "I'm a lot of things to a lot of people" -- the dear girl is reading from that dim script I occasionally dangle before her opaque eyes. -- "You're a lot of things too. The lot of you."

"Of course we are, Fay dear. Nobody's perfect," says Nelly so softly, so well-meaningly, attempting to leaven yet again with logic an evening gone terribly wrong.

"*I* was," says Fay. "I was perfect. I was a lovely child. A beautiful child. Gentle. Gentle in every way. Loving. I was a loving child. Trusting. I was trusting too. Beautiful. Gentle. Trusting. I was ...an angel."

I wouldn't go so far as to say *that,* peaches.

"Fay dear," whispers Nelly, "we've all had too much..."

"Indeed we have," says Rita.

"You can talk!"

Suddenly Fay's arms are flailing! "*You* can talk! The unknown actress who rocketed to oblivion as the unknown alcoholic dilettante author! You haven't sold a story and you can't even make a good cup of coffee!"

"I make coffee for my friends!"

"Really?! Who might they be? You've got no friends. You didn't speak to a soul till I came here. You told me. And nobody spoke to you."

True enough, Ritterhouse, me sage side-kick.

Fay's eyes are a most peculiar mauve now. Perhaps it is that light reflected from Taylor's shimmering carpet via those blue-pencilled light bulbs? She glares at her silent audience, her face that familiar tragic mask. "No one in this house spoke to anyone else in this house before I came. You were dead to one another. Decaying corpses..."

Well I wouldn't go so far as to say that either, love.

"You were entombed."

Nor that.

"I brought you together. I am the catalyst. You should have hated one another. It would have been healthier than your indifference. I am the bloody catalyst!"

Well done, Fay!

Fay draws herself up. "I came in friendship!"

Which is true, to a point -- as well as somewhat beside the point. As though *she* had anything to do with it.

Swinging the wine bottle crazily at her side, Fay moves majestically to the centre of her magnificent carpet (and, *at last*, into yet another square). "I was a beautiful child!" she screams, "A beautiful bloody child! I was a bloody angel!"

I simply cannot argue with that.

Hugh and Jenny and Bill start toward the door. Nelly motions to Bill she'll stay.

"Thanks for nothing!" screams Fay at her erstwhile friends.

"You can live for a year on what you'll get for Mrs Taylor's rug!" cries Rita.

Only a year, darling? Think again. And again. And once more for good measure. And yet again!

Fay rounds on Rita. "Get out!" she screams, "Get out! Get out! Get out! I want no hard-hearted failures in my house!"

"*Your* house?!" cries Rita.

Decidedly, Rita, emphatically so. Don't you read the newspapers? Oooops! I'm getting ahead of meself.

"Though I speak with the tongues of men and of angels, and have not love," cries Fay, "I am become as sounding brass, or a tinkling cymbal!"

Directly under Fay's feet, under that paper floor, some drums go bang, some cymbals clang and some horns they blaze away! Though, of course, unheard. Wake up, all of you darlings! Conflict! I crave conflict! Let us entertain you!

"You're mad!" cries Rita.

"You have no love in your hearts!" screams Fay, "He who hath not charity deserves no mercy!"

Taylor, fuzzed over, stares at her empty wine glass. Rita weaves back to Taylor's chair, helps her up, takes her to the door.

"I'll burn you down!" screams Fay, "The lot of you! I'll burn you all down!"

Good Nelly watches anxiously as the door closes on everyone, including Bill who was most reluctant, m'dears, to leave her alone with Fay.

"Let me put you to bed, Fay, dear."

Fay hugs her wine bottle to her stomach, pulls violently away from Nelly. Nelly tries again, gently touches Fay's arm.

"Unhand me, villain!" screams Fay.

"Fay, dear."

"I'll burn them down!"

"You'll do no such thing."

"You need a bath, Nelly. You pong! You smell!"

Nelly jerks back and even in her drunken rage Fay senses error.

"Oh, Nelly. I'm so sorry. Please forgive me. I'm not myself. I've troubles I never speak of."

But try, ducky, try!

"Unspeakable troubles. Above endurance. Troubles above human endurance."

"I know, dear," says Nelly so softly, "I know, dear."

No, you don't, Nelly. You've no idea. Nor, really, has Fay.

"Please," whispers Fay, searching the room for me, her game old tinted tormentor, "Please!"

Nelly is perplexed, attempts a little laugh, doesn't manage. "Let smelly Nelly put you to bed" soothes Nelly.

"I am not myself, Nelly."

You can say that again.

"I know, dear. Your house burned down."

"Did it?" whimpers Fay.

Nelly embraces Fay, pulls her close.

"Did it?" sighs Fay, her sad little over-lipsticked mouth twisting into a bright red slash of a grin.

"Yes, dear, it did. Your house burned down."

Fay buries her face in Nelly's breasts. "Oh Nelly!" she sobs, "Oh Nelly, I'm *so* glad!"

We must find comfort where we can, m'dears.

Selah.

17

Taylor flattens her ear to the door, susses Fay is out there, feels it in her arthritic old bones, barks:

"What do you want then?!"

Milk bottles rattle from below.

"Milkman's on his way," chirps Fay, "I spy with my little eye your money in the milk bottle, Mrs Taylor. May I use your telephone?"

Taylor inches the door open a crack, peers out, "How much money would you say is in the bottle?"

"My goodness, sugar! Enough for a month!"

Taylor unlatches the chain, sticks her head through the door, gleefully surveys her empty milk bottles. "A whole month?"

"At least a month," chirps Fay gazing at the empty bottles. Taylor cackles, motions her in. Taylor enjoys her little game with the milkman. It's worth a bit of fleeting peril with a witch.

"Paid in full?" barks Taylor.

"Golly! A veritable embarrassment of riches!"

Fay darts past Taylor to the telephone where she speaks sotto voce as Taylor slams her door and bolts it just in time.

"Mrs Taylor?" says the milkman through the door.

"Paid in full," cackles Taylor, her mouth against the door, "I have a formidable witness."

You don't know the half of it, dearie.

It is fortunate for Mrs Taylor that the milkman is a patient man with a recalcitrant granny all his own.

Later the same morning Rita clomps about in a négligée. She's horrifically hung-over, puffs at her cigarette as she checks her mirrored image for signs of incipient invisibility. All's well... for now. She clomps to the kitchen, brews that special coffee she wouldn't serve to a dog.

Hugh, naked in bed with his traditional morning erection and either a tea or a coffee (I can't quite focus this morning -- too much wine last night). Pining for defined Abs, he peruses a physical culture magazine while Jenny, sweat-suited (more about *sweat*, much later) on her back on the floor, both pert breasts beautifully intact, lifts petite barbells.

Nelly, in a pyjama-like creation (two-embossed-sunflowers-with-a-pink-watering-can-between), answers her door. It is Bill and a box of up-market custard tarts (Nelly adores custard tarts! So do I!). She smiles. He smiles. Her kettle whistles hopefully from the kitchen.

Fay places her seven coloured marking pens -- bound by one of her ubiquitous rubber bands – into her cardboard suitcase. Perhaps she'll need them. She has no idea why (but *I* do, though I'll probably forget why if we don't get this fribbin' game on the road soon).

Fay's booty from last night -- practical articles like dishes, kitchen towels, pots and of course the lovely handmade teapot from Nelly -- are in their arrival boxes stacked just inside Fay's door (I must add, a very grateful door) (a grateful *door*?). Ours is not to reason why, m'dears. Ours is but to do and *die*.

Fay goes to her window, peers out, fidgets, waits. Waits. Listens to Rita's typing from two floors below.

> Doolittle Desiree's house had not burnt
> down at all. It was London that was burning.
> Desiree was sure of it. London was burning
> down around her! And her alone.

types our obtuse Rita, coached by flickering, flagrantly unobserved flames amongst her clicking keys, her fine coffee and a smoking cigarette tight beside her. Taylor thumps from above but Rita only smiles (as do I), and continues.

> The fire would of course eventually reach
> Desiree. But not just yet. It was only London
> that was burning. She, Doolittle Desiree, was
> safe. For the moment

Rita sips that coffee, takes a long, satisfying drag on that cigarette, exhales, sings:

> London's burning!
> London's burning!

Fetch the engines!
Fetch the engines!
Fire! Fire!
Fire! Fire!
Pour on water!
Pour on water!

An open lorry screeches to a stop, pulls up on the pavement just outside.

Grist?! Rita-writer leaps to her window. A husky man jumps out and bounds up the steps. Moments later Taylor cracks her chained door, glares at him as he descends with Fay's stack of boxes balanced on Rita's old foldable table.

Across the hall, Hugh and Jenny laugh as this husky, (and *hairy*) man puffs by with Hugh's drop-leaf table and two kitchen chairs. All is going as it should -- but only Taylor knows this. Oscar Taylor foretold it. No. He is not the fool she has often made him out to be.

I should hope not too, dearie. But watch your mouth in future.

A few moments later, the removals man descends with Nelly's chest of drawers strapped on his back. Nelly is drawn by the clunk and clatter, opens her door as he passes and she and Bill, both munching those up-market custard tarts, watch. Bill laughs nervously, relieved at the unexpected departure of this searing reminder of his human weakness.

Glory in that weakness, Billy. But know it can be hazardous. Worms turn, Billy. They do, honest injun! Particularly in sagas where the walls are paper, the ceilings have a life of their own, doors are grateful and a certain rug has an emotional range more suited to the stage than the floor.

Nelly nestles into Bill's side but grieves, guilty eyes cast down, sharing yet more of *poor little Fay's* pain.

Bill's laughter from the hall draws Rita to her door and as the hairy man descends with Bill's small serviceable armchair Bill laughs harder. He could have used that chair but he's glad because it pleased Nelly to help Fay -- *whatever* Fay is.

After much coming and going and much (*dangerous*) laughter from all except Nelly, the removals man at last descends with Mrs Taylor's amazing carpet on his back. Rita is outraged and immediately sets herself in his path. The poor man stops, perplexed.

"Mrs Taylor," calls Rita to Taylor who stands giggling at the first landing with Hugh and Jenny.

"Yes, dearie?!" answers Taylor, as yet crystal clear this fine Saturday morning and wondering what all the fuss is about.

"Do you know what your carpet is worth?!"

Merrily: "Yes, dearie! That ain't the point, is it?"

"What *is* the point?!" calls Rita, still holding her ground before the perplexed furniture shifter.

"We'll know soon enough, won't we, dearie?!" replies Taylor. "Let him go. He's such a nice man. Only doin' his job."

"Do you know what *you* are doing?!" calls Rita.

"I know exactly what *she* is doing," replies Taylor switching her cane ceiling-ward.

Rita gives up, steps aside and the man struggles out the door with that singular carpet which has begun to unroll and shoot tiny shivers of crackling light in all directions. Light that no one bothers to see. Even had they bothered they mightn't have seen it. *Clear* lenses are required. Preferably lenses unencumbered by a soul. Which, happily for them, they all possess. Hang on to 'em, my dears – those soul-thingies -- as long as you can. 'Cause one day…

Everyone is laughing now. Then Fay appears.

Silence.

Precisely as when she arrived, her paper carry-bag and leather bag hang from one arm and the jam jar of withered but somehow intact flowers is in the hand of that arm -- a shivering, shaking, white-knuckled though splendidly formed, hand. With her cardboard suitcase swinging on her other hand Fay descends the stairs, eyes steely, straight ahead. "They're staring at me," she whispers, "False friends, all. I would have given them anything, done everything for them..."

Indeed she would have. And then some.

"What?" says Fay, "What was that?"

"She's talking to herself," says Rita, "My God! I can hear her from here!"

As Fay passes, Jenny feels that vibration. Shakes herself. It's unpleasant.

"Anything wrong, Jen?" asks Hugh.

"Nothing at all," lies Jenny. Damn it! she gasps to herself, I never lie to Hugh.

Get used to it, lovey.

Taylor cackles, she's seen Jenny shiver. Taylor hasn't been this lucid since, since...whatever. That witch woman seems familiar. This clarity is unnerving!

As is all clarity. Think about it, m'dears, clarity -- unnerving at the least. And, oh my! To see ourselves as *others* see us? Perhaps we could ease up just a bit on clarity?

Fay descends the last stairs, halts abruptly in front of Nelly.

"Oh, Nelly. Nelly-welly."

Bill slides his arm around Nelly's waist, cuddles her protectively. Rita, from her door, watches too. Hugh and Jenny and Taylor rubber-neck from the first landing. The hall is a tiny amphitheatre reverberating with a monstrous crowd only Fay and I can hear. Our little Fay is the gladiatorial main attraction, that withered bouquet her only weapon.

"Nelly-Welly, this is for you," whispers Fay, refusing to wilt under the stern frowns of the others. She sets down her suitcase and hands Nelly the forlorn bouquet in a jam jar. Nelly accepts the half-dead flowers, embraces Fay but (Oh my gosh!) accidentally spills water from that pesky jam jar right down Fay's back.

"How could you?!" screams Fay (with a little help from yours truly). She springs backwards like a frightened cat, hisses, streaks out the door. She pauses on the steps, eyes misting then brimming then glaring at them all, particularly at the devious Nelly who has deliberately poured that water down her back! (Doesn't Nelly know that water douses fire?) Fay rips her name card from its slot on the brass plate, glares a sizzling encore and stomps down the steps.

"Coffee?" says Rita, "Anyone for coffee?"

This *is* magic! Our new Rita?

But they're *all* spellbound, m'dears, in one way or another.

Rita holds out her arms, friendly, beckoning -- so completely out of character -- but a grist-milling writer on her way up.

Due to me alone. Or don't you *believe* me? My advice, oh ye of little faith: don't risk it.

All the occupants of the house gather in Rita's living room. To gossip?

Whatever.

Taylor, whose clarity has flagged, is not certain how she got here but Rita sticks a cupcake in her hand and a coffee beside her and Marmite and Bovril have never tasted so good.

Soon everyone is drinking coffee and chatting and gulping cake which seems to come from nowhere though it appeared somehow in Rita's tiny freezer. And so *much* of it! Ach it was almost like the water into wine of the night before. They all laugh and compare notes about the departing Ritterhouse Fay. Who is she, what is she? Taylor knows. Or appears to know but she ain't sayin'. So don't ask. In any case, she has, face smeared with goodies, vacated her mental premises – might be back by evening. We'll see.

Fay's open lorry, safely loaded and tarped down, pulls away but her -- Rita's! -- kettle dislodges itself and clatters into the street (hoping somehow to find it's way back? Not necessarily a jest, m'dears). Fay, whose eye, *like mine*, is constantly on that proverbial sparrow or anything else she can get her mitts on, instantly directs the driver to stop.

Screaming and gesticulating, Fay flies from the lorry into heavy traffic to retrieve her precious kettle. Horns hoot hysterically and drivers curse and collide. Rita's guests flock to her two windows to watch. As Fay chases her bouncing kettle Rita sings:

> London's burning!
> London's burning!

One by one, Hugh, Jenny and Bill join in. Even Taylor, surfacing for the moment, and cued by Rita, begins to sing.

> Fetch the engines!
> Fetch the engines!

Fay's lorry blocks the road. The traffic chaos grows shriller. Fay hovers stubbornly in the midst of it, polishes her precious kettle on her mousy cardigan sleeve, muttering what would be unintelligible to anyone but me, and so very like an incantation.

Darling Fay! Your incantation is *all wrong*. But ach! if you ever got it *right*! If you'd listened properly…

Fay is certain she sees flames writhing from every window of Number 13. "It's a veritable conflagration! But I have escaped unharmed!" she screams deep in her throat where no one but I can hear.

Never mind, dear. One day...

"What," says Fay, "One day *what*?

> Pour on water!
> Pour on water!

sing Rita and Jenny and Hugh and Bill and Mrs Taylor, not because they are unfeeling or cruel but simply because they are relieved?

Nelly's in the kitchen, holds Fay's drooping little bouquet under the tap but all the petals, in unison, drop right off and form a suspicious pattern in the sink, curiously like a word. The word 'beware'? But unobservant Nelly without her glasses does not see it, she's thinking. Gosh! Nelly hadn't meant to pour water down 'little' Fay's back. What on earth was Fay thinking?

If our good Nelly only knew. If, for that matter, Fay herself only knew.

That now shining though severely dented kettle having been retrieved and polished, Fay leaps in and her lorry (or 'truck', if you will, m'dears) grinds on. Nelly, at Rita's window, can just make out the back of Fay's mouse coloured head in the lorry's cab beside that husky, hairy man as they disappear in a cloud of exhaust. "Oh, Fay," sighs Nelly. Bill turns to her. She shakes her head, says "Poor Fay. We could have been such good friends."

Problematic, dear. Problematic. Ask Billy. On second thoughts, don't.

Two floors above, just under the eaves of the house, a thin grey ribbon of smoke curls into my beckoning breeze.

PART TWO

18

"Do you know what the Lord saith?!" cries Fay in a wild ecstasy with which I had nothing (or not much) to do.

She crouches beside big Ted, her husky lorry driver as they make their way in clanking fits and starts down the traffic swollen road. She pulls her threadbare cardigan tight around her and bleats, "Well, *do* you?!"

"Huh?" says Ted.

"He saith..." cries Fay, eyes flashing as she leaps into our next sizzling square, "The Lord *saith* vengeance is mine!"

Oh dear. I should have seen this coming and it's totally beside the point. Someone is making mischief. Is it you, my darlings, my ducks, my sweeties? Or is it just some alien singularity on the loose? They don't build hoosegows the way they use ta!

A gloriously red fire engine clangs by in the opposite direction. Fay's head snaps sideways to watch.

Fay! We must never exult in the misfortunes, however fiery, of others. You naughty gal!

Ted eyes Fay for the briefest moment, as though he'd heard me -- she is not hard to look at. She might be receptive to a snog. Or even more.

"What are *you* staring at?" snaps Fay, whose good will for all mankind has evaporated like a dew drop in Hell.

And rightly so. Considering.

"What?" says Fay, "What was that?"

"I didn't say nothin'," says big Ted.

All its inhabitants huddle together in the sharp morning air watching smoke curl lazily from beneath Number 13's paint-peeling eaves. Jenny mutters "bugger this!" and feels that odd vibration. But only *very* briefly.

Rita had seen this coming from day one. Never mind, it's more grist – from whatever source.

Bill, besides the enormous relief he feels at Fay's departure, wonders if he could be to blame for this mini-conflagration. Those newspapers he was reading in the loo beside his electric fire (and he has *such* a lot on his mind)...

Hugh worries that Jenny is shivering inordinately, wonders if she is coming down with something.

Yes, my tight-cheeked sweetie, *something*.

Taylor has already forgotten about their little fire. Never mind, in a few minutes she'll remember again. Then, in another few, forget. Thanks, mercifully, to me.

And poor Nelly grieves for her lost new friend. But *I* say, Nelly, good riddance to mad rubbish – at least for now. You all need a breather.

Fay jerks towards Ted, mumbles "Our bodies are temples!"

Sweet Jesus, Fay! You're going haywire!

"That is why we must eat properly."

I repeat, I had *almost* nothing to do with this.

"Keep the old plumbing in order, eh?" laughs Ted. Fay is not amused, whimpers:

"Me hungry."

Rather primitively put, honeybunch.

Ted pulls a paper sack lunch from under the seat, tosses it into her lap.

"Be my guest."

Fay is miffed at Ted's nonchalance but dives in and snatches out a sandwich. She's ravenous. Mouth full, she splutters "I was starved as a child!"

She was, too. Well...as good as.

Aforesaid red fire engine screeches up (pardon the shorthand, m'dears, sagas are a chore). Taylor claps her hands, cackles, waves her cane. "The witch!" she cries happily. "It was the witch did it!"

Fay snuggles back into the frayed, sprung seat of Ted's lorry, deftly unbuttons the top two buttons of her blouse, pulls away her cardigan, turns to Ted, "I was starved as a child but I'm very fit now."

Ted eyes Fay's cleavage, crowds the centre line and must swerve to avoid an approaching bus.

Teddy. Poor darling.

Leave him alone! He's mine!" screeches Fay.

Manners, dear!

"The loo! Fancy him reading The Sundays on his loo!" shrieks Taylor.

"The Saturdays," corrects Rita, "It's Saturday, love."

"I'm a liar!" spits Fay and chokes down the last of Ted's sandwich. Ted brakes the lorry and they swerve dangerously to the kerb-side and skid to a stop.

"Huh?"

"We are going nowhere!" screams Fay.

"Huh?"

"The address I gave you is fictitious!"

Like everything else in this crazy world, sugar. But it's only a game.

"I am homeless."

"You're what?!"

"Are you deaf? I'm homeless! No fixed abode!"

Fay sobs, kicks the floor, hammers her perfect fists on the windscreen. Ted attempts to comfort her but she pulls violently away. "Don't touch me! I don't deserve to live!"

We'll see to that soon enough, Fay, ducky. But meanwhile, poor Ted. Poor, hairy, hungry young Ted! You ate all his sandwiches, you greedy-guts!

"Drink, anyone?" says Rita as the fire engine pulls away and everyone climbs the steps to the house, "I could use one!"

When *couldn't* you, ducky?

They all make their way once again to Rita's to be minutely studied by this fledgling scribe. It is a fair trade-off for a few drinks and/or party snacks and a bit of boring talk. Humanity in action. Even if they are all, unbeknownst to themselves, strangely condemned. It's grist, darlings, grist. Though I admit the whole set-up has been somewhat stage-managed. Guess on it. Then move back, m'dears, to a safer distance, whilst our friends, herein, move perilously on.

"Fancy reading the Sundays on the loo!" growls Taylor, on Rita's arm, "Fancy laying the Sundays on his bleeding electric fire! God Almighty! What's the world coming to?! He could have got us all incarcerated!"

Incarcerated is not quite the word, my white-haired poppet -- unless applied to Fay.

Taylor glares at poor Bill who, fortunately or not, has lost only a couple of bath towels, a shower curtain and an unopened pack of toilet rolls -- which *could* be usable, charming Billy, though a bit of ash and scorch might be uncomfortable down there where it counts.

"I didn't lie about my name, Teddy."

Fay's sobs have mercifully diminished to sniffles. She dabs a few reptilian tears from her cheeks and allows Ted's huge hairy arm to rest upon her shoulder. "Ritterhouse, Fay. I was named after a woman who was abducted by a giant ape. You've awfully big hairy hands, Teddy... I like big hairy hands."

Fay shoots him a vulnerable little grin and, grin securely set, gazes up into hunky Ted's eyes. A compassionate man, he hugs her closer. He is a potential friend. But after what happened at that hideous party last night -- and this morning, water down her back from her very best friend! -- was friendship worth it?

You decide, darling.

"I will!" cries Fay.

"What?" asks Ted.

"Shut up!" says Fay.

"Hey, take it easy!" says Ted.

"I wasn't speaking to you," coos Fay, "Teddy honey, Teddy, darling, Teddy, sugar."

"Mrs Taylor? Mrs Taylor?!" says the milkman. Taylor nearly betrays herself with a cackle. When he has gone she inches her door open and climbs laboriously down her cane to snatch up her milk and cream. Though she is quite clear this morning, possibly because of all the excitement of the fire the day before, she has not given one thought to Fay. Possibly because -- and she has no idea why because she hasn't for years -- possibly because she had suddenly decided to clean and trim the wick on her paraffin lamp. She had spent an early morning hour doing just that. Oh, yes. Now she remembers why: Fay was enchanted by the lamp, touched it, commented on it. That's why. But why?

I know. So will you. Later. I have a gamey story to tell. A *searing* saga, as said (pardon my occasionally florid prose, m'dears, and bear in mind that I am rather a daffy dilettante in the prose département).

Hugh is, pre*dick*tably, pleasantly erect and yawning. He bends, flexing becomingly his firm, round, delineated, buttocks Ach! He reaches for his milk, misses, reaches, flexes 'em again. I am inflamed!

"Come back to bed," calls Jenny. "For God's sake, it's Sunday!"

Hugh takes up the milk, shuts the door and shoves his boner beneath the elastic band of his briefs so she won't tease him. Then, sleepily setting the milk by the bed-sofa, he crawls in beside Jenny who is already asleep again, dreaming of those odd vibrations; dreaming -- certainly not by choice -- of Fay, who, incidentally, has not forgotten her. And, as above, not by choice.

Rita lingers in bed. She yawns, stares up at her ceiling, listens to Mrs Taylor's padding feet and thumping cane as she goes about her morning ablutions. Rita stretches, moans a satisfied little moan, wonders where Fay came from, where she has gone. She wonders if she was too harsh on Fay. Perhaps she was. She wonders that, if there is a God as she suspects there just might be, she will suffer for her actions. She will indeed, God help her -- God or no God.

Sentimental Nelly, in baggy pyjamas, empties the petal-less stems and a shrivelled little fern; these poignant remnants of Fay's petite bouquet, into her little rubbish bin and begins a thorough search for her recently missing black silk scarf. The scarf flatters her. She needs all the flattery she can get now that Bill seems interested.

Somehow she knows she owes her new happiness to Fay. She looks again for the scarf, finds instead a tangled knot of red wrapping ribbon. She thinks another heart-tugging thought for Fay, drops the ribbon in beside the sad remains of Fay's bouquet and, daydreaming of Bill, lets go the bin's foot-operated lid which closes with a sharp clang that reminds her again of Fay. Ritterhouse Fay.

The Ritterhouse Fay, please.

Bill is on the loo with the Sunday papers, an electric fire aimed at his naked legs. He wonders how he could have laid the Saturday papers on this electric fire. He'd never done it before. Never. Then -- "Crikey, my door was unlocked! Fay was the last one down the stairs."

Husky Ted hunches on his sofa in his bulky, boxer shorts. He too has awakened with an erection.

Sorry m'dears. I know boners are a hang-up of this little Ms but as the mighty Mae West once said: a hard man is good to find!"

However, it is his back not his basket that is bothering big Teddy. Plus he's had an extremely uncomfortable night attempting to squeeze his six-foot-four, muscular frame on to the sofa preceded by an interminable Saturday afternoon amidst the frenzied whoops and whinges of this madwoman who calls herself Ritterhouse Fay.

But Ted is a patient, caring man, ever ready to assist the down and out. He understands what that means. Fay's house burned down. Didn't it?

His eyes wander over Fay's fine carpet, half rolled out, with her meagre furniture and those few boxes piled carefully on it. Everything she owns, she says, in this whole wide world (considerably more, m'dears, than she had exactly three days ago – count 'em). Crowning it all, atop Nelly's chest of drawers sits Rita's dented though much polished kettle.

Ted takes a closer look at Fay's rug which, flattered, flirts outrageously (in its way). Ted is a seasoned removals-man and knows a valuable carpet when he sees one. How did shabby little Fay get her hands on such an up-market carpet? (pay heed to my delightful internal rhyme, m'dears and ye shall be spared)

Fay found Ted through a handbill he'd slipped under the doors of every flat in Pimlico. For better or worse, thinks thorough Ted, who gets up, carefully folds his blankets and pulls on his trousers over that sagging but still sumptuous erection (humour me, darlings). For better or worse, yes. Ted was always a soft touch (no pun intended!). Although maybe, the times they are a-changing, after yesterday, a-changing.

In his tidy kitchen he fills and switches on an electric kettle, takes down two cups, cuts some bread and drops it in the toaster. Shirtless, he tiptoes to his bedroom where Fay sleeps in his double bed. Kneeling, he whispers softly, "It's morning, love."

Her eyes are tight shut. Behind them, indescribable (so I won't bother!) dreams unfold. She turns away, moaning.

"It's morning, love," he whispers again.

Fay sits bolt upright, snatches her blanket to her neck.

"It's just me," whispers Ted who is now certain this woman needs professional help.

Fay stares at him for a long moment then whimpers in her child's voice, *our* child's voice:

"You should put on a shirt, Mr Kong. In a maiden's pwesence."

"Coffee's on."

"Instant?"

"Soon as I can get it."

Fay moues her favourite little, much-coached-by-me-moue and peeps "Where am I?"

Big Ted is puzzled. "My flat, love."

"Of course," replies Fay, trembling, confused but remembering.

I *am* a bit tough on her. But it's for *our* own good, nay, our very salvation, m'dears. Not to mention amusement.

"I got to work today, love."

Big Ted isn't smiling.

"Where are my things?" cries Fay, "My rug?! My suitcase!? My kettle?!"

She leaps from the bed, pulling the blanket over her bra and Nelly's baggy, mauve panties. "Where are my possessions?! *Who* undressed me?!"

Ted shrugs his shoulders and pads to the kitchen.

Blanket flying, Fay darts into his tidy little living room, spots her belongings. Sighing with relief she throws herself upon her carpet, caresses it sensually. It seems to caress her in return.

Probably does, darlings, I don't know *everything*. Although I *am* everything.

Fay grabs her precious kettle, snatches up a corner of her blanket, rubs it lovingly over the kettle, polishing, polishing. "Where am I?" she whispers, "Let's get this straight. Where, precisely, am I?"

Good question, Fay. But let's put that on the back -- forgive me -- 'burner' for now.

"Who are you?" asks Fay, painted nail to trembling lip, terrified eyes to the ceiling where a cerulean blue blotch (me) moves out a nearby window where I hover, quasi-visible against the sky and peer in – not wishing to miss anything, but desperately needing a fucking breath of fresh air!

"Who are you?!" cries Fay at the window, apparently piqued at my desire for a brief, refreshing turn.

"You what?" asks Ted, entering with a small, neat tray of coffee and buttered toast and two paper serviettes.

"Not you, Teddy."

Ted sets the tray on a tiny table, sits.

"You are too kind, sir!" chirps Fay suddenly at her cheeriest. She must make amends for her earlier rude behaviour and selfish rejection of poor hairy Ted's shy flickerings of interest. Everyone has needs. She will make it up to him. Soon. When *her* need (*me,* m'dears) moves her. Yes, soon. "These lapses." She mutters, "Where do they come from? My intentions are pure!"

This said with such conviction it takes my newly refreshed breath away.

Fay tucks the blanket around her, catapults from her fine carpet and drops herself in a chair beside Ted and the coffee and that *yummy* buttered toast. Ted is developing into an excellent friend. He is already on her gift list -- the new one, actually. The old one has been, rightly, mentally incinerated.

"Real butter?!" cries Fay, snatching up a slice and wondering for an instant just what would be an appropriate gift for Teddy-new-friend, "Real butter melts in a very special way."

"It's Sunday, love."

"Of course it's Sunday. Yesterday was Saturday. Is this real butter?"

As real as you are, Fay.

Fay munches -- if she ignores my impertinent intrusion -- it will go away. Though it never does. Though she invariably thinks it will. Why is that, Fay?

"I got a job in Manchester. I'll be gone for three days."

"Oh Teddy! Oh Mr Kong! Three whole days! What ever shall I do with myself?!"

"Find another place to crash."

"I beg your pardon?" squeaks Fay, crumbs tumbling from her mouth into her tell-tale-grey bra.

"I don't fancy sleepin' on my own sofa no longer than I got to."

"Teddy. Teddy *darling,* there has been some extraordinary misunderstanding, some debilitating mistake. I'm not myself, you see. My house burned down."

"It looked okay to me yesterday."

Ted has done some heavy thinking on the subject, he's uncomfortable because he's never enjoyed being the bearer of bad news.

But there are limits to compassion.

Are there, Teddy? Are there really limits to compassion? *Should* there be?

"Silly boy!" squeals Fay at her most playful, "That wasn't my house!"

"Anyhow, love, that's how it stands."

Fay quaffs her coffee, gulps her toast, munches as Ted tumbles from her new gift-list. But all need not be lost. Smiling, she allows the blanket to slip slowly from her shoulders to the floor. She *must* salvage something of this stillborn new relationship – a hug, a kiss? Perhaps just a grin? But something. That's the rule of the game, isn't it?

Game? Say I. I know of no game. What game? (She mustn't know we've a game here, m'dears)

"Liar, liar, pants on fire," whispers Fay to me as she moves in close, settles herself on one of Ted's massive knees, drops one hand to his crotch, squeezes, then plants a long, kneading kiss on his bristly mouth. She sighs and lisps "Oh, Mr Kong. We'll work out something. Won't we?"

19

> It was London that was burning but Desiree was safe. For the moment. Giving the lorry driver a burning look, she climbed into his lorry...

types Rita who pauses, puffs on her cigarette, says "Strike 'burning'."

She X's out "Burning", types above it: "Smouldering".

"Giving the driver a smouldering look," reads Rita, from this much-amended page, "she climbed into his lorry."

Rita applauds herself, gently slaps her face to see if this is really happening -- it's going far too well.

Yes it is, Rita. It's done with smoke and mirrors. Enjoy it while ya can.

Fay feels no action beneath her hand on big Ted's crotch. Not a jot nor a wiggle. *Nothing* is happening! Rien, m'dears, all is rien! (As though we didn't know that!) Incidentally, 'Rien', for the great unwashed, means *nothing*!

Ted gently pulls her hand away. He rises, but only from the chair. Fay slides to the floor with a thud, exclaims "What the dickens?!" Thinks: he's gay! Gee willikers, how wrong can ya be?! This makes it somewhat more difficult, of course. But there are other ways. She must clap Ted heartily on the back, encourage attendance at the Ballet and musicals and various body-building clubs -- buy him a few Judy Garland CD's. Be a real pal to him. I'll be a fag-hag, she muses. He'll become utterly dependent upon my genial largesse. It will be a superbly symbiotic relationship. Fay claps her hands, exclaims "Goody!"

She wraps the blanket around her, thinks: Yes, I'll be a real pal. As soon as I am on my feet I'll succour him till he drops! She means it. She could be infinitely helpful, selflessly revealing Ted to himself. She pants with the possibilities of it! A calling! At last! And I'm bound to get a brotherly hug or a chaste kiss and golly that's better than nothing.

Big Ted shakes his head, says "It's Sunday, love. I'll be back Wednesday night. You got three days."

But, thinks Fay, if he is to evict me, then how --

"Get some clothes on, love. You'll catch your death."

Fay rushes into Ted's bedroom, throws on her blouse, her shabby black skirt and cardy and launches herself at the kitchen where solace is sure to be found. *Warm toast and melty butter, warm toast and melty butter*! drones through her head, dulls the uncertainty of this awful, fretful day in which anything can happen.

And will!

"Shut up!" cries Fay and rams bread into the toaster and switches on the electric kettle and glares at a jar of instant coffee -- not even good instant coffee -- until the kettle sparks and a tea-towel explodes into flames and she screams. Towel-wrapped Ted comes running from his shower. Fay flattens herself against the wall opposite as he rips the kettle's cord from the socket and douses the small fire with a pitcher of water. "Fire follows Fay," she murmurs, well knowing that witches are nearly always burned at the stake, "Fire follows Fay."

Tears stream down both cheeks, spotting her untidy blouse. She'd only wanted to help him. Look what happened. "Me so unhappy, me want to cry," she moans.

"Sorry, love," says Big Ted, "I been meaning to fix that electric kettle."

Fay waves frantically out the window as Ted drives away in his battered lorry. She's undeniably sad to see him go. There were such...possibilities...here. She must think of something soon or she'll be homeless in a trice (well, a *thrice*). Her dainty index finger leaps (as usual) to her lower lip, rests there. "Think, Fay! Think! Think! Think! Oh there must be a solution to my seemingly intractable dilemma," she whispers at what she takes to be a friendly wall. The wall is silent, won't even grin – has no imagination at all. Fay, you ain't in Number 13 anymore!

"What?" says Fay, "What was that?"

You should have been more conscientious with your homework, darling. I really can't help you here. Number 13 is miles away.

"Who *are* you?" says Fay. "I've really got enough on my mind at the moment. You're distracting me like the dickens!"

Your rug, darling Ritterhouse, your rug might be of assistance.

"Oh, go away!" cries Fay, tearing that contemplative index finger from a quivering lower lip that immediately begins to curl into a grin, "But I've thought of something! I've got an idea!"

You've got an idea?!

Fay rushes to Ted's bedroom, finds a number scrawled on a bit of paper at the bottom of her tattered paper carry-bag, dials and fidgets irritably as she waits. Then at last, "May I speak to Mr Abdullah Shamaly?... Ritterhouse Fay speaking... Ritterhouse Fay!"

She waits, fidgets as Mr Shamaly's kindly visage turns in her head. She fidgets more, looks about Ted's flat, shakes her head -- she could so have improved his lot in life..."Mr Shamaly! How good to hear your voice!...Ritterhouse Fay speaking...Fay!...Oh Mr Shamaly. You *do* remember...Abdullah, darling, I've got a problem...Yes, I did see the flat. I was a naughty gal and lived there unauthorized for three whole days just to see if I would like it... Oh, Abdullah, I knew you would understand...you *are* kind... Well, Abdullah, I did not like it...and I've got the keys right here for you but I'm indisposed...nothing serious, just the sniffles."

Fay sniffs significantly.

"But my little colds are often life-threatening and I wondered if you could come and get it?...The *key*, Abdullah, you naughty boy! We could...yes, another 'glass of wine' together. I did so enjoy the last time...Lovely. I'm staying with a friend at...Oh, Abdullah! You are a darling! I'm staying with a friend at..."

I politely allow Fay a bit of privacy to finish her crucial call. Besides, I know what will come of it. Also, telephone monitoring can be a mite difficult when one is hovering about in the air outside looking in. And nowhere near our beloved Number 13. There *are* limits. In any case, honestly, Fay, you hardly know the man you're speaking to. Though both of you might strenuously disagree.

"Leave me alone! I'm on my own now and I intend to do quite well for myself!"

*Our*selves, ducky. *Our*selves.

Ignoring me yet again, and with a satisfied smile, Fay signs off with a revoltingly audible kiss and slams the telephone receiver into its quivering cradle.

Ach! Why does the word *cradle* summon up the image of a manger? Darlings, is there some recondite religious significance hidden here in our little game, our petite saga? Or is it only a random reference to the tiny thatched witch's shrine; erstwhile companion of that very carpet upon which my darling prosopopoeia now kneels? Oj! I must rest for a bit. My so-called *brain* pivots perilously near fuse-out. Pardon me whilst I grab a few Z's.

Snort! Refreshed I continue.

Fay snaps open her cardboard suitcase and lovingly unfolds the silver embroidered crescent-mooned blue velvet table cloth, caresses it, presses it to her face, kisses it, holds it up, swirls herself into it, sighs and begins to repeat sounds that aren't words -- sounds that have intruded pleasantly into her head. She has no idea from where these peculiar -- incantations? -- have come.

Nor should she, Fay my darling prosopopoeia, know. Not yet. Hold tight, m'dears! We're adventure-bound!

Fay lifts her arms, inspects herself in Ted's wardrobe mirror. Her face glows, her lips redden. She becomes more than she was, seems taller, larger, even...beautiful.

Clutching the velvet tablecloth around her shoulders she rifles through Ted's wardrobe drawers; peering at this, poking at that. Inanimate objects are trusted friends who can do one no harm.

How silly of you, Fay. If they can help, they can also hinder. Trust no one, *nothing*. Betrayal lies everywhere. Even in the inanimate. I know.

"What?" peeps Fay, turning her head towards the wardrobe mirror, meeting her own troubled eyes, "What was that?"

Jenny is still asleep. Why not? It's Sunday. Sweat beads on her forehead as she flees the black-clad Fay who approaches, retreats, approaches. Jenny tosses about on the bed sofa. Her arms jerk, her hands become white-knuckled fists, hammering at her pillow.

Magic wears off slowly. Even sloppily applied magic, mediocre magic. Take it from me, m'dears.

"Jen?" whispers Hugh, close beside her, "Jenny, love?"

Mrs Taylor, minus her cane, carries a potted geranium to her half-open window, is about to set it in an empty window box when it slips from her stiffened fingers and topples out, plummets. She screams as the pot shatters not a foot from Rita who ascends the steps below.

Close call, Rita. You've me to thank for your narrow escape. Me to thank, *actually*, for the whole bleedin' incident.

Rita drops her shopping by her door and rushes (as scheduled) up the stairs to Taylor's flat.

"Mrs Taylor! Are you all right?!"

Rita knocks. The door swings open. Taylor slumps motionless at her postcard table.

"Mrs Taylor? Are you all right, dear?"

Taylor, vacant-eyed, does not answer. Rita says:

"Your geranium nearly brained me."

"It's not my brain," mumbles Taylor, clearing somewhat, "It's my wrists. They've give out. Goddamn my wrists."

She fumbles with her fingers, smoothing at her paper-dry, wrinkled skin, "I was airin' 'em. Geraniums need air. Just like people."

A sweep of Taylor's cane takes in two more geraniums on a nearby table. "Thrice a week. Summer and winter. Rain or shine."

"It was only a little accident, dear. Perhaps your jardinière needs fixing."

"My what?!"

"Your jardinière, your *window box*. I'm glad you didn't hurt yourself. Or me."

"It's me. I've done it before. I drop 'em all the time now. It ain't my brain. Or my window box. It's my bleedin' wrists."

"Can I make you a cup of tea?"

"You seem bright enough, darlin'. Can you?"

Rita chuckles, goes to the kitchen. Taylor throws her head against the back of her chair. "I'm even leavin' my door open now. I can't remember nothin'. That witch'll come right in and axe-murder me and throw me in a ditch. I don't know why I let her in before. Something made me do it," says Taylor wearily, momentarily forgetting Oscar Taylor's prophecy. "Something made me leave my door open."

Something?

"It ain't like me. The milkman could've sashayed right in!"

"What, dear?" calls Rita from the kitchen.

"That Fay woman is a bleedin' witch."

Taylor's fuzz clears: "That's why I give her my carpet. Mr Taylor said only a witch deserved that carpet and that's why he sent it to me. He wrote me right after and said it was cursed. Said to put it in a closet until a bona-fide witch come along and asked for it. I'm a amateur. He said only a bona-fide witch would want it."

How right he was, ducky.

"Can't hear you, dear," calls Rita from the kitchen.

"So, bein' a rank amateur, I put it in a closet and give it to the first bona-fide witch that come along. Ritterhouse what's-her-face. Marmite on some bread, please!"

"Can't hear..."

"MARMITE ON SOME BREAD!" shrieks Taylor.

"I heard *that*."

"Where's my bread and Marmite?!"

"We're nearly there. Do you know that this is the first time I've set foot in your flat and we've been neighbours for..."

Taylor's rheumy eyes wander sadly to her remaining geraniums. "My wrists have give out. How shall I air my posies?"

Rita kneels beside Taylor. "I'll air your posies."

"You?"

"Me."

Taylor, cautiously: "No strings attached?"

"No strings attached."

"No money'll change hands?"

"No money will change hands."

"You the one who types?"

"I'm the one."

Taylor smiles a ghost of a smile. "I'm the one thumps the floor." She holds up her cane.

"I know. Oh, I know," says Rita with a mock-frown.

"Your typing don't bother me one little bit. I just love to thump."

"Good," replies Rita, warming to the cantankerous old woman, "I'll be doing a lot of typing. I'm writing a novel about Ritterhouse Fay."

"Who?"

"Her house burned down."

"The witch-whatsis!"

Rita laughs, Taylor doesn't. Fay is serious business. Plus it takes one to know one.

"I know a witch when I see one," says Taylor with a look so intense it shoots a chill right up Rita's spine, "Where's my tea?!"

Rita returns to the whistling kettle as Taylor shouts after her. "Ritterhouse Fay is a witch and I've seen her before!"

Not necessarily, darling. But then, again...

Fay yanks an enormous pair of vivid blue satin pyjamas from Ted's wardrobe drawer. "Excellent taste in sleeping apparel but then he would have," she murmurs fondly and holds them against herself, matching them before the mirror to her blue crescent-mooned tablecloth. Delighted, she drops the pyjamas on the bed and skips to the kitchen where she rummages through every drawer and cupboard and at last finds a bottle of wine. She frowns, cries, "A *screw-on* top!" -- not realizing they've at last become semi-fashionable. But it will have to do. She opens the wine, tastes it, frowns again, and pours it into a large pitcher to which she adds several heaping spoons of sugar, sampling the wine after each and muttering something unintelligible. She pours a large glass for herself, sets the pitcher in the fridge and trips gaily into the living room. "I shall make an account of everything I've borrowed from Mr Teddy and pay him back, handsomely, a hundredfold!"

Yes, darling, just as you made an account of Nelly's black silk scarf.

"What black silk scarf?"

The one you stole.

"You're mad! Leave me!"

Fay slides herself onto the soft nap of her superb carpet, leans on one elbow, sips cheap, sweetened wine (Ugh! How we do suffer for a tiny evening's entertainment) and stares happily into the carpet's intricate patterns; stroking, purring like the ancient cat she feels she was, or well might be even now. She used to think this. Not so much lately. Not since she was released...or transmogrified or...whatever. It's all very hazy, isn't it, Fay? Like a puff of hot smoke. You and old lady Taylor have a lot in common, haven't you? A bad memory, for a start. But then Taylor is far older than you are, Fay. Or is she?

"Get thee to a nunnery!" cries Fay, "I must relax for the ordeal to come."

So, content, Fay sips and strokes, strokes and sips. Now they're both purring, Fay and her carpet. Domestic tranquillity at its height. Sheer bliss. But suddenly, at the corner of her eye, something is not quite right! "What *is* it?!" she demands of her glorious rug, "What is not quite right?" She presses her nose into its corner, squints. "What *is* it?!"

She quaffs her wine, whimpers and peers ever closer into the carpet's glimmering weave. This whole corner is slightly -- ever so slightly -- faded! The design is not even quite the same either. This carpet has been mended! Fay's sharp cat eyes have ferreted out a fatal flaw!

That's why the old hag parted with it so easily, bimbo.

"What?" asks Fay, "What was that?"

I, shit-stirrer that I am, am silent. But the carpet, whose imperfection has been so cruelly exposed, weeps, tufting damply here and there.

Happens to all of us sooner or later, darlings. We're all frauds one way or another, aren't we? Humanity is only skin-deep.

"Mrs Taylor is not a hag!" cries Fay (finally!) to Ted's tidy living room, "Mrs Taylor is simply an extremely old person who requires succour which I intend to provide. One day. When I'm on my feet again."

Fair enough, ducky. Everything is a means to an end – I mean *the* end.

Fay's angry. She turns the edge of her beloved carpet, sees on the underside the discrepancy in the weave. Why hadn't she noticed it before? She presses her cheek against it, stroking it tenderly, kneading it softly between her fingers.

"You're not perfect," she whispers into the grieving rug. Her eyes flood. Her nose runs, she wipes it on her sleeve, sobs "You're not perfect! You are not perfect!"

"But..." stammers the carpet in the tiniest voice, "but I'm..."

Fay hears nothing through her sobs. In any case, she'll know soon enough. We can but hope.

Hugh is troubled, climbs the stairs to his flat. Finds Jenny on the bed sofa with her mini-barbells studying one of his yummy muscle magazines. She looks up, smiles and blows him a kiss. He returns it, drops his briefcase by the door and disappears into the kitchen.

"Scones in the oven, says Jenny, "Almost forgot it was my turn to bake. Raisin."

"Bravo! At last!" says Hugh, not quite rising to the exclamation point in his voice.

"You love raisin scones. What's wrong?"

"My new boss is in love with me. He was here the other day, Jen. I never meant for this to happen. It just crept up."

"Richardson was here? I didn't know that."

"I didn't tell you, Jen."

Jenny puts down her magazine -- they were always supposed to tell one another everything.

And always had – *before Fay.*

"Do you love him?"

A bus pulls up and Nelly, in a springy mood -- she's been springy for the past two days -- climbs the steps with a large bag of groceries. Rita, smoking, conjecturing, at her window, waves pleasantly. Nelly waves back and springs right up the steps. She doesn't feel forty today. Nor does she look it. Though her colourful kit could use a major tweak here and there.

Somewhat later another bus arrives and Bill, laden with flowers, hops off. He's springy too. Hasn't been so springy in years though he's still got a lot on his mind.

This transformed Rita lingers at her window, tanking up with a couple of ciggies for another bout at her typewriter. She waves at Bill and smiles knowingly at the flowers he holds up with a gesture at Nelly's window.

One day someone will bring flowers to you, Rita, but don't hold your breath. Now get back to work. You've got a novel to write about Ritterhouse Fay. First the money. Then the men. One follows the other either way you look at it -- if you're smart. And of course, if men are what you want. "Yes, please," whispers Rita into her cigarette smoke, hardly aware she's spoken.

Fay hitches Big Ted's enormous blue pyjama trousers high above her waist, sashes them empire-style just under her shapely breasts with one of Ted's bright-buckled belts. She takes two thick rubber bands from her paper carry-bag -- collects them by the handful, waste-not-want-not. She slips one over each ankle, pulling up and ballooning out each much-too-wide and much-too-long pyjama leg to give a harem-trousers appearance. From her cardboard suitcase she snatches Nelly's pilfered black silk scarf (You're a liar, Fay! You *did* take it and I saw you!). She ignores me and places the scarf over her nose. She ties it at the back of her neck and surveys herself in Ted's wardrobe mirror, giggles, "Me so happy me want to cry! Me so lovely to look at!"

Fay claps her hands again and again. And yet again! Really, Fay! Show some restraint. You're so like me. But then you ought to be oughtn't you? Astronomically speaking, of course.

Nelly is attired in her finest, though she longs for her black, silk scarf -- where could it have gone? She must buy another. She lovingly puts the finishing touches on a table for two, wonders (*so* anxiously, m'dears!) if her cooking will be a complete failure, and is lighting the candles when she hears a gentle -- how like him

-- knock. Springing to the door (still springing!), she opens it. It's Bill! With flowers!

Nelly smiles radiantly. Bill smiles radiantly. "Darling," says Nelly. "Darling," says Bill. They stand for a magic moment entranced. Suddenly embarrassed for her happiness, Nelly motions Bill in, turning slightly from him to brush away a tiny tear of joy.

The rest is up to them, m'dears.

And to me, of course. To *me*, of course.

20

Fay does an elaborate, barefoot turn on her splendid but so imperfect carpet. Has it been corrupted by its proximity to that little thatched witch's shrine? If it has, Fay is not to know. Not yet. Perhaps never.

Gosh! As Nelly would have said, anything is possible. Especially these days.

Dear, dear Nelly -- why must the innocent suffer so? She still, even in the throes of her new love, suffers for Fay far more than she should. Ach! One urgently hopes goodness *is* its own reward. For there is much suffering to come. All in due course -- if that sort of suffering can be thought of as 'due'. Job suffered, did he not? In a good cause? Debatable, m'dears. Though a biblical model is always a useful validation of our tricky thesis. Gets one off the hook, doesn't it, m'dears? Do I hear a 'yes'? Back there amongst those indigo shadows that simply won't sit still? Show your face, darling. I'm not a monster. Yet. Nor are you. Yet.

Fay has, whilst I babbled on, fashioned her velvet tablecloth into a turban, the excess of which tumbles over her shoulders to the floor. "I'm quite replete," she has said to the wardrobe mirror just a celebratory moment ago (inaccurately celebratory – things could have been so much easier for her if only she'd …).

On a chest at the edge of her carpet is a plate of badly cut bread and that pitcher of cheap, sugared wine. Not even cheese or a soda cracker. A light-year from Nelly's lovingly set table. But Fay's house burned down. Nelly had said so herself, hadn't she? At least Nelly's honest. "Not like some people I know," says Fay.

Know, dear? Like some people you *know*?

"Leave me alone! I haven't time! I haven't time!"

Indeed she hasn't, for the doorbell rings and Fay thrusts her pilfered black silk 'veil' over her nose and straightens her tablecloth turban -- it's a tad bit heavy for her delicate neck. She adjusts her pyjama harem-pantaloons, rolls up Ted's enormous pyjama sleeves, heartily approves her mascara-koled eyes. "I am replete," she murmurs again just as inaccurately, for she is no more *replete* than I (nor should she be), and opens the door and bows deeply, *deeply* before the frail, *frail*, eighty-something, flowers-and-wine-laden

Mr Abdullah Omar Shamaly. "Salaam alay-kum, Abdullah!"

Abdullah Shamaly is delighted. He proffers the simply *gorgeous* bouquet and the bottle of finest wine but Fay remains frozen in her deep bow. Shamaly glows. His eyes gleam and his heart thumps joyfully. Here at last is a woman who clearly perceives what it is to be a woman in a genuinely Bedouin sense. Hardly able to contain his superannuated ecstasy, he declares: "Alay-kum salaam! Rise, my dear, from your semi-recumbent posture."

Mr Shamaly, well-read, has a sense of humour, has perused -- his mind, nimble as a young athlete's -- many a classic comedy. So have I. And so, if luck has it, have you, m'dears.

Fay rises as commanded, but slowly, sensuously, her eyes, for that is all Shamaly sees of her face, "smouldering", as Rita-writer wrote, "with promise".

"Enter at your peril," breathes Fay from beneath her fluttering black silk veil.

Peril? Correct on all counts!

"What?" cries Fay, "What was that?"

Shamaly proffers the flowers and wine for which Fay offers another, though not so deep, bow. She ushers him in with a sweeping gesture of the floor-length rear portion of her blue velvet turban and spirits the flowers to the kitchen. Then, head bowed, hands clasped as though in prayer, she summons Shamaly to seat himself upon her fantastical carpet. This he does with some difficulty as he is, after all, an older man. A *much* older man.

"The darling, the perfect darling," murmurs Fay as she lowers herself to the carpet beside him and places the wine he has brought on a tray beside two glasses and a corkscrew. The carpet glimmers and, though unbade, prepares itself for duty. Shamaly takes up the corkscrew but Fay snatches it from him, bows her head and proceeds to open the wine. Which, thank God, will be served in place of that sugary rubbish in the bleedin' pitcher (and she can easily witch the new wine in a nanosecond – if that, indeed, is the sort of thing she does and far be it from me to tell tales out of school). "I could just love Abdullah to death," whispers Fay behind her *black veil*. Who is she kidding? That's Nelly's pilfered scarf, darlings! The slut has stolen it! Tush – my language!

"I'm rubber, you're glue," pipes Fay, at a fluff of floating cerulean, "Every bad thing you say to me bounces right offa me and sticks to you!"

I murmur "Phooey!" and find a suitably tidy corner to rest my weary whatevers.

Abdullah, of course, has been on Fay's projected gift list for several days now. Several years now, she might wish us to believe. Because Fay has absolutely no sense of time. Nor should she. Because, m'dears, we all know that everything that has happened or will happen, happens in the *here and now* (although our Abdullah might not agree with me). There is no past, no future. It is all, darlings, simply *now*. Ask Einstein. A lovely man. I'm having him for dinner tonight...err...I mean, having him *to* dinner tonight.

Abdullah Omar Shamaly watches Fay with growing anticipation as she expertly pops the wine cork, pours two glasses, hands one to him and has already, under cover of her *veil*, quaffed hers and poured another before he can bring his own glass to his lips.

"I am a woman of strong appetites," murmurs Fay, drawing upon a simply endless supply of coals from Newcastle and patting her lips beneath Nelly's silk scarf with a toilet tissue table napkin.

"You are a rose at its height," sighs Shamaly meaning every single word of it.

Fay, one slim finger sliding suggestively round the rim of her glass, "I was a florist."

She brings the wine-wetted finger to her lips, sucks it while Shamaly, rapt, gazes ardently at her. He is such a lovely old man, thinks Fay. I am hopelessly devoted to him. He is a darling -- definitely first on my gift list, as I, one earnestly anticipates, am as securely established on his.

Tits for tat, love?

Fay quaffs her second glass, mutters "hush!" and pours another, each time, delicately raising her veil to drink. Our darling old man is enormously titillated.

"Then," breathes Fay, her hot breath instantly conquering the ever diminishing distance to Abdullah's already burning cheeks, "I was a beautician."

Fay grabs the sorry little dish of ragged bread, snatches one for herself and thrusts the dish at Shamaly. But he only has eyes for Fay as her black veil moves seductively up and down with each languorous munch of bread.

"Then my house burned down," mumbles Fay, still chewing. "I was not insured, of course, because my resources were as slim as my waist and had flowed, a flagging brook into dire necessity: the professional care required by my dear mother after sister Jane's murder. My beloved sister," adds Fay, swallowing with some difficulty as she has again bitten off more than even she can chew, "my beloved sister was signally done in by a woman who wore tweeds and brogues and kept hounds."

So you've said, my repetitive Rapunzel, and said and said.

"Hounds?!" cries Shamaly, "*Dogs*?! But dogs are anathema! I abhor dogs!"

Abdullah Shamaly winces, caninially derailed from his dogged adoration of the enchanting Fay.

"With the notable exception," chimes Fay brightly at my instantaneous coaching, "of the sleek Saluki!"

Shamaly is instantly re-charmed and exclaims:

"Ah! A royal breed!"

"Bred for hunting in the high desert of Turkistan since time out of mind," continues Fay informatively.

"My dear!" exclaims Shamaly, seizing Fay's hand, "You astonish and enchant me!"

Oh brave new world, darlings! Have I not outdone meself!

"What?" says Fay, "What was that?"

"I said nothing, my enchantress," puffs Shamaly more accurately than he knows.

Fay demurely removes her hand from the bewitched old man's scaly though fervent clutch, pours another wine for each of them. She stirs hers with her little finger and, her seductive tone at sublime odds with her subject, speaks:

"The Saluki is the oldest known breed of domesticated dog, having originated in the Sumerian Empire of 7000 to 6000 BC."

The venerable Shamaly gapes worshipfully as he moves closer, laboriously sliding his shrunken shanks across Fay's wondrously aroused carpet. Fay flaps her lashes, bows her head, glides gracefully away, but not too *far* away, whispers:

"Then I was a librarian."

Fay speaks the truth. As she knows it.

"What?" murmurs Fay, "What was that?"

As though in answer, the carpet beneath the two of them ripples slightly, morses out yet another staccato hue -- is noted, unfortunately, only by me.

"I wouldn't be easy to live with," says Nelly, blushing brightly, squirming slightly, "I'm kind of set in my ways."

Nelly and Bill clink their crystal wine glasses, gaze deeply into one another's eyes, drink.

Nelly turns her head, not to avoid his tender gaze but because she has never been looked at in quite this wonderful way. "Never," she whispers faintly to the window that *really* needs a wash -- wish she'd seen to it before. What will Bill think?

"My support payments are crippling and my ex-wife, well, I believe she actually detested me. So there it is. Be warned. But I can cook."

"So can I," answers Nelly, her left eye ticcing. "Cookies only. Oh, yes – and boiled potatoes. And haggis, the occasional haggis. I hope you like haggis. We're having haggis."

Rita's typewriter echoes from across the hall and Mrs Taylor immediately thumps from above. Nelly and Bill laugh, hold hands, tenderly regard one another for another miraculous moment.

"Shall we mention it?"

Everybody already knows, kids!

"Not yet," says Nelly, "I want a secret. This is the first important secret I've had since I was a child. I kept a diary then too, just like poor Fay. But only for a week."

"A diary?"

"When I was in love. I didn't want anyone to know."

"Why?"

Nelly swipes at her now severely ticcing eye, takes an exceptionally nervous sip of wine. "Because," she stammers, "...because I thought it would dilute my joy."

She turns away, embarrassed.

I am startled at such depth in this sweetest accessory to our purpose.

Bill moves closer, takes her in his arms. They kiss resoundingly. It is magical.

Of *course* it is, darlings. Stay tuned!

Fay is indisputably statuesque at a window (one of our favourite poses). She gazes into the darkness and, pinky extended, nibbles on the very last sorry slice of bread. A candle, in whose faint light Fay shimmers, gutters on an upturned jar lid. Abdullah Shamaly painfully shifts his other shrunken shank, continues to recline uncomfortably but devotedly on our magnificent, slyly undulating carpet, whispers, eyes glued to Fay's fanny, "You are a woman among women."

Fay turns abruptly from the window, rustling Ted's vivid blue pyjamas and snapping her tablecloth turban's tail with a great thwack. She exclaims "Abdullah! I am the marrying kind!"

The guttering candle flame flares up, casting on cue, a bright, unearthly glow. Shamaly laboriously drags himself from the carpet, leans on Fay's looted drop-leaf table. "Remove your veil, my dear!"

"No," murmurs Fay, hanging her head in a fabulous pout, "It would be unseemly."

Abdullah Shamaly sighs, feels an odd vibration very much, though not precisely like Jenny's, reaches for wine to quell it. But Fay leaps over, snatches the bottle from him and kneels. With her turbaned head suitably bowed and one hand clasped reverently over her breast she pours him another, offers it submissively.

"Unseemly, my dear?" repeats Shamaly as he seems to sip carefully but is actually an adamant teetotaler, having covertly jettisoned his first wine into hairy Ted's potted Sanseveria. "Perhaps you are right, my angel."

Fay glitters outrageously at Shamaly's gentle flattery, returns to the window, assumes an additional alluring pose. She is achingly admired for thirty seconds then, solemnly heaving her shoulders back and her veiled and turbaned head high, speaks: "The women of the desert wear their earthly treasures about their swan-like necks and on their slender wrists and graceful ankles in intricate chains of silver and gold. I have no silver, Abdullah, I have no gold. I possess only the greatest treasure a woman can offer. Herself."

My God, I'm good when I need to be!

"Hush!" hisses Fay.

"Oh! My dear, dear...errr..." Poor Shamaly falters.

Fay, sharply, from the window: "Ritterhouse, Fay!"

"My dearest Ritterhouse..."

A curt murmur: "Fay, *please*."

"My dearest Fay. Will you marry me?"

"But you have a wife."

"I shall have another."

"I'll need a house. My house burned down," replies Fay bewitchingly as superfluous shadows dart yon and hither from my so-called *armpit*.

"I shall give you another house, my dear, my dearest..."

Another falter from the fervent old fop. Sorry, darlings, Fay would never have referred to this dear old man so recklessly but this sort of thing does get me hackles up! I mean, *she* must be three hundred years older than he is! (I jest of course)

"My dearest..."

Again he falters, flops back on Fay's imperfect, pulsating, even devious rug.

"*Fay*! My bleeding name, Abdullah, is *Fay*."

"Fay, Fay, Fay," whispers Shamaly, "Fay...Fay...Fay..."

"I already have the keys, Abdullah."

"Keys? What keys, dearest Miss?"

Fay is now ready to talk business and swoops down upon her astounding carpet directly opposite Shamaly. Panting with desire and some effort, he immediately slides closer and attempts gently to paw her. She again slides demurely away. But not too *far* away.

"I have the keys to the house I must have. I have just come from the house I desire with all my poor battered heart."

"But my dearest dear! You did not like it there. That is why I have come for the keys."

"I was unhappy only because they who lived there were so unhappy. But Abdullah, now I believe I could make them happy. Very happy. *So happy they would cry*," adds Fay under her breath, meaning in the nicest way of course, every word of it.

This is a bit much for weary old Abdullah to take in all at once.

"You could make them happy?" he asks, his rheumy eyes ogling those voluptuous mounds immediately below the hastily unbuttoned top of absent Ted's pyjamas.

"I know I can make them happy if only I had the chance."

Shamaly grabs Fay's hand, covers it with kisses. "You shall have the chance, my kind and dearest Miss!"

Fay tears her hand away. "But it must be *my* house!"

"Indeed it shall! Oh indeed it shall be!" rasps Shamaly, grabbing Fay's hand again and clutching it and Fay to his hyperventilating chest.

"In *deed*?" she whispers, "I was a solicitor's assistant, monsieur, I know of these things. An actual deed? In writing? Legally? Under the law?" breathes Fay into Shamaly's over-perfumed, over-embroidered, under-sized and somewhat musty waistcoat.

"Oh yes, my dear!" snuffles Shamaly, as his ardent kisses move up absent Ted's pyjamas' sleeve. "It is a shabby little house only partly renovated. I have many more substantial. But if you desire it, it shall be yours. I am a man of honour. Under the law it shall be yours."

Fay jerks her hand away from the panting old dear. "Then, and only then, shall I be yours," sighs Fay, eyes askance at a seemingly *endless* row of squares she must soon manoeuvre; a glittering, starlit highway in the sky.

Returning from this too brief astral contemplation, she softens because, regardless of what others might think, including mischievous, megalomaniacal me, she esteems the worthy Abdullah Omar Shamaly.

A glitch on my part, m'dears, a simple glitch.

Fay takes both of the dear old man's shrivelled hands, first one then the other, in hers. "You must go now, my husband-to-be, before I lose my way. For I am only a woman."

Far more, darling! *Far* more!

"What?" says Fay, "What was that?!"

"A woman among women!" shouts Shamaly, beside himself with octogenarian lust, "Please remove your veil!"

The old man lunges and paws pitifully at hairy Ted's blue pyjamas' leg. Fay pulls away, shoots up and stands majestically over him, seems to have grown a foot taller, "Not yet, Abdullah. Tomorrow. Bring the legal papers and a witness."

"You shall be my second wife, dearest Miss."

"Second?!"

"Yes. The second. Possibly. Probably."

Fay bows low. "I am honoured."

Shamaly commences to lift himself from Fay's magical carpet but his aged bones are not up to it -- even with the assistance of a polite arse-ward, upward thrust from the carpet itself -- and he flops back with a thud. Fay, ineffably tender towards this helplessly infatuated old man, gently helps him up. Fay has her moments -- when I am not tormenting her.

Shamaly begins again, though less adamantly, to puff and paw at Fay's hastily assembled, though wizard, kit.

"You enchant me," he whispers as Fay softly fends him off and murmurs: "Tomorrow, darling. One P.M. -- by two P.M. all paperwork in order, I shall be yours exclusively."

"You astonish and enchant me," he says, "You are bewitching."

Eyes glinting their traditional mauve: "I *am* a bit of a witch."

Which is no news to no one.

Sorry, darlings. Was that redundant?

21

Rita pushes herself back from the typewriter, stretches and grins from one gypsy-earringed-ear to the other. She rips a page from her typewriter, adds it to the bottom of a neat stack of pages, the top page of which proclaims:

Her House Burned Down.
a novel in four parts
by Rita Lambert.
Part One

She places the pages in a large brown envelope addressed to "Pazazz Magazine", dances a jig as she licks a few stamps and slaps them on the envelope. Whistling, she throws on a Chanel sequinned, aviator's jacket, skips happily into the night. Her shiny-bottomed jodhpurs, with my compliments, glimmer anew in the street lamps as she trips towards the nearest post box.

Fashion note: Rita has always had a certain *penchant* for all things French. Hence, her Chanel jacket (as above); a second-hand, Jacques Louis gown (not worn since she grew out of it); her #5 perfume; her preference for 'boudoir' over 'bedroom'; and, of course, her old pal, Monsieur Courvoisier, who never lets her down (Like some men she knew. But that's another story).

Bien! Let us now *continue*.

Mrs Taylor squints in the morning light, attempts and fails to suppress a giggle. Her ear is mashed tight against her bolted door as milk bottles rattle in the hallway.

"Mrs Taylor?" repeats the milkman, "Mrs Taylor?"

She giggles again, hisses "Silence is golden, goldy-goldy-golden," shuffles away to air her posies.

Turbaned Fay perches on a stool before Ted's wardrobe mirror. She is exhausted from incantating the whole morning disturbed by my constant but apt admonitions. This sloppy slut simply will not get her incantations right! It is almost as though she hurtled directly from Hell to harass and humiliate me for my own, however scant, shortcomings. There is dichotomy here, m'dears, but yours truly is simply too pooped to pursue it. Besides, it bores the hell outta me.

Generously -- for her body is a *temple* (I've been meaning to ask her about that) -- Fay applies Nelly's purloined lipstick. A knock at the door startles and the lipstick skips right over a tiny but extraordinarily becoming mole -- a mole identical with... but that's *almost* another story. Oh, I may as well admit it. A mole identical with mine and not a silly millimetre from the very spot mine lies. That is *all* I'm going to say, m'dears. Pour maintenant. My French, he is not so tres bon. But, as in all things, I persist and somehow prevail.

Fay stubbornly (invariably to her cost) refuses to acknowledge me and hastily wipes off the erring lipstick, reapplies it, approves, and shoots to the door which she opens. Bowing very low, this time sans-veil, she speaks solemnly to the floor:

"Salaam alay-kum!"

Fay retains her nearly prostrate bow, awaits her dear Shamaly's "Alay-kum-salaam".

"I said," repeats Fay to the floor, "Salaam alay-kum!"

This darkly handsome middle-aged gentleman is aghast, can only stare at the ravaged top of Fay's jerry-built turban and manage "Alay-kum salaam."

Fay straightens up so fast the turban flies from her head but handily catching it she sees this well-dressed stranger is not her ancient lover, cries "Where's Shamaly?"

"I am Mr Shamaly's personal assistant. My name is Hassan Ammari."

"You must forgive me," peeps Fay at her contritest, "I had a small disaster in my kitchen this morning. I am not myself. My bacon caught fire."

"Bacon?" gasps Hassan Ammari, "You eat *pig meat*?!"

"Good heavens no!" cries Fay, modus-operandi mutating in a millisecond (loved that phrase!), "I was preparing breakfast for an unfortunate old lady who lives down the hall and who has recently lost the use of all four limbs."

When in doubt, darling, exaggerate. I do. Bless me, I just did.

Fay motions Ammari to her carpet. "Please sit down."

Ammari glances down his nose at the magnificent carpet. "Such a fine, ancient rug should be placed under glass, not sat upon."

The carpet dutifully scintillates a glittery, grateful response which of course goes unnoticed: By Fay who is intent upon

Ammari's comment; by Ammari who is momentarily baffled by this bizarre being who calls herself Ritterhouse Fay.

Fay decides instantly she is pleased with Ammari's assessment of her riches from Granny Taylor's closet, directs him to the sofa where he stiffly seats himself. She reclines decorously upon the carpet, carefully draping her turban tail over its flawed corner as Ammari takes some papers from an expensive looking and certainly-not-pigskin briefcase.

"You are an expert on rugs?" asks Fay.

"Yes," replies Ammari, "They are, actually, my part-time vocation."

The carpet again responds with a shimmer, again unnoticed, even by this professed expert.

"Here is the deed to that house, Number 13..."

"Yes!" replies Fay snatching away the document.

"Made over to you, freehold," continues Ammari, "Free and clear and signed by Mr Shamaly.

"With witnesses?"

"With three witnesses, as required."

Fay examines the deed, checks each clause with unabashed pleasure. Ammari, grim, watches her, hands her several more pages.

"Sign these, please."

"What are they?"

"The maintenance agreement."

Fay's eyes become slits. "Maintenance agreement? I agreed to no maintenance agreement."

"You are to receive the monthly fee stated here for two years beginning today, subject to your availability and revocable at Mr Shamaly's displeasure. You will also have no claim whatsoever to any other possession of Mr Shamaly's, real-estate or personal. Is that perfectly clear?"

"Yes," mumbles Fay, pleasurably pondering that 'monthly fee'.

Ammari hands Fay a pen. "Sign here, please, in triplicate."

Fay scribbles her name on each page and hands all three back to Ammari who returns one to her with a cheque. "Here is your copy of the agreement and your first month's maintenance. You realize that this arrangement would not be recognized as 'marriage' in a court of law?"

"Oh yes!" replies Fay, perusing with squinting eye and leaping heart the sumptuous sum on the check. She'll be able to buy thousands of presents for her erstwhile friends.

Whether they want them or not.

"Belt up!" mutters Fay, one squinty eye vainly darting to my position of a *full split-second* before -- darlings, I do move fast!

"Belt up, damn you!"

"I beg your pardon?" says Ammari, looking up from his papers with some irritation.

"Nothing," murmurs Fay, not wishing to draw attention to roiling colours gathering about the pointy fronds of Big Ted's astonishingly healthy potted Sanseveria. "I was just going over my shopping list."

"Our business," says Hassan Ammari, "is now complete, I believe."

He *believes*?

"Hush, you! What can I get for this rug?" says Fay, her eyes still asquint cheque-wise, her heart bumping.

Rather smooth, that, non? *Eyes asquint, heart bumping*?

Hassan Ammari, curious because he is an ardent, and even widely recognized rug-lover who has wisely made a goodly bit on the side from carpet expertise and invested it even more wisely in a substance known as (mark this m'dears) 'black gold', lowers himself sedately to his knees at the rug's fringed and friendly edge. Fay reluctantly slides her bottom off the corner flaw to allow him a more accurate examination of her now blushing, subtly billowing, magical carpet.

Ammari, who in spite of himself has also been noting Fay's bottom with some interest, now examines that particular corner so recently vacated by Fay's shapely bottom. Both spread-fingered hands shoot heavenward as he exclaims "Allah be praised! Oh! Indeed! Allah be praised!"

With which we can heartily agree.

22

"Richardson proposed," says Hugh, bounding through the door and flinging his briefcase in a corner.

"Proposed?"

"Fellatio," says Hugh with a laugh.

"Did you accept?" asks Jenny.

"Do you think I'm mad?!"

"Then you didn't?"

"Of course I did. He's a gem of a boss. Knows his business."

"It does seem so."

Jenny stops mid-push-up, wipes her forehead. "But do you like him?"

Hugh smiles, playing with her, "I adore fellatio."

"Duh! But do you like *him*?"

"A lot. If that's got anything to do with it."

"Scones in the oven, sunflower seeds."

Did I actually hear myself say 'scones in the oven, sunflower seeds'? thinks Jenny who continues "Bring him back for dinner."

"He wants *me* for dinner," says Hugh, smiling again and plunging into the kitchen. "Would you mind terribly if I had a lot on the side?"

"The scones are lovely," says Jenny, preferring to ignore the immediately above.

Hugh, from the kitchen, munching: "Better than mine."

"I painted them with egg-yellow, makes 'em shiny."

Egg-yellow? thinks Jenny, Did I actually say 'egg-yellow, makes 'em shiny'?

You'll be saying a lot of uncharacteristic things, Jenny. Get used to it. For the duration. A board game has only so many squares, love, and its secondary play-tokens are generally just slotted in wherever they randomly fit.

"Huh?" says Hugh from the kitchen.

"The scones. I painted them with whipped egg-yellow. Rita suggested it."

Jesus! Listen to me, thinks Jenny, No wonder the boss's blowjob is so attractive. Have I become that boring?

No, dear, *I* have. As I simply haven't the time to spend super-fruitfully with you two minor, though significant in your way, players (though they do account for one-fifth of our task). I've made sweet Hughie somewhat uncharacteristic too, with his frank, though fetching, sexual admissions. But all, it seems, to no avail. They bore me simply shitless.

"Oh?" replies Hugh, "Egg yellow! Riveting!"

"Shut up. Rita's written a story about Ritterhouse Fay. Sent it off to Pazazz."

"Ritterhouse Fay, huh?" says Hugh, entering with a steaming tray, "Have a most superbly buttered scone. Now there was one strange lady."

You may as well know now, m'dears, your august narrator is queer for scones.

"*Woman*," corrects Jenny, "Fay was one excessively strange woman." When in doubt, thinks Jenny, when in doubt, fall back on Feminism.

Jenny shudders, feels -- correctly, m'dears -- unbelievably boring, almost feels an odd vibration, fights it, wins. "Rita says Mrs Taylor is certain Ritterhouse is a witch."

"A witch who knows exactly what she's doing. She got away with one marvellous rug."

"And some furniture."

Honestly, you two! Get on with it!

"Poor deranged individual," sighs Hugh.

"The bitch nearly did your kitchen in. What a fabulous feast that mess she left would have been for itinerant cockroaches."

Ach! You've put a naughty idea into my head. Merci, Jen. But later, gator, when my so-called *legs* are straighter (a soupçon of ur-slang is never out of place).

"Jen, what'll I do about Richardson?"

Jenny, chewing:

"What would you like to do?"

"Don't know."

"Look. Either he's attractive or he ain't."

"I've already said he is. But will it make a difference? What about us?"

"What *about* us?"

Jenny looks away and chews thoughtfully for a moment -- doesn't like the subject, turns back to Hugh, "I think she is. I think Ritterhouse Fay is an authentic witch."

Jenny, what would you know about it? Stop changing the subject. And, by the way, *ho*-hum.

M'dears, it is increasingly difficult to deal with these kids when ones raison d'être (and vice versa) must, due to our curious circumstances, lie in the delicious/malicious though innocent machinations of Ritterhouse Fay, my darling prosopopoeia. But just now there is a story to tell, indeed a saga. And a game to play, and sometimes we must be patient with supernumeraries who are a smidgin cardboard (though I'm doing my damnedest). Because, who among us has not met a creature who, however real, however certain of his/her authenticity, is nonetheless cardboard? Look around, my darlings, look around! And for heaven's sake stop fooling yourselves! You might be cardboard too.

But I digress. And so must – inevitably -- you.

Ritterhouse Fay huddles into a corner of Big Ted's little sofa as my mauve/indigo/orange light-show flickers wholly unappreciated and diabolically difficult to duplicate at this distance from our venerable Number 13.

Fay is tucked cosily away under that blue velvet tablecloth-cum-turban, now a voluminous shawl. *Too many people about.* Ted's tiny flat is packed. Fay is attempting to take all of this in. The too many people are customarily *inside* her head. Now they're here, *outside,* for all this cruel world to witness. So she hides herself under her magical crescent-mooned velvet tablecloth and is magically though only momentarily safe. From what, darling Fay? Fire? Oh, yes, we know. Fire follows Fay -- needs to be extinguished. But, *honestly!* With high pressure water shot from a height aimed directly at ones head?!

Really!

A British Museum technician with a tri-podded, huge-lensed magnifying camera hovers, clicking away, over Fay's carpet. He consults intermittently with another BM man, his boss, who crouches beside him and consults with another technician who jabs information into a tiny hand-held computer. The BM boss peers with astonishment into the flawed corner of this fantastical rug. Said rug, it should be noted (by us-in-the-know), is pleased with all this sudden attention; has been waiting for approval for a millennium in various closets, caves, vaults, and what-have-you's; Mrs Taylor's closet being simply the latest. So the rug curls, ripples, glows, preens, shuffles at least an inch along hairy Teddy's tidy, thoroughly waxed and polished floor. The BM photographer has no idea why he must continually readjust his focus. Frankly, m'dears, if our carpet were a snake it woulda bit him! Woulda bit all of 'em!

Which could easily have been arranged. Most people deserve a sharp bite on the arse to wake 'em up. Take it from me, my little chickadees. As you know, I speak only from experience.

In any case, m'dears, Hassan Ammari babbles excitedly into his tiny telephone whilst Fay, from her blue velvet sanctuary, watches as from a passing cloud.

I've had her on 'hold', darlings. So much else is happening just now.

The BM boss rises from the carpet, approaches the Fay-shaped heap of blue velvet which shakes itself from its reverie and speaks.

I allow an archaic: "Glad tidings?"

So biblical, dear, you do take after Mumsy.

"Shut up!" hisses Fay.

"I beg your pardon?" says the BM boss.

"Not you, sugar," grins Fay at her jauntiest.

The BM boss nods. "It isn't actually the carpet, as you must know... though the carpet itself is priceless."

Fay's eyes dance a jolly jig at 'priceless' then return to waking-dream-come-true-mode. What is she seeing behind those opaque, mauve and *soulless* eyes?

Don't ask. But if you must, be warned. 'Tain't necessarily so.

The door bursts open. Two reporters, one with a miniature television camera, rush in. The TV man immediately trains his camera on the carpet in question while the other reporter speaks to Ammari who directs her to Fay.

The BM boss drops to the sofa beside Fay, continues. "When Arabs captured the ancient Persian city of Ctesiphon..."

"How do you spell that, please?" cuts in the reporter, brushing a hank of oily hair from her eyes as the TV cameraman moves in.

"Sotheby's?...Mr Cartwright, please...Hassan Ammari. He's expecting my call," says our spiffily dressed Persian rug expert.

"When the Arabs captured the Persian palace of Ctesiphon in 635 AD," continues the BM boss with an envious frown at Ammari, "its fabulous 'Winter Carpet', which was reputed to have been at least nine thousand feet square and said to have magical powers, was divided into thousands of pieces and distributed as spoils among the conquering soldiers..."

The cameraman cuts in, leads the BM boss to the carpet. The BM boss looks harried while the reporter, swiping that oily hank from her eyes, questions him. And our Fay, secure, distant, watches from her miscellaneous cogitations, other voices circling her head, rippling amongst the silver embroidered crescent-moons of her velvet sanctuary. "Me so happy!" she sighs, "Me so exceptionally, so extraordinarily, so excruciatingly happy!"

Savour it, Fay! Roll in it like a sow in slops!

"You'll not ruin my fun!" hisses Fay, "Whoever you are!"

"Yes! Yes!" whispers Hassan Ammari into his cell phone (*or mobile* -- say it in your heads, darlings if it'll help), "Ms Ritterhouse has agreed," says Ammari, "...Henry, you are too kind. I'll expect that in writing *well before* the auction...Thank you."

"If," says the BM boss to the reporter as, followed by the TV camera, he makes his way back to daydreaming Fay, "If I can be allowed to continue."

The reporter, vainly brushing that floppy hair from her eyes once more, thrusts a tiny microphone at the BM boss who is disturbed that Fay seems to have gone to sleep. She *hasn't*.

"Ms Ritterhouse?" he says.

"Yes?" peeps Fay, eyes closed, inner voices buzzing nearer than she'd prefer. But harmless. For now.

That's what you think, ducky. Every day, a little death, as they say.

"What?" says Fay, "What was that?"

The BM boss crouches beside Fay. "Shall I continue, Ms Ritterhouse?"

"Do."

"The largest..." says the BM boss.

"I adore carpet research," murmurs Fay with a curious smile.

"...The largest section," continues the BM boss, "of the divided Ctesiphon Carpet went to Caliph Omar, leader of the conquering army. This piece is now in the British Museum. The second largest, and missing, piece went to Ali, the Prophet Mohammad's son-in-law and..."

The BM boss has grown very red about the neck. He loosens his collar, pats his perspiring forehead with a frayed though nicely initialled hanky.

"And?" asks Fay who is unnaturally calm as she is, after all, wrapped in her special blue velvet tablecloth.

"And?" she repeats, "Et?" (compliments of moi, m'dears, and my revamped maternal Frenchiness)

"What?" says Fay, "What was that?"

But whatever it was, and *we* know what it was, it has slipped surreptitiously beneath that welcoming, wiggling, newly confident, positively coital carpet for a midday snog!

The BM boss shoos away the technician with the magnifying camera, shoos away the technician with little computer, lowers himself stiffly to the floor beside this glorious, gloating, now gyrating rug because he is too faint to crouch any longer. He strokes the flawed corner of the magnificent textile which sighs and flickers beguilingly. He says: "And here it is. Mohammad's son-in-law's fragment of the carpet."

The reporter, brushes her hair from her eyes, gasps, gapes, says: "Is that 'Mohammad' as in 'MOHAMMAD'?!"

Duh!

The BM boss nods perfunctorily, the reporter gasps and gapes again, the TV cameraman gasps, gapes, moves in close, takes in our carpet's *flaw*. Fay does not gasp or gape but smiles serenely if repetitively. The BM boss rises, drops himself again on the sofa beside Fay. The reporter sticks her mike near and the BM boss says:

"This patched corner is but a tiny fragment of course, of the original, fabulous 'Winter' carpet of Ctesiphon. But what a fragment! It was, a thousand years ago, expertly woven, complete with the initials of said son-in-law, into another extraordinary carpet -- the splendid little carpet you see here -- obviously to conceal it from enemies. It is reputed to retain magical powers and Mohammad himself is said to have rested his head many times upon it. This rug is the Islamic equivalent of twenty Shrouds Of Turin. But *our* fabulous fragment is *not* a fake."

The reporter: "Thank God!"

The BM boss: "Correction. Allah be praised. Now, if you will excuse us all, the owner, Ms Ritterhouse, has graciously allowed the British Museum today alone for our examination."

He moves away with the hint of a frown at Fay who couldn't have cared less even had she seen it. The reporter, tossing her hair back, moves in quickly to Fay.

"I could do wonders with that mop of yours," says Fay.

"What I would like to know," asks the reporter, beckoning to the TV camera and poking her mike closer, "is what you plan to do with your carpet."

"I shall..."

The BM boss overhears, looks hopefully at Fay who eyes him impassively and adds:

"I shall put it up for auction."

The BM boss's hopeful look fades -- where would the British Museum get *that* kind of money? The reporter and television cameraman whisper to one another, move in very close. Fay loves it, is no longer frightened, feels safer than ever, even allows her velvet tablecloth to slip from a shapely shoulder.

"How does it feel to be so lucky?" asks the reporter, "Speak into the mike please, love."

"Oh, I've never been lucky," replies Fay, loving to be so definitively addressed and mentally scrawling 'reporter with crappy hair' on her tentative gift list. "I believe in destiny."

And well you should, dear. As I've preordained *everything*.

Fay frowns away my whisper, adds, "This is the first good luck to cross my path."

"Better than a black cat though, isn't it?" replies the reporter.

"Is it? I love cats. Especially black ones. Black cats make best friends."

Questionable, darling, but we'll allow it to pass.

"Where did your carpet actually come from?"

"I played upon it as a child in Adelaide, Australia, or was it Alexandria, Egypt? Or Altoona, Indiana? (and that's only the *A's*, m'dears) It's been in my family for centuries. From whence it came I know not."

Fay throws back her head, guffaws, startles the reporter, "Perhaps it was conjured by a witch! A witch named Taylor."

That just popped into her head -- nothing to do with me. Though everything has to do with me. Figger it out.

"Odd name for a witch, 'Taylor'."

"Is it?"

"What will you do with all that money? All the money you'll get at the auction?" asks the reporter.

Fay, the child, peers dreamily about the room, peers at the overexcited BM team kneeling at the edges of her titillated treasure, peers at Hassan Ammari, animated, arranging, on his cell phone; peers directly into the television camera, peers at a group of curious neighbours gathered at a window, peering in. She pulls her blue velvet tablecloth close around her, shivers. Does she see that flickering, flame-engendered shadow fleeing across the wall of Ted's little living room?

We can never escape our pasts, can we m'dears? They cling like sand to our oily arses.

"What will you do with all that money?" repeats the reporter.

Fay looks up. Has this woman with the awful hair said something to her?

"What?" asks the reporter pulling several strands of that unruly hair from the corner of her mouth, "will you do with all that money?!"

Exit the dreaming child:

"Anything I please!" cries Fay, standing, "Anything I fuckin' please!"

That's what you think, love.

Fay giggles at her rare obscenity, drops back and slides into a far corner of big Ted's sofa. There is something awesome about her. Or is it just that she is, or soon shall be, astonishingly, even mythically wealthy? The reporter feels an odd vibration.

Talk to Jenny about that, ducky.

Fay winks the tiniest of winks at no one in particular. The reporter and cameraman see the wink, draw back from Fay, not aware they have drawn back. Some implausible, high-pitched voice screams deep in their heads "Me so happy!"

"Do you know what the Lord saith?" Fay asks. The reporter, who shivers in the throes of a mounting odd vibration, shakes her head. Fay says: "The Lord saith..."

The reporter pulls yet another hair strand from her mouth, feels faint. "God! I'm going to be sick!"

She rushes, accompanied by the cameraman (they're an 'item', m'dears), from the flat and jettisons over tidy Ted's pitifully small, though neatly weeded bed of flowers.

"The Lord saith vengeance is mine," whispers Fay through her cupid's bow lips. Nobody is listening. And of course nobody but us has witnessed the subtle change in Fay as she steps, amusingly but unseen, into yet another square of her nasty, boo-hoo, and much too short (as said) life – because nobody but us, m'dears, knows her.

No. No one *ever* listens to The Ritterhouse Fay.

More fool they.

Back at Number 13 a geranium flies from Taylor's hand, topples out the window, plummets through the orange sunset air and shatters on the entrance steps below. Two geraniums down, two to go! Count 'em.

Such fun, m'dears!

Rita spills her evening cognac all over her shiny-bottomed jodhpurs, mutters: "Bugger me!"

You should be so lucky, peaches.

Jenny drops a mini-barbell on her instep. Hugh leaps to her assistance with a cool, wet cloth. She cries "Owwwww!" as he rubs her foot and hugs her.

She'll soon need a lot more huggin', kiddies.

Hugh's boss, Richardson, irretrievably smitten, is about to dial Hugh's number and ask humpy Hugh to a "working dinner".

Darlings, is 'humpy' still common parlance?

Ho! ho! ho (plus a bottle of rum)!

Nelly slips in her bathtub, falls. Bill, two floors above, slips in his, falls. Both get bruised elbows. Nothing serious.

That will come later.

23

Fay twirls on the pavement outside Ted's flat, sings "Me so happy! Me so incredibly happy!"

The pavement, too, would rejoice if I had my way. We're moving on, m'dears, all of us. And God bless us, every one!

Our Fay is bathed in the same orange sunset that currently washes over Number 13 -- out of sight but definitely *not* out of mind. "What a world!" sings Fay, "How incredible are the works of man! How that little wormy-thingy turneth!"

And turneth and turneth and turneth!

Fay gazes protectively at her worldly belongings: Nelly's chest of drawers and artful ceramic teapot (that black silk scarf lies safe in Fay's dowdy cardy pocket); Hugh's drop-leaf table; Bill's serviceable armchair and Rita's card table -- talismans all -- as they parade past in the steadfast arms of two gorgeous, mauve-uniformed young men who set each piece gently in the rear of a posh lorry; much as Fay herself would have set them there had she been a handsome young man. Which she well may have been only two weeks before. At least in her dreams (*My* dreams). Ach! Those disquieting dreams she has been experiencing lately. Flame-lit melodramas in which she seems to...to...metamorphose?

These blank spaces in her head! They fill in intermittently but too soon are empty. Fay's recollections can be very unreliable. Not at all like the strong arms of these handsome, mauve-like-Fay's-eyes, uniformed young men.

I prefer it that way, mes enfants. You know me.

Parked just in front of this striking, mauve, gold-lettered lorry is a stretch-limousine occupied by another uniformed young man with longish, white-gold hair (ringlets, m'dears, *ringlets*! Just like hunky William Katt's in Brian De Palma's superbly scary, cult-classic, 'Carrie'!). Fay's delighted glance lingers for a moment on the back of his shining head. A longing look, so like, indeed indistinguishable from, her Mum's. I take a bow. *You* interpret.

Directly behind the lorry a security van pulls up. Two more uniformed, gesticulating, tiny-telephone accoutred young men get out. They are armed and menacing. "Wheeeee!" cries Fay, "An embarrassment of riches! Wheeeee!" (then, precisely as before, darlings) "An embarrassment of riches!"

Obviously, Fay! Then I sing: Give me some men who are stout-hearted men and... well, just *give* 'em to me! Why shouldn't my workaday game-plan contain a perk or three? And remember, love, Mamá is calling the shots.

"What?" cries Fay, "What was --"

Her reply is lost as down Ted's steps comes the Fabulous Fragment Carpet, longing for its vital other, the acres-sized Ctesiphon Winter carpet from which it sprang an eon or two ago. But it would have been far too bulky to deal with here (even sagas have their limits). Though this, too, m'dears, could have been arranged if so ordained by you know who. Or you know *what*, as the case may be.

So the carpet/rug, then, is imperfect. Like Fay. But perfect once -- like Fay. Impressivo -- like Fay, whose name is soon to be on the lips of anybody who watches television, surfs the Net, reads a newspaper, games their smart phones, or even listens to a lowly radio.

Fay waltzes along with the reliable young men who bear her carpet and flirts with the menacing, armed, security men who guard it. Ammari was so considerate to arrange so many boring details -- not that these lovely young men are boring.

Fay teases the young men, sings to herself, sings to them, hums, whistles, perfects her little jig; her feet and opaque eyes dancing in unison (if opaque eyes can be said to dance) (Which of course they can if I so will it).

The armed security men -- sensing menace from every quarter -- are not amused. The reliable young men are. Fay is certain she was once compelled to amuse men who were not reliable. So this is welcome. A joyful variation. Her shadows have lifted, shifted. But quo vadis, Fay?

Only her maker knows. So ask me, why doncha?

"What?" sings Fay, her head and heart lifting in the glorious orange light, "What was that?"

She turns back, watches, caresses her shimmering carpet until it groans with pleasure and promises -- in vain -- *powers unlimited*; promising all, until it is silenced, stuffed safely into that security van destined for the vaults of Sotheby's.

Fay tugs her velvet tablecloth tighter around her shoulders. Her mouse-coloured cardigan is not adequate to the cool evening dew that settles glistening upon her mouse-coloured hair. She waves goodbye to the security van and its unamused young men who mutter "nutter" -- fortunately, to themselves. She waves goodbye to her reliable mauve uniformed young men in the posh mauve and gold lorry. Reliable as ever, they wave back. Fay giggles, her cheeks glow pink against the ubiquitous orange, a positively *Tamayo* tableau. Has she seen these young men before? They seem so familiar. Not to worry, they will see her again -- whether they like it or not. Charmed money shrieks and helpmeets take many forms in life as in Art but are not, unfortunately, m'dears, always recognized as such.

N'est-ce pas?

Orange-aglow and dewy, Fay motions to her dishy chauffeur who hops smartly from the limou and assists her into the cream coloured, glove-leather back seat. Wasn't it considerate of Abdullah Shamaly to provide a car? (Fay supplied the chauffeur.) Why shouldn't Abdullah be generous? She is his wife, well, one of them, and a billionaire (possibly, darling, possibly) in her own right -- soon. Though she'll have to do something about the 'wife' part as old men often smell and are not firm though this has not heretofore been the case with her dear Shamaly who, though his waistcoat is a mite musty, is as after-shave-fresh-friendly as a fussy wife could wish. But Fay has had enough of that other kind, those infirm smelly old men, to last a lifetime. All nine lifetimes which, soon but not too soon, will be peeled from her like onion layers till nothing exists but a core: a glowing ember that sustains our game and, unbeknownst to her, defines our *task*.

On the seat beside her, Fay spies Rita's kettle as requested. My God it does need a shine! She grabs it and vigorously rubs it against her cardy. The white-gold chauffeur watches Fay from his rear-view mirror and waits patiently for his orders as he checks his perfectly manicured fingers.

Ach! A face suddenly appears at the stretch-limou's window. It is our Big Ted! He's come back from Manchester early (that job fell through) and he's baffled by this limou in front of his flat. This is not stretch-limou-land so he looks in. Christ! It's Fay! She sees him from the corner of her eye, continues to polish Rita's kettle against her cardy.

"Fay?" gulps Big Ted, "Is it you, love?"

Fay polishes. The kettle gleams and happily reflects her grinning face.

"Fay?" says Big Ted, in whose very own blue pyjamas Fay has so recently, so successfully, conjured and in which she remains,

"Fay?"

Fay turns to him as he kneels beside the limou. She buzzes the window down a crack, only a crack, stage whispers (much against her will because Ted is still on her gift list though *not* on mine, as hirsute gentlemen are not my cup of tea): "Your back is hairy, Mr Kong. That was our whole problem (prompt I). Your great, hairy back. Hair belongs on apes. In jungles. Byeeeeee, Jungle-boy!" cries our Fay, "I'll have your jim-jams luxury-laundered and returned!"

Fay is, for the moment, of course, under my lacerating influence.

She buzzes the window which thuds shut in Ted's face. As her deeply considerate other-nature briefly reasserts itself she attempts to reopen the window whilst shedding an inner tear for Ted. To no avail. Under my harsh direction her attention is directed to her chauffeur whose eyes she now follows in his rear-view mirror -- *so* like that errant bus driver who, in another life it seems, refused to turn his head and smile. She must hunt that bus driver down, give him a gift. *Such* a gift.

"The Savoy, Chauffy!" cries Fay.

"Yes, *ma'am*!" replies the chauffeur, brushing a white-gold ringlet from his clear blue eyes.

"I could do wonders with that mop of yours," says Fay. But believe her. She's done wonders with Rita's now glistening kettle, so shiny it seems to hover in the air beside her. Fay has a way with things.

So here stands Ted, ignorant of all recent events -- he's been on the road. Here he is, alone at the kerb in front of his flat watching Fay's limou speed away from definitely-not-limou-land. Poor, hairy, big Ted.

Crazy Fay hasn't seen the last of you, has she, Large Teddy?

"No," says Ted as though he's heard me. Perhaps he has, perhaps he hasn't. Darlings, I've better things to do than humour a hirsute furniture shifter. No matter how big. Me? I'm off for some stompin' at the *Sa*voy!

Precisely forty-five minutes later Fay's limou swoops to the kerb-side of the Savoy Hotel -- compliments of Hassan Ammari who stands to make a few bob on auction day -- it's on paper too – witnessed. He has other plans as well (a bit dodgy though, and definitely southern hemispheric), to be discussed later. After all, Fay isn't rich quite yet. Although she does have her first maintenance check and a complimentary vehicle from Abdullah

Shamaly; one of the inevitable perks of haremhood. We must look after Mummy's little girl.

The Savoy management has been alerted by ever-considerate Ammari to expect anything. They are not disappointed. Still polishing Rita's kettle and with her velvet tablecloth slung over her dowdy cardy and -- Oh My God! -- clad in Ted's bright blue rubber-band-cinched pyjamas and her dirty acrylic bunny-fur slippers (recently rediscovered by one of us – not sure which), Fay enters the lobby of the Savoy almost precisely as Sheba entered ancient Memphis. Only Sheba (a close acquaintance, m'dears) -- or a witch or a mad woman (take yer choice) -- would enter the Savoy lobby so attired. Funny old world, ain't it?

Fay pauses, takes it all in. "Me so happy," she murmurs, "Me *excessively* happy."

A man behind a desk, hurtles to Fay's side (not that he'd *meant* to hurtle), snaps his fingers for an upper echelon assistant to carry Fay's shabby cardboard suitcase, her paper carry-bag, her worn leather bag. All that is missing is Fay's sad bouquet, that miniscule memento of misery, abandoned to the ungrateful Nelly. Off my gift-list she will come! When I have a moment to myself, thinks Fay.

But do consider this, Fay. Keep her on the list for now. There will be a fitting, highly original, gift in the near future. Bespoke, so to speak. In a month or two? Shall we make it *two*? A gift that will settle all scores, real and imagined...Ach! Did I say that? I meant a gift that will right all wrongs – well, some of 'em.

Fay brushes these alien thoughts aside, but acquiesces (as she must) and mentally reinserts the ungrateful Nelly at the very top of said list -- where she would have remained in any case, had I not interfered. I am deeply dichotomous.

But aren't we all?! Plus I'm a busy little bee seeing to our -- here it comes again, m'dears -- seeing to our *task*.

The Savoy assistant who has just reached for Rita's kettle gets his fingers firmly slapped. The kettle is Fay's magic lamp -- or something. Is every object from Number 13 now enchanted? Fay considers this prospect for a merry millisecond. Must be. From where else has all this good fortune sprung? "How *else* should I be so larded with luxury?" sings Fay.

Don't be naive, darling. Improperly credited, *I* could get nasty!

"Huh?" says Fay, twirling towards yet another fleeting shadow, "What did you say?"

Fay's dishy chauffeur, still accompanying her, is dismissed though Fay hasn't seen the last of him either. She'll see to that. He seems *so* familiar.

He should be, sugar. We both shagged him.

Oh, dear! I mean: Of course he is, Fay. You hired him personally. What a busy, *busy* day!

Sweet Jesus! Who am *I* trying to impress?!

The Savoy assistant leads Fay to a lift whose polished brass doors swoop open to reveal yet another reliable young man. "What a perfectly enchanted world," sighs Fay.

Arriving toute-suite, the assistant unlocks the door and Fay hurries in and immediately snatches up the phone, clutches her shiny kettle to her breast so that the assistant, still at her side, cannot snatch it away, speaks:

"Can you put me through to a qualified architect? ...Suite 13, Ritterhouse, Fay."

Fay slams down the telephone, glares at the assistant who has a wart on his nose and reminds her of witches. She's had her sodding fill of witches!

Ça m'amuse, mes enfants!

"I don't speak French!" shouts Fay.

Neither do I, peaches!

"What was that, Madam?"

"I wasn't addressing vous."

"Oh. Sorry. We hope you will be very comfortable here, and if..."

"You're dismissed!" hisses Fay. He's balding, must be at least forty-five, bad skin. That wart! He's dismissed!

Goodness! I'm changing, thinks Fay, and not for the better... Why did I speak so harshly? He is only a fellow traveller through life's multi-vales of tears. What can I do to make myself a better person again? (We've all felt this way at one time or another, haven't we, m'dears?) Unfortunately Fay's edifying thoughts are lost in the whisper: Be yourself, darling. Be yourself. Fulfil your, our -- dare I say it? -- destiny. Perform your *vital task* and keep your cake-hole firmly shut.

Before the upper echelon be-warted assistant can say a word in his own defence, Fay has plunged into the exquisitely fitted bathroom where she squats and vigorously commences to polish the toilet seat with a very large, squeaky-clean, non-frayed and astoundingly fluffy bath towel.

The poor, upper echelon assistant, unconsciously fingering that hairy growth on his nose that has let him down yet again, hurries into the corridor as unobtrusively as possible. As he's a big man and carries himself well, wartless, who *nose* what heights he might have scaled?

I cause the tasteful corridor carpet to ripple slightly and throw him briefly off balance. I hate warts too though I do insist upon installing them right and left. I'm such a naughty girl just now. And so excitable!

24

But think, Fay! You must throw yourself down on that comfy, white, Louis Quinze-copy sofa and contemplate! Ponder! Ruminate! Cogitate! Consider! Reflect! Do you *really* wish to exchange your wonderful, potentially powerful rug for masses of filthy lucre? Think, my dim ducky! Ach! An act of such moment could so easily be construed by the great unwashed as a pact with the devil! Heavens! One could be burnt at the stake! Are you certain, Fay? About this... auction? Think on it, my puppet – err...sorry – *poppet*.

Fay's confused assessment of my recently proposed dilemma (directly above) spins round her like butter in a working churn; hardening to spread-consistency but soon melting under my hot, scrutinous, anti-glutinous gaze.

"You must tell me who you are," murmurs Fay, "I am so confused"

Get on with it, sister! So what is it to be?!

"Then it is my decision alone?"

Ostensibly, ducks, I answer as I sip a convenient potion and gloat accordingly. Darlings, I've got the world on a cat-gut string.

"Lucre makes that world go round!" cries Fay, more independently than I'd expected, "I'll just take the money and run. Whoever you are, wherever you are, whatever you are, to Hell with you!"

Fay casts a frightened look about her lavish suite but I am nowhere to be seen. Because, darlings, the devil is in the details.

"MOHAMMAD" CARPET TO BE AUCTIONED

says The Telegraph on Monday, from the bottom of page three.

BRITISH MUSEUM SEEKS GOV GRANT
TO BUY "MOHAMMAD" CARPET

suggests The Evening Standard on Wednesday from the top of page two.

MIDDLE EAST VIES FOR

"MOHAMMAD" CARPET!

shrills The Sun on Thursday from the top of page one.

"MOHAMMAD" CARPET SOLD TO UNKNOWN BIDDER FOR ONE BILLION!

shriek the front pages of every other newspaper in the world on Sunday.

"Britain has literally had the carpet pulled out from under her," sputters an earnest young man on the BBC Sunday Evening News. "And we had", he continues sardonically, "one whole week in which to make up our minds! Whew!" He pretends to wipe his brow. "An unknown Arab buyer, said to represent the government of..."

Fay switches off her telly, giggles, claps her hands. She pats the mammoth blue plastic curlers in her mousy hair and snuggles back into that fine Louis Quinze-copy sofa. A massive box of finest Belgian chocolates nestles in the lap of her tatty blue chenille bathrobe and her dirty pink-acrylic, bunny fur-slippered feet rest on a low, marble, Empire table carved with a wreathed 'N' -- the single initial of that long-dead despot, who turned arsenic-green prior to kicking the proverbial old oaken bucket.

Fay sighs, adjusts her blue curlers again and gazes dreamily over the Thames at London which now, so she believes, belongs to her. The doorbell chimes. "Come in," she purrs, because she knows what he looks like. They had faxed his photo. She'd insisted she see it before she engaged him. "Hugs and kisses are just around the corner" cries Fay. "He's a doll!"

A voodoo doll, dearie! And aren't you going to dress for the occasion?

"Glory!" cries Fay, "It skipped my mind!"

Par, m'dears, for the course!

> Ach! Lots of money's awfully nice
> But something's missing
> One needs spice
> Feeling listless? What's the matter?

A worthy herb intrigues the platter
The spice that's missing, call it *Class!*
This will solve your problem, Lass
Lots of money's awfully nice
But lots of money won't suffice

This young man will fill the bill
Move in, darling
For the kill!

"Belt up!" cries Fay at the innocent Thames though the culprit is obviously much nearer to hand!

"...so we have, it seems," quips the telly, "yet again dropped the ball -- I mean the rug -- and a magic carpet has flown. For shame, Britain. Tut tut tut. And tut again. And yet again, tut!"

Rita gasps, switches off her telly, hears Mrs Taylor thumping, yanks on her jumper.

Hugh is back.

"How'd the second working dinner go?" asks Jenny as he closes the door. "Work up a sweat, did you?"

He throws a newspaper at her, "Oh Jesus! A billion pounds!" cries Jenny as she takes in the full-page photo of Fay dabbing tears of joy from her heavily koled eyes. "Meet Fabulous Fragment Fay!" she reads, "Oh Jesus! A billion pounds!" she repeats, then, after a moment, "How'd it go? Your meeting with Herr Richardson."

"Well."

"Is something about to happen?"

"No more than's happening with Fabulous Fragment Fay," says Hugh. They laugh, neither wholeheartedly. Though each has had a modicum of experience, bisexuality is largely uncharted territory. But Hugh, it seems to Jenny, has already boarded his exotic canoe and is well on the way up his erotic Amazon. Or up something or other.

Here's some more:

Jenny and Alicia have only paddled about in circles though their respective dinghies are decidedly seaworthy.

In any case Hugh and Jenny laugh. Again, neither wholeheartedly. But let's move on, shall we?

reads Mrs Taylor from the local free newspaper that is faithfully slipped under her door. "Fabulous Fragment Fay!" reads the caption under another large photo of velvet tablecloth-draped Fay.

Taylor drops the newspaper, laughs. "Now it's the money that's cursed! Filthy lucre! Every pound! Every penny! And the money belongs to her! The witch! Mr Taylor knows what he's talkin' about! Oscar is no fool!"

With which I'd heartily agree.

Taylor cackles. There is a knock at her door. She freezes, eyes narrowed. "Milk at this time of day?!" mutters Taylor to herself as she shuffles and thumps to her door.

"Mrs Taylor?" says Rita.

"That's me all right!" cackles Taylor, still amused at witchy Fay's embarrassment of riches.

"It's Rita. I have something to tell you."

Taylor inches open the door. "Well what's stoppin' you?" Taylor thrusts the newspaper in Rita's face, catches Rita's elbow in the crook of her cane, draws her in.

"Don't they mean 'Fabulously frag*mented* Fay'?" says Rita, "That money should have been yours, Mrs Taylor."

"Godalmighty! Wouldn't want it! The witch has got the money and the money is cursed. Now you're here you may as well air my posies."

Rita opens the window, sets the two remaining geraniums in the window box.

"There's special sweeties in the kitchen. From Jenny," purrs Taylor, pleased she can remember Jenny's name. "Fancy a special sweetie?"

Taylor is feeling wonderful this evening. As clear in her head as that day several weeks before when she had the presence of mind to fob off the cursed carpet on *Fragmented Fay*. Taylor likes the phrase, it's got a ring to it.

"You're a darlin'," she shouts at Rita who is in the kitchen setting those special sweeties on a dish, "You're a darlin' for helpin' me. It's my wrists, you see."

Taylor holds up both gnarled, vein-knotted wrists. But Rita's in the kitchen. "Not my brain," continues Taylor, "I bet you could do with a nice hot cuppa. Come to think of it, so could I."

Rita puts the kettle on, decides for her own sanity it's best to drop the subject of the thieved carpet, begins to wash several grimy cups.

Taylor is drooling with anticipation for her sweeties, her nice hot tea. Hunched over her postcard table, she kisses several cards and drops them into that red carry-bag. The others she flings savagely into the rubbish bin by her feet.

"I bet you would like to know why I'm sortin' out all these cards!" says Taylor, "I jist bet you would like to know why give a smooch to some of 'em and I don't give a damn about the others!"

"Be there in a minute, love," calls Rita from the kitchen.

"Well," continues Taylor, "I smooch the cards that're signed with pretty little hearts and arrows. I jist love them little hearts and arrows!"

Taylor smiles mysteriously. Rita, still in the kitchen, doesn't see the smile. Doesn't hear.

"Where's my cuppa?! Where's my special sweeties?!"

Rita enters with Jenny's home-baked tarts, sets them on the postcard table, returns to the kitchen. Taylor smacks her lips, grabs a tart, munches noisily. "I was co-hearsed into payin' that bugger of a milkman. He said he would bring me to the attention of the authorities so I paid him for two weeks only. Now I give him the silent treatment. The sod says he's got a grandma just like me but I won't answer him. Phooey to him!"

Rita brings in cups and milk on a tray, returns to wait for the kettle.

Rita, love, a watched kettle never boils.

"Yes," says Taylor. "The silent treatment. For silence is golden and that's a fact and if you think I am about to tell you why I smooch my hearts and arrows and don't give a flying fart about the others you got another think comin'. For silence is golden and I think my posies has got enough air."

Rita leaves the kettle -- for a watched kettle never boils -- fetches the geraniums from the window box, sets them on their table, says "What pretty geraniums -- and they smell lovely! I never knew geraniums had such a sweet scent."

"Never too late to learn," says Taylor.

"I'm older than you think," says Rita.

"Hell, I knew that!" snaps Taylor, "Here, you better have my spare key. Just in case you want to air 'em and I'm sleeping or... indisposed or keeled over and dead as a doornail. I won't use my door-bolt nor chain anymore so you can get in."

Think twice about that, my very old dear – could be dangerous.

Rita takes the key from Taylor then brings in the tea, pours.

"Have a tart," says Taylor, "Before I eat 'em all."

"Thanks, no. I'm slimming," says Rita and pulls up a wooden stool, sits beside Taylor who pats Rita's hand, chews noisily for a moment, says:

"Someday I might tell you."

"Tell me what?"

Taylor begins to chew. She is suddenly not so clear as a moment ago. What was Rita's question? Never mind. Taylor loves home-baked tarts. Taylor used to bake them for Fay. That was years ago and Taylor couldn't remember even if she tried. She is ninety-nine or one hundred or something. Much has happened since. Although she can't, for the life of her, remember what it was.

I see to everything, darlings.

25

The serenely masculine young man, bending over in his thigh-hugging jeans (*I'm* the wardrobe mistress of this sagacious saga!), explains a large architectural drawing. Fay lobs an occasional chocolate into her gob, studies his firm bottom. He turns expectantly to her. She studies his plump crotch and at last notes the architectural drawings laid out on the low table.

Fay had, upon arrival contacted from the uppermost reaches of society, the above. Class. Funny how that idea dropped right into her head, ain't it? 'Twill do wonders in the next few squares, m'dears. Let us not forget whose game this is -- for whose ultimate purpose and amusement. At the moment, I am not amused.

"The flat would be..." says architect Archie, kneeling, acutely accentuating that plump pouch which bunches up becomingly, trapped between his strong, firm legs (precisely which comely component of said pretty package does the bunching is munchably moot. But we shall savour it for a mouth-watering moment -- pardon my detail, darlings, but let's face it, a girl's got to *live*), "... the flat would be widened to cover nearly the entire roof of your building," he continues, "and the remaining roof area would be converted to a decked, south-facing terrace suitable for planting."

"No one, repeat, no one is to know who the new owner is," says Fay, ripping her ogling peepers from the young architect's convivial nether-parts to his big brown eyes, "Or the deal's off. Is that quite clear?"

"Perfectly. As you requested."

Fay kneels beside Archie, studying him (who *wouldn't*, m'dears?) and, oh, yes, his *plans*, and leaning slightly into his firm jeans-hugged flesh, murmurs "The wall to the terrace (tiny nudge) will be completely glass?"

"Yes. Just as you..."

"Floor to ceiling?" whispers Fay, moving closer and grasping the plans; her elbow, accidentally intruding into a soft warm place.

"Yes," he says and moves sharply away, "but retaining privacy with a border of potted trees along the terrace periphery."

"What a lovely word, periphery!" cries Fay, "I shall instantly add that to my vocabulary!"

"Be my guest," says Archie with an odd glance that Fay

fortunately does not see.

"What?" says Fay, "What was that?"

"I said 'be my guest'," says Archie.

"Trees along my periphery. I love trees!" exults Fay who bends slightly and shamelessly studies the becoming contours of the kneeling architect's pressed-against-the-low-table-genitalia (again the gentle question of *what* is doing *which* arises and *I* am enormously titillated). "My dear sister Jane climbed trees," Fay continues, "She fell once. Flat on her face. Knocked out her two front teeth. It made absolutely no difference to the woman who wore tweeds and brogues and kept hounds. Did it?"

"Apparently not," says Archie with another quizzical look. This tatty blue-curlered, creature, he thinks, is certifiable. But she's rich. And famous.

An embarrassment *with* riches, dear boy?

Fay sighs a sad, contemplative sigh. "That was the woman Jane lived with."

"I see."

Yet another soupçon of local colour, m'dears.

"I believe the woman preferred Jane without her two front teeth, don't you?"

"It is not inconceivable," he says as Fay's eyes flick from his fabulous fore to his elegant aft for a pleasant reprise then flick back, where they rest, well, m'dears, *restlessly*.

Fay is a fool for love (Like mother, like daughter) -- my influence is difficult, if impossible, to resist.

Archie glides to the far end of the sofa and crosses his legs, plays momentarily the fledgeling actress dodging dishonour on the casting couch (ask Rita about this!).

"Never mind," says Fay. She kneels up from the floor, slides back into the sofa beside him. "Never mind. It mattered not. In any case the woman murdered dear Jane."

Our myths, darlings, we must hold fast to our myths. They sustain us.

"Chocolate bon-bon?"

Fay proffers another chocolate. He again declines. She says:

"Do you climb trees?"

"Only when I'm sozzled."

"Physical exercise is a serious matter," replies Fay through her teeth, a smidgin irritated though wishing desperately to make contact, *high class* contact preferably, but human contact, any kind of contact. "Our bodies," she continues most shibbolethically, "are temples."

"Oh yes, of course," he stammers, "I only meant..."

Fay bats her eyes, smiles indulgently, places him, tentatively, on her gift-list. "Then you are forgiven. Choccie?"

This time he takes one, chews nervously. This is a big job. It's high-profile -- I mean, Fabulous Fragment Fay! Photo opportunities galore! And he is *so* photogenic!

Fay will now speak sharply -- for the moment. She's read in one of those endless long ago discarded brochures (though *I* still hoard them) that business affairs must proceed without softer emotions, without intimacy. However, she will soon put an end to that, bring humanity back where it belongs, into the boardroom. But *later*. For evening casts softer shadows and daylight is harsh and unforgiving to even the creamiest complexion.

"Work to proceed seven days a week as stipulated?!" barks Fay, "Time is of the essence. One must strike while the...!"

"Two full-time crews have been engaged."

"How long will it take?" (A gentle, somewhat ambiguous wink here. Just to prove she's human)

Really, Fay, *Class* seems such a costly commodity even if it *was* I who slipped this poetical gilded-bug into your shell-like ear.

"Six weeks?" replies Archie. "The project to reach completion in six weeks?"

He's hesitant.

"Six weeks?!" shrieks Fay, "God created the whole earth in six days!"

"He had a distinct advantage."

Fay glares at him. Archie is flustered. Tense silence. Has he gone too far? "This sort of thing," stammers the worried-about-his-photo-opportunities young man, "usually takes at least six months. Six weeks is phenomenal."

"It must be sooner. Put them on overtime, your most skilled workers."

Fay's eyes dart desperately here and there searching for a satisfying peek between those stubbornly crossed legs (I do lead the poor child a merry chase). "It must be sooner," she repeats, "Put them on overtime."

"They will be on overtime, Ms Ritterhouse, seven days a week. Special permits must be sought."

"Then seek them! Seek them!"

Archie's nervous. He uncrosses his legs. Ach! Fay's eyes rest pleasantly loins-level. "Put them on twenty-four hour days. Put on three crews. Four!"

She pops another chocolate, offers him one, he declines. "I can pay. *Everyone*," says Fay and resumes her overt exploration of his young, ostensibly firm body, "I'm rich and chock full of bribes, darling."

Oh, Fay. You go too far. You'll be apprehended, ruin our game and we've hardly begun.

"Shut up!" cries Fay.

"Sorry?!"

"Not you, sugar." She clutches his knee. He re-crosses his legs. Damn!

She says:

"You must be wondering what it's like to be so rich."

"I hadn't, actually," says Archie uncomfortably, aghast at Fay's outré behaviour. This of course is but an assumption on my part, m'dears, as everyone knows the rich *are* different than us and I do tread recklessly attempting to duplicate their thought or prattle. As, I must admit, I find both unutterably boring.

Notwithstanding my tiny tirade, Archie pulls the large architectural drawings up over his legs, thighs, crotch and nearly to his chest, "I'm quite wealthy myself," he says, "You know, Dad and all."

Fay, with new respect:

"As rich as I am?!"

Young, handsome architect, from beneath his blanket of drawings:

"Probably. Land, don't you know. Mayfair etc."

But he wants to 'Make It On His Own', doesn't he Fay?

"What?" says Fay, "What was that?" She turns her head, searches for her covert purple prompter, sees only an ambiguous shadow that might have been *anything* (such is her meagre experience).

"What?" she asks again, "What did you say?"

"Land," he repeats, "a surfeit."

"Not you," replies Fay. "I didn't mean you."

He shrugs, pats down a protective fold in the plans.

Fay is suspicious. Who could be as rich as she? She's never heard of as much money as her carpet swept up, even after taxes which she will of course avoid paying – we have our ways. Who ever said you can't fool all of the people all of the time?

She fixes Archie with her cold, mauve stare, says, "If you're so bleeding wealthy why do you bother to work at all?"

"I've got to do *something*, haven't I? Can't just slope about wearing me old school tie," he replies and tucks the architectural plans carefully over his lap, thinks: She's eating me alive!

Slow down, Fay! (That was me)

"I'll do as I please!" (That was Fay -- I've been a bit hard on her. Or is it the money that's changed her?)

Another odd look from Archie.

Fay jumps up, tugs her dowdy chenille robe closer, pads, dirty bunny slippers flapping, to a window, taps absently at her blue plastic curlers. "Now that I am excessively wealthy I shall explore philosophy, whose rewards will fall like ripe fruit into my lap."

Fay tosses him a highly polished apple from an oddly glyphed silver compote that wasn't there a moment ago. "Tempting, isn't it?" says Fay. "I have them flown in from Washington State in the good old U.S. of A."

Is this woman real?! That rag of a robe! Those hideous curlers! Those bunny-rabbit slippers!

I'm afraid it's my fault, Archie. Fay needs taking down a peg or three!

Our poor Archie must say something, so he says, at a somewhat higher pitch than intended:

"*Philosophy*?"

Fay, at the window, strikes a pose. She's forgotten her big blue plastic curlers et al, assumes the morning sun is playing in her mousy, newly shampooed, combed-out hair, says:

"I studied psychology. Why not philosophy? I can afford books now. Philosophy tomes, I am told, are large, heavy and expensive. Now I can afford them without a moment's thought -- leather-bound. And tutors! The whole Nobel Laureate will spring to my aid if I so ordain. I can, if I choose, hire an entire university faculty. The Nature of Things cannot be *that* difficult."

No, darling, its really quite simple. Numbingly so. Frighteningly so. *Unbelievably* so. Even from wayyyy out here.

Archie, a university graduate himself (well, almost – you know the super rich), pretends to be engaged in his drawings. This woman is talking such rot!

No worse than yours, darling, last night at Janie Hogg-Smythe's soireé at Claridges.

"Of course," continues Fay expansively through her favourite Savoy window to her very own Thames, "being of a somewhat religious turn myself but logical to my fingertips, I tend towards Thomas Aquinas."

Archie looks up, interest flickering. Yes, he's heard of Aquinas, just. A catholic bloke isn't he?

Fay turns from the window, has his attention, concludes: "Aquinas subordinated philosophy to theology, natural law to the revelations of Christ and I am completely certain he believed in divine vengeance."

Fay pops another chocolate into her cupid's bow but it is the serenely masculine and only marginally Classy (mea also culpa, m'dears) Archie who gulps.

My darling prosopopoeia, it seems, has been reasonably well-tutored already.

Might I gloat? For just a moment?

In any case, so much for 'Class'.

Sorry I brought it up.

26

Rita is musing at her window. She loathes that scaffold web on the now battered facade of Number 13 (*Loathing* again, Rita? We must do something about that – immediately). Rita muses, furious yet hopeful; buoyed by a notion that she may soon become a paid author. She may not know a lot about writing but she certainly knows what she likes – the money! New faith in herself is crucial at this juncture and all experience is, well, *experience*. So she is resigned to the dreadful din of building, knowing, somehow (ho ho ho) that Pazazz will respond positively to her work. She has the oddest feeling about it. A *good*, odd feeling. Successful authors can afford face-lifts and a face-lift can lead to almost anything. Perhaps even…Romance? She owes all this in the strangest way to Ritterhouse Fay, her inspiration. She muses on my Fragmented Fay, who is her muse, muses on Fay's money, every amusing penny of it.

Lost in her musings Rita suddenly realizes she is staring directly into the knees of a well-dressed man -- she looks up -- in a hardhat -- who is gazing down at her from the scaffolding. "Sweet Jesus!" splutters Rita. He smiles at her. "Jee-sus!" she says and turns away to collect herself -- can it be true?

He squats, taps at her window, says:

"Rita?!"

He takes off his hard-hat, cries "Rita, let down your golden hair!"

"Jesus H. Christ!" cries Rita and throws open her window. He climbs in.

Mrs Taylor kisses yet another postcard and drops it into the red carry-bag. Mr Taylor stares unblinking from his tortoise-shell picture frame (such a handsome man – *in his way*). She turns, squints at him, "Why, Oscar Taylor, why?"

Poor, forgetful woman. Poor aged crone. It's better like this, dear. Less painful. The truth hurts etc. But I digress.

Suddenly Taylor remembers why! Then: Why *what*? So like Life, ain't it, m'dears? Perhaps she'll remember this evening. Meanwhile she'll just keep kissing these goddamned cards, the ones with the hearts and arrows, just keep kissing them and dropping them in this goddamned red bag. The others she'll discard with epithets. This evening she'll remember why again. She always does. Almost always.

And don't try to blame it on *me*!

It wouldn't be fruitful.

Though perhaps it *would*. Nudge, nudge.

"You haven't changed," says Ian.

Rita slams down the tray, "Christ, you could lie."

She hands him a coffee, "Well sit down. Stop prancing about."

Ian, smiling: "What luck."

"Luck? Whose luck? All it would have taken was a phone call. I've been in the frigging book for thirty years."

Ian, still smiling: "I've been in California for thirty years."

"Lucky you."

"We married."

"Oh, did we? Lucky her, then. Lucky rich American Ann."

Rita stirs her coffee, startled that Ann's name had leapt so easily from her unsmiling lips.

"She left me last year."

"Took her bankroll with her, did she?" Rita blinks, panics. "God, Ian! Sorry. I'm ridiculous. Pathetic. (Sip) Were we blessed with issue?"

"No."

"Sorry, love. I seem to be permanently disgruntled since the age of fifty (you just need a drink, m'dear). How long have you been back?"

"A week. Fell right into this job through an old connection. I intended to look you up."

"Forgive me. It's so good to see you. So good, that I'm behaving like a perfect bitch."

"You always were," he says with affection, "a *perfect* bitch." He takes her hand. "Good to see you too...more than."

She withdraws her hand -- must keep at least a crumb of dignity -- and motions at the scaffolding. "What the hell is going on here? Nobody will tell me."

"We're rebuilding a flat. At the top."

"I know that, love. But for whom?"

"Haven't the foggiest. It seems to be top secret."

"You're making a hell of a racket. They've no plans to move us out, have they? Because Rita won't budge an inch."

"Rita never would. As far as I know she won't have to."

Rita is comforted, calms. Ian says:

"Do you know what I remember?"

"I'm rapt."

Me too.

"At your mother's. You and me. That winter. Tapping at the window to frighten the jays away so the blue-tits could eat those bits of sausage we'd tied in the tree."

Rita twirls, sings:

"Tapping the jays away! Unhappy jays away..."

She stops abruptly, "Don't remember a thing. Top your coffee?"

"Better get back to work. I'm on trial."

"Don't you dare go yet. Who are they, Ian? Really? Who are they knocking this sodding house apart?"

Ian shrugs, rises. "Wish I could tell you, love. Wish I knew."

Rita pushes Ian back into his chair, "Stay put!"

She's not going to lose him yet but spies the postman climbing the steps.

She hurries into the hall, returns shaking an opened envelope at him. "I've sold my story! I've sold my first sodding story! They like it so much they're putting it in their next issue! They want to commission more! They want a part two! Ian, Pazazz Magazine! They want a part two!"

Rita reads her letter again. Ian watches her, says:

"Then we're lucky today."

"Ummn," says Rita, her nose in her wonderful letter.

"The both of us," says Ian, "Lucky."

Rita looks up from her letter, beams. "Yes," she says, "We are lucky, aren't we?"

For a while, darlings. *Luck* is so fleeting. Savour it. Gulp it down. Roll in it. But be sure to thank *me* for it. Else the jig is up. And for God's sake show a bit more interest in what's happened to *him*. Ask a few questions. Delve, dearie, delve. Get some background on him. You're a writer now, though only a pawn in our game of squares. Ritterhouse Fay, my darling prosopopoeia, is the queen (Whilst *I* am the empress!).

Her young architect, 'Archie', has gone. Question: How do young architects who fail to graduate become architects? Answer: Mayfair manages.

Of course, they gotta be cute too. But somehow, he's a

disappointment. Oh, his ideas were adequate but... "But I feel no different," says Fay. "Should I not be somehow altered after this close encounter with Class? Should I not have acquired by osmosis a certain sheen?"

Probably not, darling. It's all done with smoke, mirrors and Swiss accounts, you know.

"It was my unfortunate behaviour," says Fay and shoves another bon-bon through chocolate-smeared lips. "Why was I so aggressive with the poor boy? I only wished to be business-like. Then, golly, all that sex stuff came swarming in. It's not like me. I just want to be friends. Just a kiss or a hug. Honest. I'm a good girl, I am."

She is. Really. When I leave her alone.

"What?" says Fay, "What was that?"

Her big blue curlers lay scattered over the architectural drawings on the low marble table. She sips from a large tin of Danish beer, half studying the drawings, half contemplating Archie; those tight blue jeans. She wonders what it would be like to be a man for a change, baggage bobbing between ones legs -- what an odd thought, Fay. Where did that come from though of course we know. "God!" she squeaks, "perhaps I've already *been* a man?! Have I? Can't remember."

The slag has had this thought before. And it's no secret to me, ducky.

"Maybe I'll try it some time, being a man -- now why did I think that? Did *I* think that? Ah well, just now I'm awfully busy."

Hair-of-hag! I taunt, tired of *Class* alternative amusement. Besides, m'dears, Class can't save one from destruction – hence the French Revolution. But Hair-of-hag *can*!

"Hair-of-hag?"

You'll need it, Fay. The time will come when you'll need it. Better to be prepared. Hair-of-hag!

"Hair-of-hag? Please, *why* did I think that?" says Fay.

There's so much to do, Fay, to keep the ball rolling -- the great round stone rolling uphill. To amuse. A fate to fill. Your destiny to dredge right up. Whoopdee-do!

"I've accomplished so much already," says Fay. "So much in so little time but there is so much more. Friends. Gifts. Kindnesses. Acts of supreme munificence. Kisses and hugs. Rescues."

Rescues? Ach! Then you *know*, Fay. You *do* know?

"What?" says Fay, "What was that?"

Then you *don't* know. It's better that you don't know yet. Everything might seem too simple. The game would be forfeit.

It's all right there on the table, isn't it, love? For the taking. But meanwhile...

Meanwhile, Fay swears she will never take a lukewarm bath again. Never. Goddamn them for making our wayward waif take baths in lukewarm water. And other things too delicate...too hideous to mention. Things better forgotten if only she could. Ach! If only I'd let her forget the beautiful child she *was*. She could have been perfect *now*. They wouldn't allow her to stay that way. None of them. For this they shall pay.

Goodness, m'dears! *I'm* terrified!

"Shut up!" cries Fay and pops another chocolate. Sweets were forbidden too. Damn them. Who is them -- they? Those horrid people at Number 13? Them? "I tried to be friendly there. I gave of myself. Brought them together. They should love me. I am a fiery angel. Don't they know that? Damn them. People are all the same, should be regularly struck -- Like I was!"

Like gongs, I add, in my cowardy custard way.

Vengeance belongs to God, Fay. And don't you never fergit it!

> Vengeance is mine, saith the Lord and Fay
> pales, she sets down her beer to varnish her
> nails...
> She'll ponder revenge, God,
> Some other time, later
> Tonight she is slated
> To trick with a waiter...

(sorry, m'dears I simply couldn't resist that)

But my Fay, painting a delicious blood-red on each wonderfully sharp, long fingernail, nevertheless contemplates making vengeance *her* very own. And soon. These are poor Fay's, painted Fay's, bitter Fay's, exact thoughts.

I should know. I put them there.

27

"What do you think, huh?" asks Hugh of Jenny after Jim Richardson's departure. Hugh is gathering up paper plates, plastic forks, chopsticks.

Ho-hum, but what can ya do? So on we go with our Unisex Twins – kinda boring, ain't it, like drawing that Community Chest card, but necessary to the game though had *I* been the Parker Brothers I would have jettisoned that boring Community Chest card long ago.

"He's got a sense of humour," says Jenny, spooning food intractable to chopsticks.

"And you're so tactful," replies Hugh.

"He must know how the other half lives."

Of course he does, darlings!

"Of course he does," says Hugh defensively, "He was married once."

"Do you like him?"

"Sure."

"I mean very much?"

"Yeah," says Hugh, "I do."

"But do you plan to shag him?"

"You mean again?"

Rita rolls a sheet of paper into her typewriter, types:

MY HOUSE BURNED DOWN
Part Two

A mighty crash from above. It's been going on all day. "Goddamn them! It's too late to be making that much noise. There are laws against making that much noise after ten P.M.! Goddamn them!"

Rita sighs, clenches her teeth and continues, the rat-a-tat-tat of her aged mechanical typewriter echoing through the paper-walled, paper-floored house.

The latter does bear repeating, m'dears, again and again. For is it not the means to our jolly, though upon occasion anxious, six-flat-edifice's very raison d'être?

Mrs Taylor sleeps in her postcard chair. Oddly, the noise fails to wake her. But she is very, very tired. Not the fatigue of accomplishment, or mischief making -- those days are long gone. But the fatigue of simply hanging on. After eighty, she has often said (to herself, of course), it's a full time job.

Tell me about it, sugar!

Taylor's paraffin lamp glows cosily on its small table just beside the chock-a-block closet that for many years embraced that exquisite carpet, spirited so recently away by the angel or devil, or witch: The Ritterhouse Fay.

If Taylor were awake she would hear Rita's rat-a-tat-tat. She would hear the building crew directly above her head as they demolish by the light of the silvery moon the rear exterior wall of Fay's miniscule flat which is to be extended in all directions right across the roof nearly to the mews behind. Taylor would then thump the ceiling a few times and the floor several more to let labouring Rita-writer know she was there, that she's happily remembered again who she is, that she hasn't keeled over, ain't dead as a doornail. But Mrs Taylor is sleeping, dreaming of The Fay. Taylor's lips twitch as tiny puffs of air escape between them and her eyes dart back and forth uneasy under wrinkled lids. The paraffin lamp continues to glow cosily. Soon it will need another wick-trim. We must keep an eye on that pesky lamp, darlings. It simply must be kept in tip-top working order. For 'tis a major player.

"When can I meet him?" asks Nelly. She's fervent, afloat in new found love. Bill is in his kitchen making sandwiches while Nelly lies serenely in his bed having never, *never* been treated quite like this -- I mean, glorious ham sandwiches made to order! And it's past one A.M.!

I should be so lucky! But then, of course, I *am*.

"Bliss!" whispers Nelly so accurately, "Bliss!"

She sits up and stretches happily, her long arms reaching far above her head. "When can I meet him?"

"Soon, love."

Bill's really piling on the mayonnaise. Nelly really likes mayonnaise.

"How soon's soon?" she asks, pushing her nose into Bill's pillow, savouring Bill's clean-soap smell.

"Soon," says Bill piling on more mayonnaise, wondering how, why, such *good* fortune -- such a tender and fine and kind and loving Nelly -- could come to him after so much ill.

Then ask me, love, I'm just here, beside your tatty little fridge. Ask *me*.

"Soon? I'll meet him soon?" calls Nelly. "Good".

"Mustard too?"

"Masses! I feel tarty."

"Good," says Bill, piling on more mustard.

Nelly gazes about Bill's small bedroom. She's so happy, so content. So...needed. Then, suddenly sad, she says:

"I wonder what poor Fay will do with all that money?"

"*Poor* Fay?" replies Bill, "I suppose we'll never know."

Oh but they will. Every crash of those infuriating demolition hammers directly across the hall brings my Fay nearer.

"I did feel sorry for her," says Nelly. She stretches again, sighs, studies the uncovered toes of her large feet at the foot of the bed. "Fay was so childlike. A poor lost child. She couldn't help it."

"Help what, love?"

"The way she was. It was her background. Her terrible life. All those murders and fires and things."

"I don't believe a word of it, love, it never happened."

Think on that, Billy. But with an open mind, m'dear, an *open* mind.

"The meek do inherit the earth, darling," says Nelly, "Don't they?"

"If you say so, love. But there was nothing meek about Ritterhouse Fay."

Oh, Bill, you are so wrong. So devastatingly wrong. Fay is the way she is simply because of *the way she is* (or is it because of the way *I* am?). Ponder, poppet. In any case, Billy, our Fay is a pussy cat. Part *meeee*! Part *owwwwww*!

Bill is adding gigantic slices of pickle to each ham sandwich as he ruefully contemplates that split minute of bliss with Fay on her glorious (though he was not to know), enchanted carpet. He was momentarily bewitched, he's certain -- he's not the sort of bloke who messes about with indigent strangers.

"Yes, there was," says Nelly, "Meekness underneath. Deep down. Fay was meek deep down."

Dear Nelly, more apt than you know. More apt than Fay herself knows. Perhaps more apt than even *I* know. But not bloody likely.

Bill enters, hands Nelly her mayonnaisey, mustardy sandwich, sits on the bed, says "So very deep down it doesn't matter."

"It always matters," sighs the kind, blameless Nelly. "We owe her a lot, Bill. She brought us together."

"Through no fault of her own."

"Through every fault of her own," replies our ungainly sage.

Think again, love.

Nelly takes another bite and, chewing: "I'm so glad you've got a son. When do I meet him? I want to set a date. Now."

Bill lays down his sandwich, grabs Nelly and hugs her. Mouth full, she protests. He rolls into bed beside her and both of them lie there, flat on their backs, happily noshing their astoundingly good ham sandwiches -- naive Nelly, swimming with thoughts of undying love, Bill, swimming with yet more.

But shouldn't they know better at their ages?

You tell them that!

Directly across the hall the door on Fay's old flat swings to and fro, diagonal on one hinge, its dusty black plastic "6" in the debris on the floor beside it. A heavy canvas flaps noisily over remnants of the now missing exterior wall and a black cat who'd leapt from the roof of an adjoining house (or from somewhere beyond), is frightened by the flapping, cowers, not knowing whether to crouch, hiss and strike or spring away. The second building crew has at last gone home. There will be exactly one hour of quiet till the next crew arrives. Ask Rita if you don't trust me. I'd honestly understand if you didn't trust me, sweeties.

Though it *could* be risky for you.

28

"Mrs Taylor? Mrs Taylor?" pleads the milkman (he'll be retiring soon -- his father before him had also dealt with this infuriating old woman), "I know you're in there and you owe me."

Taylor grins, whips a hand over her mouth, listens as he retreats down the stairs.

"Silence is golden," she whispers, "Silence is goldy, goldy, golden."

Taylor is confident the milkman has gone, opens her door a crack, snatches up a milk and a cream and nearly drops them when a great crash from the workmen echoes from above.

"It's the witch's doing," she mutters to herself as she closes her door and locks it securely.

She's right, of course. But which witch, droopy-drawers?

Ach! Here is our Fay lying on her tummy on a massage table chewing at a large, half-peeled banana as she is delightfully pummelled into our next square by a cheerful, uniformed masseuse whose only task amongst these mortal coils, is simply *that,* m'dears, to pummel Ms Fay into the next square. There are numerous less noble callings, believe me.

"I was forced upon my own resources at an early age," says Fay, her voice buzzing with each blissful blow.

"They say," says the masseuse, "What is it they say?" She pummels and ponders. "Oh yeah," she says, "They say that necessity is the mother of invention."

"Don't you mean," replies Fay swallowing a large lump of banana with some difficulty for it is problematic to eat while lying on ones tummy being battered on ones arse (take it from me, darlings!), "Don't you mean 'necessity is the invention of mothers'?"

"Oh. Is *that* what they say?" replies the masseuse, squinching her forehead much in the manner of Fay when perplexed, "I thought they said..."

"Well they didn't," snaps Fay who bites off another chunk of banana, chews contemplatively for a moment, adds: "My mother pretended she needed me long before she actually did. I was her constant necessity."

So far, so good, love.

"Oh dear," says the masseuse, still squinching. Fay shifts a chunk of banana to a more convenient corner of her mouth and spews on: "My mother invented her need to keep me constantly by her side."

So? What about it, my darling prosopopoeia?

"Her need was *invented* to deny me a life of my own."

Tough talk, Fay, but mind. Mummy's tolerance needn't be as infinite as she is.

"Thus," spews Fay, "necessity is the invention of mothers."

Aren't you being just a wee bit tough on Mumsy, my tenebrous little tart?

"What?" says Fay, "What did you say?"

"Oh dear, oh dear," sighs the masseuse not missing a pummel.

"Mum was mental, of course," adds Fay (mendacious girl!), now shifting another chunk of banana into chewing position and chomping excitedly as she speaks, "Finally, I mean. But not in the beginning..."

"Not when she was denyin' you a life of your own, you mean."

"Correct! Have you never heard of a Bill of Grievances? It's a very subjective term, of course."

The pummelling pauses, "What's that then?" asks the masseuse, increasingly nervy. This banana-spewing woman has an odd squinty look about her even if she *is* rich.

"A Bill of Grievances was a list Mummy typed each evening and I was forced to read the following morn before breakfast."

Ach! Memories!

"Before breakfast?! Lor'!" says the formerly cheerful masseuse in a righteous mini-rage.

"Now," says Fay, "Anyone who can type is certainly in their right mind, aren't they?"

Yes and no, darling. Yes and no.

"What was on the list then?" pipes the masseuse.

Fay, at the very precipice of acute irritation: "One could not use a typewriter and be totally round the bend, could one?!"

Pummelling away: "What was on the list then?"

"Only everything I had said and done during the previous twenty-four hours, that's all! And everything I was to do in the next twenty-four. And she was constantly, even as I slept, whispering into my ear!"

You're mixing up your tutorials, darling – nothing to do with Mummy.

"Oh dear! Oh dear!" cries the masseuse.

"It was as though I was being...brain-washed. I couldn't put a foot right. Nothing suited Mummy (Your Mummy has high standards, darling!). I could hardly relieve myself in comfort. If I was from her sight more than five minutes it was instantly construed as Abysmal Neglect."

"What was that, love, errr, Madam?"

Fay, chewing another chunk of banana surges on. "It was *I* who was the abysmally neglected! I was the orphan of that peculiar storm! Tell me this. Children are little humans with souls, aren't they? Little souls that shine right out through their dear little eyes."

Back to the soul bit, eh, Fay? Give it a rest, ducky.

The poor perplexed masseuse can only massage away.

"Are you listening to me?!"

"Oh yes, Madam!"

"I had an authentic soul," sighs Fay, spraying a bit of banana spittle over the edge of the massage table. "Bruised and bleeding, I buried my tiny soul deeper and deeper -- so deep that my eyes were no longer a window to it."

Where *do* you get these stories, these...myths?

"Do you hear me?! Mummy became..." cries Fay, munching banana and squirting hot tears, "...my mother became, with her Bill of Grievances, a poisonous mist that floated around my head at breakfast and elevenses. A mauve mist lit by fire!"

A reasonably accurate description of your fantasy, darling, though that's no way to speak of a dedicated Mom.

Fay, triumphant, cries:

"But I noted her not! Though I did lose my soul in the process."

Fay obviously, at this point, knows more than she ought. Where have I gone wrong?

The masseuse stops pummelling and reaches for a hanky in her light blue nylon uniform pocket and, tears streaming, blows her nose.

"She wasn't mental then!" sobs Fay, "She could type!"

Fay twists, looks up wet-eyed from the massage table and with a wave of her half-eaten, bruised brown and flapping banana, cries:

"Then Jane was murdered!"

"God help us!" cries the tormented masseuse, "Who was Jane?!"

"My dear sister Jane meant all the world to me!" shrieks Fay in a spray of tears and spit, "She climbed trees and was slaughtered for her efforts."

This is simply too much. The poor, overly sensitive and now far from cheerful masseuse, hands covering her horrified eyes, bursts from the deluxe, private massage room to be sick. Fay lies there on her stomach, tears racing down her nose. She swallows the last of her banana and pushes its peel over the edge of the massage table where it falls with a dull flap to the floor.

She lies there for a long while thinking about lost, windowless souls, hair-of-hag, fires, Class warfare, and why she has become so embittered in so short a time -- especially considering her recent good fortune. "I was a perfect child," retraces its well worn path into a vacant corridor of memory through which, she is certain, her soul has only recently fled. How could she see said soul through the window of her eyes if it has flown like a witch on a broomstick?

Ah, Fay. Perhaps it has not flown. Perhaps, dear, it lingers near, a sinister, not so silent personal provocateur?

"What?" mutters Fay, shaken, "What the dickens was all that?"

She wrenches herself up from the massage table, slams a large towel around herself and sits there, legs scissoring wildly back and forth over a deep purple pool that was once floor; once a sweetly sincere series of shipshape squares sighing for satisfaction (Oh my!). She slumps there in her hurt. Her hair blows wildly upward from that roiling ruckus of floor and she contemplates vengeance, specifically including all the residents of Number 13. Particularly Rita. That sour, alcoholic slut, Rita. "I'm changing," cries Fay. "My goodness, how I am changing!"

Don't play innocent with me, my fugacious pet. I didn't promise you a rose garden. *The ceremony of innocence is drowned!* I croak librettorally.

"Leave me alone!" shrieks Fay, "Get a life damn you! Whoever you are, get a life!"

I *have* a life, ducky.

"Huh?"

I *have* a life, Ms Ritterhouse Fay. Yours.

29

Rita makes several valiant attempts to type but amidst the early morning rumble of construction her flighty muse has flown. "Goddamn them!" she cries, "Goddamn them!"

God has nothing to do with this, dearie. Don't flatter yourself. But I'll do what *I* can. Who am *I*? Don't be cheeky.

Mrs Taylor cannot hear the crash of shattered walls tumbling above her, is riveted still on the shadowy figure that pursues her. She jumps in her sleep, frets, cries out and flings herself into a handy abyss. Anything to avoid The Fay who looks precisely like her very own great granddaughter who was abducted by gypsies. Or is this only nightmare residue from some gothicky novel read long ago whilst eyes and I permitted?

"It's Sunday!" hollers Jenny at two workmen who shuffle by shouldering unwieldy planks of wood, "Construction workers do not work on Sunday!"

Jenny and Hugh, Jenny clutching a pastry box, stand in the open door of Fay's unfinished penthouse. One of the workmen lays down a plank and approaches. He pulls a small calendar from his coveralls, reads it and squeals:

"Blimey! She's right! It *is* Sunday, lads! Clever little lady!"

"Up yours," mutters Jenny to his back as he rejoins his crew.

Rita is still stymied and aching for masses of grist. She's insatiable! She calls from below (and, m'dears, I can hardly stress adequately how completely unlike Rita, Rita has become.) "Coffeetime!"

Hugh and Jenny start down the stairs, meet Mrs Taylor at the landing. Hugh, despite her grumbles, assists Taylor, with promises of goodies to come. Jenny has insisted the old woman be 'integrated' into their group whether Taylor likes it or not. Don't ask Jenny why, darlings. She hasn't the vaguest.

There is a lot of strange, purposeless energy capering about these days at Number 13.

Oh, and everywhere else of course. Copy that, m'dears.

Nelly and Bill are already at Rita's and in animated conversation with Ian, a welcome newcomer to our enchanted group. All are startled by a great crash from above. All look wearily up.

"Someone's in a hurry to move in," says Rita to Ian in a way that makes it obvious they are now more than just good friends. "Even our dedicated construction manager doesn't know who the lucky tenant is."

Hugh attempts to help Taylor to a chair and because, presently, she has no idea who he is, she menaces him away with her cane as Jenny disappears into the kitchen with her pastry box and returns with a large white cake the top of which, in blue icing, reads:

AUTHOR! AUTHOR!

"I'll be on the stands tomorrow," says Rita and is roundly applauded by all except Taylor who is not sure who Rita is either. "I couldn't have done it without Ritterhouse Fay," says Rita with a hint of sarcasm.

And *me*, Rita. Get your bleedin' priorities straight or you'll suffer for it. Remember it's my saga. My game! My Fay! Mine! All mine! And that goes for this goddamned house too!

Mrs Taylor surfaces, shouts:

"The witch! The bleeding Antichrist!"

That familiar odd vibration ripples through Jenny. She takes a sip of hot coffee to dispel it. No luck. Takes another. Still shivers, something is definitively askew.

Nelly doesn't like to think of 'poor little' Fay as an Antichrist. Anyhow, what *is* an Antichrist? Fay can't help being what she is. Who can? Nelly agrees Fay might have been perfect. We're all born perfect. In spirit anyway, thinks good Nelly.

Think again, ducky.

Bill knows what his forgiving Nelly is thinking. How could he not? Her kindly thoughts pass as transparently across her face as a billboard in Piccadilly Circus. How lucky can you get? thinks Bill.

Nelly grins at Bill, knows he is thinking about her, takes a bite of Jenny's (though Hugh actually baked it) excellent cake, loves Bill even more now than yesterday, thinks: How lucky can you get?

Hugh is worried that Jenny is shivering and doesn't seem happy. Is she upset about Jim Richardson? Something's got to give,

Hugh is sure.

A lot is going to give, but not what you expect, my bulgy-briefed beefcake.

Jenny wonders if Hugh is thinking about Jim Richardson. Wonders how she'd feel if he were.

Start wonderin', sugar.

Mrs Taylor wonders where Oscar Taylor found that damned rug, wonders if Oscar knew what the devil he was talking about (of course he does!), wonders if she's done the right thing giving a billion pound rug to Ritterhouse Fay, wonders if Fay really is her granddaughter (or daughter?), then fuzzes out again, gets cake icing on her bristly chin and coffee on her bathrobe, wonders where she is, how she got here.

We *all* do, darling, from time to time. But it passes.

Rita shudders, grabs Ian's hand, drinks her coffee with the other, feels safer than she felt yesterday. Knows she is not invisible. Never was (her ectoplasm theory was rubbish). Knows that she has materialized beautifully and is as tangible as anyone in this room -- ask Ian -- but wonders what Ritterhouse Fay is up to. Cannot get Ritterhouse Fay out of her mind. Wonders, and this is really odd and she must speak to Ian about it now that she has an Ian to speak to -- wonders if they are all, in mortal danger.

Well that's the whole point, ducky!

That evening, our resident Antichrist boringly attired in her mouse-coloured cardigan, blue velvet tablecloth over her shoulders, pink, acrylic-bunny-fur slippers, evening shadows playing over her scowling though still attractive face, screams into the eight-carat-gold-trimmed Savoy telephone. "When-when-when-when?!... It is one month today! One month of living out of my suitcase! (when hasn't she?)... Ritterhouse Fay is not accustomed to living out of suitcases! (Liar! -- how do you know what you're accustomed too? That's *my* watch!)... Two weeks!" cries Fay, "You have two weeks! Or I shall sue for breach of contract!"

Fay jettisons the telephone which lands with a muffled thud on carpet that pales beside a certain shimmering (and excitable) floor covering hovering high above the Arabian peninsula, about to begin its landing approach.

Half of Fay's elegant suite has disappeared under mountains of half-unwrapped items of excruciating luxury; dresses, shoes, silk, pearl-encrusted bags, jewels to shame Dorian Gray's (and don't *I* know it). She rolls her eyes over a particularly opulent, undulating hillock, calms as she sees, buried beneath a chinchilla coat, Rita's kettle. She pulls it from the mauve satin folds of the chinchilla's lining, caresses it, tenderly polishes it on the sleeve of her mousy cardigan. Recondite phrases -- with intricate glottal stops -- leap from her throat while thoughts of gentle rapprochement with everyone and everything nibble at her often indistinct perimeter (there's a mouthful, m'dears -- such gravitas! Mama gloats accordingly!). But I'll put the kibosh on that rapprochement business, won't I just! Fickle girl!

"What voice from yonder window calls?" shouts Fay, somewhat calmer than her last rude outburst, "Who are you? Do you mean me harm?"

Before I can answer with a poke or a pinch or a pop to the chops, the doorbell chimes and she's off.

"Why if it ain't Shamaly Abdullah with a bouquet of the reddest roses imaginable! Long time no see, Abdullah!"

Fay motions him in. He looks tired, thin as his sparse moustache as he makes his way through Fay's maze of up-market merchandise and tangles his toe in a slim, rhinestoned dress-strap. He pauses to catch his breath and extricate himself then sits, wearily scans the stupefying disorder of the suite.

Take it from me, she never kept her room tidy as child either – fire was a blessing, m'dears.

Fay immediately rushes her roses into the bathroom basin and returns to find the pale, frail Abdullah wiping his brow with a fine, silk hanky. His usefulness has declined with his health, m'dears. Or should that be vice versa? Nature has its ways.

"I love your taste in hankies, Abdullah."

"You will pardon me, dearest Miss," the old man says with some effort, "I am not well."

"Wives," snaps a hostile Fay who seems to have leapt directly from my so-called *brow* and who remains standing, arms stiff at her side, "can be a punishing burden."

"I am sorry I have not come to visit you sooner."

Fay nods a single, stiff nod though, in truth, her manacled heart cries out to him -- this crucial old love whose days are numbered.

I weep, oh, darlings, I *weep*. But the rules of the game must be adhered to. Many must fall by the wayside -- mind the next square!

Fay offers him a chocolate. He declines. She stuffs two in her mouth for good measure, munches quietly while Shamaly wipes his brow once more. Has he come to reclaim his house? Or...

That was me, m'dears, shit-stirring.

Fay flushes, rises to the bait, her chewing quickens. But Mr Shamaly draws a small jewel box from the breast pocket of his finely tailored suit and she relaxes, squeals with pleasure. "Prezzies!"

He wheezes: "I have brought you a token of..."

Fay snatches the box from him.

"Abdullah! How stupendously thoughtful!"

She snaps open the lovely little box, snatches out an exquisite jewel-encrusted fish on a fine gold chain, holds it between her dirty fingernails -- *still* sooty, Fay?

She is delighted, ignores me, immediately hangs the jewelled fish around her neck. "How apt," she cries, "A little fish. Like me. A little fish out of water. Stranded. High and dry in a thirsty land where no water is."

Metaphorical water douses fire, dearie. You'd be a goner if you *weren't* high and dry. But how *very* poetical.

"You are a wealthy woman."

"Yes, ducky. When it rains, it apparently pours."

Careful, slag, stay out of that rain.

"What?" says Fay, "What was that?"

Only the ceiling responds with an abrupt shift of colour and a petite quiver that goes *entirely* unappreciated. But so easily conjured in such luxury! With the generous assistance of that divine Louis Quinze-copy-sofa.

Fay pops another chocolate (she never gains an ounce -- want to know her secret? I'll bet you do).

"You are young and seemly, my dear," says Mr Shamaly most inaccurately and who must catch his breath to wipe his watering eyes.

"Why have you come?"

"Our contract, my dear Ritterhouse."

Fay suddenly rises, marches briskly to a window, says :

"London at night. Let us not waste it. How 'bout a little drinkie instead?"

"A Vichy water, please. I have been tempted to stray and I am paying for it. Yes, I have been tempted to stray from the path."

Honestly, love, who *hasn't*?

Shamaly watches silently as Fay trembles slightly. They drink.

"Are you kind to children?" she asks.

"I have no children."

"No children?"

Shamaly shakes his head. He's thought a lot about it.

"Tough luck, love." mutters Fay, "I could have had hundreds. I'm as fertile as a fucking ferret."

That's what you think, sugar!

"Who said that?!"

"I beg your pardon, my dearest Miss?"

"Nothing."

Fay quaffs her drink, wishes she could have put *fertile as a fucking ferret* more genteelly, pours another, quaffs it, pours another, pours a Vichy for Shamaly who has not touched his first. He declines with a tired wave of his veined old hand. She steadies herself, sets down his glass, snatches up her own. Must fill this agonising silence. "Speaking of children... (Stirring her drink with a finger) I am trying to forget that I was ever a child."

"Why, my dear?"

"I had forgotten too. Before I moved into that house. That dreary house with all those unhappy, lonely people."

"I am sorry. You could have had your choice of dozens of houses."

And a palace if I'd had my way. You must realize, m'dears, that our -- Fay's and mine -- relationship is very strange and very beautiful. What is it they say? Ach ja! A love/hate relationship! How *can* one separate love and hate? They are eternally one. Like the cream in my coffee. Fay, who *is* love, is also a seeker after love. I am the hateful one. But for a reason, darlings. If it *is* a reason. Oh dear! Why must we have reasons?! I tire myself unduly, must husband my resources. Must belt up for a mini-second. Time flies so quickly here, don't it?

"I did not have a model childhood, Abdullah."

Childhood, Ritterhouse Fay?! Were you *ever* a child?

"What?" says Fay, "What was that?"

"I said nothing, my dear," replies Shamaly.

Fay quaffs her whisky, pours yet another, says with feeling "Those poor people. They never spoke to one another until I came."

"So very English."

"Honestly, Abdullah, I've malice towards none. I was a beautiful child. A loving child. I was an angel."

Now we're getting somewhere.

Fay quaffs even this whisky, pours another (excess being a common vice of witches – not to state categorically that our Ritterhouse Fay is a witch). She sways back to the window, narrowly misses catching a dirty bunny slipper on a half-unwrapped Valentino something-or-other -- chants softly, sing-songingly to the dancing lights in the Thames:

> It's more than funny
> When honey has aged
> And it's mouldy and old
> Clovered or saged
> And the bees are fleas
> And the wax is sold
> And the queen is caged.

My eyes are wet, darlings. That was one of Mum's favourite incantations. Had it been properly intoned it might have levelled the Savoy in a trice.

Fay purses her lips, sips, spills Johnny Walker Blue on her cardy sleeve.

"What a beautiful poem," whispers Shamaly, moved to the tips of his clammy toes.

"I wrote that myself," answers Fay, lying through perfect teeth as she plucks from her cardy an abnormally large lint-ball (or a cinder, m'dears – she's continually combusting).

"What does it mean?" asks Shamaly, dabbing again at his streaming forehead, shuddering and peeping covertly at his watch.

"Sometimes I feel as though I'm running down, Abdullah."

Only when *I'm* fatigued, my simple slattern. Only then. And I know the feeling, love. You come all over *queer*.

"It's about running out of resources, Abdullah, like running out of oil."

But let's not go there.

"I have never run out of oil, dearest Ritterhouse."

"*Fay*, please! My name is *Fay*!"

Fay weaves to the bar, sloshes whisky (whisky being the drug of choice of *my* generations – mark that plural, m'dears)…yes, she *sloshes* whisky in and around her glass, peers as alluringly under the circumstances as possible at Abdullah, says: "I am a flame. Rising Phoenix-like from..."

We mustn't get ahead of ourselves, lovey.

Fay hesitates, plants her shivering knee firmly against the sofa, steadies herself again. Is that a fire reflected in the window? Is London aflame? *Again*? Is this 1666? 1939? "I don't want to set the world on fire," she sings, "I just want to start a little flame in your heart."

Careful, dear one.

Shamaly puts a hand into his other breast pocket. Another jewel? Fay sways far too far to one side, sways back (an old habit). Her eyes dance their traditional gimmee-dance.

"Our contract," says Shamaly, wearily slipping the folded paper from his pocket, holding it aloft.

Fay drops herself into a chair opposite, replies "Come to claim your pudendum of flesh?"

That was me, m'dears. A little appropriately timed darkly comic relief.

Fay is disappointed with Mr Shamaly, was certain that motiveless goodness did exist in some far-off land (beyond Pluto?). "I liked Abdullah," she murmurs, "A great deal. He has been..."

Shut up, Fay!

"What?! Don't you shout at *me*!"

Look at him, Fay!

Shamaly's face is a death-mask. He watches Fay pityingly as she strikes vainly at phantoms, like fruit-flies buzzing around her head.

Darling! Adjust your sites, the target is me!

Fay pulls herself up from the chair, feels unwell, tries not to show it. Her eyes on Abdullah, she sways across the room.

"The bedroom is this way, sweet-cakes," she intones.

She'll let bygones be bygones, m'dears. She swings, teasing, between the bedroom and entrance doors, pointing first to one then the other. "The bedroom's this way," she slurs, pointing to the bedroom door. "Or," and with a limp gesture towards the entrance door, "or is it this way?"

Just follow the bouncing ball, Missy Fay.

Shamaly, silent, watches. Fay is less sure of herself.

"The bedroom is this way," she whispers, alarmed at the frighteningly skull-like shadow rising directly above the dear old man's half-bowed head. This lethal shadow suddenly bursts, evaporates.

Fay blinks, shields her eyes from a billion particles of exploding need.

Shamaly pushes aside a still price-tagged black lace nightie, shakily rises from the sofa. He rips their contract in two, flings it into the air. "No obligations, dearest Miss. The house, of course, remains yours."

"Please," says Fay, pointing to the bedroom, "The bedroom is this way."

Fay is breathing hard, is frightened, doesn't know why. She seems to have some peculiar penchant for older, very *much* older, men (I *was* naughty, wasn't I?).

Shamaly shakes his head, wipes his brow again. Fay pleads. "The bedroom is this way."

She opens the bedroom door, stands there shivering, pondering potential cuddles and kisses that might never be. She smiles desperately, means it. Her miserable past flutters in her head, a mad moth.

Abdullah Shamaly puts two fingers to his lips and throws a little kiss to Fay.

"Please!" cries Fay, "The bedroom is *this* way!"

Shamaly, so frail, so ill, so old, makes his way through the shimmering, undulating hillocks from Bond Street, past Fay to the door.

"Abdullah!" cries Fay.

But, waving weakly over his shoulder, he is gone.

She flings herself on her bed, moans, whines, cries out, screams bloody murder -- for *one* minute. In two, with my useful, high-kicking choreography and The-Show-Must-Go-On ringing in her ears, she's sitting before her dresser mirror studying her face in oh so loving detail; her cheeks, the silky sheen of her neck, her perfect teeth, her well-formed ears, her lush eyelashes, thick eyebrows. All, gifts from me, m'dears, so do show me a little respect. I may, upon occasion and with good reason, be hateful, vindictive and horrifically destructive but I assure you I am a fully credentialed Sugar-Mommy and strive continually in the best interests of my ward, my darling prosopopoeia! (See dictionary for further definition; I haven't a moment to spare)

Fay unclasps the little jewelled fish around her neck, dangles it before her nose then drops it into that tatty cardigan pocket. Ach! The woman has no fashion sense.

She empties her scuffed leather bag on the dresser, finds Nelly's lipstick, applies it, going over her lips several times (carefully avoiding our mutually awkward, but under ideal circumstances, titillating, mole). She tears off a bit of tissue from a box on the dresser, folds it into a tiny rectangle, tucks it under her upper lip for an excellent pout. She rehearses the pout for a moment. Men *love* a pout, go crackers over a pout! Ask that stunning, gifted though much deceased actress, Gloria Grahame. If Fay had had Gloria's pout precisely three minutes prior, Shamaly would be at her feet right now, frail or not, ill or not, old or not. After all, we do share certain attributes. But think what you will, m'dears. It'll pass the time.

"Huh?" slurs Fay, "Wha' was that?"

Fay had cared deeply for her ebony kitty, her sister Jane, her mother. No. Possibly not her mother (for which she'll pay -- wait, strike that!). Her... grandmother? Fay, like Mrs Taylor, is a serial fuzzer-outter. Runs in the family. It doesn't pay to care. Doesn't pay to *remember* either. Remember one thing and everything else comes buzzing back like a swarm of angry bees. Fay is swollen with painful memories. She's been stung too many times to care too much for anything that can't be turned into cold hard cash or a decent meal or a place to crash for the night. *Or a good shag, darling?*

"Contrary to popular opinion," opines Fay, "I am replete with either a hug or a kiss!"

Yeah, baby.

So why does she care about this sick old man? Fate. Obviously, it's Fate, thinks Fay. "I mean, I wasn't born yesterday."

Now don't go jumping to conclusions, hon'.

In any case, the above are Fay's exact, not wholly inaccurate nor wholly sober, thoughts from the gleaming, bubble-jetted bathtub where she now lies, increasingly cynical -- but *aware* of it as never before. Lessons from life crowd around her like bees to honey (that apiarial allusion again, m'dears!) though she has no inclination to absorb metaphor at the moment as she is up to her silky neck in fragrant, expensive and most importantly -- warmer than allowed where she came from – bubbly bath water. A squat, cut crystal glass of Blue Label (my all time favourite) beckons on the tub's edge. Fay takes a mega-swallow and hiccups. All is well for the moment. She even feels like singing. Until she notices Abdullah Shamaly's roses in the wash basin, sheds an instant tear of loss and, swaying, pulls herself up, stretches from the tub for a rose. A magnificent, crimson, *comforting* rose.

But, ach! She pricks herself, slips, plunges, cracks her leg with a sickening clunk on the tub's edge, plummets, compound-fractured to the tiled floor, screams.

The control on her mauve cashmere electric blanket throws a tiny shower of sparks over her bed while Fay, half of her twisting in agony on the cold, en-suite bathroom tiles, sniffs burning blanket and screams louder.

"Fire! Fire! Fire!"

It is just like the old days. No one comes. When they did, they were armed with fire hoses to blast her senseless against a wall lit with flames.

Not quite it, dear. Close. But not quite it. Ditch the water. It came later. If it *did* come later. No one has a patent on clarity. Even me. I'm getting a bit old myself, peaches. But what's eternity to sempiternal *us*?

30

Fay screams from watery darkness. The pain is so intense she can't move. She is trapped, half-in, half-out of that treacherous bathtub, and her mauve electric blanket, not to be upstaged, has fused a circuit. The Savoy sub-manager in charge of electricity is now knocking politely on the door of Fay's suite. Writhing puffs of smoke spring like weeds from the edges of Fay's bed while the tiniest of fires has begun at its centre (Zounds! Have we clues herein for that small -- but smoky – newspaper/toilet tissue blaze in poor Bill's bathroom?).

ZOUNDS? m'dears, did I just say *ZOUNDS?!*

A bit more smoke will soon activate the fire-prevention sprinkler system. Can't end it all here, can we? Too much effort has gone into this petite baguette -- or should that be bagatelle?

Humour us.

Ian disapproves of smoking but nonetheless lights Rita's cigarette. A burst of hammering slams down from above. Rita winces. "Sweet Jesus! Will they never stop?!"

She sips her cognac.

Ian watches her sympathetically.

Rita, with a guilty smile: "Told you I was grumpy."

"You've every right to be, love."

Note, darlings: Though copulating regularly, our two golden-oldies are not on *completely* comfortable terms yet, just that wee bit wary of one another -- you know how things are at that age -- hence the stilted conversation when they are not otherwise, more intimately, engaged. Thirty years separation has certain disadvantages.

"You're not grumpy, love."

"If you hadn't been such a liar I would have married you long ago."

"I never asked you."

Rita raises her glass, "In vino bloody veritas."

You aged darlings, get out of the bleeding drawing room!

They laugh (one would hope) at Rita's cliché remark and she reflects for a moment, wondering what to say, wondering if her bark *is* worse than her bite or whether she really has ended up a churlish old baggage.

"What's your ex up to these days? What's that American divorcee up to?"

"The same thing she did when we were married. Sleeping about."

You're just jealous, honey.

"Poor Ian, you must hate her. (Sip) I know I did." Rita smiles. "No. I don't hate anyone, anymore. Not even the Ritterhouse Fay."

Why does Fay invariably muscle into everything? But Rita's conversation has dried up today and Ian isn't saying much either. Was their love affair too hot not to cool down?

Rita drinks too much (That was Ian). Ian is worried too (What a *nanny*!), about her smoking but her cigarette has gone out so, disapproving, he re-lights it. She puffs it back to life and looks mischievously at him, says "Incidentally. If you ever meet Ritterhouse Fay, don't give her a match."

They laugh again. Ho-hum! Let us leave and allow our friends (*hopefully*!) to engage in discourse not requiring either Rita's smoking, Rita's drinking (honestly! He drinks too – just wait!), or Fay, understandably ubiquitous Ritterhouse Fay, our preternatural protagonist, to whom we now, with unconcealed relief, repair! Mummy sorely misses her.

A pretty little manicurist (*hand*maidens are indispensable in our game) dries the fingers of Fay's left hand as Fay sits immersed in a voluminous white silk smock from which, most uncomfortably, protrudes her immense, splinted leg. Her right hand lies soaking in a soothing, lukewarm finger bath as bitter memories linger of her extraction from the bathtub by that awful man with the wart. That wart (with my compliments, sugar) and all its metaphysical implications! There it was! Looming larger and larger till she swooned! (I am nothing if not merciful)

"Like hell you are!"

"Oh dear," says the little manicurist, have I said something?

"No," sighs Fay, and with my help banishes these warty ruminations.

"You've lovely nails," sighs this pretty little manicurist who holds up Fay's fingers, squints at them.

"I used to bite them," says Fay, feeding on the compliment like a jackal on a corpse, "Don't ask why."

Now we're going to have some fun, m'dears.

"What?" asks Fay, "What was that?"

Nothing, darling.

"Do tell!" squeaks the manicurist, still squinting, evaluating, "Tell us about them lovely nails of yours."

"I used to bite them so they wouldn't break off whilst I scrubbed floors as a child of six."

"Six?!"

"Years old," sighs Fay. "I was sent out to work. It brought in a few bob."

A few bob, darling, *bob*? You *have* heard of our delightful decimal system?

"My goodness!" cries the dear little manicurist, still squinting but also squinching her brow very much like that masseuse had, several days before, very much like Fay often does, very much like I, and my own so-called *eyes,* do. "Where on earth were your parents?!" adds the little manicurist."

Beyond Pluto, ducky!

"Mummy was in a sanatorium."

Fay looks away. It is genuinely difficult to continue as authentic though entirely inaccurate feelings pirouette in her gut.

"And your father?" asks the manicurist, simultaneously shuddering and squinching, "What about him, then?"

"The only thing I ever got from my father was Athlete's Foot."

The manicurist gasps and accidentally pricks Fay's finger with her fine, Swedish-steel cuticle-prober.

"Ouch!" pipes Fay who has taken very nearly all she can take -- this includes her badly broken leg, that man's enormous wart, as well as a bonfire in her bed. The bonfire, if I may so digress, was a blessing as the fusing electric blanket had brought said be-warted sub-manager straight to her door. Perhaps not quite straight, as he had first inspected four other suites on the same circuit before his arrival at the screaming, half-in, half-out, buck-naked Fay's...

"Ouch!"

"God! I'm so sorry," squeaks the little manicurist.

"I was forced to wear Papá's septic socks because we couldn't afford any for moi," says Fay.

When did I ever teach you my fractured French?

"Ugh!" moans the manicurist, wincing sincerely at the thought of fungus, any fungus (She does *toes* too).

"His socks came to my knees and I had to hitch them up with rubber bands I had stolen from school. (That old rubber band trick, eh, Fay?) The infection spread right up my childish thighs."

The manicurist, in some awe, nods her head in deepest sympathy.

"I was taken out of school as a health hazard to the other children," says Fay, "It left an indelible mark on me."

The Mark of the Beast?

"You poor dear!" shudders the manicurist, again pricking Fay's finger with her fine, Swedish, cuticle prober.

"Ouch!" says Fay, nevertheless basking in the manicurist's serious concern. "But I survived."

Just, darling. *Just.*

Pretty little manicurist, merrily: "Good for you, dear!"

"The fungus then spread under my nails. Spread from all that scratching. Fungi do itch!"

Tell me about it!

The manicurist drops Fay's left hand, peers hopefully at it from afar. "But you're lovely shaped nails, dear."

"These are all new," sighs Fay happily, "The others were so deformed they had to be removed one by one like Chinese torture. A hideous experience for a tiny child."

The manicurist breathes faster, takes up Fay's right hand, probes.

"Ouch," says Fay.

"Sorry," says the manicurist, "It's just that..."

"They soaked my nails for days and days in hot, chlorinated lye-water. My fingers became so soft I felt they might drop right off if I so much as plucked a bogey from my pert little nose."

The manicurist is chagrined. Fay is enjoying herself.

And so am I. That being the sole reason (well, *one* of 'em) for this delicious detour. One must take pleasure where one can. To recreate, so to speak. As I do, darlings and have always done. Besides, when the time is ripe the little manicurist will, without knowing it, nudge Ms Fay into our next square.

"Then they tweezed my softened little nails right out with tiny tongs. Daddy was a religious zealot so anaesthesia was out of the question."

"Oh!" cries the distinctly queasy little manicurist who fumbles her prober yet again.

Ouch," says Fay, gliding at a dangerously oblique angle into the waiting square, "But God has his tender mercies."

"Thank God!" says the manicurist.

"Oh I did!" says Fay, "I said my childish prayers every night. Every night until my house burned down."

The manicurist stops probing, waits expectantly for more. Fay pauses, withdraws into a private moment of purest, perfectly postured pain, then continues:

"I lost my father in that fire. Plus four tiny kittens we couldn't afford to feed."

"How awful! How truly awful! To have your house burn down! How awful!"

"Not at all, you silly cow!" spits Fay, "That is what I was praying for!"

The little manicurist is aghast. She takes up Fay's fingers, begins to work on them -- for two reasons only: because this is her job, isn't it? And because she feels the oddest vibration telling her she ought to. Or else.

Fay does not see this innocent creature's strangely awry face because Fay's eyes are closed. She is laughing to herself. Dreaming of sugar-plums?

Never mind, sugar plums will come soon enough. So will sour grapes.

Jenny and Hugh, my favourite papier mâché couple, lie sprawled on the floor, armed with chopsticks. Feast your eyes on Hugh! He's a living doll. Curly hair and biteable buttocks and *all* that happens so magnificently between on his flip side. But those morning erections, m'dears, in those tight red shorts! Au secours! Help! Help! I'm mincing, not drowning!

And Jenny, as delicious a concoction as any healthy male (or female) might require for admission through those pearly gates of paradise; dark eyes sparkling with intelligence (I'm doing my best here, m'dears, bear with me), lips brushed with cherry, cheeks with roses, a lithe though compact body to rival Fay's, and obedient muscles the envy of an athlete of either gender.

So chopsticks equipt J and H tug carry-out from bulging cartons placed about them on their worn carpet -- a far cry from that other well-known floor covering of yore.

"We *sat* on that carpet! What would *we* do with a billion pounds?" continues Jenny making conversation in lieu of what she really wishes to ask: what happened between you and Jim Richardson at your "working dinner".

Poor Jenny is now tongue-tied when it comes to matters of the heart (I saw to that – I simply had to make these two more commercial because we're stuck with them and I haven't the inclination to reconnoitre). So a little soap opera conflict here greases the squeaking machinations of these, our sexy young supernumeraries.

"Immediately write a check to Inland Revenue for five or six hundred million," says Hugh in answer to Jenny's previous query simply ages ago! (How do they remember what the fuck they're saying?!)

Honestly, Hughie, the super-rich never pay taxes!

Hugh's having terrible trouble with his chopsticks (a soupçon of conflict for your enjoyment, m'dears). He wouldn't have minded at all if Jenny had asked what had happened at his working dinner. (Read my lips, darling. *Nothing* happened – not that time.) Why can't Jen and I speak frankly to one another anymore? Thinks Hugh.

"God! That much for tax?" gasps Jenny.

Repeat: The super-rich, my naive little bimbo, never pay taxes!

Jenny ignores me, of course, continues to use her chopsticks expertly, as in all things, except frank interrogation -- though their relationship is meant to be completely open. It *was*, of course. Before *we* came. What happened? Besides those damned vibrations? Everything changed that night. Or so I've heard. I'm a newcomer myself.

Hugh nods, yes, that much for taxes (Yawn). Jenny says: "That leaves only countless millions. You can't buy anything for countless millions."

Pardon me, m'dears, whilst I slap myself awake!

"We could deduct as business the three point seven million we spent on take-away this year," says Hugh wishing that Jenny would -- damn it! -- ask an explicit question about Jim Richardson, "That would free up another million or so."

Fuck deductions! I have told you repeatedly: THE SUPER-RICH *NEVER* PAY TAXES! I do everything I can to beef-up this borrring situation! I melt the walls and place those proud Lions of Delos at either side of the bathroom door. But, darlings, to *no* avail! Why *do* I get myself into these...?

"Goody!" cries Jenny, "Enough for one whole room at the back in Camden Town!"

"With a loo across the garden."

"What garden?"

Hugh and Jenny smile cosily at one another but are deeply

ashamed that their conversation is so poverty-stricken, so uncomfortable, so...cardboard. So *common*. Perhaps, like Rita and Ian, H and J are just running out of steam? Well, I'm sorry, m'dears. I need a rest too but the game, however fitsy-startsy, must continue as everything herein, as it is in life, is a means to its end.

Goddamn it. Is it Hugh's obvious attraction to Richardson or those vibrations, thinks Jenny. Goddamn it, thinks Hugh, does Jenny actually believe I'll leave her for a blowjob? We've been over that a hundred times! She's had her moments too, with Alicia. I've never said a word about them. Maybe I should have.

It's not as though Jenny should feel completely secure with Hugh as they've only been living together on and off for eight months, and not as though he should feel completely secure with her either. She's had those moments -- some quite serious -- as above. But Hugh and Jenny have always been such good pals. Sex was simply a dividend.

They *love* one another, fer christ's sake!

The crash of a falling plank shakes their ceiling, their walls, their floor, unites them. Jenny drops a chopstick and checks her watch. "Bastards! It's midnight!"

"Let's complain," says Hugh.

"To whom? To bloody sodding whom?!"

So, m'dears, alliteratively speaking, Fay from afar, fucks up family life.

And, remember, the super-rich *never* pay taxes!

31

Fay awoke less than a minute ago. She's in huge, purple plastic curlers, climbing on to her crutches in her shabby chenille bathrobe (Even Taylor's chenille is nicer. Why doesn't Fay wear the satin négligée from Versace in that half-opened box on the floor? Ach! Who knows what lurks in those indigo depths? *Besides* me?

Fay plods laboriously on splinted leg, every bone-screw squeaking, into the cluttered living room of her suite, through packages from every posh shop (she counted them) on New Bond Street. (Just a reprise, m'dears, to verify her astounding wealth – I *still* can't believe it – though I arranged it.)

"Enter!" shrieks Fay to her chiming door with all the breath she's got left.

In rolls Fay's breakfast on a shiny trolley propelled by a smartly uniformed young man. The elegant tray is set with crystal, delightfully translucent china and silver. Delicately arranged flowers jiggle over several morning newspapers. The smartly uniformed man notes with alarm Fay's alarming appearance, attempts a smile, pushes the breakfast trolley to the centre of the room directly beside Fay, exits as shot from a gun. Fay gives the trolley a splint-buttressed push and sends it thumping against the sofa towards which she heaves herself and has snatched and chomped down a delicate slice of buttered toast before her chenille-clad botty whacks white leather. She dollops great, mad scoops of butter on a second slice until she spies a newspaper headline in boldest black hovering directly over the next square:

OIL BILLIONAIRE
ABDULLAH SHAMALY DEAD

That'll teach you, Fay!

"You are cruel! Mad and cruel! I did nothing to deserve this!"

Darling, into each life a little rain must fall. You were warned some squares back.

"Why must I suffer?! Why do you torture..."

Original Sin, ducky! You're dripping with it! What went round, comes round! Particularly on a treadmill, love.

Fay screams, grabs up the newspaper, topples backward into

our next square, reads more, then casts the paper to the floor and kicks away the breakfast trolley with her good leg. On her knees she drags her new chinchilla from its huge gilt box and sinks back into the sofa and pulls the coat up to her chin and shuts her eyes tight. Her cheeks go red then ashen then white. The room swims in remorse until the telephone rings. Fay pulls the chinchilla up to her nose and rolls back and forth wracked with great, gulping sobs. The telephone continues to ring (it is Ammari with yet another money-making scheme). But she doesn't answer it, sobs longer, louder.

How she sobs! Shakes and sobs! Sobs and shakes!

"Oh leave me alone, will you?! Can't you see I'm in pain?! Don't *dramatize*!"

Well shoot me at dawn, darling! I was only trying to help!

It's another day and Fay's tears are long dried and the late saint Abdullah is filed away in some, I note with chagrin, *inviolate* place in her head. She reclines as comfortably as possible, considering. Her enormous splinted leg protrudes from beneath another silken smock -- this one's the bright vermilion of a certain poisonous Guyanese toad. The leg in question rests propped high on a fine plush stool while she luxuriates under a hairdryer and attempts to remember a latterly fuzzy period that has skipped her mind. She plummets for a moment into inky darkness rounded by fleeting, flashing forms shrieking unintelligible commands.

How like Mum!

She stares into this murk at her half-formed fingers, half-formed feet, screams in her head. "What have I done?! Why am I being punished?!"

Ach! An excellent question, my dear. Go instantly to the head of the class.

"And the heat is unbearable -- it can't all be coming from the *infernal* hair-dryer!"

I adore that adjective, Missy Fay.

The solitude in this private room in a posh salon is yummy -- would be once Fay rids herself of these things in her head. There was so little privacy...before. In darkest Stygia. Although one could not, mercifully, see the beings that prodded, poked, pricked, pierced and impaled one.

Fay now abandons with a sigh this treacherous stroll down memory lane and begins to read Country Life, a really excellent alternative. The cheery hairdresser, yet another helpmeet to our pernicious purpose, peeps in at her, grins, flounces away. Fay drops Country Life, picks up another magazine, thumbs through it, finds herself (literally finds *herself*, m'dears!) at a two-page spread:

HER HOUSE BURNED DOWN
by Rita Lambert

Rita Lambert! Fay reads on, her rosy lips tightening over perfect teeth:

> "Warm your coffee?" said Janet, wondering
> what on earth this strange, mousy creature
> who called herself by her surname could
> want. And want she most certainly did!
> "Why yes, please," simpered Doolittle Desiree,
> "I noticed you had some excellent blends on
> your shelf."
> "It's my coffee she's come for," thought Janet
> but Janet said:
> "Oh. Those. They're ancient. I wouldn't give
> them to a dog."

In Fay's spacious, elegant flat at Number 13, several workmen hammer a dazzling wall to wall carpet in place as Fay, *my* hammer in her head, skips a page, reads on:

> "Perhaps Walter would notice you if you asked
> for help," said Doolittle Desiree, "People are
> always generous when one is desperate."
> Desiree pursed her prim little lying lips,
> smiled her cutest, most helpless little smile
> and lisped: "It never fails for me."

My hammer grows louder.

Workmen slam down several sections of scaffolding at Number 13. In the vast new street window of Fay's spacious new living room, a young, muscular lad, arms over head, stretches, his jeans ascending to enfold that delicious warm thingy nestling between his muscular thighs. (Sorry, m'dears, it was time for Mummy's mini-moment. Ach! Now she can, on her so-called *knees*, crawl on.) This delightfully endowed young man looks down at an up-market van. A superb white leather couch -- a perfect copy of the one in Fay's Savoy suite -- and white marble end-tables (ditto) are wending their way up the entrance steps on the shoulders of several more young men.

Rita scowls through the remaining planks at her window. Mrs Taylor, vague and above, aims her wrath at the office building opposite. Suddenly, Fay comes to mind and Taylor shivers, is convinced she'll see her soon. Knows she'll see her soon. As it takes one to know one and Mr Taylor's prophecy is correct etc. For when was Mr Oscar Taylor ever wrong?!

I'll vouch for that, m'dears.

Jenny, home for lunch, shivers too. From sexual jealousy? Or is it simply an odd vibration?

They're one and the same, m'dears.

Hugh, at Jim Richardson's flat for a business lunch is, this time, having more than business, more than lunch. Jim, just 'out', shy and unsure, has nonetheless unzipped Hugh's fly, clasped Hugh's moist erection, gently pulled back Hugh's foreskin. Hugh is now reaching for Jim's you-know-what, wondering if Jim is going to kiss him. He'd love to be kissed first. Jenny always kisses him first.

> Doolittle Desiree, shocked and stammering, backed away from Nina. "My house burned down!" gasped Desiree.
> "Oh really?" said Nina, pulling the bedclothes over her surprising, *two* perfectly formed, firm breasts, "And were you in it?"

reads Fay as my head-hammer crescendoes, far louder than the hammering in her new flat. Louder than all the hammers dismantling the scaffolds outside. Louder, indeed, than all the presumably presently pounding hammers in London.

Fay, if she weren't furious over the magazine crumpling in her fists, might even have seen the progress at Number 13. She knows the construction and fitting schedule by heart. She's got a photographic memory and built-in, radar-quality sensing. She's "a bit of a witch". So why not? Isn't witchcraft the one and only key to her present miraculous situation? What else could it be?

I could tell you everything. But I won't. One can't cut a good story short. Be patient. Listen, m'dears. Listen. And if any of you have divined the outcome of my saga, keep your dainty traps shut, or -- as they say in the jejune though often jaunty jargon of our mega-tawdry day -- I'll have to *kill* you.

Rita, too, is furious. Furious at the hammering, the fall of scaffolding, the clomping of furniture up the stairs, the return clomping down, the shouts and guttural gossip of workmen, their obnoxious, eardrum-bursting radio music, their leers. She's trying to write, sod 'em all! She's an author now, with a budding career rising from the rubble of her former lonely life. She thrusts her trembling fingers at her typewriter, pounds. From above comes the familiar thump of Mrs Taylor's cane. Really! How *can* she? When there's so much else to complain about why must it be my puny typewriter?

"Just letting her know I'm alive," mutters Taylor, "She might think I've succumbed. She might think them god-awful noises is my body tumblin' down the stairs dead as a doornail."

How prescient of you, my dear.

Taylor chuckles having obviously not heard me. Rita, below, laughs and relents. "Mrs Taylor simply wants to let me know she's still about," says Rita, "Get a grip on yourself. You're a paid author and everything is grist for your mill."

Ain't it just? Won't it just be?

Fasten your shiny-bottomed jodhpurs, Rita. It's going to be a bumpy ride.

Fay's eyes blaze. "How *could* they?! How *could* they?"

Not very original comments, admittedly. But we're in a hurry.

"Fuck off!" screams Fay, at a perfectly innocent indigo shadow. Misdirected wrath, darling, is no better than no wrath at all.

"Whoever you are!" screams Fay, "Fuck off!"

Our libellous magazine protrudes, savagely shredded, from her two claw-like, fists. Shredded like her kindly plans for the dubious denizens of Number 13. Ach! The hammering in her head positively thunders. "Fuck off!" she cries again and again, "Fuck off! Fuck off! Fuck off! Fuck off!"

You, Missy Fay, had better watch your cloven step!

Slinking out through the half-open sliding glass wall to the spanking new roof terrace beyond, that blackest of cats pauses and looks about with huge, mauve slit-eyes then moves lithely to the potted trees that edge the roof terrace. The shattering crash of several large planks flung into the lorry below startles! The cat leaps through the potted trees but alas, over the edge of the roof. It plunges three stories to the ground, lies there, still, a tiny trickle of blood oozing from its black-whiskered mouth. Suddenly it is up, the very picture of health. It bolts away to die another day -- even a fool knows it's got eight more lives to lose.

> "I've only got a bed," whispers Doolittle Desiree as she kneels, shall we say, "vulnerably"? on old Mrs Belcher's looted rug staring directly at the aroused Albert's, shall we say, "sweet surprise"?...

Bill has told Nelly and Nelly has told Rita about Fay and Bill. Jenny has told all too. Hugh also couldn't keep his big mouth shut. Rita has, cackling to herself, added the rest, sold it for *money*, rejoiced over poor Fay's pain, thinks Fay. "How *could* they?!" exclaims she who was a perfect child, could have been a perfect adult yet was somehow -- aborted? What *is* that word? -- Shanghai-ed. Yes! Shanghai-ed. Shanghai-ed by what? Whom? People? What people? These people! "How *could* they?!" (Not again, Fay. Move on, ducky. The next square awaits your dainty hoof.)

Fay rips Pazazz magazine into ever tinier pieces, casting them about in a frenzy of loathing. "I tried to be friends! They were, to a person, all reinstated on my projected gift-list!"

They were, indeed. Got my vote.

Fay kicks away the stool supporting her splinted leg and the leg crashes to the floor, its clustered titanium screws straining against bone. She screams in pain, curses. Her hair-dryer sparks, smokes, catches fire. Her vermilion silken smock flying, she leaps away, screaming louder, balancing crazily on her crutches. Deception! Cruelty! Mendacity! How *could* these people?! She'd only wanted to be friends! To help them!

When she was able, of course. When her ship reached harbour.

The hairdresser rushes in, sees frenzied Fay fragmenting before her very eyes as Fay huddles in another chair, incantating, ripping to shreds all the magazines she can lay her hands on. Fay screams again. A bottle of shampoo bursts in the terrified hairdresser's hand. The hairdresser, scared witless by Fay's singularly savage look backs out of the room, cries:

"Fire! Fire!"

"Fire!" shrieks Fay, "I'm a goner!"

Sorry, m'dears, too many Westerns..

"Save me!" screams Fay, "Whoever you are!"

It's not time. Not yet, sweetie. And I wouldn't count on it.

"What?! What was that?!"

The hair-dryer continues to spark and burn. Flames and smoke pour out. Fay stops screaming, is fascinated by the flames. Suddenly, for a refreshing change, *cerulean* shadows circle in wild-goose formation. The smoke doesn't choke. Trance-like (ho-hum, it's happened before), she studies this small conflagration, tries to manipulate the licking, writhing flames with one piercing look. Thinks she does. Perhaps she does. Those wild geese shadows begin to honk:

> You got those ce-ru-le-an blues
> Ain't never been so blue...

A well-dressed woman rushes in, attempts to remove Fay from the room. Fay claws at her, is transfixed by the flames, won't move. The woman runs out, calls for help, returns. Two more well-dressed women rush in, try to drag Fay from the room. Fay curses them all, spits at them, their sleeves catch fire. The three elegant women scream in unison.

For some reason known only to Fay (and me) she shouts "Sissies!" at these heroic, these three well-dressed women who are attempting to rescue her. "Sissies!" she screams, "You're all a bunch of pampered, over-priced sissies!"

Is there a lesson here, m'dears?

The racing cerulean shadows evaporate. Fay shrieks until over-come by the acrid, sweet smoke of exploding hair-mousse and she is carried senseless from the flaming premises.

Should I feel guilty?

Darlings, no one is blameless.

Okay, so schedule my execution. But be warned, I'm slippery as a greased sow and as smelly as her sty.

Everybody is celebrating at Number 13. The scaffolding is down and the new construction is complete (so they believe). Six weeks of rattling walls, shuddering ceilings, catapulting planks, buzz saws, electric drills, worker's shouts, loud music and plastery powder on stairs, shoes, trousers and skirts -- have all ended. Only six weeks?! That took a bit of magic too, m'dears.

The grateful tenants, excluding Mrs Taylor who is present but not grateful (*never* grateful – and don't *I* know it!) as she has already forgotten the noise and confusion, are dispersing into the hall from their now traditional Sunday coffee at Rita's (Fay's and my doing, of course, and unaccredited of course).

Bill and Nelly, hand in devoted hand, are about to adjourn to Nelly's flat opposite for a comfy post-meridian lie-down. Rita and Ian linger lovingly just outside Rita's door as Jenny trades recipes with Rita (a simple, though imposed, domestic touch, m'dears for those of you who respond to such things, and your number, I hear -- I *fear* -- is legion). Hugh attempts to assist Taylor, much against her will, up the stairs. She'd rather fly. At the moment, thinks she, at some time or other, *has*. I can't deny it, honestly can't deny it. Though I'll not confirm it either.

The morning's conversation, aside from discussing their well earned nascent tranquillity plus who can be about to occupy the now completed, luxury flat on the top floor had turned, as usual, to Fay. What will she do with her new wealth and wasn't life strange and unfair to drop a fortune into such undeserving claws? Although good Nelly does not agree with this assessment but still feels for poor, confused, frightened and child-like Fay.

Really, Nelly! Though there is merit in your machinations, you dear, daft poppet.

Jenny and Hugh had been unusually quiet -- with each other at any rate, m'dears. Though Jenny was quite forthright about how their tenant's rights had been literally trampled on. Silent Hugh had Jim Richardson in his head or, to be blunt, in his briefs. *Seamy* detail, but fun. N'est-ce pas?

Ian, though he was in charge of the construction work, agreed with Jenny that a lot of money must surely have greased a lot of palms to circumvent ethical building conduct. He added that he had kept the noise and inconvenience down as much as possible and would himself have quit but he needed the money. Rita said she would hate to imagine what the last eight (or was it six?) weeks might have been like without Ian's... err...intervention.

Yes, Rita, fifty-something and almost invisible, had executed an about-face. She might soon attempt to quit smoking (again).

And her drinking...well she'd work on that too. Every writing manual agrees (and I've read a few, one of which resides in my left so-called *breast* pocket) that ones characters – even those of the cardboard variety -- must all, in some way, *develop*. So, in the interests of effective gamesmanship cum wouldn't-you-like-to-know...

"Sweet Jesus!" cries Rita who weaves suddenly round, turns white.

"What?" asks Ian and grips her waist. Is she having a seizure?!

"What is it?!" cries Jenny fastening on to reeling Rita's arm.

"What?" say Nelly and Bill simultaneously moving close. Hugh, who has seen Rita stagger, leaves Taylor securely attached to the stair rail, bolts down the stairs to help if he can (He's had first aid nurse's training, m'dears).

Rita is speechless, swept by some terrifying presentiment. She sways again, removes her arm from Jenny's grasp, points through the bronze-framed newly installed glass door at the street, cries:

"Jesus H. Christ!"

PART THREE

32

The curly-white-gold-haired young chauffeur (hand-plucked, m'dears), stands stiff at attention beside the Rolls-Royce limousine and waits for instructions. They are succinctly shouted. But by *whom*?

As if you didn't know!

With the curious eyes of every occupant of Number 13 (save Taylor) upon her, a shining woman emerges from this glistening limou amidst the gut-tugging adagio of Ravel's piano concerto in G major which lilts from the limou's labyrinthine glove-leather interior. This luminous woman is superbly coiffed, made-up, wondrously wrapped in an ankle-length chinchilla that flaps luxuriously in the wind.

A far cry from the tatty, sooty black skirt of yore! Ach! But she's got a huge splint on her leg!

The white-gold chauffeur steadies her then reaches into the Rolls and hands her something.

"Good God!" cries Rita, "That's my kettle! It's Ritterhouse Fay with my sodding kettle!"

Gasps all around! *All* around, m'dears! Who wouldn't?!

To the haunting, halting strains of this concerto's adagio bursting full-volume from that spectacular vehicle, Fay, ably assisted by this mauve uniformed young man who carries her crutches and shabby cardboard suitcase (the very same!), hobbles up the steps of Number 13. Rita's kettle dangles from one diamond-braceleted hand. In the other is a perfect, long-stemmed rose. At the now highly polished, new brass call-box, they pause. "Chauffy" places a gilt-edged, engraved card, "Ritterhouse, Fay" in slot six, and opens the glass door.

Rose held high before her like a shield (wilting bouquets are a thing of the past) and smiling benignly straight ahead, though awkward on her splint-leg, my darling prosopopoeia, bone screws whining (a little techno-spice never hurt anyone), enters. At the bottom of the staircase she whispers in Chauffy's ear and he takes the kettle and one crutch and bounds up the stairs with the suitcase.

Fay grasps the stair rail, pulls herself slowly, step by clumsy step up to the first landing where she stops and hovers in her splendid chinchilla, tilting awkwardly on her crutch, gazing down at everyone. I care about you all, she thinks, so deep inside -- as Bill might have said -- it hardly matters, then she says aloud, "I've come to enrich your lives."

In her fashion, m'dears.

"What?" asks Fay, "What was that, you cowardly kibbitzer?"

I stifle a voluble smirk.

The residents of Number 13 are stunned, silent. But they think:

> Rita: "Why the fuck does she want to live *here*?!" (Wouldn't you like to know, Rita.)
>
> Ian: "So this is who I've been working for." (Greater surprises are in store, Ian.)
>
> Bill: "Oh my God!" (You once made a big mistake, 'Billy'. You'll pay for it.)
>
> Nelly: "Poor Fay. She just wants to be friends." (You'll see, Nelly. Soon enough -- though there is truth in what you say.) (Or *was* truth in what you say.)
>
> Hugh: "She's completely mad!" (Think again, Hugh – you've no idea.)
>
> Jenny: (Can't think. Feels, in place of a thought, an odd vibration.)
>
> Taylor: She's backed against a wall, terrified. Wondering if her 110-year-old-husband, Oscar, was only a febrile figment (I assure you, love, that this is *not* the case). She wonders, however, if this *is* the case, how this Fay-thing could be their miscarried love-child. Did it somehow survive?! That ring of chanting women took it away, thrust it into the flames. But it emerged... No! NO! NO! Taylor, mercifully, fuzzes out.

With a shy smile Fay lifts her perfect rose aloft for one poignant moment -- while time stands still (Actually *does*, m'dears) -- then casts the rose from the landing and disappears up the stairs. The rose, losing but one petal, falls just before the bottom stair. Nelly advances hesitantly, picks it up, is savagely pricked by it, drops it.

Take a hint, Nelly!

But she doesn't.

Sucking the blood from her finger, she gingerly takes up the rose again, turns, looks uncertainly at the others who stare dumbly at one another.

The door bursts open and in comes Nelly's chest of drawers in the arms of the mauve uniformed men. Nelly looks at Bill. "That was mine," she says.

"I know."

"Sweet Jesus," says Rita, "My kettle and your bureau. The gall."

Jenny is about to say something, shudders, doesn't. Nelly's chest of drawers disappears up the stairs.

"Good luck to us all," intones Rita, theatrically -- and why not, she's a bleedin' actress. Plus she's got Ian now. Well, sort of and if she loses him and her writing is just a flash in the pan she could go back and grace the stage -- any old stage, maybe the first stage outta here! Jesus, she'd grace the goddamned telly! If she got any offers. Which would, of course, depend on *me* – for the time being, m'dears. For the *duration*.

And gosh! Nelly's got Bill -- Bill's got Nelly. Jenny and Hugh have got one another too, in their fashion. Though there is movement on that front just now. So, all considered, here are the makings of a formidable anti-Fay faction, like that Band of Spartan soldier-lovers!

Forget it, m'dears. Just note the ever so subtle quivering of the outer edges of the staircase and the nearly imperceptible, ongoing variations in the height of each stair and you'll see why. And it ain't from the heavy footsteps of those lovely, mauvey men. Creep down the hall some evening, gang o' mine, quite late, and if you listen carefully the muted conversation between the walls and the ceiling is most revealing. Or not.

Hugh and Jenny assist Mrs Taylor, near catatonic after this close brush with the Fay-thing, up the stairs to her flat. Jenny shivers still, as various bits of familiar furniture, gifts to Fay at that party some weeks ago, drift by in strong, mauve arms. Why she would want it now is anybody's guess (though I assure you it's crucial – or *could* have been). But Taylor, suddenly semi-conscious, knows *everything*, blinks several times in abject terror, gulps. Then, the poor, poor old cow, swoons and is caught in the four serviceable arms of solicitous Hugh and shuddering Jenny. See, m'dears? These tots aren't *completely* useless!

On her roof-spanning terrace Fay sits and sips from a behemoth bottle of Johnny Walker Blue (my own imposed taste I am bound to admit again and again) and snuggles into her magnificent chinchilla thinking the gods only know what. That black cat, casing the joint, peers suspiciously from between two potted trees.

Through the glass wall of her fabulous flat Fay watches the last of her furniture -- Hugh's drop-leaf table, as it happens, being set in place. The mauve-uniformed removals men (colour is so important, ain't it, m'dears?) nod to her. She nods back, winks, then whispers to the furniture, "Long time no see".

The furniture et al, pouts at first – it wasn't pleasant being crammed together like sardines even if it was an *up-market* storage facility.

The removal men leave, pocketing their substantial tips, having unpacked everything according to precise instructions. Money shrieks, doesn't it? We're a wee bit old fashioned about money.

Fay's gaze wanders to the transparent bathroom where Chauffy, fully visible, showers in all his white-gold glory. She studies his smooth, wet nakedness, savours it (as do I), sips from her bottle. He flashes a libidinous smile, begins to soap his bouncing, blooming dangling things.

Lightning splits the sky followed instantly by deafening thunder. That black cat, startled, jumps into Fay's lap and curls up in warm, costly folds of chinchilla, purrs and purrs. "Darling," whispers Fay into the ebony creature's twitching ear, "We're home. We're nesting. But the question is, 'Where have *you* been?'"

You might ask that of yourself, Ms Ritterhouse Fay.

"What?" says Fay, glancing into the gathering stormy darkness, "What was that?"

I am merrily mute.

Then, rain! A deluge! Great sheets of it whipped to a frenzy by a freak whirlwind as black sky is shattered by blinding light and the terrace trembles with the simultaneous crash of thunder. The cat deserts Fay, leaps through the potted trees and over the edge of the roof to its second death.

Fay doesn't move, hunches here in the downpour, sipping from her bottle, ogling her showering chauffeur. They're showering together, aren't they, m'dears?

Fay giggles, doesn't mind that her enchanting chinchilla becomes rat-fur in the rain. "Me so happy!" she whoops to the wind, to the slanting torrents, "Me so exceptionally happy me want to cry!"

Still she sits, her elegant coiffure winding in the wind. Sits and sips and lifts her glass in a toast to the gods and to divine vengeance. Though she's not completely sure she still desires vengeance. What our dear Fay-creature desires (what all of you desire, m'dears) is to be loved -- anything for a hug. Or a kiss? My God! Is that *so* important?! I've lived a millennium without anything remotely approaching that myth of deluded self interest, *love*. But Fay *will* be loved. In a manner of speaking. Soon. When Chauffy finishes his shower, towels dry his godlike corpus and she, the fallen angel, beckons. "But that's not *really* love," murmurs Fay, momentarily sidetracked, "Real love is not for sale."

Ain't it? God bless her, wherever You are. If You can. It *ain't* her fault! Oh really? I ask myself, then whose bleedin' fault is it?! This self-interrogation causes me to blush as I answer, *Mine*, of course!

"What was that?!"

Fay rises, peeps into her potted mini-forest, "Was that a jolly little wood nymph whispering in my ear? Come out, little wood nymph. Where the dickens are you? Golly! Is my lovely new house bewitched?"

Duh.

Fay is so charmed she will think about vengeance tomorrow. "Never avenge today," she chuckles to herself, "what you can avenge tomorrow. As tomorrow...is another day!"

In any case, though music swells I've forgotten the Tara theme and decide, just now, to give it a miss. Besides which, tomorrow never comes, does it, m'daffy darlings?

However, it is just possible Fay's route to revenge will return and reveal itself mid-loveless-coitus. Primal instincts often go hand in glove (or is that an anachronism?).

Ask her. If you dare.

33

I'm singin' out the storm!
Singin' in the wind!
What a fantastic feelin'!
I'm Ritterhouse again!

Fay's elegant coiffure is no more. Great chunks of mascara skid down her cheeks. Lightning flashes. Thunder crashes. Still she sits. Sips and sits and sips.

Waiting for her instructions, m'dears.

"Instructions?" says Fay, "*Instructions*? I take instructions from no one!"

I comment on this with a sharp slap of sleet across her chops.

"Ouch!" cries Fay.

White-Gold, still towelling himself, watches her warily through the glass wall of her state-of-the-art bathroom.

"Coward!" she shouts, "Come out! Let us sing in the rain!"

She's mad. He's certain of it.

So am I. Almost -- like mother, like daughter. Or should that be, like '*mother*', like '*daughter*'?

"She's mad as a hatter! Why, Ian? Sod it! Why has she come back? She could live in a palace! Why has she come here? She's deadly. I'm sure of it."

That, from Rita, our resident Cassandra. One-issue-Rita marches rambunctiously about, puffing furiously at her elegant long holdered cigarette as:

With rain on my face
And wind in my hair!
You'll have to admit
I'm finally there!
Oh happy me!
Where I've longed to be!
I'm home at last!

perforates Number 13's closed windows, paper walls, floors. Rita gapes helplessly at Ian who shakes his head. She drops herself beside him on the sofa. "We're in danger, lover," she says, "All of us. The woman is rich and mad."

An *almost* unbeatable combination, sugar.

Ian takes Rita's cigarette from her, places it in an ashtray, silently embraces her.

"Say something, sod you," says Rita, "say *something*."

"I love you. I never forgot you."

"Liar."

Rita yanks herself from Ian's arms, jumps up, snatches back her cigarette, puffs maniacally, paces back and forth waving her cigarette. "Did you just say you loved me?"

"Yes."

"I love you too, always have -- Ritterhouse tried to burn us down once."

"Did she?"

"Possibly," says Rita. She frowns and looks up, softens, "I mean it. I do love you, darling, so beware of this aging spinster."

Ian holds up a hand. "I'm shaking, see? But prepared for any eventuality."

"You'd better be, love. I'm not your only problem."

"You're not a problem, you're the solution."

An embrace is due, m'dears. So they take the hint for a casual cuddle then Rita (she *will* do this!) breaks away again, says "Ritterhouse has come back to kill us all. Did you see Taylor? She knows a witch when she sees one."

And, m'dears, Rita knows nothing of the little witch's shrine hidden at the back of Taylor's closet. The closet that held the rug. The rug that got away. The rug that Fragmented Fay filched. Neither does she know about Oscar Taylor's prophecy; his instructions to his estranged wife, she of the directly above -- *if* they were instructions.

Fay is mad and bad and supernatural to know. How else would a penniless vagrant with a multi-dubious past wind up with a billion pounds? How else?

Well, m'dears...

With rain on my face
And wind in my hair
You'll have to admit
I'm finally there!
Oh happy me!

I'm home at last!

warbles Fay through walls and floors and putty-crumbling windows of Her house.

"The bitch doesn't have enough sense to come in out of the rain," cries Rita hitting the nail on the head once again. Writers often do. Though I'm a fledgling... thinks Rita in a creative-writerly way, ...I'm feathering fast.

Good for you, Rita.

"That woman!" she cries, "That monster!"

But what has poor Fay ever done to Rita, besides being excellent material, super grist for Rita's roiling writer's mill? Just the facts, please. Ex-actors do tend to chew their own scenery.

"There, there, darling," says Ian to Rita's look of direst despair.

"She's got high explosives in that great splinted leg -- Don't patronize me!"

"Sorry."

"No. I am sorry, my darling. I'm being utterly stupid, aren't I?"

"Possibly. Possibly *very*."

Rita guffaws, she's retained her sense of the ridiculous. Though, in this case there's nothing ridiculous about it.

Absurd, perhaps?

"Ian?"

"Yes, love?"

"Did you really, a moment ago, *really* say you loved me? Real words to that effect."

"Yes."

"Christ! I *thought* you did. And what did *I* say?"

"We'd better go, love," says Bill. "Danny gets upset when I'm late."

"Bill, why did she come back? Here?"

Poor good Nelly doesn't know what to feel. Never mind. Soon, and sadly, she will.

Hugh and Jenny are worried too. They're crouching beside Mrs Taylor who slumps, eyes glazed and swollen, arthritic knuckles white, clutching the oaken arms of her postcards chair. Storm lashes windows crazily lit by lightning. Fay's song careens through the raging wind, seems to envelope the whole house:

HOME AT LAST!
HOME AT LAST!
I AM-HOME-AT-LAST!

"Mrs Taylor?" says Hugh.

"Mrs Taylor?" says Jenny.

Taylor doesn't move, doesn't blink.

"Shall I call a doctor?"

"You call a doctor, young man and I'll have your ballocks!" barks Taylor not aware, obviously, that Jim Richardson recently has.

"Feeling better, dear?" asks Jenny.

Taylor fairly spits! "Of course I ain't feelin' better, you twit! How can I feel better with a witch hangin' over my head like a sword?!"

Taylor snatches a hanky from her sleeve and blows her nose hard. "Twit!" she adds for good measure.

"A witch?" says Hugh to Jenny.

"Address *me*, young man! I ain't dead yet though I soon shall be! So shall we all!"

"What do you really mean, 'witch'?" asks Jenny. She's beginning to feel one of those now chronic odd vibrations. She must see a doctor about this -- is she pregnant?

"Witch or Antichrist," says Taylor, "Take yer choice."

Taylor has completely forgotten that minute of clarity -- or was it fantasy -- suggestive of her, Taylor's, miscarried motherhood. How *could* one so accuse the bona fide product of ones very own womb?

"Let's start with 'witch'," says Hugh.

"The Ritterhouse woman is a cur-sed witch. That's why I give her my carpet, don't you see?"

They don't. Hugh and Jenny are beginning to think it is Taylor who's nuts, not Fay. After all -- Fay may be a bitch but she's not necessarily a witch.

"Mr Taylor said to give that carpet to a bona fide witch and that is just what I done."

"I should have been that witch!" says Jenny.

"Ain't funny!" says Taylor, "The curse is serious!"

"You're telling me," laughs Jenny who is worryingly late this month, joined by Hugh who's suffered through enough of Jenny's to know she's a tiger every new moon (don't talk to Fay *or* me about new moons).

"The Ritterhouse witch has come back for a reason. We're that reason!" cries Taylor. "She's cur-sed and the curse has come with her. The curse of the carpet! That's a fact! Mr Taylor knows what he's talkin' about. So does Tabari."

"Tabari?" asks Hugh.

"Don't you know nothing?!" screams Taylor, "Tabari is a ancient writer of history. Mr Taylor has read every word Tabari ever wrote and Tabari says that carpet is cursed!"

"But Fay sold the carpet, Mrs Taylor," says Jenny, "She hasn't got it anymore."

"Now it's the money's cursed! Every pound. Every penny. Ritterhouse has spent some of that money on this house. This house and everybody in it is cursed! Ask Mr Taylor! Ask my Oscar!"

Ummnn. But where do we find him, m'dear?

Taylor doesn't look at all well. The whites of her eyes are shot with red. Great blue veins pulse at her yellowed temples.

"Where is Mr Taylor?" asks Hugh who, though he believes none of the curse story, is worried for Taylor's health.

"How the hell should *I* know?!" screams Taylor.

Jenny and Hugh look hopelessly at one another.

"Last time I heard he was studyin' Voodoo in Santo Domingo. He never addresses his postcards. The postmarks are the only clues I got to the sonofabitch's location! He travels like a *devil*."

You may be barmy dear but your nouns, proper or otherwise, are nonpareil.

"What shall we do, Mrs Taylor?" asks Hugh, referring to the seemingly parlous state of Taylor's health.

Oh happy me!
Where I've longed to be!
I'm home at last!

sings Fay through the walls, windows, wind.

"Move out!" screams Taylor, "Move out if you value your lives!"

Poor Mrs Taylor. Sorry about this, me ol' Honey. But, as you well know, or should know by now; what went round, came round. Or something like that. Something very like that. It bears repeating as it is our *thought for the day*.

And the night.

34

From her sparkling new solid bronze window frame -- I'm a dedicated materialist, m'dears and I don't care who knows it -- Fay stares down at Ian's departing car. She has a perfect right to watch. It's a boss's perk. She even has a secret plan to help him beyond his wildest dreams. Yes, he's already on her gift-list. All she needs is a hug. Or a kiss? Or a fervent night of bliss? She'd better slip him onto her *wish*-list too! And write a poem about him as well -- she's already got the rhyme.

She watches for a moment more, decides she has better things to do -- flings herself on her king-size, separately-wrapped-steel-sprung-satin-mattressed bed beside Chauffy -- prepares to do them.

It's bliss time again, m'darlings.

Mind if your inveterately vivacious voyeur lingers just a bit?

Chauffy lights a joint for Fay, lights one for himself, takes a deep drag, stretches. His white satin T-shirt hikes up from his briefs, exposing his navel and the golden hairs curling down to what counts, for Fay, in a hu-man. Fay will have the joint then she'll have the chauffeur. Possibly Ian as well -- hasn't quite decided. She'd chosen him from his photo. She likes older men. She likes younger men. She likes men. After all, she may have been one.

What do you think of that, darlings?!

"I'm going to die."

Rita is here because she heard Mrs Taylor's pitiful crying, didn't like the way the old lady looked this afternoon, has come up to comfort her. Taylor huddles in bed, blankets up to her chin, certain again that she's Taylor, certain she's got a husband named Oscar but just as certain she's about to die. Clarity is not welcome today. Taylor's earlier fuzzes were more pleasant.

"I'm going to die," she repeats amidst her unwelcome clarity.

"We're all going to die sooner or later," comforts Rita.

"Sooner," says Taylor, "And that's a fact."

"You ought to lock your door," says Rita.

"It's the witch's doing -- makes me forget. I don't want to die."

Taylor twists in her bed, grunts in pain -- her arthritis is playing up, "I want to see Oscar Taylor again. Give him a piece of my mind.

He was a naughty boy. I don't want to die."

"You are not going to die."

Rita takes Taylor's hanky, wipes Taylor's eyes.

"Now you're here will you air my posies?"

"In this rain?"

"They love rain."

"I'll air your posies."

"Goody," says Taylor. She feels much better. A little human contact does wonders. Why didn't she think of this 30 years before? Cry a little and they all come running. "And while you're at it," says Taylor, "fetch us a sherry. You know where it is."

Ah, Mrs Taylor! How like Fay all that was. But really, old love, who is manipulating whom?

"What?" says Taylor.

I believe she heard me. Didn't mean for that to happen. I haven't spoken to the old bat in eons though I am rather fond of her. *In my fashion*.

Rita opens a window, is struck by a blast of rain. She puts the geraniums in their window box, shuts the window.

"I seen you in a play once," shouts Taylor from her bed.

"You did?"

"I never said nothing about it."

"Why? Didn't you like me?"

"Nope. You pranced about like a flibberty-gibbet."

Rita laughs, says "You were not alone in that opinion, I was often, towards the last, at least three sheets to the wind."

Make that *four* sheets, lovey.

Rita brings in two sherries on a tray, sits beside Taylor's bed.

I must respectfully pause here to say that Rita was actually (or *is* actually) a quite astonishingly inspired and completely powerful actress. She simply has a bad image of herself. Alcohol and loneliness, one feeding the other, can bring down the most towering of figures -- has. May do so again if Rita is not careful. However, in my beneficence I have chosen to give her another whack at creativity. This time in the books rather than on the boards. Her progress, I am happy to report, is admirable. An apt pupil, she. But a trouble to Fay. With whom Fay will be forced to deal. Soon. But on with our mesmerizing moment:

Taylor seizes the sherry, gulps it down, "We won't die tonight, will we?" she asks, blowing her nose into a discoloured hanky.

"No," says Rita, "Not tonight."

"How do you know?"

"Because we're having a cream sherry tonight."

Taylor smiles. "One thing at a time, eh?"

Rita pours Taylor another sherry, holds her own up in a toast. "One thing at a time."

"Who'll air my posies when I'm gone?"

A burst of giggling from directly above causes Taylor to drop her glass, panic and grab Rita's hand, cling to it with both of hers. "Not her! Please, not *her*! Don't let *her* touch my posies!"

He stands shaving at her gold trimmed, shell-shaped wash basin. "Fay loves smoothies," giggles Fay to his rippling, well-muscled back. Fay has recently begun to refer to herself in the third person. It's less painful (and more *accurate*). Provides just the distance she needs -- considering what she plans to do, what she's already done, and what she's been through.

Squares, darling, lots of 'em. It's as simple as that. If you'd only open those scary mauve eyes a bit wider.

"Shave it smooth for Fay," she whispers and stretches and sips champagne. "Hurry it up. Fay is impatient. Don't keep Fay waiting. Ritterhouse Fay is a dragon."

Was a dragon, dearie. It was only an experiment and it was very long ago. It was not successful and it's really none of your fucking business.

"I never said it was," pouts Fay.

"What did you say?" says Chauffy turning from the mirror, smiling another libidinous smile as she's not bad to look at if she'd only keep her mouth shut, stop muttering to that *surfeit* of invisible guests (though he wouldn't have put it quite so literately).

"Ritterhouse Fay is full of surprises," says Fay who sings-songs: "Her mummy was mad -- Her daddy was bad -- Her sister was sad -- Uncle Oscar was...was..."

Yes, Fay?

She breaks off. Her eyes darken to deep purple and glisten yellow like a cat's in the dark.

"Chauffy, did you have a mother?"

"Huh?"

"Skip it. God, you're slow."

"I'm known for it."

"Well you'd better strike while the iron is hot. Or the hot iron will flatten you."

"Huh?"

"Skip it. (sip of champagne) Chauffy?"

"Yeah?"

He's still shaving, taking great care over the skin he/she/it or whatever loves to touch.

"What's your mother like, Chauffy?"

"Pretty."

"Like you?"

"Uh-huh, last I seen her."

"When was that?"

"Can't remember."

"Did she love you?"

"Yeah."

"Did she hug and kiss you?"

"Can't remember."

"I can't remember either," replies Fay, "sometimes."

Count your blessings, my sweet, my temporary tart.

Chauffy finishes shaving, wipes the remaining lather from his silken face, rinses the fine gold handled razor -- gift from Fay -- places it in its fine leather case. He takes a gold handled brush from the case, brushes his ringlets, studies himself in the mirror. Likes what he sees. So does Fay. Or she would if she could see that face, that hair, those smooth, muscled buttocks. But our Fay sees nothing. She's gone to sleep, the half-empty champagne glass still tilted in her hand, the mauve satin sheet tangled wet around it.

Chauffy studies himself appreciatively in the full-length mirror, pulls up his designer shorts, pulls them down very suggestively, enjoying the effect (and so say all of us!) pulls them up, pulls on his designer jeans, his designer shirt and jacket -- all gifts from Fay. Careful not to wake her, he sits on the bed, slips on his designer socks and designer shoes. He tiptoes to the elegant gold-tapped basin, grabs his fine leather shaving case, tiptoes to the door, tiptoes out, tiptoes down the stairs, lets himself out as quietly as he can. Fay, even while asleep, could be hearing something, seeing something. He's not sure what. She sees things, hears things. She's said so. He's inclined to believe her. But she gives nice, expensive gifts and pays him well and that suite at the Savoy ain't nothing to be sneezed at.

Nicer than the street, ain't it, pal?

And Fay never asks more in return than he is prepared to give, which is nothing of importance to him. I mean that's all gone, isn't it? Unless one means a warm spurt of he'll-never-miss-it-viscosity now and again.

Anyhow, it's miles better than that gutter. Where she found him. Just after she'd got out from -- where was it she said? She wasn't very clear about that. But she had a little ready cash then and they'd had a good time for a few days though it is all rather hazy. Then she disappeared -- for a long time. Then she got really rich from that rug, found him. Who the fuck cares where she fucking came from?

Good thinking, darling. But what you don't know can hurt you. Though whether the monster will ever turn on *you*, her convenient squeeze, her insignificant other, is up for grabs. My grabs. And I'm grabby. But we'll see, mon petit, we'll see.

Rita is washing her face when the front door closes. Who could it be at this hour? (Quick, maid, to your grist-mill!) She swiftly pats her face dry, slaps on moisture cream giving her sags a visible, if temporary, lift. A car door slams. Still applying fragrant moisture cream, she rushes to the window, pulls the curtain aside just in time to see the Rolls rocket away.

She sighs, drops before her dresser, looks younger. How young? Still not young enough to be Doolittle Desiree in her own production of Her House Burned Down. But younger than she was before Ian stepped out of the scaffolding and back into her life and assured her she's not even ectoplasmic -- that she's totally palpable. He should know -- he's palped her more than once. Rita chuckles, switches on the telly, finds the only channel still on -- she can't afford cable. Perhaps when they make a film from her stories she'll bring in cable and buy a computer -- she's heard about surfing the Internet. But at the moment it's just -- if you'll pardon the expression -- a *crazy* dream (italics, m'dears, as you've already no doubt noticed, are always an *important* part of my day).

Perhaps she could surf to that distant shore where Fay rose, complete, from a colossal clam shell in the swirling waters? Sweet Jesus! Fay again! Hold it down, Rita. A writer's imagination can go *too* far. Besides, metaphorical water douses metaphorical fire, doesn't it? Fay was born in fire, not water. Get back on the track, ducky.

The "F" sticks on Rita's typewriter too. She'll be needing that "F" when she writes about Fay (and I don't mean "F" for "Fay", m'dears!).

But how very lucky Rita's been. Selling part one of her novel. Savour it, Rita. Make it last, love. Fame is flipping fleeting.

She lights a cigarette, sticks it in her holder, finds a book, climbs into bed. You mustn't smoke in bed, Rita. You could burn your bedroom down. One pyromaniac per building is quite enough.

Through the walls, windows, above the wind:

"CHAUFFY! CHAUUUUUUUUUFY!"

Fay's lovely bronze framed window has slammed open on the street and her head thrusts out at the oddest angle. Leaning on her crutch she wails pitifully again:

"CHAUUUUUUUUUUFY!"

Rita who had just begun to doze, bolts upright, her heavily ashed cigarette flying from its holder. Perhaps Fay has prevented Rita being burned alive in her own bed. You'll never know – though *I* do.

"CHAUUUUUUUUUFFY!" cries Fay to the street. Her voice reverberates on that faceless building opposite, doubling, redoubling in a poignant echo.

Rita kneels on the floor snatches up her burning cigarette, sticks it back in its holder.

"CHAUUUUUUUUUFFY!" wails Fay in a tone of unutterable sorrow. Universal sorrow. A no hugs and no kisses, not never no how, sorrow.

Rita attempts to rise from the floor but slumps back against the side of her bed and begins to cry. Fay's plaint is so desolate, so ineffably forlorn, so...

"CHAUUUUUUUUUFFY" wails Fay.

Rita sobs helplessly. A thousand lonely nights bear down upon her. Nights she may never have to experience again. But what if...? Fay's terrible loneliness becomes Rita's very own.

"CHAUUUUUUUUFFY!" wails Fay, "CHAUUUUUUUUFFY!"

Rita sobs her heart out too.

And so should you, my dizzy dears.

For all mankind.

35

"Room service?" mutters Fay sleepily into her tiny telephone, "Room service?"

She abruptly realizes it's morning and she is definitely not at the Savoy, slams down the phone, screams:

"Chauffy! Chauffy!"

She struggles with her great leg, grasps her crutches, lifts herself from the bed and onto square umpteen. "Bastard!" she shrieks, "Bastard, where are you?!"

She pulls on a radiant red silk kimono (Chauffy hid her old chenille one in the closet, m'dears), crams the phone into a pocket and limps from room to room shrieking "Bastard! Bastard! Where are you, bastard?!"

Fay! How you've changed! I feel almost guilty.

"What?" says Fay, "What?!"

You've changed so! Where is your (this is difficult, darlings)... Fay, where is your (titter) purity? Your altruism? Your perfection? Has...errr...*life* been cruel? Why are your tender sensibilities so colossally calloused currently? Have you been...errr...burned? Again? Yet *again*?

But Fay is thirsty and will not be deterred, even by a raft of ceiling-crawling shadowy somethings I've conjured for our mutual delight. She snatches open the door of her giant fridge. It's filled top to bottom with the most expensive gourmet foods and every dairy product imaginable. She was always short on dairy products (gourmet foods too), where she came from, intends never to be so again.

"I'll never be thirsty again!" she screams cinematically and grabs a pint of milk. Balancing on a crutch, she takes a huge swallow, slams the milk on the kitchen counter, slams the fridge shut, limps to a costly white leather chair, hurls herself into it. "Bastard!" she shrieks, "Bastard!"

Don't overdo it, darling.

"What?" says Fay, "What was that?"

She looks about for a moment -- perhaps Chauffy's hidden himself in the closet? Speaks to her from the closet?

Like so many we know, m'dears.

"Chauffy?"

But no, he's not in the closet. So she plucks the phone from her kimono pocket, dials, "Nelly Wilkinson...thank you."

She waits several minutes, lets it ring. Frowning, she rings off, limps to the kitchen again, carefully examines its superb equipment; every electrical kitchen convenience known to technology. She opens the freezer. It, too, is packed with food as requested and she grins happily -- she likes it when her requests are obeyed, not like the old days when she had a number not a name. 1-6-4-5-2! rings in her head compliments of yours truly.

"Shut it, you!" she mutters and finds a package of frozen breakfast rolls, slams them in the electric oven and sets it to its highest level. She bangs open a shimmery, brushed aluminium cupboard door, revealing what might be a sumptuous food display direct from Fortnum and Mason (which, indeed it is, m'dears – delivered just yesterday). From the shelf she yanks a tin of fine coffee and a jar of jam, sets the jam on her hand-painted-Italian-tiled counter and pours some coffee into a glistening Miele coffee maker which is delighted to be, at last, of use. A sudden scratching at her terrace door startles, causes her to spill a bit of the water she adds to her over-ambitious coffee machine which, grateful to be a player in our game, bears this watery inconvenience with a spirit suitable to even the most major of appliances.

Ach! Isn't this good fun?! I often get hung up on kitchen machines – the homemaker in me is a sucker for sales-brochures so bear with me, those among you whom I might humbly address as 'my domestic dears'.

Fay limps to the terrace door, slides it open. Seven-lives-left leaps in, springs to Fay's white leather sofa, curls up, shuts its eyes. Fay shuffles to the cat and drops herself with a great plop on the sofa beside it. She attempts to pet it but the cat hisses and with a lightning swipe scratches Fay's hand. She grimaces, pulls back but she's not angry. No, not Fay. She watches Seven-lives lick its paws and preen. Fay also licks -- the blood from her own hand. "Fay isn't angry," whispers Fay, "Fay understands circumstances beyond our control."

They're unavoidable. That goes for *you* as well, m'dears.

The cat continues to preen.

Preening herself -- a child's pink plastic hairbrush (hers? from another time?) was handy in her pocket -- Fay watches. After a moment Seven-lives crawls into Fay's lap, begins to purr.

A delightful chime beckons from the coffee maker. As gently as possible Fay removes the sleeping Seven-lives from her lap, limps on her crutch to the kitchen. But the cat awakens and follows, winding in and out between Fay's legs.

Fay warms and pours milk into a crystal bowl, opens a jar of caviar, forks it into the bowl. Seven-lives jumps back from the splash then darts in to gobble this gourmet treat while Fay watches affectionately, whispers gently:

"Fay was a hostess. Do you know what a hostess is?"

Fay pours herself a coffee, generously laces it with cream, returns to the cat, says:

"A hostess sells kisses."

Seven-lives finishes the milk and caviar, looks up at Fay, meows. Fay says:

"You don't mind dining with a hostess, do you?"

Oh, my! How desperately poignant. How *satisfying*. My so-called *eyes* are wet! My heart goes out (and down – as I traditionally watch from above) to my misunderstood Fay, my darling prosopopoeia. Ach. Should we be held responsible for what we do? Because isn't what we *do* what we *are*, m'dears? Ask any adjacent ancient Greek. Should we be held responsible for what we *are* then? Shouldn't that blame rest rather higher up in the preternatural pecking order? Brings to mind the murderer who cried: *God* made me do it! -- Or should that be: God made *me*, and I did it?

Pretty pickle, that. I don't relish it.

Leaning as close to the cat as her splinted leg allows Fay whispers "Are you a hostess too?"

Seven-lives brushes lovingly against Fay's ankle, meowing as Fay limps to the white leather sofa. The cat follows, leaps on her lap, purrs raucously until Fay's head jerks back, sniffs. Smoke! She pulls herself up, toppling the cat who hisses and falls. Landing, of course, on its feet.

Fay scrambles on her crutch to the oven, snatches out her smoking breakfast rolls, throws them into the stainless-steel state-of-the-art sink and slams the tap on full. She is met with a terrifying explosion of steaming water.

Oh my!

"Damnation!" screams Fay appropriately as something dreadful twists in her head. A memory of water bombarding her, forcing her against a wall. And flames.

I hover directly above in my mauve smog, seeding variegated horrors into Fay's fertile, burgeoning terror. She screams, tears open a cupboard door and searches frantically, her appetite rising crazily with this dreadful happening. She spots a potted pheasant and savagely pries off the lid, tears out a chunk, jams it into her mouth, chews and sways, grasping a perfectly lovely brushed aluminium drawer-handle for support.

Splashed water spreads and drips from her lovely kimono. Seven-lives cowers in a corner, curious, and of course, cat-hungry itself, watching with its big slit eyes as Fay devours the conveniently boneless pheasant. What excessively black cat could resist boneless, potted pheasant. I'm sure I've never met one and I've met a lotta cats! *All* black as sin. Black is de rigueur, m'dears, out here beyond Pluto.

In her bathroom Fay snatches an initialled towel from a gold-plated rack, squats with great difficulty, her huge, splinted leg thrust out beside the sculptured toilet, proceeds to polish its already high gloss, limed oak, especially-bum-contoured, electrically heated seat. She polishes for a moment, pulls herself up and hitches down her pricey panties and plants herself upon this shining techno-wonder WC. Can she pee her lonely poisons away? She'll try (can't blame a girl for tryin', can we?). She catches a glimpse of herself in the mirrored wall, looks deeply into her mauve eyes searching for that errant soul. The eyes are windows etc, her grandmother said -- yes! It *was* her granny looking suspiciously like Mrs Taylor. Fay peers harder at the mirrored wall -- still sees nothing, begins to cry. Why would Granny lie?! Granny had *promised* that crystal clear optic window into human infinity. Fay cries harder. Sobs! Shrieks! Moans! Wails! Peers! Pees! The house shakes with Fay's unhappiness. Why won't they love her?! Because she is soulless? (Don't be boring, dear) Why did they attempt to have her put down? Who, Fay?! Who attempted that?! Odd laughter rings in her head, unbidden, unwelcome. Unstoppable.

Until I decide to stop it. Which, mercifully, I do. Nobody's all bad, darlings. Not even the devil. Not even me. Or do I, *characteristically,* tell a lie?

Fay slides herself off the toilet bowl -- a feat when you're dragging pounds of splinted brace and a hundred titanium bone-screws. She tilts her head over said bowl, vomits her heart out. Heart? Does Fay have a heart? Of course she has. Or did. Or thinks she has. Someone knows. Someone. Want to guess? Madness. Ach! All is madness. Those interminable squares. They meet at game's end, m'dears! Meet and the game begins again (don't say I didn't warn you).

Just below Fay, in fact, directly below, Mrs Taylor dreams in her chair before her postcard mountain. A few postcards, as usual, lie scattered on the floor beside her. Taylor was in a quandary about her identity this morning. She's not been herself since Fay's mysterious return (who *has*?!). It's fortunate now that Taylor sleeps, cannot hear Fay's hysterical cries from above, though they echo through her cavernous sitting-room like the screeches of a thousand bats -- like the howls of those horrid women swaying at this very moment in her dream. Women Oscar had brought home that fateful, full-mooned night. The one of them, beautiful, angelic but with wilted wings. Her eyes, something about her eyes. And her chin, something about her chin. Women don't have whiskers, do they? Not unless they're *very* old?

That's enough, dear. Dreaming or not, that is *enough.*

Rita is not so lucky. Her concentration at her typewriter disintegrates in Fay's airborne hysteria. Rita gazes longingly at her brandy decanter, has promised Ian she won't touch it. At least not till after five P.M. -- on weekends only. But she's so nervy! could easily put her fist through one of these howling paper walls and a shot of cognac might...But no! Non! Non! Non!

Love has its little sacrifices.

36

Seven-lives, sleek and blacker than the most extremely black natural cat, nibbles contentedly from an open packet of half-thawed, premium scampi, oblivious to the evening traffic from without -- for a moment. Then fussily deserts the scampi and peruses the opened packets, the half-eaten tinned meat and spilt milk and thick butter-smears that besmirch the counters and the floor of Fay's once immaculate, techno-wonderful kitchen.

Besmirch?! -- lovely! Yours truly has been at her panting thesauri, m'dears. But ach! Where on earth has Fay's obsessive tidiness gone? Perhaps it will return? Don't hold yer breath, m'dears.

MEANWHILE: That Dreadful Something in Fay's head has at last subsided and been replaced by another frenzy of gluttony. "Me so hungry! Me so excessively hungry!" she had cried and again flung herself into any adjacent kitchen. Now, exhausted but sated, she lies sleeping, snoring -- how like Taylor -- on her elegant white leather sofa at the edge of yet another not quite revealed square, another life's possibility – how like us all, sleeping through our possibilities, letting our so-called golden chances pass us by. Rise and shine, m'dears, gather ye rosebuds whilst ye may. Before your long day's journey has instantly morphed to darkest, unredeeming, night.

Fay snores amidst a peculiar disorder of odd, continually changing colours reflected from the floor, the ceiling, the walls, glass, plaster and paper -- snores until her doorbell chimes.

Seven-lives, startled from its re-perusal of the packet of half-thawed scampi, flees to hide in Fay's bedroom under that damp but still splendid chinchilla. The doorbell chimes again. Fay stirs, sits up, mumbles:

"Chauffy? Room service?"

Thoughts too numerous and too terrifying to list, flicker and fade.

"Chauffy?" she repeats, "Room service?"

Fay wipes her eyes, attempts to focus through my winking multi-coloured lights. She is not sure just where she most recently was. The kewpie-doll clustered, Wheel of Fortune at a funfair? Ach! One kewpie stands out. It has an oversized plume in its painted hair and Fay still sees the colours, hears the voices and carousel music but they're fading fast.

The doorbell chimes again. At least a cupful of partially eaten cookies and crumbs falls from Fay's lap as she struggles onto her crutch, wobbles to the door, opens it.

"Nelly?!"

A sudden blast of friendly sunset orange, unseen by both women, lights the room.

"May I come in?" asks Nelly shyly, kind eyes downcast.

Fay stands aside. Nelly enters, understands -- bless her -- but is instantly appalled by the dreadful disarray in Fay's semi-open-plan kitchen.

"What do you want?" asks Fay, too hurt to hope.

"It's not what I want, It's what you need!"

Fay eyes narrow.

"And what do we need, pray tell?"

"You poor darling! Is no one looking after you?"

"Nelly-Welly!"

Fay wails, moans, does mental cartwheels (such an excitable creature) as she throws herself into Nelly's outstretched arms, "Oh Nelly-Welly-Nelly-Welly!"

Nelly leads throbbing, sobbing Fay to the sofa, takes her crutch from her and gently sits her down, drops beside her.

"Oh Nelly-Welly!" sobs Fay until Nelly reaches into her own cardigan pocket, hands Fay a small, naked kewpie-doll with a huge, partly crumpled pink plume on its head. Fay's sobs diminish as she contemplates this painted plastic creature. She's seen it before.

One minute ago, ducky, in dreamland!

"What?" asks Fay, still dazed from dream and Dreadful Something, "What did you say?"

"I won her at a funfair when I was sixteen."

Fay recovers, is suspicious. Why has Nelly given her this cheap obviously *old* gewgaw? What does she *really* want? But coached by her better self (nothing to do with *me*, m'dears), Fay says to Nelly, "How sweet. How very sweet."

Fay knows somewhere deep, what most of us refuse, life-long, to admit: that many things must, and do, remain inexplicable -- those who insist on all the answers are fools. Fay dabs one eye then the other and with a suspicious glance at it, tosses the tiny though oddly familiar kewpie to the sofa beside her. Daydreams, m'dears have long been known to abandon suspect and even tangible residue. This particular residue, one faded, shelf-worn kewpie, has now been duly categorized under *inexplicable* (extracurricular reading required, darlings – get to it).

I am almost ashamed to admit that Fay's icy acceptance of kind Nelly's heartfelt gift is my doing. We've simply got to get this show on the road. No time for gushing. Or even extracurricular reading (aren't I *fickle*?!).

"What?" says Fay, "Did you say something, Nelly?"

"No, darling."

Poor Fay's earlier rejection by the inhabitants of Number 13 lurches through her head like a poisoned rat. But in view of Nelly's obvious good will she again dismisses it. Vengeance, for the moment, will float safely harboured but *accessible* somewhere in her quagmire of half-remembered horrors. But total forgiveness? Darlings, I won't let Fay near it!

Perhaps I have given the poor cow too much baggage?

"Oh Nelly-Welly! It's awwwwful to be rich!"

A plaint that often echoes, most inaccurately, amongst the superbly well-heeled (who never pay taxes!).

Then, her voice increasingly shrill: "Decent people desert one in droves. That awful carpet is a curse!"

"That's what Mrs Taylor said," offers Nelly.

"What?!" cries Fay, her bottom bouncing more than three inches above the sofa.

"Or something like that," says Nelly who, though she cares deeply, can never remember precisely what people have said. "But maybe she didn't," Nelly continues, "I might have got it wrong. I'm always getting things wrong."

You can say that again, sugar.

Nelly takes Fay's hand. "I'll take tomorrow off. We'll put your house in order if it's the last thing we do."

It might well be.

"My poor, poor, little Fay."

Fay is delighted. Carefully avoiding Nelly's ample breasts, drops her head into Nelly's lap and pushes that first suspicion of Nelly into a far corner directly beside the pulsing remnant of the Dreadful Something on the poop deck of that tenuously harboured ship of vengeance. That I, m'dears, shall launch again at will. Though not *nearly* so ostentatiously as Helen.

Acutely observed? -- but back to Fay who, even as I puff stuff metaphorical, allows Nelly to stroke her hair.

Stroking, Nelly looks about at the hideous disorder of this richly appointed, absolutely wonderful but curiously soulless apartment. Nelly has a feel for such things though she wouldn't have described this chaotically disordered apartment as *soulless* Possibly: untidy. Or even, *dishevel*. Nelly loves that word (she hasn't many) – applies it inappropriately everywhere. It was I who dropped it into her ear that morning a couple months ago on the Red Arrow when she instantly materialized for Bill.

Are you putting two and two together, m'dears? Be my guest.

Nelly notes Rita's kettle enthroned in a prominent position in the kitchen – perhaps it is that peculiar hidden spotlight of mauve glinting off its perfectly polished though dented surface? Nelly sees Bill's comfortable (though down-market!) chair, incongruous in this rich setting. She sees Hugh's little drop-leaf table, likewise, and, just beside what might be a bedroom door, she sees her own favourite, pressed-not-carved-wood chest of drawers and her handmade teapot upon it. But of course, Mrs Taylor's rug has long ago departed to the Middle-East and a new life. As I warned, that fantastical rug's departure was to Fay's cost. Though neither woman knows this. Yet. I, much amused, dote on the personal turmoil said departure is likely to occasion as I crave excitement. It is so dark out here. And not yet the holidays.

Nelly, with my prompting, oddly hopes this techno-marvel though *dishevel* flat won't also be gutted.

Don't get your hopes up, darling. We've promises to keep, and miles to go before we sleep.

"Leave her alone," whispers Fay, "For God's sake, leave her alone!"

"What, darling?" says Nelly.

Fay says, "Nothing, love," as the floor, witnessed only by Fay, splits in two, revealing old Mrs Taylor at her evening ablutions. Then, as suddenly, reconstitutes itself with a scraping, longing moan.

If only the special school Bill's son is enrolled in could afford such fabulous equipment, thinks Nelly longingly, her eyes wandering over that electric heaven in the kitchen. Gosh! Is this why I came, to beg for Bill's son -- because Fay has such phenomenal means?

Put it out of your head, Nelly. You are not a calculating person. You're here to help Fay. Tomorrow you'll give this neglected wonderland a thorough going-over. You'll help poor one-legged Fay back on her two or know the reason why.

But oh, Nelly. If only you did know the reason why. If only you could avoid your Fate. If only Fay could avoid hers. Forget it, love. Can't be helped. Not when it's preordained -- though you, Nelly, are only an accessory long after the fact.

Unfortunately, m'dears, the cards are all in my hand. And, in a mustily, musical mood I sing: Sometimes I'm orange, sometimes I'm blue. My disposition depends on you.

37

The next day has dawned and proceeded into late morning as the automatic dish washer starts for the umpteenth time with a deep roar. Nelly leaps back. "These things frighten me to death!" she squeals. At last finished in the now spotless kitchen, she enters the now spotless living room where Fay reclines, slowly crunching down the last of Nelly's completely competent home-baked, you guessed it, *cookies,* and lazily petting Seven-lives who purrs in her lap (I can't over-animate this cat-fondling creature the whole time, darlings. It's tiring).

"Would you like a liqueur?" asks Fay, dreamily -- rudely ignoring me.

"Love one."

"The bar," says Fay with a languid flourish towards a large wall mirror. She aims a remote-device at that mirror and with a jarring buzz it slides aside revealing a fully stocked bar, mini-fridge, mini-sink, and ice-maker.

"Gosh!" gasps Nelly. She presses a button on the ice-maker and several ice cubes spew to the floor. Delighted, she kneels, picks them up, drops them in the shining, stainless-steel mini-sink and stands for a moment, eyes misting. "Fay, I am so happy for you. You had nothing. Now you've got everything."

"Not yet."

Some people!

"Hush!" says Fay, "Where's my Drambuie, Nelly dear? I'm a Drambuie girl!"

Fay is exulting again. Perhaps love and happiness are within reach? Through helping others? No secret, really. She has always known that the key to happiness is benevolence which consists (besides gift-lists) of, for one thing, abundant personal grooming services. She watches Nelly, thinks: I can and will do wonders for her (like *last* time, Fay?) because a friend indeed is a friend in need.

I remade *you,* Fay. But look what I got.

"Are you mumbling at me, Nelly?" asks Fay, hopefully.

"No, darling, not me," laughs Nelly and pours them each a Drambuie, sets the dainty-handled little crystal glasses on the low marble table and drops beside Fay.

"Isn't life funny, Fay? Here we are, you and me. We've known each other for only two months..."

"Seven weeks and six days," corrects Fay with the smile of a true friend.

"...and look what's happened between!"

Fay sips, looks intently at Nelly, "What *has* happened between?"

"Well, you know."

"I know what's happened to me," replies Fay, a perfect blank, "What has happened to *you*?"

"It's a secret but I'll tell you because it's all your fault!"

Fay is momentarily miffed -- hates to be accused of things. Even by a friend, a friend on her gift and/or wish-list. Particularly when she's doesn't know what these accusations are. It's like the old days all over again. Fay got the blame for *everything*. Then they hosed her down. Ach! The Dreadful Something reawakens in her head! "What, precisely," she asks, "is *my* fault?!"

"That wasn't the right word," replies good Nelly, kind Nelly (who'll never have a way with words) as she sweetly anticipates Fay's loving approval when she tells Fay her wonderful secret. "I meant that you are responsible for it."

"For what?"

Get on with it, woman, for God's sake!

"For Bill and me."

Fay drains her glass, "May I have another Drambuie?"

Nelly rises happily, grabs the kewpie doll from the sofa, goes to the bar, kisses the kewpie and places it on a glass shelf there. "She'll be happy and safe in here."

Good Nelly is overflowing with happiness she'll soon share with Fay.

Tread carefully, love.

"Bring the bottle," says Fay, "You and Bill *what*?"

Fay is beginning to hurt and it's not a pain she's familiar with. Should be, but ain't. I'll take all the blame here, m'dears.
She presses a button on her remote and closes the bar with a buzz and a thump, nearly mutilating Nelly's hand in the swiftly sliding mirrored door.

"Bill and I are engaged!"

"Set the bottle here by me (without skipping a beat) this was awfully sudden, wasn't it?"

"More sudden than you think. Bill proposed to me the day after you left."

"Did he then?"

"Yes. It was like being struck by lightning!"

Would that you were, dear Nelly, and numbed to the pain to come.

"I can't you tell you how happy I am," answers Fay.

She can't, m'dears, because she ain't.

Nelly is alight with joy. "He has a son."

Nelly and Fay gaze at one another, Nelly in rapture, Fay, expressionless, compliments of me (though I must admit it's been a struggle to keep Fay's pesky better nature in harness).

But at the moment, even I don't know what Fay is thinking. Odd, that.

"What I must tell you, Nelly," says Fay, idly stroking the purring cat's ebony head, "may come as a shock."

Nelly's rapture shifts. Her delight falters under the four unblinking eyes of Fay and her inscrutable purring pet.

"He has another in the oven," whispers Fay.

"Another what?" asks Nelly, "*Who* has another *what*?"

"Bill!" bleats Fay, "He has another in the oven!"

Nelly can't quite take this in, thinks desperately: Bill has what in an oven? A ham? A turkey? Then suddenly: A baby!

"Whose oven?" whispers Nelly, faltering. She's certain she'll suffocate.

"My oven" replies Fay, "My very own high-tech oven."

Is Fay being naughty on her own? Is she actually preggers? This is news to me!

Nelly crumples, her eyes dart first to Fay's glorious, triple-oven kitchen then with horror to Fay's midriff.

Fay pounds at said midriff which now seems somewhat larger than it appeared only a minute ago. The cat leaps, hissing, off her lap into the air, disappears with a tearing rip of claw to carpet.

"I came back to this house of bitter memories so that my incipient child can be near its daddy. Brute that he is," moans Fay, still mired in her/our early reading of Large-Print Gothic Romances -- the only books available in that long ago, strapped for funds, prison library, she'd tell you.

But *I* think not!

Fay contorts her brow, her mouth turns tragically down, "I want my child to be near Bill. Fay believes that's important. Don't you?"

Nelly wants to vomit. She jumps up but Fay grabs her hand.

"Please! Please, Nelly-Welly! Stay! Stay!"

Nelly swallows her nausea, allows herself to be pulled back to the sofa.

"You are all I have in the world," moans Fay, "Besides Bill's baby."

And your bank account, you silly boots!

Nelly's eyes flood, looking away from Fay, looking anywhere but at Fay.

"It was just one of those things. Just one of those crazy things," drones Fay, skimming the edge of a once popular song that Granny Taylor held dear, "Circumstances beyond our control. I didn't want it to happen. You remember, don't you, Nelly? The night it happened? You must remember. But I lied to you, I *did* capitulate. Said I didn't but I did. Say you remember."

Now it is time for Fay to cry. She does so admirably, in great, miserable gusts -- practice has made perfect. She's not feigning. It's the truth as she perceives it -- as *we* perceive it.

I really can't verify or deny this pregnancy, my darlings, I was relieving myself whilst said alleged outrage was or was not perpetrated.

"He forced me," says Fay, "I wasn't myself. I was a tiny fish out of water. My house burned down. My father perished with my little black kitty. My sister was murdered. My mother was institutionalized. I hadn't got even a teakettle when I came here to that shoebox of a room. I was destitute. You were kind. I have never met anybody so kind as you, Nelly, dear."

Fay slips halfway from sofa to floor, her great encumbered leg thrust out stiff before her, one hand, for support, deep in the lustrous pile of her stark white, 100 percent virgin wool, wall-to-wall carpet.

"I was thinking of you, Nelly. I swear it. I was thinking of my betrayal of you when Bill tore my clothes from my frail frame and ravished me."

Fay seems to melt before Nelly's eyes, becomes a sobbing mass, a blur of tears. The Something Dreadful swims in the air round Fay's bobbing, sobbing head then darts from Fay into Nelly, fills her, deadens her pain, soothes her doubts. And those doubts, my dears, ach! Those doubts were Nelly's last defence.

Fay wails, attempts to pour another liqueur but is capsized by the weight of her leg. She screams in pain, her little crystal glass shatters on the marble table and an unwitnessed hefty crack appears from nowhere in the door of her multi-digitalized triple-glazed wine cupboard.

Good Nelly, wipes her tears away, re-fills her own glass, holds it to Fay's lips. But Fay pushes the glass aside, lifts herself from the floor and falls backward on the sofa. Her sobs are dire, dreadful! She screams, kicks over a vase.

Kind Nelly embraces her, honest Nelly sobs with her, finally manages to speak. "I didn't believe you the first time, Fay," says this beset, honest -- let's face it – *gullible* Nelly, "I believe you now."

That Something Dreadful twists in Nelly's head too, continues to comfort, where no comfort ought to be. Something obscene, has settled in, resides in Nelly now, at least for the *duration*.

"Nelly, darling? Are you in there?"

It is Bill, through Fay's door.

"Nelly? I got your note, love. Are you in there?"

Fay regards Nelly expectantly. Nelly looks away. The black cat in the white leather chair licks its chops, preens its translucent whiskers with both black paws.

"Nelly?" says Bill, "Darling?"

But Nelly is silent. The black cat purrs and although cats can't (or don't often), smiles.

38

Ritterhouse, Fay invites you to a sumptuous party/feast at her new flat Friday evening, punctually at seven. Please come, even if it's only out of curiosity. A valuable prize will be awarded to a lucky winner.
Kissy-kiss-kiss, and hugs galore,
Ritterhouse, Fay (Number 16452)

The engraved type pulsates, glows faintly. Rita, an ostensibly observant author who should miss *nothing*, notes it not. Who, even actresses-cum-authors-of-fervent-novels, could possibly be aware of such *subtly* pulsating type on an engraved stiffy?

Ach, yes, my dears, I know precisely what a *stiffy* is. It is not for naught that I myself have naughtily flitted betwixt the dreaming spires of Oxford. Tripped merrily (but unbeknownst) on my so-called *feet* from lavish sherry soiree to lavish sherry soiree. I well know the transforming joy of a finely de-crusted, petite cucumber sandwich. But I grow faint at the thought of past frivolities. So back to business:

"Wouldn't miss it for the world, darling!" says unobservant Rita to that subtly pulsating, though highly persuasive, engraved card (*stiffy*, m'dears!) in her hand (And, darlings, I'll vouch for it. As a stiffy in the hand is worth two in the bush).

Jolly thoughts of endless grist-filled sequels prance through Rita-writer's head as she stoops to gather from the floor under the mail chute the four other identical envelopes addressed to Nelly, Bill, Jenny and Hugh, and Mrs Taylor. She drops them on the post table where they continue, inside their unopened envelopes, to swell and exhale in unison. My, how one does get caught up in magical trivia. But, m'dears, never forget that the devil *is* in the details (It bears repeating!).

And that's where I come in. Darlings, you might recall my Cassandra-like admonitions re: The auctioning of that famous fragmented rug -- my sincere, yet crucial, advice that was heartlessly flung right back in my so-called *face*? I do not suffer humiliation meekly. I am constrained to exact a small measure – considering the colossal scope of my powers – an *excessively* small measure of semi-savage revenge.

One must be a thorough housekeeper, so to speak. One must tidy up, often mercilessly, after the reckless behaviour of our ersatz subordinates. Repaint their squares. If you will, always mindful of the *task*.

Have you never, due to simple obtuseness or drink or extreme sexual depravity, made a complete fool of yourself? Ach! And suffered profoundly for it? Of course you have. Who hasn't? A common failing, I fear. So now, with my pernicious prodding, my darling prosopopoeia, Fay, will again become preposterous poseur, duped dunce, bizarre butt of her own undisciplined behaviour. There is, after all, some justice (however rough) upon this, our deeply insignificant, cerulean sphere. Alors et au secours! I am hopelessly adrift in my own luscious, gloriously incorrect lingua-franca loquaciousness.

However, be warned. The following fiasco serves only to fortify me, does nothing I fear (other than further establish Fay's nearly infinite unpopularity with her peers, with the exception of Nelly), ...nothing to steer forth our seamy saga. Think of the following as a divertissment, a dipsy-doodle detour, a gross but glossy gloat!

Which you question, m'dears, at your peril.

Oh dear, oh dear, where will it all end?

Well that's the flamin' point of it. Ain't it?

39

So, m'dears, Party-Friday inevitably arrives via a plethora of anxious squares (that I simply cannot be bothered to describe – suffice it to say that one follows another as minutes fill the hours, and be done with it).

Nelly says "But what if he *does* come?"

Dear, constant Nelly is setting dish after dish of catered delicacies from a shiny metal delivery crate to a long, beautifully decorated table, "What if he *does* come?"

"Come?! Of course he'll come!" cries Fay through the bathroom door from atop her electrically warmed toilet seat, "There's a valuable prize, isn't there?"

Really, dear hearts, what could be more unbecoming, more humiliating, than holding forth perched upon a (no matter *how* high-tech) WC? My revenge is sweet.

"Be a darling, Nelly," says Fay, "and put out more wine. I seem to have drunk it all. I'll be out in two shakes!"

Fay turns up the thermostat on her toilet seat, shifts her shapely buttocks, toasts for a moment as she chants "Party-time-party-time-party-time!"

The good, loyal, but thoroughly morose Nelly, acutely enchanted, continues to set dish after dish on that long, lively (and most cooperative) table until Fay shouts:

"If you can live without him for two weeks you can live without him forever!"

Fay has no idea how long forever can be, she's a newly hatched chick (do I reveal too much?) But ask Nelly how *longing* can extend a day.

"Ask Nelly what?" whispers inattentive Fay towards a slim though pleasantly muscular, fleeting shadow that may as well be me. But ain't.

"*Well*?" she asks, patting herself dry in the meantime.

Pat-pat-pat, m'dears, *never* rub!

"Ask Nelly *what*?" repeats Fay.

But, honestly, I haven't time for these tawdry toilet tales. So I dismiss Fay with a snap of my beautifully manicured...whatever they are. Ach! I am alive with deadly darts which eager for vengeance linger quivering in my so-called *quiver*.

Fay, of course, due to my merciless machinations, can't at the moment carry a sustained thought in a wheelbarrow. She puckers before her shell-shaped basin's mirror, applying with Nelly's long ago pilfered lipstick yet another gleaming, scarlet layer. Honestly, this woman who could afford the whole make-up department of a major film studio is a riddle. But at least she has at last abandoned that damnable dooble-vey-see.

Through the bathroom door: "I have done many things in my short life, Nelly, but only once have I cast my pearls before a barbarous brute. It happened in this house, perhaps on this very spot. You well know the night I am referring to."

"But Bill rings me!" cries forlorn Nelly, "Oh, I won't speak to him. But he rings me."

"Of course he rings you! But don't let him ring you little-band-of-gold-wise!"

Too much daytime television, poopsie.

Fay plays the doting sister to Nelly. She will shield her, gift her, coif her, transform her -- world without end, amen. Fay *will* have Nelly's love. She requires it, in any case, for the next few squares.

"Fay, you said you led him on. You did say you'd led Bill on."

"Nelly-Welly! If being attractive is 'leading men on' then we are all in peril 24/7! Consider your narrow escape and rejoice."

"But I don't want him to come. What shall I do if he comes?"

"Ignore him. After the prize-drawing he'll go away. I know men. When they get what they want they disappear like a spray deodorant."

Fay and Maman speak from experience.

"I'll leave before he comes. I'll leave now!" cries Nelly, "Your chauffeur will be here, he can help you."

"Can he?" sighs Fay, "*Can* he?"

Chauffy has deserted her more than once. But there is something magical about his allure. So she continues to supply him with his needful. Which apparently includes masses of bespoke clothing and numerous illicit chemicals obtained through dark connections in darker alleys.

"Fay, I'm frightened," says Nelly.

"Pish-tush" (where *does* she get these nineteenth century phrases?!) sings Fay whose posterior warmed, bolshy bladder docile, is before the mirror again, folding a tiny bit of tissue, placing it under her upper lip, constructing a suitable pout. Did glorious Gloria Grahame actually construct tissue-props under her upper lip for effect? Yet another urbanesque legend? You'll have to ask her yourselves, darlings. But it might prove difficult (for anyone but me). As that splendid, Oscar-winning actress, Gloria, is ever so deceased. I remember her well (I was in one of my primes), as she entertained the troops at Camp Roberts, California in 1945, bare a month before Hiroshima. She, starlet that she was then, was admirably turned out in a horizontally red-striped, long-sleeved jersey blouse, a tight, to-the-thigh-slitted, red satin skirt, black fishnet stockings and heels that could dislocate the libido of any man within a hundred yards! But forget it, m'dears. Feathery youth, for me, has long ago moulted. Ach! Life -- a little bit o' this, a little bit o' that. A bit more o' *that*...a whole lot more o' *that*...I could go on but I won't as I'm all choked up. Feigning emotion is far more difficult than experiencing the so-called *real thing*.

Nelly fills her wine glass, charily accepts the inevitable – will he come? She sits and attempts to stroke the black cat but it hisses, jumps away and hides itself beneath a chair. Fortunately the glass wall to the terrace is closed or flighty Seven-lives might well have leapt out, catapulted into the ether, directly become diminished by one.

Meanwhile, back at her lips, Fay's pout is at last suitable and a peculiar happiness dances beneath her superbly coiffed hair (I take a bow); wondrous hair that occasionally whips out to catch a fly on her pillow as she sleeps. I must see to that when I have a min. Ach! I'm a happy camper, pitching me tent in alien climes. For the *duration*.

Fay exits her en suite bathroom, dons her party dress and waltzes from her bedroom to pose prettily before an amazed Nelly.

"My God, love!" cries the immediately above two wines along, when she takes in Fay's exceptionally pregnant silhouette amidst her ribboned and tasselled, empire smock, "What happened?"

"I gwew," lisps Fay.

"You're retaining water, love," says truly concerned Nelly, "You must see a doctor."

An hour later in the kitchen, drooping Nelly stirs an enormous pot of Swedish meatballs as Hugh adds Creme de Menthe to the frosty perimeter of a giant Italian ice cream bombe and bulging Fay models her ribbony smock for Rita and Jenny. She twirls, bows deeply, straightens up. Then, arching her back and severely accentuating her preposterously parturient abdomen, she turns on her heel, says "Hugh and Nelly need me in the kitchen."

Fay disappears unseen into the kitchen pantry to eavesdrop. She hears a champagne cork pop and good Nelly, bless her, speaks. "She's been lovely to me since Bill and I..."

"She's... an odd woman," replies Hugh, not quite sure it's drink that causes the shelf to shift in his favour (compliments of the house) as he reaches for more champagne glasses.

Nelly takes a jar of premium pickled artichoke hearts from Fay's fabulous fridge, continues. "She's been terribly hurt and she's, well, she's...different."

"You can say that again," says Hugh.

"Her house burned down, Hugh. That's well…" says Nelly reaching for the word, "well…"

Nelly, a well is a hole in the ground! Damn it! Get on with it, girlfriend!

"Fay's …injured."

Fay hovers, listening in the pantry. Her eyes *well* up, tears tumble over her beautifully constructed, Gloria-Grahame-pouting upper lip.

"Her soul is...injured," adds Nelly.

Fay listens. Wipes her eyes, listens.

"Poor Fay is..." Nelly pauses. "Poor Fay is...terribly... scarred."

"Yes, oh yes!" stage-whispers unseen Fay from the pantry. "Scarred like the dickens. And sooty to boot."

"What?" asks Nelly, "What did you say?"

"Nothing," says Hugh.

Hugh is perplexed, pops open another champagne and marches it into the living room. Nelly follows with the giant Creme de Menthe ice cream bombe.

Fay's eyes are fountains. Her crystalline tears shoot out, threatening to short-circuit every electric appliance in her wondrous kitchen.

"We can delay the prize drawing no longer," says Fay skipping from pantry to living room. "We are, however, missing two human beings."

"Three," says Rita.

"Three?" asks Fay, "I count only Billy Hope-Jones and the venerable Mrs Taylor."

"Mrs Taylor isn't coming," says Hugh, "She's not feeling well."

"How sad. The poor dear cannot be long for this world," says Fay presciently.

And we should know.

"What was that?" says Fay and jerks her eyes vainly from floor to ceiling for a fleeting glimpse of mysterious me.

"Ian," says Rita, "Ian hasn't come."

"Ian? I invited no *Ian*."

"Your building supervisor and my... beau. I invited him."

"Your beau! Of course! But I'm afraid I have only enough prize tickets for..."

"Ian was never mad for prizes," replies Rita thrusting her empty glass at Hugh."

"I can see *that*, love," says Fay, with a piercing glance at Rita's waistline, "Still. Most men are."

"Are they? Well *you*, darling, would certainly know what most men want," replies Rita as her glass is topped, "What do you think, Hugh?"

"Crikey," says Hugh, as fretful fitted carpet rustles persuasively, unbeknownst beneath his fashionable American penny-loafers, "I've never been one to turn down a prize."

"Thanks heaps," says Rita splashing her champagne and wondering why Ian has not yet arrived.

The doorbell chimes melodiously and Fay glows, knows precisely who's out there. She grabs two champagnes and scurries to the door which, a champagne in each hand, she manages to open with a dexterity quite unknown to me and my so-called *fingers*.

She thrusts a glass into this handsome, middle-aged gentleman's hand, says ingenuously: "Who are you?"

"A friend of Rita's. Sorry I'm late."

"Ah! Ian! Welcome Mr Ian! I own this house!"

Fay, what an odd greeting, even for you.

"Yes, I am the owner," says Fay, "for my sins."

For *all* our sins, ducky. Have you cottoned on to *this* yet, m'dears?

"So we've heard," says Ian.

"I've extensive plans for this structure. I intend to restore it, the whole house."

"Indeed?"

"Indeed. Restore it and alter it substantially."
Over her shoulder, "Hughie! Hughie! More champagne for Mr Ian!"

Ian says "Thanks," drains his glass, accepts another from Hugh, and with a fearful glance at inscrutable Fay, feels he has gained instant insight into Rita's fascination with her Mr Courvoisier. It wouldn't be the first time, Ian. Don't play innocent with me. I'm well aware of your imbibical history.

Fay grins maniacally as her eyes wander to Ian's flies which she, sipping and mentally unzipping, contemplates for an emotive moment till her lewd assessment flicks from his flies to his eyes and she earnestly declares:

"I am prepared to rehouse all the present tenants as required by law. I have a certain renovated castle in mind."

Affirmed, m'dears! I know precisely where it is as I arranged the estate agent. I'm really rather excited about it! It could greatly simplify her/our task and smooth the way to...(I *must* calm down)!

"Rehouse everyone?" replies Ian, "That could be difficult."

"Really? I can afford *anything* now."

Fay's imagination is aflame with plans for her Number 13 friends. That renovated petite palace just up river. With its five ultra-luxurious apartments, extensive gardens, a swimming pool complex, a private cinema, individual saunas for all and a daily dinghy to deepest Londinium. She's also more than willing to set up a mini-branch of Fortnum and Mason in the stadium-size ballroom.

Talk about gift-lists, m'dears! Mark this well. It is yet another attempt to curry favour that, hope against hope – against all my odds -- will metamorphose into that superb bi-product, the biggest of apples: True love itself! So simple but at this square on our board of life, inexplicable to but a very few. Including, of course, me. Perhaps you?

"But," replies Ian, bringing down like a hovel of cards, Fay's castle on the Thames "You would require their cooperation."

"Would I?" Instant new tack: "I am prepared to buy out their leases at great profit to them."

"But are they prepared to sell?"

If you'd only persevered Fay. If you'd only listened to Mummy – clung to your carpet, shied away from Sotheby's! You would have been capable of anything. Could have buggered them all!

Hugh reaches around Fay, thrusts a champagne at Ian who accepts it and attempts to move towards Rita but is again blocked by Fay who grins and does a radical tango-turn accentuating her now absurdly large abdomen.

Honestly, how ridiculous can one get?

Then to all: "Has anyone seen my chauffeur? He was meant to tend our bar this evening."

Fay puffs out her tummy and exclaims, arms akimbo, "Chauffy! Chauffy! Wherefore art thou, Chauffy?!"

Honestly, Fay! This is embarrassing! I've conjured witless parties before but this one commences to tax. For God's sake, step into the next square, you're chasing our own tail!

Fay sticks her arm in Ian's and, breathily, lips hard by his ear:

"Come, Mr Ian. Partake of my largesse."

My God, how she means it! I'm a bit dizzy, m'dears. The drink -- my Achilles so-called *heel*.

"Belt up," mutters Fay, causing my -- how do they put that these days? Ach! Causing my *gorge* to rise.

Under Rita's watchful eye, Fay leads Ian to the food-laden table. But Rita steps in, claims Ian with a suitably dramatic big sloppy kiss while Nelly nervously sips one too many bubblies. What an odd affect we have on people.

Fay noisily gulps down a bacon-wrapped chicken liver, holds up her dripping, over-laden plate and announces:

"Sorry to be such a greedy-guts but I am eating for two! Aren't I, Nelly?"

Poor Nelly, whose thoughts swim fretfully at the bottom of her champagne glass, says "What, love?"

"I said, Nelly," says Fay, sweetly (and innocently – I *promise*) intoning each hurtful word, "I said I am eating for two."

"Oh. Yes. Yes," whispers poor, good, sad, bewitched Nelly.

"However," continues Fay, "Papá is not here. Though he was expected. I'm expecting and he's expected!"

Fay's laugh again tinkles through silence. Nelly rushes to the kitchen, Rita follows. Fay, her plate piled ever higher, intercepts Ian who is about to follow Nelly and Rita.

"Congratulations!" she cries.

Ian regards her uncomprehendingly.

"Congratulations! You've done a miraculous, positively magical, job!" Fay blocks Ian's exit to the kitchen, tilts back her head and drops a giant prawn (Seven-lives couldn't eat them *all*) down her throat, swallows without chewing, says "Congratulations on my flat, silly! You've done a miraculous job on my flat."

"We were simply carrying out orders."

"You have performed above and beyond the call of duty."

"I am happy you're satisfied."

"I am never satisfied. Grateful. But never satisfied." (And so terribly changed, she thinks, deep, *deep* inside, so terribly, terribly changed -- oh, dear, oh dear! My tongue is not my own! Why?)

Ian is silent. What can he say? Particularly as Fay is eyeing his groin and announcing:

"I have a large project in mind."

Sorry. My fault, m'dears. Couldn't pass it up. Hugh knows how I feel.

Ian manages:

"Oh? A large project?"

"It could be very profitable for those involved. I would love to discuss it with you."

Fay! Get on with it! Would that I had never arranged this party! We'll run out of squares! Another fiasco, and repetitious to boot! Am *I* not hurt by this as well?! Ach! But, in my defence: Life (like literature) has its petite longueurs.

"Discuss away," says Ian.

"My goodness!" cries Fay, "We're becoming much too serious (a kittenish moue here). It's time for the prize drawing. Hughie! Jenny! Where *are* you, Nelly?! Riiiiiiiittttta!"

Fay, her finger at her lip, looks on as red-eyed Nelly with reeling Rita comforting her and glaring at Fay, weave solemnly back from the kitchen (Let's face it, m'dears, Rita's only there for the booze and the grist).

Fay claps her hands.

"Everybody ready?"

Nonchalant nods (and shivers) all around. Fay, now a frisky border collie, harries her reluctant guests into a small circle then somehow emerges at its centre, her overfilled, ribboned smock alight with mauve and cerulean, and aflutter in a mysterious breeze.

"I am dreadfully sorry that everyone has not attended our little get-together. I do hope you will tell Billy and Granny Taylor what a lovely time they've missed. I'm speaking for myself, of course. I have so enjoyed being with you all again."

Fay, under the pretence of wiping away a tear, covertly flips the latest disintegrating pout tissue which is seriously hindering her oration, out from under her upper lip and into her hanky and, poutless, plunges on.

"I would like also to express my joy -- for there is no other word for it -- at being back amongst friends again and, as you will note..."

Up comes her recently de-splinted leg in a kick a Radio City Rockette would kill for.

"A lot has happened since..."

"A lot," says Rita.

"Some things for the better..."

"And what might *they* be?" asks Rita.

Fay simply does not hear Rita but gleams happily, for a real tear has finally appeared, welled and slid sideways over our tiny mouth-mole. We've a surfeit of moisture beyond Pluto, m'dears, oceans of tears unwept. Frozen, of course, in far circling comets and somewhat difficult – upon occasion -- to access.

Fay carefully wipes said echte tear away and gestures expansively at her lovely apartment, "...yes, some things for the better and some things..." she pats her protruding belly, "...well, we shall have to see about *this* little thing, shall we not?"

Her tinkling laugh flies unreciprocated, bouncing from rapidly multi-colouring walls that -- and I really must look into this -- that no one seems *ever* to notice. Has the escape of that rug diminished *my* power too? Don't ask unless you'd like a knuckle sandwich.

"In any case," continues Fay (and so do I), "Ritterhouse Fay welcomes you to her new home."

Bravo, darling! As I must support this poor creature occasionally for my own sake, to this end I call forth a few more mauve and indigo shades that proceed vainly to dance an entertaining jig on the ceiling and walls. My conjured colours collide unnoticed by everyone but Fay, who wisely decides not to acknowledge them and draws herself up and proclaims, "Now! To the drawing! Nelly?!"

Faithful Nelly fetches a box from the kitchen.

"In this box," whispers Fay conspiritorially, "are tickets with numbers from one to five corresponding to your flat numbers. I shall now draw!"

Fay draws a slip of paper from the box and reads.

"Number one! That's you, Rita!"

Fay thrusts the ticket at Rita and claps her hands.

"So it is," says Rita, not caught up in Fay's -- what appears to be -- honest enthusiasm.

Indeed it is. Honestly. But you know *me*…

"Applause, people!" shouts Fay, "You're a lucky girl, Rita!"

A desultory round of applause as Fay clomps, exaggerating her delicate condition, to a closet, fetches a beautifully wrapped package, returns, offers it to Rita who makes no move to accept it.

"Open it! Please!" cries Fay, clapping her hands again. "See what you've won!"

Rita hesitantly accepts the package, tears off the wrapping. Page after page of the (dare we say, controversial?) magazine story, "Her House burned Down" float to the floor as she approaches the object in question. "Up to her old tricks," mutters Rita.

My old tricks, *old* love!

Suddenly, here is Rita's now gleaming kettle which Rita holds up for all to see, and proclaims, "Always nice to meet an old pal."

"It was a horror to clean," says Fay with a grimace, still wondering how this bleeding kettle, instead of the diamond bracelet, got into that elaborately wrapped package (tee-hee), "It was filthy!"

"But you've done an excellent job. Did you lick it clean?"

"Whatever do you mean?"

"I mean did you lick it clean with your cat's tongue? Between bites of something or *somebody* else?"

Fay is aghast. Where was that wonderful diamond bracelet she had… She is stunned. She could just sit right down and cry, "Rita! What are you saying?!"

"That you eat and poop people!"

"Rita!" cries Nelly, rushing to Fay's side.

"I was raped," mutters Fay, "My house burned down. Isn't that enough for you? All of you? Isn't it enough?"

It really should be, my dears, but *some people*...in any case, think on it – let us, as Lot should surely have done, pray for the very *last* good man! Not to mention Lot's most impractical wife! – but *I* showed her, didn't I? Pardon me, m'dears – delusions of grandeur. I occasionally go off half-cocked (no pun intended, but *do* pay attention).

Rita makes for the door, Ian follows. Fay turns to Hugh and Jenny, "Just because Rita can type doesn't make her invincible! The Press lies! I was raped!"

"Get stuffed!" shouts Rita and slams the door behind herself and Ian.

"I *was* stuffed!" screams Fay most undiplomatically, "Me! Against my will! Shagged right here! On the bleedin' floor!"

She stabs a carmen red finger at the newly quivering, guilty and frightened, floor.

"Raped by the brutal Bill! Raped and ravished and I haven't brought charges!"

"Well, bugger you!" mutters Jenny.

Ach! Fay's disciplinary humiliation proceeds apace!

"Fay's trying! Can't you see, she's trying?!" sobs Nelly who rushes from the flat immediately followed by Hugh and Jenny.

For myself, I sigh, slump only semi-satisfied against a handy reverberating wall and peruse my column of slowly circling squares wondering what was the point of all this. Surely there must be a reason other than some cliché retribution? But, of course, ours is not to reason why.

Fay drops to her fine white leather sofa and glares at the door through which her *friends* have made their precipitous departures. "Friends?" she says, "These idiots aren't my friends! Who said *friends*?"

So sue me, slag. Ach! to see ourselves as others see us. Her party, m'dears, left something to be desired.

"Be off!" cries Fay. "Piss off!"

Another, though infinitely posher, party in ruins, m'dears. It does indeed seem that the more things change the more they stay the same. A universal dilemma, no?

Fay reaches into her lottery box, finds, and casts away three lots till she comes to number two -- Nelly's flat. "Dear Nelly. Dear Nelly is still a friend."

An enchanted friend, Fay. They don't count. You can't get blood from a charmed turnip.

"You're hateful! Why have you done this to Fay? Why?!"

You know why, Fay.

"I'm innocent. I was a perfect child, an angel. A stunning baby with gossamer wings and a voice like the peal of moderately sized crystal bells. Until *they* got hold of me!"

Who got hold of you , Fay?

"You defilers of innocence! You soul snatchers! You monsters!"

Your innocence palls, my mechanized Medea.

"It does not! I'm innocent as the dickens!"

Remember that you are freshly disciplined, darling. Only I know who you are and what you are so play your part like the pawn you are and Mummy won't erase you – just yet.

"Erase me?!" cries Fay, "How can you *erase* me?! I'm indelible! I am the very milk of love and human kindness! I am love itself! I'll prove it!"

Fay leaps, ribbons flying, through this now tilting, rainbowed room to her wardrobe, snatches her chinchilla coat and the diamond bracelet that has suddenly appeared, buzzes open her automatic door. With the chinchilla flung over her arm she bounds down the swaying, throbbing (and much too excitable) stairs.

After a moment Nelly's door opens and red-eyed Nelly peeps out. "Fay?" she whispers, the poor, good creature, "Fay is that you?"

Fay hunches on the first stair. Her face is buried in chinchilla. Why must every human emotion be so difficult? It seems so easy for others. Rage is the only thing she can manage *without* effort. "Is there something wrong with me?" she whispers.

Ach! Will the penny never drop?

Fay is about to utter "What?" when Nelly says, "Fay, love, are you all right?"

Fay heaves with tears that have not quite arrived. When they do she lifts her streaming face to Nelly.

"Poor little Fay," says Nelly and pulls Fay up and embraces her and draws her into her flat and closes the door.

Déjà vu, my Francophones?

Nelly leads Fay to the bathroom basin and wipes her face with a cool, damp cloth. Fay, in a tiny voice, says "The real prize hadn't been drawn yet. This is the real prize."

Fay shoves the chinchilla coat at Nelly. "I drew your number after you left. You're the winner. I'm not lying."

She's telling the truth, Nelly, in our fashion.

"It's yours, Nelly. All yours. It got wet once. But now it's dry and soft. And it's all yours."

"I can't take it, Fay. It's much too much."

"For me, Nelly-Welly. Take it for me."

"It's too much."

"Do it for Fay."

A *balmy breeze* caresses Nelly's cheeks, her neck, her wrists. An even balmier breeze might have attained had Fay not exchanged her carpet for lucre, and lost... well, let's face it, darlings...and lost, well, shall we simply say: a *great deal.*

Fay slips that fabulous fur on Nelly and the pleasure of it sings in Nelly's eyes.

"There's a goodie in the left pocket too."

Nelly reaches hesitantly into the pocket, extracts the glittering diamond bracelet. "Oh, my God!"

Fay snatches the bracelet and clasps it on Nelly's wrist.

"You're beautiful. Big and so beautiful," whispers Fay, caressing Nelly's broad, soft, now furry shoulders, "Diamonds, Nelly dear, are a girl's best friend."

And where does that leave *me,* you ungrateful...

"Hush!" snaps Fay.

"It's bliss," sighs Nelly, "It's paradise."

Paradise lost, my simple friend. Just you wait.

Fay clings to Nelly, "I was an angel, cast down. Nobody loves me, Nelly. I've got a billion pounds and I was an angel. I'd do *anything* for a hug and a kiss. Yet nobody loves me."

"*I* love you, little Fay."

"But you won't always love me."

"Why?"

"Nobody ever does."

Correct so far, Ms dipsy-doodle. Cruel world, this.

And gettin' worse. Far, far worse.

And worse yet.

Ummm. But *soooo* familiar. Ach!

40

Dolittle Desiree had developed in many ways. Her bizarre behaviour had grown, leapfrogging over convention. Her gluttony, both carnal and carnivorous had grown. But not to be outdone, her tummy had grown and she was robustly, almost indecently pregnant by Tom, Dick or Harry. Or just some dick. Any dick'd do.
"He ravished me!" cried Desiree, "and when he was sated he..."

"Buggery!"

Rita stops typing, drops her chin into her cupped hands and sighs and refuses to be coached. You did detect me in that telling little excerpt, m'dears? Although, as we mature, it becomes increasingly difficult to separate the wheeee! from the chaff.

Ian, reading, looks up from his book. Rita uncups her hands, shrugs, "Poor, pathetic bitch."

Do I detect sympathy? Is our icy mill-maid thawing?

Fay nestles in Nelly's furry embrace but pulls away a smidgin, still permitting the lavishly furred and be-diamonded Nelly to hug and lull her, but not so fervently. Is it simply too late now? For that hug or that kiss? "Goodness," whispers Fay, "I'm so…mutable, and, golly, tempus fugits like the dickens."

"What, dear?" asks Nelly, ever attentive.

"Nothing," says Fay.

And of course there is…nothing. Nothing but another square, darling. So lift your dainty feet and waltz into it. Our disciplinary divertissment is accompli. But we've other fish to fry.

Morning, for our wretched Mrs Taylor, at last arrives, but as milk bottles are rattled and replaced outside her door the terrified, snooded old lady cowers in her bed -- no lactic larks this morning for her, m'dears. Rita's typing erupts from the floor but Taylor makes not a move to grab her cane and thump, not even to announce her huddling presence amongst these mortal coils. In bed, she'd heard the party yesterday, heard Fay's piping voice rise above the rest. She'd heard the angry shouts, the creaking floors, the slamming doors (the walls too are still paper -- and oh, my dears, how paper *burns*!).

Taylor knows the witch will be coming for her soon. That strangely familiar witch -- she remembers her from some time, somewhere. It was long ago, before... Then it slips away, goddamn it. Oh, it was all right at first when the witch came and took the carpet. Then *went*. It was almost fun in its odd way, a simple carrying out of prophecy. She'd read it all on one of Oscar's hearts and arrows cards -- just one card -- Had she misread it?

We'll see, won't we Sarah?

"Sarah?!" squeaks Taylor, "Sarah?! Who called me Sarah?!"

But she soon realizes she's only heard the name in her muddled old head (to which I have permanent access). Indeed, as I have unobstructed access to every player in this Ritterhouse game.

Taylor does not see the room shift around her either. For her eyes are closed -- too much, too soon, could be too dangerous for all. Let us hold our stallions, grip them tight, my dears, whilst this willy-nilly world reels round bewildered us. All in good time. If you're impatient, why not take a flying leap. What would you do in any case to occupy your idle hours? Twiddle your thumbs? Watch a soap? *Honestly*!

Now, thinks Taylor, Ritterhouse Fay is back with a vengeance. Poor old dear. Oscar had said nothing about the witch coming back. Oscar Taylor had said nothing of that.

A sharp hammering just over her head shatters Taylor's blurred remembrance of scary things past. She shivers violently, squinches her eyes tight shut and covers her ears with her woolly mittened hands.

Fay hammers a large nail into the fine silk tapestry finish of a spanking new wall, drops the hammer, yanks a fancily framed printed plaque from a table and hooks it over the nail where it swings from side to side in my fire-flickering, freshly conjured cerulean shadows. It reads:

There is no place
Anywhere near this place
Precisely like this place
So this must be

The place.

How true, dear. The *only* place. Ach! That peculiar fire, how it does flicker on your wall! How our destinies are wrought in fire and how splendidly prescient *I* am. Unlike that Delphic dame I require no mind-altering, labyrinthine miasma to get high. *Prescription* drugs have got my vote – I write my own.

"You must be mad," whispers Fay, to the suspicious though completely innocent indigo entity just beside her bedroom door whom she perceives as me. But she refuses to be drawn, stands back admiring her plaque and humming a little tune. Behind her on the marble coffee table is a bouquet of roses wrapped in silver paper. Beside the roses is a huge mauve leather portfolio containing her architect's plans. Embossed on the cover in gold is "Portfolio".

Fay lays the hammer aside, alights on white leather and opens the portfolio to consider the shapes of various things to come.

And go.

Nervous Nelly trembles so. She can hardly hold her violently rippling morning coffee. It's almost as in the beginning when she'd first moved here, fallen for Bill. Bill has started down the stairs, approaches closer, closer, pauses at last at her door. He knocks! Should she answer? She hasn't before. Should she now?!

"Nelly?" says Bill.

Nelly's rippling coffee becomes impossible, it's splashing, she quaffs it, burns her mouth.

"Nelly, darling?" says Bill.

Nelly clutches her coffee cup in both trembling hands. Tears gather, cascade.

"Nelly. I love you," says Bill through the door, and turns and quickly descends the steps, jumps on the departing 7.55 Red Arrow and is gone.

Poor Nelly's trembles multiply, her shoulders convulse, that *Thing* twists in her head and she drops to her sofa beside the chinchilla and abandons herself to sobs. After a moment she pushes aside the chinchilla, dons her shabby duffel and dashes out the door. She'll catch the later Red Arrow.

Rita waves from her window but Nelly, who is watching her own clumsy feet take graceless footsteps that no one will *ever* admire again, doesn't see her.

"Poor thing," thinks Rita, "It's the Witch-Bitch's doing. How can we fight her? She'll bugger us over royally before she's through."

Bugger you over she will, Rita, and not at all royally. Nor -- if the truth, the whole truth and nothing but the truth be told -- *willingly.*

Hugh and Jenny nurse colossal hangovers -- they'd spent their post-party evening rolling about on their bed sofa damning then delighting in Fay and her fluttery, overstuffed smock. They descend the steps to wait bleary-eyed for the bus with Nelly. Nelly, bless her heart, nods gravely at them, attempts a sweet smile.

Their bus arrives, they embark silently and are carted away through the dingy dawn.

41

Rita turns from her window, checks her watch, stubs out her cigarette; a moment later is waiting on the front steps, certain that Fay is watching. Ian pulls up. Rita jumps in and they drive away. Fay, at her window, smiles. "I got plans," she sings, "You got plans. Everybody's gotta have plans."

My plans.

Behind her that black cat gobbles caviar from the crystal bowl, jumping only slightly at countless shadows bounding through the room. Certain black cats have seen it all. She's one of 'em.

Poor Mrs Taylor lies motionless in bed, more dead than alive, her saucer eyes frozen on her ceiling beyond which resides the witch who returned. Shouldn't have. Did. The witch who will now do her in. This very morning. The witch whom she can almost recall but can't. What a coincidence. Taylor cannot quite recall Fay and Fay cannot quite recall Taylor. Is there anything to recall? What a silly question. If you're wondering why there are so many unanswered questions it's because, obviously, there are no answers, m'dears. As Gertie Stein used to say to Alice B: *There ain't no answer -- There ain't gonna be no answer -- That's the answer!* (Instant déjà vu: didn't we just discuss this 'no answers' question recently at a morning seminar?) Ach! It's simply mankind in all its devilish diversity. Talking the talk, walking the walk, and defecating (hopefully regularly).

And of course, upon occasion, flying.

Taylor reaches for her bedside pitcher and a spoon and attempts to dissolve a cube of Bovril in a smudged cup of water. Again and again she stirs to no effect then, a brain-penetrating: "Mrs Taylor?!"

Taylor's spoon leaps away, strikes her dresser mirror, cracks it. A very evil omen, thinks Taylor.

"Mrs Taylor?!" cries Fay through Taylor's door. The cup of undissolved Bovril drops bouncing, splashing, to the floor.

Fay, just outside Taylor's door, is resplendent in her ribbony smock with the portfolio tucked under her arm, roses in silver paper in her hand. She presses her face to the door, shouts:

"Mrs Taylor?! I know you're in there. I have an offer you can't refuse!"

Taylor is terrified, clutches the bedclothes tight around her, pulls her knitted snood over her ears, closes her eyes. But instantly *remembers* that she has earlier this morning unlocked her door for Rita to air her posies, had forgotten that Rita has her own key. The witch must not come in! The witch who came back must not come in!

"You're a naughty girl, Mrs Taylor," coos Fay with every good intention in this world *and* the next.

Taylor struggles from her bed, grabs her cane, painfully pulls herself up, shuffles towards her door.

"I have extensive plans, Mrs Taylor," coos Fay who smiles as she hears Taylor's cane-thumping approach. "Extensive plans. You are included. Will you let us in, darling? Honey? Sugar? Will you let your Fay in?!"

Taylor falters, slides to the floor and slowly, in agony, crawls to her knees and draws herself up her cane.

"Golly! What the dickens can be keeping you, Granny? I know you can hear me. The walls of this house are paper. I'm going to change that, dear," coos Fay, "That's one of the many things I'm going to change. Won't that be nice? Of course you won't be here when I do, will you, darling. Honey? You won't be here, will you, sugar?"

Taylor is at last on her feet again but winces in agony, drops her cane and clutches at a sharp pain in the hand that held it.

"I am offering you a million pounds, Granny Taylor. Can you hear me? *One million pounds.* I have made all the arrangements (she has, m'dears). All you must do is sign a tiny little paper. I have it here. You can live out your golden years in the luxury and comfort of the finest retirement home on earth. Could a dutiful *grandchild* do less?"

Taylor has retrieved her cane. Her eyes are riveted to that unbolted bolt. The bolt that just might prevent the witch's entry before Taylor is ready. Taylor must bolt that door, must go to the closet that once held the fabulous fragment, must fetch the little thatched shrine, must incantate before it is too late! "Must incantate!" she mutters, "Must incantate before it is too late!"

But the witch outside her door has already begun! With her 'darling', her 'honey', her 'sugar.' This witch has got the jump on her! She, *she, Taylor,* taught the witch all she knows! She remembers now! Remembers! "Must get the bolt bolted!"

Taylor's brain spins and remembers, spins and forgets. She flounders in a whirlpool of terror, thinks: Must incantate! Must incantate!

Taylor is at the door, reaches for the bolt. A stabbing pain explodes in her head, pulls her arm back. Fay's incantations -- her 'darling', her 'honey', her 'sugar', they're all working!

"They have Jacuzzi bubble baths in every suite, sugar," coos Fay, "And endless personal posies which they dutifully air! Just imagine the blessing for those suffering from the discomfort of arthritis, honey. The food is cordon bleu and they'll serve it right in your own little dining room. Imagine! Broth d'Bovril, darling."

Now Fay is inverting the incantation! That is the next step! Now it is 'sugar' then 'honey' then 'darling'! Just as I taught her, thinks Taylor who must, *must* get her hand to that bleeding bolt and bolt it! A thread of drool dangles for an instant then flaps from Taylor's lip. Oh! Her arm is so heavy! But she must lift it to that bolt!

"I know you can hear me, Granny Taylor," cries Fay, "and I am beginning to be uncommonly pissed off!"

With a mighty effort, because her arm weighs a ton, Taylor lunges, attempts to throw the bolt. It sticks! Won't lock!

"The witch has done her job well," are Taylor's last thoughts as a sharp pain just above her left ear squeezes away the morning light and poor, perplexed Mrs Oscar Taylor falls against the door and slides to the floor and may as well be dead.

Fay has heard Taylor's glide to oblivion, says:

"So there you are! Have you opened the door for me? Can Fay come in? I have celebratory roses for you. Are you going to allow me in? Darling? (No answer) Honey? (No answer) Sugar?"

Fay tries the doorknob, jerks the door open and Taylor slumps through it with a great thud, lies there, her sightless eyes staring up at Fay. Then, so slowly, the inert body of the old woman begins to slide, *seemingly* pulled by invisible threads. It moves from the door, across the worn hall carpeting to the edge of the stairs, pauses a moment, *seems* to quiver then floats an inch from the floor. Suspended, it moves out over the stairwell and suddenly plunges, tumbling from stair to stair to the bottom, coming at last to rest against Rita's door.

But no one's home, Mrs Taylor. No one is there for your unexpected visit. I suppose we might have talked it over first, dear. Your fate. But you are at least one hundred now. That's quite enough. I mustn't grieve. Mustn't get too personal though we do have a staggering past and we are old, so *very* old, friends. And, in our way, accomplices.

Fay backs away from the staircase, upsetting one of Taylor's uncollected milk bottles and with the roses and the portfolio under each arm, does an abrupt about-face and marches up the stairs. Thoughts of terrible neglect play through her mind. Neglect of a helpless child. And acts of dreadful depravity. All due to that unnervingly still woman on the floor at Rita's door. That creature who never lifted a finger to protect her from...to help the hapless child she was. That shrivelled old centenarian lying below.

Not a very nice way to describe Granny, is it Fay?

"What?" says Fay.

You heard me!

"I've got to pee, leave me alone!"

In her bathroom Fay fills the wash basin and drops the roses, silver paper and all, into it. Unable to resist, she unrolls a long strip of super-soft, mauve-tinted, scented tissue and kneels and polishes the seat of her digitalized toilet seat to an even higher gloss. Holding the toilet seat up and well away so it won't get splashed (and/or short-circuited!), she drops the tissue in the toilet bowl and flushes it and squats on the pressure activated heated seat, grinning, relieving herself in a most delightful way. After carefully flushing the toilet again and washing her hands and glorying in this novel and entirely *human* function she takes up the roses and jigs to the kitchen.

Still grinning, she finds a heavy crystal vase and forgetting to add water places the roses in it and sets the vase on the white marble table in front of the white leather sofa upon which purrs the black cat. The cat, ostensibly content with its seven remaining lives, watches suspiciously as the waterless roses immediately droop and instantly shrivel.

Healthy cut flowers are a pet-peeve of mine. They're intimidating, darlings, smell of mortality, so I dispatch them forthwith.

Back in the kitchen, Fay slams eight slices of nutritious, coarse-grained bread into a gigantic toaster, fills and switches on the electric kettle, returns to the living room to sit by the cat. Only then does she snatch her telephone from her pocket, dial emergency and scream: "AMBULANCE! PLEASE! AN OLD WOMAN IS DYING! AMBULANCE NEEDED AT NUMBER THIRTEEN... (wouldn't want to give away the street name. It could be dangerous for a gawking public, considering our task).

Be not harsh with Fay, she has her reasons. Don't blame her. The Ritterhouse Fay has her reasons. Our reasons. My reasons. Possibly, m'dears, *your* reasons as well. So don't be smug.

42

Study poor Fay as she bulges, writhes on the white leather sofa, her face hidden under one of those serial, cool, damp clothes that our Nelly, kind Nelly, has provided. Is not Fay's pain acute? Nelly bends over her, concerned about Fay's sporadic contortions which are unlike any she had ever witnessed (or ever will, m'dears) during her brief career as volunteer assistant to a midwife.

"You've rung? You *have* rung?" asks Nelly.

"Yes! (gasp) I've rung! He'll be here in a moment!"

A tiny scream of pain.

"Oh Fay!"

"I'm aborting, Nelly!"

"Oh God! Are you sure?"

"I am going to lose my baby, you idiot!"

"Oh dear! Poor little Fay!"

"How is Taylor?"

"Dear, *dear* Fay. Never thinking only of yourself."

Fay, irritated:

"How is Taylor?!"

"In hospital."

"I know she's in hospital! Have you forgotten that I rang for the sodding ambulance?! It was the shock of my life!"

Fay removes the damp cloth from her face, exaggerates a wince for near-sighted Nelly as Nelly hasn't got her specs on.

"That bloody ambulance should have taken me too!"

Fay exaggerates another wince. Life is more exhausting when Nelly forgets her glasses (and Fay chronically forgets her elementary magic – if that's what it *is*).

"How is Mrs Taylor?" winces Fay.

"Not speaking."

"Won't (wince) speak or can't (wince) speak?"

"Can't speak. Oh Fay, I should call an ambulance for you!"

Fay begins to sob, no tears yet but the noise and contortions are just as effective. She screams:

"Daddy should know! The daddy should know! Give me my phone!"

Nelly is aghast, hesitates. "But he doesn't care, Fay. Bill doesn't care."

"DADDY should know!"

Fay snatches the telephone, punches a number.

"Hello?" says Chauffy from the back seat of the Rolls. His feet are up, a lager in his hand.

"Billy! This is Ritterhouse Fay. I am fifteen feet away, aborting your bastard!"

Chauffy, parked just around the corner, smiles, shouts, as arranged, "Go to Hell!" and rings off. Fay has held the phone away from her ear so Nelly has easily heard and can hardly contain herself, I shamefacedly report.

"That heartless man!" cries Nelly, the Dreadful Something fine-tuning this fallacious thought, "That monster!"

Fay will have Nelly's love. One way or another. So she winces and arches her back and thrusts her bulging midriff heavenward and screams. Nelly has no time to reflect -- even if she could.

"Fay! Can you make it to the bedroom?! We've got to get those clothes off!"

"I will not take off my clothes!" cries Fay, covertly consulting her Cartier -- A bit of committed alliteration, m'dears, to confirm my continuing *benevolent* presence.

"Fay, love! Where is your chauffeur? I'm not waiting. I'll ring an ambulance."

"No, Nelly! Please!"

Chauffy crashes in, hoists Fay into his smooth, gym-conditioned arms and starts away (a moment of respect, m'dears, for beauty in all its gut-grinding glory).

"Nelly, the pain is terrible!" shrieks Fay as in those divine arms, she is shifted out the door, "Get my pills by the bed!"

Nelly turns back, rushes to the bedroom, sees no pills by the bed, looks under the bed. No pills! Rushes to the bathroom, slams open a cabinet, are these the pills? No time! Grabs any pills, rushes down the stairs. But the Rolls, accompanied by Fay's fading screams, is already disappearing into the stygian, and I do mean *stygian*, night.

And, of course, yet another square.

Rita appears.

"Fay is in trouble," says Nelly, "Bill's baby."

She can say no more, begins to sob. Rita leads her gently into her flat, sits her down, places a cognac in her hand.

"Ohhh, Rita!" sobs Nelly, dipping, as could be expected, into cliché.

Rita sits beside her, takes her other hand, squeezes hard.

"It's not Bill's baby, Nelly. Ritterhouse is a self-confessed liar and if Mrs Taylor doesn't live, she may also be a murderer."

"What do you mean?" cries Nelly, that Dreadful Something twitching to life, eager to defend Fay.

"I believe Fay was involved in Mrs Taylor's 'accident'."

Nelly leaps up.

"I won't listen to this! Poor Mrs Taylor was right! This house is cursed!"

At last, Nelly! Or do you realize what you've just said?

"And who cursed it?" asks Rita.

"Fay might have been all right. The first time. You pushed her, Rita. You laughed at her. We all laughed at her. Your story. Your awful magazine story!"

"My story was true, every word of it!"

"She told me how much it hurt her. I'm to blame too. I helped you, God help me. I told you what Fay told me. I betrayed her. We all betrayed her. I'm a traitor, Rita, but I'm not cruel! Poor Fay is having a miscarriage..."

"I don't believe it!"

"...and you are accusing her of murder!" Nelly struggles away from Rita.

"Nelly, darling, please. You're wrong, dear. If you only knew what..."

"I don't want to know anything! We're all cursed! Fay too! She's only human!"

Is she, Nelly, Dreadful Somethings aside, of course?

"It's Bill's baby! And I heard him! He told her to go to hell!"

"Rightly so! That's where the mad woman came from!"

Not quite, Rita, but you're getting close.

Nelly bursts from Rita's flat into her own and slams the door.

Rita does not move for a long moment then sticks a cigarette in her ivory holder, lights and puffs. "Poor Fay?!" She exclaims, "Merde!"

Tiens! Then *you* speak French too, Rita?

Curiouser and curiouser.

Have you been too harsh on her, Rita? She did try -- seemed only to want love. No! She was a scheming bitch -- showed it time after time. She broke up Nelly and Bill -- good Nelly and innocent Bill. A miscarriage? Bullshit. And now Mrs Taylor. Was it Fay who caused it? If Taylor dies...

You've got to know people to write about them, Rita-the-scribe, so don't complain. Fay made you a star. Of sorts. Yes, she did! Just as she said. Life's like that, me *old* beauty -- full of erratic chance. Fay was the catalyst. Brought you all together only to unite against her. It's natural she should wish to separate you again to defend herself. Are you listening to me, Ms Rita Lambert?

Rita consults a scrap of paper on her writing table, picks up her phone, dials.

"Mrs Oscar Taylor...she was admitted this morning...a stroke or...yes, thank you."

Rita sighs, waits, takes from the mantel a recent snapshot of herself and Ian walking barefoot on a beach. Gazes longingly at it, hopes...wonders...

"Oh...Could you give me that again, please?...Mary of Teck wing, room 304...no, sorry. I believe she is married but I've no idea where he...Yes, of course. I have her key so I'll check and ring later... Thank you."

Rita hangs up, takes a long drag on her cigarette, leans back, exhales, eyes the brandy decanter on the mantel. She'd like to say hello to Mr Courvoisier tonight but it isn't the weekend. She promised Ian.

Don't muck it up, love. A career ain't everything. Though some of us goblins might not agree (joke!).

Nelly lies sobbing on her bed, mottled face in rumpled pillow, a film cliché of abject misery, m'dears. Rita would instantly recognize this, she's used it almost word for word in her brief, tumultuous career as the aspiring writer of a feverishly encouraged, fervent novel. Particularly in the yet unpublished part two. Fay would also recognize this literary convention. She uses it in life -- only while others, of course, are present -- and when she can get that echte salzwasser flowing.

But darlings, it's not Fay's fault. Then whose fault is it, you ask? Pass the buck, skip into your next square, ask no questions, and you'll get no lies. We must all of us sigh for Fay, cry for Fay. Tears, m'dears, are the commonest of currencies. Especially *these* days. We are all of us in this board game together. If you don't think so, you've got another think comin'. Honestly, why must I constantly accent the obvious?

So here lies Nelly, face buried in her pillow, sobbing out her huge shattered heart. She at last rises, dabs her swollen eyes and begins to pack a small suitcase, only a few things. She wonders what ever happened to her black silk scarf. Certainly would never imagine it tied as a veil over Fay's cupid's bow as Fay munched ragged bread and bogus butter and bamboozled this very house from the gnarly grasp of the late -- and very sweet in his way -- Abdullah Omar Shamaly.

Oh what a tangled web we weave when first we... Ach! and phooey! Let's roll the diddly dice.

Nelly finishes packing, snaps her suitcase shut, sees a toy lorry she had bought for Bill's son, Danny. He's sixteen. In that special school he'll make good progress -- He's doing better in this new school than in the last.

Bill had so much on his mind when he came here. He wasn't himself. Like Fay, whose house had burned down, Bill's life had burned too, been gutted. All this seems long ago though it isn't -- unless two months be reckoned so. Two months that went by unnaturally fast. Einstein's theory of relativity was correct, thinks Nelly, having absolutely no idea of what she's talking about except that *everything* is relative. Yes. Of course it is, dear, and a little knowledge is a dangerous thing. Particularly when the sky is falling.

Nelly ties a ribbon around the toy lorry and tags it "For Danny" and sets it beside her door.

Back at the Savoy, Chauffy, white-gold ringlets gleaming, clad in his briefest of briefs (mauve like Fay's eyes but not opaque), pours a drink for Fay. He watches her through the bedroom door as she removes her huge, red angora cardigan and reveals the ribbony smock and ogles him. He grins at her. She does not return his smile but studies him curiously, as inspecting a magnificent butterfly impaled on a pin -- a butterfly in tight briefs on a pin in a box. Fay's *very own* box. She moves out of the bedroom toward him...

She was so innocent once, so perfect. All men and women were, weren't they, my dears, perfect? Well, you tell me. I'm a novice (joke).

Fay approaches Chauffy, arms akimbo, back arched, tummy a parturient parody, eyes unblinking, laser-like and glued on her pierced butterfly. She moves ever closer. Chauffy finds himself backing away -- he has been wary of her ever since that first time though she had literally hoisted him up from the street after he'd been beaten and dumped from a car by three brawny clients. He'd looked up into her opaque, mauve eyes, become wary on the spot. It hadn't changed. She is even more frightening now but he feels he owes her something. Odd, that.

But not odd to us-in-the-know, is it, my dears?

Fay twirls and rips a contoured rubber cushion from beneath her smock (had she only known, she could have produced the same effect sans crude and tangible props) and flings it savagely at her poor butterfly who spills the drink he is about to hand to her. Then, gently, cooing as only Fay can coo, she pulls him towards the bedroom.

"The bedroom's this way," she stage-whispers and the words echo curiously. She recalls saying the very same words in the very same place. This happens a lot to Fay -- she and Taylor are so alike in their fuzzings-outs and fuzzings-ins. They're related, aren't they? Somehow? Everything is relative. Ask Nelly.

"Let's recuperate," whispers Fay, "Three days? Chauffy? Is three days enough?"

She's pulling down his briefs, she's had practice pulling down briefs. *And* pulling them up. After all, she'd worn Y-fronts, hadn't she? And she secretly always wanted to be, like Pinocchio, a *reallllll* boy. And wasn't her father a man? She thought she saw her father once, through a puff of smoke. He was wearing lipstick. And those big, awkward shoes. But she could have been wrong. Fay often is. It's built-in, m'dears.

"No," says Chauffy, "A week. I want a whole *week* in Monte Carlo."

I just adore Monte!

White-gold is rising under her fingers, to Fay's own occasion.

"A week is too much," whispers Fay who enjoys manipulating foreskins every bit as much as Jim Richardson. She's only seen him once, that second day at Number 13. Doesn't even know his name. But will. Will.

"A week is too much," repeats Fay, "I've got so much to do." She gives Chauffy's ding-dong a sharp tug. He cries "Oww." She says "I've got so many things to do."

He says, adamantly (be careful here, Chauffy) -- he says adamantly, taking her hand from his swelling penis:

"No. A *week*."

Fay is expressionless. "A week," she repeats mechanically and rises from the bed and pours a drink, returns, throws it in his face.

She sits again, rolls a special ciggie, lights it, puffs and, grinning, holds it in.

"Anything wrong?" he asks, sweat and scotch beading on his flushed forehead. He's worried, terrified actually.

He should be.

Now she's gulping chocolates, two at a time between each puff, chewing, exhaling sweet smoke, grinning that same unnerving grin. He's pulling on his briefs.

"Darling," she says, though it is difficult to understand her through half-chewed chocolate, "honey," she says, "sugar."

She swallows the chocolates with a gulp and barks, completely intelligibly, "Three days of recuperation is sufficient."

He couldn't agree more.

"I've got better things to do," hisses Fay, "than sit around and twiddle your willie, you stupid bastard!"

Now she's grinning again, though she wonders, *sincerely* wonders, where all that came from -- cruelty is so unlike her, so alien. But the minutes, the hours, the days, months, years, millenniums – they corrupt, degrade. She's nothing special, our Fay. Couldn't hold a candle to eternity though I'm certain she'd try – if she's anything like her old Mum. Pardon me whilst I don't shed a tear. I'm not as amused as I might be after so much effort. I tire of the animation of my darling prosopopoeia, The Ritterhouse Fay. Nee Feckless Fay who forces a chocolate into Chauffy's cake hole; is so full of grins, so full of plans. She crams another chocolate into him. If she can chew three at a time, why can't he chew two? "Stuff Monte Carlo," she says, "Stuff Monaco."

Down come his briefs. "Fay's hungry."

Sweet Jesus! So am I! See my so-called *mouth* gape open, my sharp *teeth* glisten? See my hot so-called *breath* cast steam in the absolute zero of Kelvin? See roly-poly Pluto command my window?

Nelly, rigid with nerves, shivers before her mirrored door, derives no comfort at all from the magnificent chinchilla that envelopes her (or the glittering bracelet in its pocket!). In one hand is her small suitcase, in the other, two letters. She opens the door, sets the suitcase beside it, reaches back for the toy lorry and starts up the stairs. She squats, places the little lorry by Bill's door and slides one of the letters under the door, the other under Fay's door. She descends the stairs, picks up her suitcase and walks out. Clumsily, of course, and so heart-wrenchingly aware of it.

C'est la vie, dear Nelly. C'est la vie.

So let us bid adieu to Fay's primary partisan as the orange December sun sets on a grieving Number 13; Ach! Moaning mortar, bawling bricks, puling paper walls and frantic floors, dolorous dooble-vey-sees, inconsolable carpets, weeping windows, sad stairs, drooping drains, the whole schmoozing schmear, m'dears. Everything is so out of balance. Ach, the entire heaving house knows and mourns the loss of an eminent soul. I hasten to add: an *unaffordable* loss. Although, we are on course. Perfectly on course as the squares fall so obediently, so seductively before our so-called *feet*.

> Dearest Bill,
> Goodbye. I can't live here anymore. There is too much unhappiness. You should have been better to Fay. She needed you. But I'm no one to talk. I'm a traitor. Here's a present for Danny. I hope he likes it. He is such a sweet, loving boy. I would have liked to know him better.
> More love (for what it was worth)
> Nelly.

Bill puts down Nelly's letter. He's sick, brings a hand to his mouth, rushes to the kitchen -- can't make it to the bathroom. Gripping the sink, he chokes. Can't vomit. Only chokes. The dry heaves, m'dears. If you've had 'em, you won't fergit 'em! The sympathetic ceiling stares down, would weep if it could -- might later. We'll see.

Nelly disembarks from her taxi at Paddington Station and a moment after cannot find the right platform through tears of loss.

43

Three days later Fay, in a new sable coat, svelte, sans smock, stoops inside the door of her flat to pick up Nelly's letter.

> Dear little Fay,
> I hope you got to hospital and are all right. I didn't know where you went or I would have visited. I rang everywhere. I apologise for Bill. He is a good man but he has a lot on his mind and has made a big mistake. I apologise for myself too because I have not been the friend you thought I was. I said things to Rita about you that she used in her awful story.

Fay's eyes blaze for a moment, the fire subsides (it's much too early darlings, to be *reborn*) is replaced by a spectrum of writhing indigo flecked with mossy, froggy green that sets my colour wheel spinning. Mummy must amuse herself – and *you*, of course. But back, m'dears, to our resident vandal who continues to read Nelly's tear-stained letter:

> I betrayed you when you needed me most. I am so sorry, Fay.
> On the enclosed I have signed over to you my lease. I cannot live here anymore. I will send for the rest of my things in a few days. Please forgive me.
> Love, Nelly.
>
> PS: I looked everywhere for my black silk scarf. I wanted to give it you but could not find it. It would have looked lovely with your red angora. I am sorry it all turned out this way. Goodbye, little Fay.

Fay throws Nelly's letter to the floor, cries "Where's my chinchilla, traitor?! Where's my goddamned diamond bracelet, traitor?!"

As we all know, darlings, when love goes wrong, nothin' goes right.

This little fracas would never have come up had Fay retained those err... special advantages she so readily surrendered for auction cash. But it's all in the game, eh? Eh?! Just say *yes*.

A few minutes later Fay is moving swiftly about Nelly's flat poking into drawers, peering into cupboards and closets, poaching the last of Nelly's wonderful homemade cookies (biscuits for those of you with short memories!) from their prettily flowered tin. Cookies again! God-almighty! Seems I can't live with 'em, can't live without 'em!

On Nelly's living room floor, opened and scattered beside her is the portfolio: "The magnificent future of Number 13" as Fay, mid-coital-cogitation, described it to Chauffy the very night before.

But 'the magnificent future of Number 13?' Number 13 only? Why, in view of her glorious possibilities, has she set her sites so low?

It wasn't *she*, m'dears. It was *I*! That scatter-brained uncooperative slattern is clueless. She, with her good intentions, her neediness. We all have needs, Honey. Give us a break. Ach! If I must I'll wring my amusement from her with a cheese press!

Fay snatches the last cookie from the tin, chews, squats on the floor, pencils out a detail on her plans and sticks the pencil back in the pocket of her new sable. She liked the chinchilla better and she'll buy another soon but she's a bit concerned that some animal-rights-fanatic will throw paint on it. She understands why they do these things. Fay of all persons, understands. She would too. Has. But then, Fay has done everything, been everything. So she supposes. And I suppose we, at the moment, must suppose with her. In lieu of any *substantial* corroborative misinformation. Substantial, meaning in this case tangible. Chew on that for a while, my dears. It's crucial. But then, *everything* is.

"Nelly?"

Fay's heart jumps, she chokes on the cookie, leaps up and rushes to the kitchen for a glass of water.

"Nelly?" says Bill through the door, "I can hear you're in there. Nelly, darling?"

"Hello, Daddy, long time no see!" cries Fay throwing open the door.

Bill jumps back from Fay's gut-twisting grin. "What the hell are you doing here?!"

"Nelly and I are friends, in case you hadn't noticed."

"You are a nasty bitch, aren't you?"

"I was the mother of your premature little..."

"Like hell."

"Our foetal son survived just long enough to realize he'd come to the wrong place..."

"Cruel bitch."

"...He left instantly for fairer fields."

"Lying bitch."

"I'm rubber, you're glue! Every bad thing you say to me bounces right offa me and sticks to you!"

Bill moves towards Fay who retreats. Rita has heard Bill shout, pokes her nose out, can see them both clearly through Nelly's half-opened door.

Grist! Rita, grist!

"What are you doing in Nelly's flat?" says Bill.

"Don't you want to hear about our aborted son? Our miserable miscarriage? The details? I'm the woman you ravished! Remember?"

"I wouldn't touch you with a ten foot pole!"

"How's about a three inch twig? You budded, buddy, but you never bloomed."

"I never...!"

"Well it wasn't *my* fault, was it?"

"My God, you are a wicked woman."

It's not her fault, Billy! Blame *me*! Honest injun!

Fay, who simply cannot see herself as 'wicked' (who *can*, darlings?), winces, and not for effect. "I'm a fish out of water," she squeaks, colouring and recalling a childhood visit to an aquarium -- not to mention poor, departed Abdullah Shamaly's more recent gift of that tiny jewelled fish (which she would wear if only she knew where it was).

It's in the pocket of that shabby cardigan you will insist on wearing!

"What?" says Fay, "What was that?"

Her eyes swivel round looking for me. She's faint, leans against a door to steady herself. Why has she been called wicked? Really, why?

"I jumped out of the water and I landed here," she bawls.

I'll vouch for that. To a point. Change the essential element from which you darted, ducky, and you've got *my* vote.

Rita, watching it all through her door, cannot wait to return to her typewriter.

"You're mad," says Bill.

"Not mad," whispers Fay, "Not mad. I'm only grounded, darling. Stranded, honey."

Fay screws up her face and two authentic tears, with my dubious blessing, tumble down her flushed, over-rouged cheeks, "I'm suffocating, sugar!" she cries and grabs Bill's arm. "I've a billion pounds, monsieur!"

He pulls away, makes for the door.

"A billion pounds that say YOU LOSE!"

I'm afraid that was me again, m'dears.

Fay follows, slaps his face. "I'll have you put away! I'll sue you for sexual misconduct! I'll have your flat for my potty-room! I'll have this flat too! She's given it up! This traitor's flat will be a sandbox where my kitty does her poo!"

Atta girl, lovely!

Bill slams the door in her face -- if he'd stayed he might have struck her back. He leaves as quickly as he can. "Billy!" she cries from Nelly's sofa, "Billy! Come back!"

Fay! What is it you do to people? They're forever slamming doors in your face -- or should we say "faces"?

"Please!" says Fay. "Whoever you are! Please!"

Now it is Rita who grabs Bill's arm. "I heard her, Bill. You're not responsible for this. I'll tell Nelly. She'll understand now, won't she? We know for sure now. Ritterhouse is bonkers."

Bill is shaking, close to tears. "Where is Nelly?"

"She left with a suitcase, love."

"I'll find her."

Bill is out the door. On the street he spots a bus paused at a signal, jumps on as it pulls away.

"Riiiiiita!" cries Fay emerging from Nelly's flat, "Long time, no see!"

Rita's door slams.

Yep. Right in Fay's flushed face.

"Can't blame a gal for tryin'," calls Fay to Her House as she sashays up Her Stairs, Her portfolio under Her sabled arm -- safe for a moment, swaddled in the fantasy that she is something special. And *anything* but wicked.

I wouldn't completely disagree. Or we could all be tarred with that same brush. But then, again. We all *are*.

Early next morning Rita awakens to a clatter from the corridor, opens her door, wipes her eyes and finally focuses on two men shovelling sand from a wheelbarrow on to the carpet of Nelly's still completely furnished flat.

"What the hell is going on here?!" cries Rita.

"Ask *her,* darlin'" shrugs one of the men, sticking his thumb up the staircase. Rita turns. Here is Fay in her sable and bunny-fur slippers, her hair in pink plastic curlers and the black cat in her arms. Ignoring Rita, she descends the stairs, glides by and tosses the cat through Nelly's door onto the growing pile of sand.

"Do your poo, darling," coos Fay, "honey, sugar. Do your poo for Mummy."

Fay twirls and ascends the stairs, leaving Rita and the two men with their shovels and mouths suspended. Kitty poos then leaps through the open window to the street, is hit by a car, lies there for a moment, jumps up, races back through Nelly's window and up the stairs for its daily dose of caviar. Three lives gone -- six to go.

Plus several feline squares, pussycat, before you purr your last.

44

Poor Granny Taylor -- trapped in a web of tubes threading in and out of every flagging orifice of her frail old body, surrounded by a battery of beeping, babbling, brutalizing, machines -- fights for her life.

"The witch," she murmurs, half conscious, "The witchy, witch, witch."

Rita, who has been here every day, takes Taylor's hand, holds it. How odd it is to care for someone you hardly know. How I've changed, thinks Rita.

A very little success goes a very long way, dear.

Soon Taylor, unaware of Rita's odd caring or even her presence, falls into a deeper more perilous sleep.

"Oh dear!" cries Fay, as the door of Hugh's flat slams open and Jenny gapes at the dazzlingly jewelled and fur festooned Fay. "Oh, dear!" cries Fay, "I didn't know you two were in!"

Fay has, in her surprise, dropped the portfolio and her master key but Hugh appears and politely retrieves both.

"Thanks, sugar," she exclaims and makes to enter but is blocked by Jenny who says:

"What do you want?"

Fay laughs her *merry* laugh. "I've come to inspect the premises, Honey. As you'll note in Hugh's lease it says that I, as legal owner, have the right of periodic entry to ensure that the leasee, Hughie in this case, is properly maintaining said premises."

"The lease states," says Hugh, "*with prior arrangement with tenant, owner may inspect the premises.* I've just reread it."

"Sorry," says Fay. She sighs, brings a hand to her forehead, "I was so busy losing my baby..."

Bless her! Her mouth turns down, trembles reliably, "*So* busy that the fine print just swooped by me."

Fay smiles a fraught smile, one of her very best, and Jenny feels that odd vibration again, quivering just behind her kneecaps.

"We may," says Fay, holding the portfolio before her, "be able to improve upon said premises. Paint, kitchen cabinets, that sort of thing. Mr Abdullah Shamaly, Allah be with him, was an extremely absentee landlord. Allow me to enter, pretty-please?"

Jenny is now giddy with vibrations, couldn't say no if her life depended upon it (Which it ultimately does if Fay's mission fails. No! I shan't reveal Fay's mission yet! I'm a stubborn old thing, yet extraordinarily glamorous in a singularly unearthly way).

Jenny glances anxiously at Hugh, steps aside and Fay, portfolio aloft, marches in crying "You *are* kind!"

Hugh and Jenny exchange glances, and Jenny, whose odd vibrations have now reached a sensitive area just between her shoulder blades, says:

"We were sorry to hear about your..."

"My miscarriage," coaches Fay.

"Yes," mutters Jenny, still beset.

"Oh it could happen to anyone," chirps Fay, "Whatever happens *will* happen." Then cheerfully, her head in a kitchen cupboard: "You'll need new paint here or the woodwork could suffer irreparable damage."

And will, darling. And *will*, soon.

"I painted just a month ago," says Hugh.

"Who on earth chose this *colour*?"

"I did," says Jenny.

"I see," says Fay and briskly disappears into the bathroom.

"I hope she drowns in the WC," whispers Jenny, throbbing only lightly at the moment, into Hugh's ear.

"What was that?" exclaims Fay from the bathroom -- her hearing remains phenomenal -- "what did you say?"

In unison: "Nothing."

"You need a new WC. And the tub. Ach du lieber himmel!"

Ach du lieber himmel, little chou-chou? Have we deserted our gallic badinage? Although, if memory serves me keerect, mein Papá was a bit of a Kraut -- hence my chronic *Ach-ing*!

Hugh and Jenny burst into giggles. They fail to see my shadows romp or to hear that tiny shrill voice echoing in the kitchen sink drain or to note the floor rising ever so slightly up then down with Fay's every breath. Or is this *my* imagination? But there's so much goes on, isn't there, my dears? So much that just slips by us. Whole alternative universes of frenzied clandestine activity. Ask any metaphysician, ask any astronomer, ask any astronaut, ask your next door neighbour (on second thoughts, don't – she's indisposed). But do ask *me*. I'm a prescient pussy cat.

"Yes, the tub," says Fay, "Oh my. All chipped and stained with lime-water -- what is so *bleeding* funny out there?!"

Fay's cheery face appears at the edge of the bathroom door. Being helpful is such a tonic! "I've an idea. We'll install a new water closet and a new tub in a lovely shade of mauve."

Fay is trying so hard. All she desires is a little loving kindness plus a hug 'n' kiss, plus...what? She's not sure. These words just sang pleasantly in her head. I'm giving the girl a break, darlings, the next square is dismal. So let us grin and bear it. We're all in this together.

Fay exits the bathroom, stands triumphantly before Jenny and Hugh, opens the portfolio on both arms. "I'll even throw in a new wash basin to match. What do you say to that?"

"You've got to hand it to her. She *is* trying to be reasonable." whispers Hugh.

"Mauve'll show the scum," says Jenny who is now fighting vibrations with some success.

"Scum? What scum?!" says Fay.

"Soap scum."

"Jenny, darrrrling! Is it not in the bathroom that we worship the temple of our bodies?"

"Only *very* occasionally," replies Jenny with a naughty grin.

"You do intend to keep your bathroom hygienic? Give it a thorough going-over now and again, jettison all the errr…inflammables?" says Fay.

"We promise," replies Jenny seriously, through no fault of her own, "we promise to maintain said premises and jettison all inflammables."

Not *all* the inflammables, surely?! Including Fay?

"I'm comforted," sighs Fay.

These spontaneous human expressions are necessary but tiring. For the both of us.

"No, they are not!" squeaks Fay, still nominally comforted.

"White is a better colour," says Hugh.

"What was that, sugar?" asks Fay.

Fay has dipped abruptly into one of her mini-reveries, caught herself, re-emerged with a half-memory of ancient spells – writ in a huge purple book somewhere. Whilst incarcerated, of course, and simmering at low flame.

Puzzled and dizzy from these random ruminations, she continues to gaze absently at Hugh.

"White," says Hugh, "is more modern. Jenny and I would prefer white."

Fay wipes her forehead, staggers the tiniest bit, braces herself against a wall, thumps it. "Can we raze this wall then?"

I yawn. I'm *awfully* sleepy just now so Fay duly slumps a silly smidgin more, eyes drooping. So like mine.

Hugh, reasonably:

"It's the wall to the kitchen."

Fay lazily consults the portfolio. "So it is."

She fights her stupor and knocks heavily on the wall, a cup is ejected from a shelf on its opposite side, shatters. Fay ignores it and continues, words deliciously slurred:

"I will build you an open-plan kitchen."

That voice in her head is positively buzzing now (I'm merciless even whilst exhausted). With her nose in the portfolio Fay backs through the kitchen door. "We'll have a smart little breakfast bar right here where you can sit of a spring morn on nice high, chromium stools -- with backs on of course, to support your vital lumbro-sacral...areas. Nice high stools from which to dangle your toes as you drink your morning coffee and just take your time and ignore them when they say *time's up*."

But Fay, dear. When it's time, it's time.

"A lovely place to sit," says Fay, "where they daren't...set you afire...and hose you down..."

Fay wipes her forehead again, her eyes roll up into her head, reappear in a squint.

Hugh, ever a gentleman and sensing Fay's *terrible* unease and, even, vulnerability, says "That sounds great, doesn't it Jenny?"

Jenny, with a shiver, "Yes."

Fay instantly recovers, claps her hands. "You will need to be re-housed, of course."

"What?" says Jenny as the room tilts, tilts back. Jenny and Hugh gasp, grasp for support then forget.

"Re-housed."

"Forget it!" says Jenny, "No can do."

Fay seems to have lost her grip. She wipes more sweat from her forehead with tiny jerky movements, soot, stigmata-like, appears in the palms of her hands. Where have these *hands* been?

I know.

"Temporarily re-housed. Temporarily only! For the *duration*!" cries Fay, puffing for air, "Don't you trust me?"

"Mrs Taylor says you're a witch," says Jenny.

"Mrs Taylor is in hospital!"

"Rita says you put her there."

"Absurd. It could have been much worse. Mrs Taylor is fortunate I was around."

"Is she?" asks Hugh.

"It was she who sent *me* to hospital. She frightened my child to death."

She actually believes she was with child?!

Fay grimaces, falls backward. Jewels jangle, sable soughs (Darlings! Am I not a *wordsmith*? And with so *little* practice).

Hugh catches Fay, leads her to a chair where she sits clutching the portfolio to her furry breast and fidgeting with her tiny jewelled fish (She finally found that fish -- must have overheard me).

Hugh says earnestly: "Can I get you something?"

"You can get me back my baby boy."

Fay looks up. Her eyes are muddy with mascara (*borr*-ring!). "Sorry," she adds, "You can get me a glass of water. Plus maybe just the tiniest bit of scotch for a chaser (Alcohol is such a passé high, m'dears but let's get on with it -- one can't teach an ur-cat new tricks). I'm a whisky girl today. Jenny, if you would. I'll reimburse as necessary."

Jenny is in full control now, frowns but reluctantly exits to the kitchen.

"How fortunate you are, Hughie. To have somebody. Anybody. It is a sacred trust. Cherish and do right by your significant other. Do right by your scalliwag squeeze."

Fay laughs, sits straight in her chair, summons a comforting memory of Hugh's earlier kindness, straightens a page of plans in the portfolio, wipes stigmata-soot from her hands, shifts her sable, adjusts her jangling jewels then looks up to note that Hugh is studying her.

Ach! Who wouldn't be?!

She grins engagingly, exaggerating as she always did for near-sighted, now departed, Nelly, thinks: Hugh could grow to like me. A lot. He's still on my gift list.

Hugh looks away. Jenny arrives with a glass of water and a whisky chaser, decides to pour a whisky for all tiresomely concerned.

The unutterably boring above, my dears, is simply to illustrate Fay's...Oh my! I'll be caught short! Off to the loo! You go figure it out.

Rita's exhausted, been to Pazazz's spacious offices in Paddington to discuss her promising future. Nevertheless on her arrival home, tired as she is she unlocks Taylor's door and goes directly to the kitchen where she fills a watering-can and returns to water the geraniums and carry them to the window box for airing. On the floor by the bedroom door she sees a toppled cup and the stain of dried Bovril. Bending to retrieve the cup, she notices the cracked mirror on Taylor's dresser. Was it cracked before? She can't remember.

In the kitchen she washes the cup, returns, rinses away the Bovril stain, sees a small stack of postcards on a sideboard, picks it up, reads the top card:

> March 17, 1947. Sweet Patootie, just a note to tell you I'm alive. You know what to do with it. Fondly, Oscar.

Rita reads the next card in the stack:

> April 21, 1948. Darling, Honey, Sugar: how long has it been? You know what they say, "Absinthe makes heart grow fonder". Or is it Absence? Ha-ha. Do the usual with this but don't get burned this time. And don't blame those poor women. They were only carrying out orders. Fires need dousing, dearie. Especially when things are out of control. It's an unnatural fact. Fondly and responsible in my fashion! Ha-ha. Your Oscar.

Both cards are scrawled with hearts-and-arrows. Rita shrugs, drops them to the postcard table and returns the geraniums from the window box. She locks Taylor's door, hears Fay's giggle hurtle from Hugh's flat opposite, pauses for a puzzled moment then starts down the stairs.

Pauses for a puzzled moment. Ground-breaking prose, darlings. Listen and you'll learn as I whistle whilst I work!

Later that night Rita sleeps alone -- Ian is out of town on a job. A shrill, wall-piercing voice from the hall startles her awake. It could only be Fay's. Rita sits up, ears pricked.

"I have always thanked God for little favours," burbles Fay to her wobbling accomplices, "but tonight I shall thank you! My dear, dear friends."

Ach! Love hath conquered all.

Hugh and Jenny, either drunk or bewitched or both, help tipsy Fay to her door. Fay giggles wildly, swings her arms which must be caught to keep her from tumbling down the stairs.
If she fell would she take flight?

A question that lingers, m'dears.

"Huh?" says Fay and giggles and slips to her knees. Hugh pulls her up again and Jenny holds her other arm. "Thank you, dear friends, for aiding Ritterhouse Fay, 1-6-4-5-2, on her merry Fay-Wray way."

"1-6-4-5-2?" slurs Jenny.

"You got it, sugar! The Ritterhouse Fay, 1-6-4-5-2 but whose counting?!"

"What do you mean, '1-6-4-5-2?" says Jenny.

"1-6-4-5-2 is my number, bimbo! What's your number?"

"I haven't got a number."

"No number?! Of course you've got a number. We've all got numbers in the sodding Book of Life! Ritterhouse Fay, 1-6-4-5-2! Present and accounted for, matron!"

Who, I ask, can argue with that? With a straight so-called *face*, I hasten to add.

Fay pulls away, sits on the top stair of her landing. "What's your number, Hughie?"

"I haven't got a number either."

"My God, you numberless people bore me poopless! Have you never been incarcerated?"

"No," replies Hugh.

"Incinerated? Roasted on your own petard?"

Not quite, Fay. But close.

Fay's face suddenly drains of colour, freezes, as enervated by my heavy schedule I have temporarily withdrawn Fay's support. I am tired, darlings, but let me attempt, through sheer malevolence, to plod on:

So, strangely silent (say I), Fay offers no resistance as Jenny and Hugh take her by both arms, lift her to her feet, place her in front of her door where she fumbles and drops her key. Jenny picks it up but Fay snatches it away, clumsily unlocks the door herself, falls through as it opens. They reach in to help her from the floor but she slaps away their hands, rises unsteadily and dead-eyed, recites:

> There is no place
> Anywhere near this place
> Just like this place
> So this must be the goddamned...
> The damned...place.

Not really, sugar, it's just an open prison. You know, like the ones we, every Jack and Jill of us, blithely inhabit.

Fay closes her door, opens it again, says:

"Thank you, my friends. My dear friends. Thank you for being my friends. Searching for Granny is risky business."

Errands! Errands! Such a bother.

Fay's door closes uncharacteristically softly. Hugh and Jenny, hand in hand, sway for a moment catching their breath, each mutely considering all the things they would like to have honestly asked one another today. Then they wonder whether they have been duped, yet again, by this -- Jenny is certain of it -- this...well, she's at least mad isn't she? And why...why have they agreed to... No. This is all too much!

Hand in hand they haltingly descend to their flat, find Fay's forgotten portfolio, open it, sit, and swaying still, read.

"Crikey!" says Hugh, "Rita's flat is to be a garage!"

A savage hammering at their door! Jenny freezes.

"Hello?! Hello in there?!"

It is Fay. Hugh makes it to the door, just, opens it.

"Pwans, pwease," lisps Fay.

"Huh?" says Hugh.

No lisping now! "My goddamned portfolio, if you please!"

Jenny hands the portfolio to Fay who steadies herself on the rail, then sashays up the stairs, suddenly, and curiously, sober.

After some time, during which Fay has been vainly hashed and rehashed, Jenny wants to say: What is really happening with Jim Richardson? Can you still love me, Hugh?

But honestly, it's as if someone had slapped duct-tape over her mouth.

Hugh wants to say: Why did you encourage all this with Jim? Are you trying to fob me off on him? Are you trying to get rid of me, Jen?

But he's been duct-taped too.

Sex is one thing. Love, another. And sex, at your age, my two capering, cardboard cuties, seems far more important than it is.

Neither of them says a word. They simply unfold the sofa-bed, undress, climb in and smile guiltily through those taped lips at one another. Both trying to forget what they promised Fay. The solemn oath. Signed in blood. Real blood. Human blood. Though Fay's blood *was* a curious mauve.

Must have been the lighting, huh, kids? My God! Isn't it all just *too* ridiculous?! I shall be more alert in future. Fay, it seems, is capable of recharging herself -- like one of those delicious cars, the ones with both combustion and electrical motors. Being infinitely literary, as I valiantly strive to be, does not preclude a searing interest in *motive* technology. A pun, darlings! Cherish it. Particularly when there are so many inexplicable (and murderous) motives about. But then, darlings, that's a sign of the times, isn't it? Or is it? You tell me.

Ah! To be, or not to be. That's a *question*?!

45

Jenny and Hugh wait, bedraggled, beset, at the bus stop -- Jenny stayed the night as she often, though not *so* often lately, does. She's confused. She lays this at Fay's door. But when she attempts to reason this out, reason won't come. She shivers, damn it! *Shivers*!

With Hugh it is a different story. He rather enjoys Fay's wild ways. A crazy lady here and there adds zest (How très gay, darling, even for a bitchin'-butted bi-boy). And Jenny's been so quiet lately. So aberrantly taciturn when they're on their own.

Hugh and Jenny are soon joined on the street by Rita who listens, outraged, to Jenny's news from the previous evening. Rita's flat to become a garage?! Rita gives them sad news of semi-comatose Taylor whom she is on her way to visit in hospital. The bus arrives.

Ach! Fay at her window has seen and heard. Her eyes are acute, her ears, more so, Marcel! They all spoke so amicably to one another. Why does no one speak amicably to her?

Hugh and Jenny were kind last night, kind to the Ritterhouse Fay. They've both risen precipitately on that murky gift-list. "Perhaps an automobile between them?" muses Fay, "one of those electric/petrol wonders? Top of the line, of course, with four-zone automatic air conditioning and a super CD/MP3 deck to play the adagio from Ravel's piano concerto in G."

Is Fay's taste in music somewhat too profound for this too temporary tart?! My cunning little copycat! Your desperate digressions, well intentioned as they are, drain me. Traipse on, darling, into the next square. But then, have you anything *else* to do?

"Yes," murmurs Fay, "A visit to my lawyer. But what business is it of yours?"

That's for me to know and for you to find out.

"Belt up!" hisses Fay and slaps on her sable.

"I've aired your plants, love," whispers Rita to the sleeping, tube-webbed Taylor, "watered 'em too. Everything is as it should be, love."

Taylor's eyes pop open but seem to see nothing. "*Is* it?" she whispers, drool gathering at the corner of her shrunken mouth, "*is* everything as it should be?"

"Yes, love," says Rita who wishes she'd had a grandmother who hadn't died so soon and left no time at all to be loved. Rita is thinking a lot about love lately (*how* like Fay), feels terribly inadequate in the hugs 'n' kisses department, is trying to make up for it. Ian...

"The witch," whispers Taylor, "Mr Taylor's postcards... Don't let...the witch."

Taylor's eyes flutter shut. She begins to breathe deeply, harshly, lips flapping. She falls into her chronic dream of mutable Fay as a snarling black cat, as a screeching raven, as a...

Rita pats Taylor's hand. "Granny," she whispers, "I'm here, Granny Taylor."

Taylor's dream image of Fay fades for a moment under Rita's soothing touch. Then reappears as a burning doll. A doll she, Taylor, recognizes. Ach!

Well you should recognize it, my dear. It's an authentic closet case -- been in your closet for donkey's years. Tucked beside that rug. Whoops! That rug abandoned ship. Old woman, are you certain you did the right thing?

I'm really quite naughty, my dears. But this old gal and I have a history.

Fay, as though summoned, unlocks Taylor's door with her master key and lays the portfolio open on the Postcard Table. She skips (yes, *skips* -- according to instructions) to the kitchen, finds an over-ripe orange in the fridge. Snooping and sniffing she wanders about the flat, trailing orange peels after her. "Ummnnn" she mutters, "Ummnnn," and again arrives at the postcard table where she sits, pokes a so-called *toe* (whoops!) into the next square, withdraws it. Which is *extremely* irritating.

She divides the orange into three sections, sticks one in her mouth and scribbles a note on the plans. She flips a page, studies the next, pauses to wipe dripping orange from her cupid's bow lips. In retribution for irritating me, I have made this orange uncommonly acidic. She pulls a face, wipes her lips again, rises and, sighing, goes to an interior wall, kicks it. "Yes. This is a bearing wall."

I've been demoted, thinks the wall and pulsates an angry vermilion, I was once known as an *over*bearing wall.

Fay scans the wall, loving it with her eyes, and is filled with profound satisfaction. The wall responds, fades to mauve then to comfortable cerulean. "This is my wall and my house," whispers Fay, "Others may live here but they do so at my pleasure."

Our pleasure, ducky. You are now proceeding (I prod her ahead with a mini-blow to her so-called left kidney) into the next ordained square of this game, this saga. Sagas, my dear, do belong to their narrators, do they not?

"I haven't the vaguest idea what you're blathering about," says Fay and plonks into her mouth the penultimate section of her *sour* orange. Then, treading on ever more dangerous ground (she'd best start watching those p's and q's), she returns to the kitchen, opens the fridge again, tilts a pint of milk to her mouth but dashes it to the sink. It's sour too! (Ho! Ho!) She opens a pantry -- precisely like the very old days -- looks for cookies, goodies of any kind. Her Granny always had something scrumptious here. Nothing! Fay frowns, slams the pantry door, looks as though she'll cry, doesn't, kicks that wall instead. Whoops! The wall weeps. Careful Fay. She's hurt her so-called *foot*!

"Why am I so self-destructive?!" asks Fay, "Me not so excessively happy just now."

At the postcard table Fay sits and grumpily pulls her sable closer -- she's naked under it and it's cold in here. Who turned off the bleeding heat? She reaches into the red plastic carry-bag on Taylor's chair arm, pulls out a card, reads:

> October 12, 1963. I refuse to feel guilty, my dear. It had to be done considering the situation. I care deeply for you in my fashion but your family! That family! Especially... "F" (!!!!) You did get yourself into rather a pickle with those -- were they women?!
> We must remember that one man's meat is another man's meat errr...poisson (Joke) and I wasn't your cup of tea.
> Fondly, in the fullness of etc, Oscar.

The card is scrawled with a heart, but the arrow through it stabs Fay. *Oscar*!

That name rings a sinister bell! That woman in brogues was there, was cruel to her -- was lipsticked and whiskered! Who was she? Was she poor sister Jane's hound-keeping, heavy-footed, oath-belting murderer?

Poor Fay, all this unleashed in her head by a name and a heart with an arrow through it -- clumsily drawn at that. But everybody has an Uncle Oscar somewhere, haven't they, Fay? An Uncle Oscar who *must be stopped*! "Where am I," asks Fay, "just now, at this bloody moment. Where am I?"

You're just leaving square umpteen, darling.

"But where have I been?"

I'm silent. Let her stew for a moment.

Then after that moment: "But where have I been?"

In the previous square, darling, I mutter then dutifully plunge the room into inky darkness to illustrate that oblivion is much the same wherever encountered and *where* one has been or even *what* one has been is not nearly so important as where one is going and what one will become.

This ebony vacuum I create circles menacingly around Fay. Distracted, she stuffs the last wedge of sour orange into her mouth, is calmed by a most nutritious squirt of good old (though sour) vitamin C.

"Rita?"

Fay, about to swallow, coughs up the bit of orange.

"Rita?" says Ian through the ajar door.

Fay scrubs her lips clean with sable, says:

"Come in!"

Ian sees Fay, "I beg your pardon," turns immediately to leave.

"Mr Ian! Long time no see!"

Ian nods, pauses, a billion pounds beckons, draws him back. He's only human. Perhaps it's not only the money. He was a weak man in the past -- didn't always do the right thing. Fact is, m'dears, hardly *ever* did the right thing. Rita will have her hands full (and so will he). But the course of true love never did run smooth, did it? Remember, there is potential in everyone. We've just got to dig it out. Tear it out! *Slash* it out! Somehow.

So Ian, feet of clay firmly planted in past regrettably bad habits (nobody's perfect though Rita will attempt it), watches Fay with a -- how shall we put it after all this revelation? -- Ach! Watches Fay with jaundiced eye as she gestures majestically at her portfolio and says:

"These are the extensive plans I mentioned at my soirée. The last time we met, sir. It was, I believe, during the Crimean war, sir."

"What?"

"When I last saw you, silly! Ages ago. It was a figure of speech, an allusion. You are familiar with allusions?"

"Yes. Illusions as well."

Not *that* familiar, old son. You're walking a plank, love. Mind how you tread. There are sharks below (and above!).

"You're making merry of me!" chimes Fay archaically, determined that her *voluminous* experience as a prison librarian be not wasted. Words do paint such lovely pictures. Words were once all she had. Unuttered words circling about in...smoke? Thick, indigo, choking smoke?

Ian stares at Fay. She is accustomed to being stared at, enjoys it. Once they stood her on a box and spat at her and poked her with sharp sticks and...

"Well, Mr Ian," says Fay. Her/our eyes are wandering naughtily from his unconsciously clenched fists to those fetching flies of his, behind which lurks at least fifty percent of the source of life in all sentient beings.

Now that, my dears, was a *seminal* statement.

"Mr Ian, don't you wish to see my plans?"

Fay laughs and extends the portfolio.

"I was looking for Rita," he says, "I thought she might be here."

"Pray, why?"

That odd choice of words, we do so enjoy it.

"What?" says Fay, her eyes darting to a dark niche in the room, just by the chock-a-block closet that held...

"Rita airs Mrs Taylor's geraniums."

"*Airs* them? I knew Rita put on airs but I didn't know they extended to gardening."

Ian doesn't speak.

"I had a miscarriage," murmurs Fay searching for a sop. All she gets is a dry "Yes?"

Sweet Jesus, Ian! A little milk of human kindness might be appropriate here. But all Fay gets from you is a blank face. So, in view of your heartless indifference, she chirps: "But I'm rarin' to go now, partner!" and rattles the portfolio once more.

Ian is curious (let's be generous and add spellbound leavened by greed), comes cautiously to the table where she pushes her plans and a bit of nippled tittie before him (compliments of your own merciless mistress of ceremonies).

"I'll start here, on the ground floor, opposite Rita. This tenant has given up her lease."

"Nelly?"

"Was that her name? Yes. Well, sugar, I'm afraid we've lost her. It was sad. I was deeply fond of what's-her-name. Until she stole my ankle-length, chinchilla coat and a priceless diamond bracelet."

Ian studies the plans, ignores Fay.

"Her flat, currently kitty's poo-box, will be my chauffeur's quarters (that Savoy suite is *so* expensive). Next to my garage."

Fay smiles innocently.

"Garage?" says Ian.

"Page four, lover."

Ian turns to page four. "But this is Rita's flat."

"Whoopth!" lisps Fay, "It wath?"

"I believe you'll have trouble there."

"We'll simply have to wait and see, won't we? Well, howsa 'bout it, guvnor? When do we start?"

Tiny flashes of light glitter here and there from the crack at the bottom of that closet door. Fay sees them, Ian doesn't. As soon as he's gone, she thinks, I must inspect. I wouldn't want something rotten in Denmark."

"I don't think I'd be interested in this sort of work, Ms Ritterhouse" says Ian.

"Oh do call me Fay."

Fay squinches her forehead, brings that finger to her lip. "Oh, golly, Mr Ian! Your employer will be ever so unhappy when I take my business elsewhere. I've other jobs too. Dozens of them. With the kind help of the poor, late Abdullah Shamaly's associate, Hassan Ammari, I have acquired extensive holdings, nearly doubled my money, monsieur. All those projects! Are you certain you won't reconsider?"

"You're a tough nut, aren't you, Fay?"

She's a nut, Ian. Full stop (or 'period' as the Americanos say).

"Maybe. But when I'm cracked open I'm soooo nice."

Fay moves closer, Ian jerks away.

"What is it you're after here, Ritterhouse? Why can't you just slope off and leave these people alone? What in hell are you trying to do here?"

"A five letter word, Mr Ian: M-E-R-C-Y."

She's right, my friends. It's for their own good, believe you, me! The inevitable is just around the corner. I do have to agree with Fay here. Though I'm partial. But who isn't?

"Mercy?"

A severely perplexed Ian is almost at the door when Fay screams. "I hope you'll reconsider your decision, Mr Ian! A billion and growing goes a long, long way!"

Fay, darling, you have an unnatural interest in money. Let it not distract you from your mission.

"What?" says Fay to the glistening shadow by the closet door that seems to, what is the word?

Ah, 'pulsate'.

"Mr Ian!" cries Fay, but he is out the door, closing it softly behind him.

"Mercy," whispers Fay on her way to that closet door for a snoop, and the milk of human kindness (didn't *I* just say so?). "God's teeth!" continues Fay, "I could be the prodigal, returned, and this is the thanks I get. I've come to save *them*, one and all. And Granny. I want my Granny. I WANT MY BLOODY GRANNY!"

She *has* come to save them. One and all. And she *does* want her Granny, desperately. Poor Fay. But we don't always get what we want, do we? Beware of *Answered Prayers*, said the volcanic Truman Capote-catty-petl before he blew his top and kicked that latin-lovin' lava-laden bucket.

46

A pullulating shadow lingering at the corner of her eye seems to jump as she throws open Taylor's closet door and blinks, certain she hasn't seen what she certainly has. "I mean, really!" pops into Fay's head, followed by "What the dickens?!"

Pullulating shadows are none of your business, love, back off.

Fay's shivering, she's frightened. She obediently backs out of the closet, returning the extremely heavy latch (Make a note of *that,* m'dears) gingerly, as though it might bite her (it's definitely an enemy, Fay). Keeping an eye, as commanded, on that heavy latch, she backs across the room, drops herself into Mrs Taylor's oak chair and mumbles something unintelligible. Something very like: "Abra-katzenjammer".

In that somehow familiar closet Fay had felt something, seen something sinister, something that could only be explained as a threat to the continuing existence of my Ritterhouse Fay. My Fay who is the very personification of love. But love, m'dears, has ever been fleeting.

She spies a box of matches amongst the postcards piled over Mrs Taylor's table, lights one, lets it burn to her finger, screams with delight at the pain then blows out the match and lights another. She takes her burning match to Taylor's paraffin lamp on the table by that suspicious, excessively heavily latched closet door. "My magic carpet came from here. It seems so long ago."

Ach! Memories! How they do grease the skids of our too hasty retreat from the ties that bind, these oh so mortal coils. Mixed metaphors never hurt a *soul* – one must glory always, m'dears, in diversity. As do I.

Fay lifts the lamp's glass chimney and lights it, studies its flame. "I could come to like fire."

If she practiced long enough. Why not? She was born in fire. We were all born in fire. We are the stuff of a trillion suns… an infinity of stars... Sorry, m'dears, I do digress of a balmy evening.

Fay returns to the oak chair and sits and lights match after match, throwing each to the floor where it scorches, sputters, and dies on the damp, lazily undulating, somewhat embarrassed but I hasten to add, completely adequate carpet.

And please note, my dears, that paraffin lamp as it glows cosily, lovingly, singing:

I'm bidin'
My time
For that's
The kind of
Lamp I'm...

Rita's eyes blink open, she sits up in bed, sticks her nose in the air, sniffs. Smoke!?

"Ian?! " she cries, then remembers he'd left earlier in the evening but not before relating the incident with Fay in Taylor's flat. Jenny and Hugh had seen the plans too!

Was there no end to that woman's...? SMOKE! Rita smells smoke. She jumps from her bed, throws on a robe and rushes into the corridor, sniffs again, races up the stairs and pounds at Hugh's door.

"Fire!" she shouts, "Fire!"

Hugh, in his scanties: "Jesus, Rita, it's three A.M.!"

"Something's burning!" cries Rita.

Hugh sniffs the air, rushes back, fetches Jenny. Rita points up the stairs. "It's coming from her!"

The three of them rush up the stairs to find smoke escaping under Fay's door.

"Hello in there! You're on fire!" cries Hugh.

"What about Bill?" says Jenny, "Is he in?"

"No," says Rita, "He went to look for Nelly a few days ago, hasn't come back."

"Open up!" shouts Hugh, at Fay's door, "You're on fire!"

"Break the door down, Hugh!" screams Rita.

"Open up, for God's sake!" cries Jenny, her mouth pressed to the polished, intricately carved (lemmings leaping to their lot in life) door.

But there is no answer. High-tech speakers blare Country-Western from within. Hugh rattles the door, it's locked, he backs away then charges, vainly butting his shoulder and yelping. Jenny moves him aside and, with a mighty karate kick worthy of a master, lock separates from door and the three of them burst into Fay's smoke-filled living room.

"Welcome!" giggles Fay through the open wall from the terrace where she reclines, sabled, black cat in lap, scotch in one hand, joint in the other, "Welcome, dear, *dear* friends!"

Here is Chauffy in a tall chef's hat, a wisping joint between his lips, clad only in an apron which cannot conceal his gleaming buttocks, aft, nor his becoming bulge, fore. He seems impervious to the cold – but his meat is toasting nicely, thank you. We pause for a lust-break, my dears. Ach! Then on!

Chauffy attends a splendid chromium barbecue the smoke of which has, most curiously, been sucked through the open glass wall of Fay's flat and under her door into the corridor.

"Long time no see!" giggles Fay. She is delighted. Rita screams with laughter.

"Sorry," says Hugh, wearing marginally less than Chauffy, "We thought you had a fire up here."

"We do, mate," laughs Chauffy, keenly aware of Hugh's interest in his fore and not disinterested himself in Hugh's mini-briefs (he wishes he had a pair like that – good for business), "this meat ain't cookin' itself."

"I mean a fire fire," stammers Hugh, noting in detail (Here we go again, my dears) Chauffy's broad, defined, flame-lit, superbly gleaming chest, "we seem to have broken down your door."

"Pish-tush! tinkles Fay, "Who cares?! Chauffy! Make 'em a drink, light 'em a joint!"

That's about as far as we oldsters dare venture, m'dears, from alcohol to mary-jane. Not that we *couldn't*...but of course you know all that, don't you? Or *should*, you dense, dimpled darlings.

"Not for me, thank you," says Rita, "I believe I'll just crawl back to my garage and roll in some axle-grease."

And possibly a quart of cognac?

"Rita, darling! You didn't take that garage rumour seriously?"

But Rita is out the door and Jenny, then Hugh, still lingering on Chauffy's fire-lit flesh, make to follow her.

"Nooooo!" cries Fay, "Pleassse stay! Chauffy, throw on two more steaks from Texas, the Lone Star State! We fly them in, kiddies! Direct from Dallas!"

Hugh and Jenny are tempted -- though for somewhat different reasons.

"Pleassssse stay. We'll discuss your modernized kitchen and bath. We have an agreement. You do recall? Monte for a week and your abode finished by your return. You have that in writing."

They have that in blood! Don't you remember? *Any* of you?

"Do stay, my dear...dear friends," pleads Fay.

Jenny and Hugh decide to stay, as much to see Fay in action, as for the steaks, the drinks, the weed, Chauffy's gleaming buttocks (Jenny's a bit of a butt-king herself) and just perhaps, more than a modicum of magic.

Rita, in her 'boudoir', is unable to sleep. She makes an exception, pours a cognac even though it's not the bleeding weekend (Didn't I tell you?). She takes up her French Primer. Plenty to learn here – must learn it properly one day. For when she and Ian honeymoon in Paris. She smiles, plumps her pillows and settles down for a long read but is distracted, puzzles for a moment. How did all this witch business begin? Taylor. Of course. It was poor Mrs Taylor. But there is something about the mauve glow in Fay's eyes -- opaque eyes that are windows to nowhere.

Ah well. Rita lays her French Primer on her stomach, lights a cigarette, puffs. Taking up the book again, she notices that her fingers are shaking and the print is a blur. She slams the book away, downs a brandy. Then another and another. Let us hope she does not fall asleep with a her lighted cigarette and burn the house down. Though the walls of course, fidgeting round her, would have warned her.

I've thought of everything, m'dears. Nothing will derail my 'Little Engine That Could' when we're so close to the completion of our task/game/saga of love applied and love denied. The *task*? Glad you asked. Rescue, of course! What else?

Suddenly it's morning and Rita is baggy-eyed at her window smoking -- she has survived, shaken her hangover away and risen early -- must get to that novel at her freshest. She waves to Hugh and Jenny as they wait for their bus.

"How late?" says Hugh to Jenny, waving back at Rita in the window.

"All night," says Jenny.

"All night?"

"Sure," says Jenny though she's not sure at all. How does she get them both into these things? God! He's so repressed. It was pathetic the way Hugh deferred to Chauffy. A male prostitute. Far better, a steaming, cathartic affair with Jim Richardson -- a boss who could do Hugh some good -- besides *doing* him. But...

"You are absolutely sure? No going back on it?"

"Absolutely sure," says Jenny who isn't at all sure (It's tough being an old fashioned girl, ain't it love?).

"Where will you be?"

"With Alicia."

"Why do you get me into these things?"

"Jim is a nice man. So are you. You have to get to know one another."

And you, Jennykins, have a few soft nothings to whisper in Alicia's shell-like ear, n'est-ce pas?

"Know one another?" says Hugh, "Your full-potential bullshit?"

"Using ones full potential is not bullshit."

Oh, for heaven's sakes, you two! Get on with it!

"I almost think you're tired of me, Jen," says Hugh with a weak smile.

"Life's like that. Hey. What about that week in Monte?"

"Ritterhouse'll never come through."

Jenny shrugs, hates herself, hates her phony psycho-shit. Hates the present shallowness of their conversation. Hates the drunken, blood-pact promise they both made to Fay to accept a new kitchen and a free holiday -- something *fishy* about it. What am I doing? thinks Jenny.

Pleassssse, children!

"Oh, Jen," whispers Hugh in her ear, "You aren't trying to get rid of me, are you, Jen?"

"Darling. I am trying to keep you."

She hugs him, thinks: Am I? Reassures herself: I am.

Honestly, Jenny, by now, who the fuck cares?

Fay watches from her window. Can she hear them? Probably. They're just a couple of crazy, mixed up kids, aren't they?

Mixed up *boring* kids, dear. I should have devoted more time to them, fleshed them out.

Fay's been there herself. About a million times in a million years. Funny feeling, that. Isn't it Fay? Sex across the millennia?

"Why do I suffer, why do I burn?" asks Fay. "Why must I be continually crucified upon a cross of fire?"

A universal question, ducky. The best I can do, just now, is: Because it is written, love. Somewhere -- I'll look it up. It is written that you will burn. Again and again. If I so choose.

"Who are you?" asks Fay, "Please. Who *are* you?" begs Fay, "Please tell me who you are."

Mum's the word.

Rita leans out of Mrs Taylor's window, sets Taylor's last two geraniums out for airing. She has already visited Taylor in hospital this morning. No improvement. Poor old dear, thinks Rita. Sooner or later we all end up on a bedpan.

Dear Rita, you 'emerging' authors should be more observant. Mrs Taylor voids her bodily fluids and poisons through various plastic tubes, love. *Honestly*! Do join us, dearie, in the twenty-first century! Do your fucking research!

So Rita, blithely oblivious of emergency room hygiene, is watering, airing Taylor's geraniums and tidying up.

The damp old carpet, she sees, is covered with spent match-sticks -- obviously from Fay. What can be done about it? It's Fay's house. If she wishes to burn it down, so be it.

Torment, too, apparently, has its perks.

47

"Hello, stranger!" cries Rita jolted from her thoughts at her window by the appearance of an ecstatic Bill springing up the front steps.

He looks up, waves.

"She's fine. I'm fine. We're getting married next Sunday. Very simple, just the two of us. We *must* be simple; Nelly, to marry me in the first place and me to marry again at my age."

Bill, darling, think better of yourself. You're a catch too!

Rita tops Bill's cup. "You'll come here after?" asks Rita, "You must. We'll have a little reception. Ian and I and Jenny and Hugh. We've all been through so much together. For old time's sake?"

Really, Rita. *Old* times? You've only known them for a couple of months.

"I'm not sure Nelly will come here again. I'm just back for a few things. We'll send for the rest. We're staying with a friend. We're buying our own flat."

"That's wonderful. Where?"

"Kilburn side of St John's Wood."

"Lovely! St John's Wood. I almost got married at a chapel there. Forget precisely where it was. Forget precisely who *he* was. He certainly forgot where *it* was -- and I'm not speaking about the bleeding chapel."

Rita guffaws. "But you will ask Nelly? We've all been through so much together (You already said that, love – been nipping?). I'd be sorry if we couldn't celebrate with you. We're all so -- well -- joined now, as if by magic."

Bulls eye!

"I'll ask her, Rita. But I won't promise anything."

That's right, love. In any case, promises are made to be broken, else why should we make them?

Bill checks his watch, "I've come for a few things from upstairs -- I'm in a bit of a rush. We're due at the new flat in an hour to sign papers."

"I'm so happy for the two of you, Bill. Nelly is a lovely woman. I'll miss you both."

"We're both pretty set in our ways, maybe too old to start over..."

"Nonsense!" cries Rita who knows all about old, all about

starting over. But most about being set in her ways.

Bill hurries up to his flat, finds himself face to face with Fay immersed in her portfolio. She is startled, backs away, slams the portfolio shut and tugs her sable closer around her.

"Long time no see, Billy."

Bill is silent. The air crackles around them (compliments of guess who) and the walls shrink back in terror at a potentially unpleasant confrontation.

"The prodigal Daddy returns," snaps Fay, ignoring me.

"You do get around, don't you, Ritterhouse?"

"Only a routine inspection of the premises as specified in your lease. How is..."

"Nelly is fine. Nelly is lovely. Nelly is kind. Nelly is good. Nelly is all the things you'll never be, Ritterhouse. We're getting married next Sunday, a little reception at Rita's. Don't bother to come."

Billy! Now why did you have to go and tell her that?

"Billy! Really?! How wonderful!"

Fay is delighted. She adores Nelly, her very only friend on our spinning sphere. She wishes her every happiness. Bill too. Why should she hold it against him that he sullied her and absconded. Why should she care about that priceless chinchilla, those precious diamonds?

Why indeed?

Bill finds a small suitcase in his bedroom, begins to toss in clothes. Fay follows him and leans provocatively (doesn't she *wish*!) against the door frame. Another square beckons. She sticks one foot into it, pulls it out quickly – it startled her, seemed to burn her toes. She sniffs the air – no smoke. Yet. Sets the foot back into the square. Can't defy Destiny. If only she knew what Destiny was. If only any of us could separate our destinies from that avalanche of miscellany that threatens daily to engulf us all. Ach, m'dears, I wax pseudo philosophical. 'Pseudo' is, in fact, as near as I can get to *anything* as I, like Ms Fay, have my reasons. But lucky Fay has only to follow the bouncing squares and I have other fish to fry (or have I said that before?). But such is life. As though any life, my pets, holds intrinsic meaning. Unless that meaning lies in ones love of another and another's love for one – Ach! that occasionally pleasant game of hide and seek. But such pie in the sky is not to be easily grasped. You don't simply stick in a thumb and pull out a plum. Particularly via an ephemeral hug and an empty kiss (no matter how juicy) or a corrosive coital connection (adds Mumsy with alacrity!).

"There was a baby, Billy," says Fay, both of her feet finally standing shakily in that next dodgy square, "It wasn't yours. But there *was* a baby."

"Get out. Please."

"I was raped by that lorry driver, Billy. That hairy monster of a lorry driver. He had black curly hair all over his back, Billy, like an ape. I've brought charges against him but you know how it is these days. They prefer to believe beast, never beauty. They *never* believe me."

"How odd," says Bill and continues to pack.

"They say I asked for it, Billy."

"Why am I surprised?"

"Billy. Why are you so cruel?"

Bill! *Please* be gentle with the woman. She's hurting.

"You can have my lease too. Stick it with Nelly's, tie them with a ribbon and shove them up your arse."

"Billy, really, that was uncalled for."

And dangerous, Billy, très *dangereux*!

Fay sets the portfolio against a wall, moves towards Bill. Very close, she licks her lips. He ignores her, says "Nelly sold that chinchilla you gave her. And the bracelet. We've put it all on a flat."

Fay slips out of her sable. She is clad in her skimpiest underwear, her firm, magenta nipples poking out through lacy mauve peepholes. She *will* confuse sex with love. Didn't we just discuss that? Darling Fay, if you refuse to listen…

"Take this one too." Says Fay, thrusting this second fabulous fur at Bill.

Ignoring her near nakedness he takes the proffered coat, tosses it on his bed. "Thanks, we'll buy a car too."

He turns away, continues packing, angrily assessing that crazy sand-pit Fay has made of Nelly's flat. Fay moves in, presses herself against his back, waits, eyes closed. He twists round, faces her. "You still love me!" she whispers. It seems for a magic moment he does but when he places his hands on her shoulders and turns her firmly away from him, and marches her into the hall -- well. What's a gal to do?

So she shivers in her skivvies, nostrils flaring, fit to spit.

And *I* don't like it much either.

"Belt up!" whispers Fay, "Let *me* handle this!"

Bill returns with her sable, drops it on the floor in front of her.

Before he can get away she slaps his face with a terrible wallop. He quietly closes the door. The door opens again. She smiles expectantly, meets his eye. The portfolio comes sailing out, joins her sable on the floor and the door slams shut. Fay tries it, it's locked. She pounds on it, presses her mouth to it, screams:

"Ask Nelly exactly how she comforted me! Ask her how she comforted Ritterhouse Fay the very same night you tried to rape me! Ask Nelly! Ask Nelly if she enjoyed it!"

Fay has no idea at all, *none at all*, why she says such hurtful things (nor should she, m'dears). She hasn't meant to. "I don't mean to," she murmurs truthfully into the locked door, "And it's not true. Not at all true what I just said about dear Nelly. What has come over me?"

The walls nod affirmatively, knowing full well that I, indeed, am responsible. Oh my darlings, forces, *almost* beyond our ken, are busily at work on our oversized board game, the parameters of which seem to spread exponentially -- endless squares of choice that must be expended! Your faithful old tart grows increasingly weary. So humour me, m'dears. Pat me on my arse and give me a shove. Merci mille fois!

Bill shakes his head, continues packing. Fay pounds at the door, pleads for several minutes. Anguish morphs to rage and she gathers up the scattered portfolio and flies through her own door, directly opposite.

Chauffy lies naked on the white leather sofa. What a delicious sight he is with his artificial tan (those ultra-violet solariums are perilous, darling – could give yer knob a nasty nip!). Ach! His white-golden ringlets and those lithe limbs -- a seductive sight, at the moment, to anyone it seems but Fay. The poor boy opens his mouth to speak.

"GET STUFFED!" shrieks Fay.

"Yes please," answers Chauffy who is soundly thumped with the portfolio.

Fay rockets to a window, throws it open, screams, slams it shut. The semi-skyscraper opposite quivers in sympathy for poor, throbbing Number 13. "What *have* we got ourselves into?" whine the walls and floors. Don't play innocent! I answer. You're no more virgin than I am. Your shattered hymenic accoutrementi could pave the way to Pluto!

That blackest of cats, overwhelmed by Fay's house-shaking shriek, has already leapt once again from the terrace to its fourth death. Resurrected, it will return in the evening to Fay's kitchen -- via an alleviatory visit on Nelly's sandy strand -- for its ration of caviar or frozen scampi or whatever. Much like, but not *quite* like Fay in the old days. For Fay ate putrefying food from rubbish bins. She rubbed decayed fish, like war-paint, across her forehead. Or so it appeared to Fay. But that's another story, never to be reprised. Although me old mate, Nostradamus, might thoroughly disagree. But pessimists bore me shitless, m'dears. They are *so* pessimistic.

48

Fay is dressed to kill and angry as hell and doesn't care who knows it. She's abandoned much of what's left of her goodness though a searing soupçon of said remains (see directly below). Here she is in her Rolls, careening towards a speciality supply company in London W1 via her lawyer's for some unfinished and very surprising business (to be explained *much* later as it is simply too contradictory to be believed at this point).

Don't ask why. "I wouldn't tell you even if I knew!" spits Fay. I permit a smile to creep languidly across my so-called *chops*. Chauffy, at the wheel, is both frightened and amused by the mad glint in her eyes but dares not let her see he's watching in his rear-view mirror. Clear thinking, Chauffy. Keep it up and you'll survive. Might even prosper.

"Yes?" replies Rita, "Can I help you?"

With identical bewildered frowns the two men lead Rita into Nelly's Flat. A thick carpet of sand covers everything, in places piled as high as the sofa. Suddenly, with a disturbingly un-cat-like howl, Five-lives, who has been lying in the claw-shredded nest of what was once Nelly's fine (though severely coffee-stained) antique quilt, rockets past them and into the street where she is instantly struck by a speeding car and catapulted to the kerb. Expect her back. She's a few lives left. But who's counting?

"We've come for," begins one man who consults a smudged notepad, "Mr Hope-Jones and Miss Nelly Wilkinson's furniture and articles."

"So what's this then?!" says the other man with a hopeless gesture at this mini-desert, this cat-soiled, sand-trap of a flat.

"It appears," murmurs Rita, sniffing the air, "to be a particularly capacious cat-box."

Deft turn of phrase, Rita, my fledgling writer. You do me credit.

As the last of Nelly's and Bill's furniture and belongings are set into the lorry, up rolls the Rolls and disgorges a radiantly smiling Fay. She comes from a morning with her lawyers, having successfully dealt with that unauthorized, surprisingly contradictory and deeply munificent though secret business just mentioned. She has also made a rather more than naughty little detour -- to be dealt with later, m'dears. She waves to the pair of cat-odour-beset removals men, cries cheerily "Long time no see!" and glides by with a purple and red-ribboned package in her lavishly furred, jewel-dripping arms. Christmas carols from her limousine's stereo accompany her regal, quasi oriental *Wolfman Meets Frankincense* ascent up the steps of Number 13 (a bit of low humour, m'dears, never hurt anyone). Or did it?

Rita sobs, Ian mists mightily, attempts to comfort her, hugs her, kisses her cheek, whispers in her ear. She is inconsolable. But then, he's competing with young Judy Garland (Ach! How I adore her, mes enfants, and I don't care who knows it!). Yes, from Rita's telly, the fabulously young and chemically innocent, Judy sings "Have Yourself A Merry Little Christmas" to a sobbing five-year-old Margaret O'Brien. In this glorious old film (you've seen countless re-runs on your telly, m'dears) little Margaret is desperately unhappy that she'll be forced, with her whole family, to move from their beloved early nineteen-hundreds St Louis home to faraway New York City. Rita is certain *she* will be forced to leave Number 13. But that's not why she's crying. She's crying because *all life is loss*. Even with Ian beside her, *all life is loss*. Particularly when seen through the bottom of an oft filled, though now nearly empty brandy snifter. Put that in your ivory cigarette holder, Rita, and smoke it. It's a universal brand. The stuff that nightmares are made of. Better yet, ducky, put it into your novel. Any self-respecting author would.

I'm only trying to help.

Fay is watching the very same film, is weeping, but is not so sympathetically attended as Rita. Because Chauffy is high as a Kilimanjaro mountain goat. And although our succulent bimbo-with-balls cuddles close against Fay squashing his luscious loins into her tatty chenilled thigh, his interest has childishly wandered to the remote control, with which he buzzes open, then closes, the glass wall to the roof terrace and dims and brightens consecutively every room in the flat. He finally opens the built-in bar yet again with a resounding thump. Beware, Chauffy! For there, on a shelf beside a bottle of Irish Mist, is Nelly's pink-feathered Kewpie, tiny hips frozen in an accusing sashay. It is fortunate for Chauffy that Fay's eyes are riveted upon the telly and a terrifyingly tender close-up of little Margaret O'Brien's tear-drenched face.

Chauffy's attention wanders farther still. "What's that then?" he mutters.

Fay is irritated, "What's what?"

He points. "That."

"A cat, stupid," squeaks Fay, drowning amidst a colossal sob.

"What's that cat sleeping on?"

Fay and I weep, lost in this magical film, ignore him.

Wonderful film!

"What?" says Fay, "What was that?"

"What's the bleedin' cat sleepin' on then?" asks Chauffy with no sensitivity at all, at all!

"A prezzy!" snaps Fay, her eyes not deserting the telly screen.

"For me?"

"For Billy and what's-her-name!" hisses Fay with a glance at the purple and red package upon which Four-lives snoozes and, in the strangest way, dedicates. "They'll be married tomorrow."

Fay is of two minds (so what's new, sugar?) about Nelly and Billy but they will have their come-uppance. Just as she has had her multi-come-uppances, world without end, amen. Make that sans amen, m'dears, and hold the mayo.

As the film progresses, dear little Margaret O'Brien hurtles into a snow-blanketed garden and begins, hysterically beating down with a large stick, the many snow-*persons* she had earlier so laboriously fashioned with her own, blue-with-cold tiny, mittened fingers. "Right on!" screams Fay in a frenzy of hate for snow-persons -- or any persons, including Chauffy. Because persons, all persons are so damnably cruel. Especially persons who hose one down with ice-cold, high-pressured water! The world is a vale of tears, her Granny used to say, but we must, somehow, find our place in it. So Fay, still searching for *her* place, turns to Chauffy, wipes her eyes, murmurs "Do you love me?"

"Why not?" he says, moving up a notch on her gift-list then pressing a button on the remote which simultaneously closes all the curtains in the flat. "Why not?" he giggles, opening them again. Fay nestles close to him, bogusly comforted. Her gift-list glistens in her head -- beside all the other rubbish, including that long-harboured ship of vengeance -- and comforts her. And so ought we.

The film father of the soon to be dispatched to New York City family finally announces that they'll stay here after all, in their beloved St Louis! Tiny Margaret hugs her big sis, young Judy.

Everybody on the screen laughs happily, ultimately sing 'Meet me in St. Louis, Louie!' (though the identity of this mysterious 'Louie' is never revealed). Rita and Ian brush the tears from their cheeks and laugh happily. Fay, two floors above, laughs happily and sidles gingerly into another square, leaving Chauffy far behind. Christmas is just around the corner.

But what's Christmas to our *Antichrist*?

Let's not think about that just yet, shall we?

Jenny in her jolly red jogging suit knocks gently on Hugh's door. No answer. With a grunt she shifts her back pack to the floor, knocks gently again. No answer. She'll not enter now even though she has her key. It could be inconvenient. She might disturb Hugh and Jim and after all, she as much as set up the whole increasingly complicated...she drops the thought, picks up her back pack, swings it over her shoulder and starts down the stairs.

"Jenny?"

It's Hugh with that traditional morning erection poking out of his briefs! Careless boy! *Dearest* boy!

You've probably begun to think I'm hung up on Hugh's merry morning member. Guilty, as charged! I admit it, m'dears. I exult in life's infinite variety – so long as it's a willy. And I am not alone, methinks.

Jenny laughs. Hugh is yawning and barely awake though it is almost eleven on this bright Sunday morning.

"How'd it go?" asks Jenny glancing again at his over-stretched briefs, "or maybe I should have said how is it *going*?"

Hugh tucks himself in as I, sighing close by, diligently spy with my little so-called *eye*.

Jenny is apprehensive, feels stupid and self defeated, "Well?"

Hugh is back in bed. "He didn't arrive. His aunt or ex-wife or something. Some emergency."

"Damn."

"I tried to reach you but you weren't there."

"Alicia and I went to a late film."

And that ain't all, dearie.

Jenny starts for the kitchen. "Coffee? You look awfully tired for just sleeping."

"I wasn't sleeping. Ritterhouse and her humpy chauffeur were bleating on her terrace all last night."

"In this cold? Shall I put some scones on?"

Hugh nods, yawns, closes his eyes.

Jenny, from the kitchen:

"Have you arranged another tryst with Richardson?"

No answer. She sticks her head out the kitchen door. "I said have you arranged another tryst with our Jim?"

She's just the tiniest bit annoyed, mostly with herself.

"Jesus, Jen," mumbles Hugh, "What are you? My pimp?"

Jenny unwraps several frozen scones, lights the oven, shoves them in with a clatter.

"Oh God! I almost forgot. It's Nelly's and Bill's little reception today at Rita's. Did you wrap our present? You do it so much better than -- Hugh?"

He's sleeping. Jenny creeps in, kisses him on the forehead. "I love you, love. But..."

A crash from outside distracts her. "Damn," she whispers, not to disturb Hugh, "Damn them. They're beginning again."

So as the crashes re-commence and the sun rises through the smoky mist of Pimlico (Several hundred persons are illegally burning real wood in their fireplaces again), we say goodbye to our cutest 'n' cosiest cardboard couple.

Rita is furious with this new noise. She hurls down the knife (she is icing a small wedding cake -- my own incomparable recipe, though she doesn't know it), sticks her head out the window just avoiding a long metal pipe zipping by on the shoulders of two workmen.

"Hey!" she shouts, "It's sodding Sunday!"

"Ain't it just?" yells one of the triple-time workmen as he bolts together a section of pipes, soon to scaffold the entire exterior façade of Number 13.

Rita slams her window shut but not before an errant scaffold-pipe shatters Nelly's window and the rip of wood and plaster echoes from the corridor as the old staircase balustrade is torn from its throbbing, perhaps sobbing, though no one cares but me, moorings.

What we have here, m'dears, is an acutely sensitive, multi-purpose house readying itself, in its way, towards its purpose. Curious? Ach! I do hope so!

Rita deserts her cake, drops into a chair. With shaking fingers -- they've been shaking since the night before -- she sticks a cigarette into her holder, lights it, sprawls there sucking-in the soothing nicotine smog; battling in her head Ian's sensible anti-ciggie objections. But there are more important matters at hand. She must attempt somehow to endure this new assault of noise from without and within -- especially within – upon the very guts of her home.

Our home, lovey. *Our* home. You are only an accessory.

49

"Jesus, Jen, it's heavy!"

Hugh is struggling with Fay's purple, red-ribboned present for those soon-to-arrive newly-weds as he and Jenny descend the treacherous staircase through plaster dust and splintered wood amidst the deafening crash of a nearby sledge hammer. (*I* would instantly have rung someone in authority about this brazen breach of building behaviour!).

A large hole explodes in the wall of Nelly's flat and a hammering workman leers out as Rita pulls Jenny and Hugh through her door.

"Tiens! Where does she *get* these people?" says Rita, "Sod her! She knew, didn't she? About the reception. Did you tell her?"

"No," reply Hugh and Jenny in unison.

Rita forces herself to remain calm, has been particularly tense these past few days. Not only because of the noise but Ian as well. Is he still as interested as he was? The dedicated bloke himself, whom Rita might have consulted before thinking such outré thoughts, would answer unhesitatingly that he was every bit as.

Men grow invisible too, anxious with age. Reflect, Rita, *reflect*. Else I shall spirit away your literary luck to some other louche loser.

The man in question is at a large punch bowl and dips a cup for each of them. He graciously offers the first to Rita who is reassured, says:

"Thank God you don't have anything to do with the building this time, darling."

Ian has, in fact, and not so mysteriously, been made redundant by his former employer but hasn't yet told Rita.

"I plan to sue," says Rita to Jenny.

"No shit?" says Jenny.

"For breach of the peace. I'll figure it out later."

Then to Ian:

"Won't I, darling?"

Ian smiles, thinks how beautiful this fifty-four-year-old is, how lucky he is she cares for him, this woman with a sense of humour; how lost he was before her, how much he wishes she would stop smoking and go easy on the cognac. Ironical, ain't it, m'dears? With his ex-wife these roles were reversed. Now he's recovered, landed on his feet. Wouldn't want his dear Rita to experience that same debilitating dilemma, though she already has. Hence, *cognac-related* unemployed actress. Sweet Jesus, Ian! Do I have to draw a picture for you?!

Anyhoo, I invariably, of narrative necessity, lurk nearby.

"Ritterhouse is remodelling our kitchen and sending us to Monte Carlo for the duration," says Hugh.

"Surely you're not going?!" replies Rita.

"Why not?" says Jenny, "We deserve it after all the crap she's put us through."

"You're a witness, Ian. These two are bewitched."

"Nobody's bewitched," says Jenny, who suddenly remembers the odd vibrations that had plagued her for several days, and continues with less conviction. "Would you turn down an all expenses paid week in Monaco?"

"You're sodding right I'd turn it down if it came from Ms Ritterhouse Fay!" says Rita and quaffs her punch in one go. "Mrs Taylor is in hospital because of her. Remember her? The old lady who got thrown down the stairs?"

You're just envious, Rita, because no one ever offered you a free trip to Monte. Ach! I take that back. Of course, someone *did* – but he was old enough to be your Granddaddy.

"We don't really know that Ritterhouse put Taylor in hospital, do we?" says Hugh.

"Good God! Does somebody have to pee in your face before you know you're wet?!"

"Not bad, Rita," laughs Jenny, "for an invisible old broad."

Rita loves this, falls about for a moment, glad she's confided her now happily discarded theory to Jenny.

Kind of livens things up, doesn't it, *my* invisibility leitmotif? Though I've *attributed* it to Rita -- wouldn't want to spar with those pesky feministas.

"I don't believe Mrs Taylor is going to make it," says Rita.

"We haven't been to see her," says Hugh, "When we rang, the hospital said..."

"I know what they say but I go anyway and sit there. She might not know I'm there but it makes *me* feel better. I've taken a fancy to the old gal. Pity I never got to know her sooner. Sweet Jesus, I've lived here for five years!"

"When I think of the time *I've* wasted," says Ian, "just waiting for my aspirin to dissolve in water."

Rita chuckles, snatches a small notebook and pencil from her work table, "I'll just stick that line in my novel, thank you very much. Pardon me." She jots down a few words. Ian slips his arm around her waist, nuzzles her cheek. She nearly coos. Elderly passions do flame on!

Jenny, who has gone to the open window to avoid Rita's cigarette, cries "They're here!"

Nelly is smartly dressed -- through the able advice of Bill's sister who knows a thing or two about apparel -- in a crinkly white linen suit with a burst of white camellias at the lapel. A far cry from Fay's disastrous though well-meant -- or so it seemed to Fay and I'll vouch for it -- fashion tips.

But Nelly appears apprehensive even from across the street. She and Bill pause there for a moment and Bill hugs her. Jenny waves wildly, Nelly waves back -- mutual friends by default, I must add. Superbly engineered from start to...projected finish.

In the hall Bill and Nelly survey the debris, the gaping hole in Nelly's wall, the broken window, the fallen balustrade, the great gaps in the hall floor as the workmen return with yet more scaffolding, yet more demolition equipment, and the relentless noise begins again.

All this building ruckus, darlings, boring and repetitious as it may be at times, is based on an inevitability as solid as a kind heart: Mercy. For there is good in all of us, even me. So bear with me. Our saga's denouement, wherein all shall be revealed, is about to commence.

Rita rushes out to hug Nelly who is weeping from happiness (how like Fay) and who hugs her back. As Nelly and Bill enter, Jenny and Hugh and Ian hum Here Comes The Bride and of course Nelly glows as only a bursting with love, forty-year-old, married for the first time can. This goes for glowing Bill too, even though it's his second. Nelly smiles and curtsies ostentatiously, blows a kiss to all and a terrible crash from the hall sends her flying into Bill's arms.

"What a beautiful cake!" cries Nelly from Bill's loving embrace, "Thank you, Rita. Thank all of you!"

Ach! This merry band of tenants, so implausibly but appropriately linked. I, like Nelly, curtsy. Applaud, m'dears, if you know what's good for you.

The shatter and shake of demolition has increased but the little reception continues apace, not realizing that the windows in Rita's living room have become as opaque as Fay's eyes.

I'm a bit of a show-off.

The conversation turns, as ever, to Fay and everyone has their say and Nelly sheds a few more tears and later, in the kitchen, says to Rita: "You were right about Fay. I'm sorry. So sorry."

Rita nods and kisses Nelly on the cheek. What a changed person is Rita since the first invasion of Ritterhouse Fay. She's nicer, our Rita. Isn't she, m'dears? Although her sociability could be a grist-gathering ruse. But why, m'dears, hasn't Rita realized that her window glass is opaque and that the lino in her kitchen is humming a sinister little ditty?

Oh, these obtuse persons! How they try ones soul! Now, indeed, is the winter of my/our discontent. Notwithstanding that I'm sprawled on a sandy shore somewhere in the Caribbean with a frosty Singapore Sling in each mitt (Haven't seen my so-called *hands*, darlings, in donkey's years – heee-haw!).

The renovation of Number 13 grows louder, as though the appalling distraction is planned to destroy, which indeed it is, whatever peace of mind the inhabitants of our could-be-humbler edifice might enjoy this Sunday afternoon; this afternoon of what could be, should be, bliss for our Nelly and our Billy.

But with Ian serving at the punch bowl, though sporadically wondering where he is going to get a job or even a crust, what might have been disaster early on becomes, with the generous ladling out of good cheer, general hilarity as everyone laughs at each additional crash or rip or relentless bout of hammering. Everyone but Fay who squats on her spotless, heated WC listening, her head oscillating in that radar screen mode, greedy to catch every sound of laughter, every sinister nuance, from the little reception; that gathering of traitors two floors below her creamy, perfectly formed, toasting-nicely-thank-you, buttocks. The walls have ears, m'dears -- and, of course, toasty buttocks too.

"Ohhhhh," whispers Fay with, as usual, my naughty needling, "Ohhhh, I am furious!" Or words to that effect – my attentions have momentarily strayed to another bum. That of a much-tanned, nude young native as he scampers fetchingly towards Neptunic delights in the frothing tropical sea.

"Rita tells me you've bought a flat," says Ian to Bill.

"Yes. Kilburn side of St John's Wood."

"Kilburn, love," corrects Nelly with a smile, "strictly Kilburn."

Good Nelly can now scarcely say a word without an accompanying smile.

"Kilburn," says Bill.

"It's tiny but lovely," says Nelly. "On a quiet little cul de sac. No traffic at all."

"I hear you owe your good fortune to a certain little animal via a certain rich bitch," says Rita.

"Chinchillas, the poor little things," says Nelly quickly, "It took so many little souls to make that coat."

Ach! *That's* where those metaphysical little blighters are disappearing to! Nelly. Such depth. I'd be proud of you, love, if you weren't so goddamned sentimental.

"You'd probably get a pot of paint thrown at you if you wore it. Anyway, it got you a flat," says Rita. "But if you'll pardon my saying so, you paid dearly for it."

"Did I? Well, it came out all right and we've forgotten about that now, haven't we, Bill?"

"Suppose so."

For the time being only, poor dears, In any case, enjoy the next *half hour.*

A particularly loud crash causes them all to gasp then laugh and Ian says "If you need advice on anything structural in your new place I'd be happy to..."

"Oh we do!" says Nelly.

"We'd appreciate it very much," adds Bill. "We've got ideas but we're not sure quite how."

"Bill wouldn't know a bearing wall from a beehive."

"Heard that, did you? We've been married (he consults his watch) exactly two hours and twelve minutes."

Bugger this, m'dears! Let's do get through this small talk and on to the gory part -- though I *am* attempting to build a certain degree of suspense.

"Let's cut the cake," says Rita who appears at my beck with a tray of coffee, having immediately prior, swilled down a cognac. Ian is too tipsy himself to have noticed.

Now *he's* on the sauce again, my dears. Where will it all end? What we need is a good solid deus ex machina (mark this!). But don't hold your breath. I'm moving as fast as my so-called *feet* can manage.

Somewhat later Rita, sensibly soused, cries:

"Prezzies, prezzies!"

Ian and Rita set the gifts, with the exception of that purple and red-ribboned package, beside Nelly. Rita returns to fetch it, grunts "It's heavy! What have you and Jenny brought?"

"Oh, that's not ours," says Hugh. "It's from Ritterhouse. She left it by our door for the happy couple."

"Take cover!" cries Rita who quickly sets the present in a far corner, "It's a bomb!"

Everyone goes silent. Nelly rises, retrieves the present and brings it back and sets it with the others. Fay, two floors above, smiles triumphantly, shifts her buttocks (which are bound by now to have red toilet seat marks, m'dears! -- digitally monitored warmth be damned!) and Jenny feels a shudder ripple up her spine, coincidental with a subtle change of shade on two cushions of Rita's cretonne sofa where she sits. Perhaps it *is* a bomb? thinks Nelly as Rita winces apologetically. Ian suffers for Rita, for Nelly. Hugh, sensing Jenny's unease, wraps his arm around her waist.

"Sorry, love," says Rita to Nelly, "I was out of order. Open it."

All eyes, including mine, darlings (as my naked native has disappeared into the trident-god's soggy saline and I am all yours), are on the large, heavy package which glimmers in its purple metallic wrapping paper and shining red ribbon. Nelly pulls the gift across the table to her, Jenny gasps and feels stupid. Rita shields her eyes.

"Nobody's all bad," says kind Nelly, gentle, tolerant and forgiving Nelly who pauses to commiserate with the absent Fay.

Rita is unable to bear it, says:

"Open it, Nell, for Christ's sake!"

Fay shifts on her cosy toilet seat to relieve a prickly leg gone to sleep, listens, smiles.

As the others watch, Nelly slowly, carefully begins -- not noting the oddest, fleeting shimmer in the ribbon -- to remove the shiny, metallic paper on Fay's gloriously done up gift.

"Does it tick?" asks Rita in her best stage-whisper.

"Belt up, darling," whispers Ian.

Nelly removes all the wrapping paper and (Ach!) here is a tallish wooden box with an ornate, hinged lid. "Lovely wood", says Nelly and stops. Something tells her not to go on (I'll take credit for that, my dears) but she does go on, and unlatches a small clasp and slowly begins to raise the hinged lid. Unease, like shaken champagne, gushes from the raised lid of the box. A terrible whining wrench of a crowbar and the accompanying crash of falling plaster explodes in the corridor. Everyone gasps.

"Get on with it, Nelly, please," says Jenny.

Rita sticks a cigarette in her holder, lights it. Ian takes it from her, stubs it out. Rita frowns but acquiesces.

The lid of the box is now open and Nelly removes page after page of packing material, each page being, as before, the first page of Rita's 'My House Burned Down' illustrated with a frightened, sooty face peering through flames, a face more than coincidentally similar to Fay's.

"She's up to her old tricks," sighs Rita, lighting another cigarette.

"Yes," says Ian, snatching it and stubbing it out, "Her old tricks."

"Yes, yes," mutters Fay from the dozy warmth of her high-tech toilet seat. Although she can't help wondering if she will, momentarily, be just a smidgen too harsh on Nelly. But the deed will soon be done in spite of what Fay may think or not think. It is integral to our task.

I clear the uselessly opaque windows (m'dears, I've no idea *what* I was thinking!) and terminate all incidental vibrations and sick-making pulsations as no one is watching anyhow. The spotlight has moved, m'dears, in the most definitive way, to saintly, positively *haloed* Nelly.

The pages of packing are gone and Nelly grasps the top of the object within the polished wood box with both hands and quickly pulls it out for all to see.

As I can't resist it, I cause the room to explode in racing shadows and crazy staccato noise.

M'dears, it just couldn't be worse!

50

No one sees my shadows, hears the staccato high-pitched chatter that only a dog (or Fay or foxes) can hear. No one notices because their eyes are fixed on the object floating in the large glass jar. The object that is my darling prosopopoeia's gruesome wedding present -- a tiny human foetus submerged in formaldehyde. A large label attached to the glistening cylindrical jar reads: Fay and Billy's miscarried infant boy.

Nelly screams, slams the jar on the table and before anyone can restrain her is out the door and into the debris of the undulating, pulsating, whining corridor where she trips, falls, rips her wedding suit, smashes her fragile corsage, cuts her hand on a shattered hall lamp (over-described but you know me).

Bill is just behind her, leaps over scattered planks, falls, pulls himself up, tries to grab her but catches his foot (in my mittened so-called *hand*) and falls again.

Nelly is into the street running towards their rented car. It all happens too fast -- the car horn, the screeching brakes, the dull thud of terrible impact as Nelly's tumbling, twirling body scuds across the pavement. Our friends rush from Number 13 and can only watch in horror.

Rita gesticulates wildly into her telephone. We can't hear her -- we're on the street with the others, Bill, Jenny and Hugh and Ian in a tight circle around the still Nelly. Bill kneels beside her, afraid to move her and possibly do further damage, if further damage is possible? -- if Nelly is even alive.

"Nelly," he whispers, "Nelly, my love."

Darlings, I am overcome! My tears shoot out like tiny globules of lava spat from a super sympathetic Vesuvio! I honestly haven't a clue why I allowed this! It was unnecessary! Our task was perfectly on course! But you know what they say, m'dears, about best laid plans. And if you don't, you should.

From her window above, Fay pouts in that tatty chenille bathrobe, pours a fistful of rice back and forth through her fingers as she watches Rita run to kneel with the others and cover Nelly with a blanket. A distant siren is just audible as the traffic clots.

Jiggers, duh cops!

Impatient car horns hoot, unaware of our mini-tragedy at Number 13. From above, an evil angel ascendant, Fay peers down.

"Poor Nelly. Poor, poor Nelly," breathes my Fay through clenched teeth, "She was on my gift list."

Why should you care, Fay? What was that turncoat to you?

"It's your fault," screams Fay, "I was good before you came."

You were *never* without me, Fay.

"Shut up!" cries Fay, "Go away! Begone! Flee!"

Three policemen drive up. The driver of the car that struck Nelly stoops, wringing his hands, is questioned. Another policeman kneels beside Nelly who hasn't moved. The third attempts to unsnarl the traffic. Fay watches, grains of rice still spilling from one perfectly formed hand to the other.

Bill, Jenny, Hugh, Rita and Ian, in earnest, whispered conversation, cluster protectively around Nelly. Curious onlookers in turn circle them, moving back as the policemen motion them away.

The ambulance, blaring through a cacophony of stalled traffic, races up, and Fay, above it all, suddenly jerks from her window as though she's seared her fingers on its bronze sill. But she remembers the forgotten rice in her hand, moves back to the window, slams it open.

Nobody sees the small shower of rice caught in a quirky wind that swirls between Number 13 and Mrs Taylor's despised office building opposite. Nobody hears Fay who shatters a great hole in her glass wall with a marble lamp and throws herself, shadow-lit and screaming, to the undulating, unforgiving floor (This house has a heart, m'dears, and it hurts for Nelly). Nobody notices Fourlives whose vital quota diminishes to three (or whatever -- I was never good at math) as the ambulance backs right over the crazy cat and, siren shrieking, screeches away.

Fay lies a long moment here on her new up-market carpet which scratches vengefully at her stomach. The noise of the street thunders through the gaping hole in her glass wall, buffets her eardrums like the bellowing howl those cruel monsters of yore made after they'd tied her hands, just before they hosed her with that cold water. "I'm not lying! I'm not lying!" screams Fay, "What have I done to be punished yet again?"

You mean besides murdering Nelly, ducky?

"It's your fault!" sobs penitent Fay, "for I know not what I do!"

Nevertheless, evil is evil.

Which brings to mind *yet again* a considerably unanswered

question, my dears: Why, really, is Fay, with her mega-means, *here* at all? At stodgy Number 13? Was she drawn back to this bewitched house (and furnishings) by the old woman who speaks with her grandmother's tongue? This crazy old bat who gave her the wretched rug that was rightfully Fay's already? Depending...

Is Fay bewitched by this cantankerous old crone who used her to fulfil some unspeakable prophecy? Ach, m'dears, ask me no questions and I'll tell you no lies. What is there to do but cry real tears, plentiful tears, human tears? An empty gesture at best. But soothing? You tell me. Nothing is feigned here, baby, not today.

So Fay lies babbling on the floor, drenched in hot, now easily produced but totally useless tears. She finds the shiny remote control beside her, presses it and with a buzz the built-in bar slides open. She dares not look up. She knows what is there (I have told her). Nelly's kewpie doll will grin at her as it shakes its cunning little bottie and condemns her. She forces herself to look at the kewpie. She needs to be punished. To be scourged, to shout mea culpa! The kewpie's outrageous pink feather is flattened in wintry wind that whistles through the shattered wall. Fay punches the remote again, the mirrored bar thumps shut, conceals her tiny, pink accuser. She buzzes it open, is accused, buzzes it shut, is exonerated, open again: guilty. Shut: innocent. She drops the remote.

"I was a beautiful child," echoes from somewhere too near. "Gentle. Gentle in every way. Loving. I was a loving child. Trusting. I was trusting too. Beautiful. Gentle. Trusting. I was an angel. I was perfect."

No comment.

The waiting squares circle lazily around me...sorry. Let's have another go at that...

The waiting squares circle lazily around our prostrate, not so perfect heroine (talk about squaring the circle, sugar!).

On second thoughts...

No...no...Definitely *no* comment.

PART FOUR

51

Snoring, m'dears?! Do I hear snoring?! My goodness, yes! Ach! It is The Ritterhouse Fay on her shapely back, snoozing amidst a vertiginous, yes! *vertiginous* tangle – see it squirm and grow! -- of animated empty bottles, upturned, upward-mobile furniture and broken vases and shattered picture frames -- testimony to a night of orgiastic guilt; all her mental and physical resources, like mad antibodies, flung violently against herself.

Fay lies here oblivious, still circled by the questioning squares -- life choices that didn't give a damn for her before *I* came along. So I'll take a bow here, scheming spoiler that I am. 'Tis but *Kismet*! Is that easier for you to grasp? 'Tis for *me*.

The bright morning sun fails to wake our submerged and fear-some Kraken. Borne on screaming wind, the din of morning traffic rumbling through the shattered glass wall also fails to wake her. It bears repeating so we'll say it again: *When love goes wrong, nothin' goes right.*

Breathes she? Is our hapless demi-child thingy yet among the virtually human?

That cat, tail held high, prowls the kitchen counter eating again from the gourmet garbage; opened tins and unwrapped packages. No caviar for you today, you careless cat! You've wasted enough lives already. You never think before you leap. You're skittish. You're so like Fay.

"I *am* Fay," says the cat in a Cathy, Wuthering Heightsish, sort of way, her mew modifying into a rancid-shrimp, raucous purr.

The doorbell chimes. Fay sits up with a jerk. She has survived! Is victorious! She pulls her bathrobe closer -- It's cold with a hole in ones glass wall. The world can be *so* intrusive.

The doorbell chimes again. Fay is stiff, cold, pulls herself up from the floor, opens the door. Whoa! Here is Ted the lorry driver, hammer and thud of demolition commencing just behind him.

"Hello, Fay."

"Why...uhhhh..."

"Ted."

"Ted." And after a long moment, "Hello, Mr Kong."

"That's me."

"Long time no see."

Fay rubs her reddened eyes as Ted takes in the dreadful disarray of the room. "What happened?"

"I was robbed and forced to submit to unspeakable acts."

Ted smiles. She looks away, says:

"I've been unconscious. What do you want?"

"Money."

"Money?! For that measly little breakfast of fatty bacon and three pieces of stale bread plus an excruciatingly bad screw-top bottle of wine and, oh yes, that horrid little dab of rancid butter!"

What a memory -- for a change!

"No," says Ted, "Not the bacon, the bread, the screw top wine or the 'horrid' little dab of butter, love."

"Then *what*? For one night spent in a lumpy bed I wouldn't have allowed my kitty-cat to pee-pee upon?!"

"No."

"If you think I'm going to pay you for moving my furniture then you're mad! You damaged my magnificent chest of drawers and dented my kettle!"

These bitter words tumble from Fay's twisted little cupid's bow as though they were her own. But they're not. Believe me. They are not.

Ted sticks a piece of paper in her face.

"What is this, pray tell?!"

"My telephone bill," says Ted.

"Your *telephone bill*?!"

"Uh-huh."

"I touched your grimy little telephone once! Once! For a local call. And Mr Ammari used his mobile or cell phone or whatever they call it. I saw him."

"Well it looks like his battery run out. I've been billed for eighteen trunk calls to the middle east."

"Why come to me?! I've been robbed! Can't you see?! I've been unconscious! What day is it?!"

"The day after. Quite a party, eh?"

"I suggest you leave instantly and take your great, hairy back with you!"

Fay! What a way to speak to a man on your gift list!

"What was that?!" says Fay, "What did you say?"

Ted advances a step, says: "I suggest you pay up before I use your supple body to make another hole in your nice new glass wall."

"You wouldn't dare!"

Ted moves closer. "Try me."

And this is all so odd coming from the *only* man in our galaxy who actually does have a soft spot for the Fay – perhaps the closest she'll *ever* come to real affection.

Fay retreats, clutching her bathrobe to her breast. "Hairy brute!"

Foolish Fay! Your fragmented rug would readily have come to your aid. Alas, it is not at hand but half a world away.

However, every scintillating, stainless-steel appliance in Fay's kitchen hears, glistens and prepares to defend her. Until I intervene and force her subtly into our next square.

Ted reaches into his pocket, finds another slip of paper, pokes it towards her. "The unsettled bill for my services."

"Ha! Services! You men are so..."

Ted menaces Fay aside, drops himself on her sofa and hoists his plaster-dusted trouser legs on the coffee table. "I've got all day, Fay."

"Oh, Mr Kong, *darling*, I'm sorry. Forgive me. I've been unconscious. I was struck on the head."

"Probably more than once, love."

How right Ted is.

"What?" says Fay to the ceiling, "What was that?"

The ceiling only smiles demurely and is promptly forgotten. Like all else in our topsy-turvy world.

Ted shakes his head as Fay fetches her purse then sits beside him, "How much do I owe you, Honey? How much, sugar?"

Ted drops both bills into Fay's lap. She winks at him and snatches them up, reads them, winks again. "This seems reasonable. Would you like a cheque?"

Ted shakes his head, sticks out his big, rough hand, says:

"Legal tender, me old darlin'."

"I believe I can manage that."

Fay puzzles over Ted's odd request. Doesn't he trust her? They were so close once. She snatches an enormous roll of bank notes from a drawer and without bothering to count it slips it into Ted's pocket and sits beside him. He fishes the roll out, counts the money, takes what is due him and drops the rest, a very considerable amount, into Fay's lap.

"I didn't mean what I said about your back, you know, being hairy," says Fay, eyes downcast, hastily repenting.

"My back *is* hairy, darlin'."

Fay flashes her cutest, most seductive -- for this time of the morning and considering the events of the previous twelve hours -- little grin, "Not *that* hairy, Mr Kong."

She suddenly adores the man. He helped her. A dear gay friend. And a friend in need is a friend...those Judy Garland CD's, those ballet tickets, why, he'll have 'em in a trice…

But Ted is out the door without bothering to say goodbye.

"I've seen hairier backs...!" screams Fay at the closed door, "...on apes!"

Then as a searing afterthought:

"IN ZOOS!"

Poor mutable Fay, she's in an awful dither, springs up and frightens that blackest of cats who leaps through the great jagged hole in Fay's glass wall, makes for its traditional flying leap through the potted trees into space, reconsiders, hides under a cretonne upholstered patio chair.

Hair-of-hag, Fay. Hair-of-hag! I hiss somewhat uncertainly into the glass-walled reflection of my own so-called eyes. Ach and goodness! Am I experiencing the briefest moment of self-doubt? Is my omniscience waning? Perhaps un peu, m'dears, with that departing rug – it was so entertaining and passing strange. But I nevertheless cheerfully (and I must admit, most musically) chant hair-of-hag-hair-of-hag and Fay is instantly on her tiny phone, nervously plucking at her linty chenille sleeve, until, in a meek whisper of a voice, she speaks. "Could you give me the number of a domestic help agency?...*any* agency...I *would* look it up myself, dear," whimpers Fay, "but I am visually handicapped...BLIND, ducky...Thank you."

This petite deception was, of course, completely unnecessary and a possible affront to those among us who are visually handicapped or even unsighted. Although, in my experience, out here where *eyes* are as useless as a pork chop in Pakistan, the unsighted see more than we know!

"Hush!" says Fay who fidgets with the remote, opening inadvertently the mirrored door on the built-in bar and is condemned yet again by Nelly's feathered kewpie. Fay gasps and buzzes the bar door shut and, as she waits, attempts to forget -- for the ensuing two minutes -- yesterday, all her yesterdays. From her telephone comes a suitably guilt-stricken voice.

"Could you repeat that?" asks Fay, writing down a number,

"Thank you, sugar. Thanks ever so. I'll send a contribution to your favourite charity."

The above, m'dears, was a glaring example of wasted effort. Had she memorized even one work-a-day incantation, the whole flipping telephone directory could have been accessed by simply tapping one Carmen-red nail against a temple – *either* temple!

By now, m'dears, you must surely be convinced that our Fay is simply an extremely negligent witch.

Well, you'd be wrong.

She beeps off her phone, sticks it in her pocket, shoots to the kitchen, opens a jar of caviar, crams it into her mouth with her fingers. She's ravenous. Chews furiously while the sing-song phrase *hair-of-hag-hair-of-hag* catapults inexplicably from wall to quaking wall. Three-lives watches, bubbling with envy, from beneath that sun chair, almost decides to join her at lunch. Doesn't. Must calm down first.

52

"Unfortunately," moans Fay, "one *must* lie. One is constrained to. One has no choice."

And indeed this is so. Take it from me/us.

"Oh yes, dear!" chimes Mrs Hawkins as she briskly hoovers by.

"Occasionally, I mean" opines Fay, her fingers dripping with caviar, her eye on Hawkins' hair (More about this later, m'dears, as Hawkins', though she need never know it, is a sort of Almost Last Chance Saloon for our increasingly desperate Ms Ritterhouse).

"Oh yes, dear, tiny white lies is always permitted in a good cause," chimes Hawkins, briskly hoovering by in the opposite direction.

"One can't be truthful the whole time," says Fay truthfully, noting a particular hank of Hawkins' red-dyed thatch eminently suitable for 'hair-of-hag'; the crucial incantations of which now lie inchoate at the back of Fay's mind, to be revealed at my pleasure.

"Truthfulness is dreary," continues Fay, oblivious to my meaningful machinations.

"Dreary, dreary, dreary!" cries Hawkins over shattered bits of window glass hoovered noisily, greedily up into the shiny, brushed-aluminium vacuum cleaner to the great relief of the much-abused, newly installed, fitted carpet.

"Not to mention, dangerous," screams Fay with some irritation as she seems not to have Hawkins' unadulterated attention (it will never be *unadulterated*, sugar, try as you may). But Fay needs reassurance. Needs it *so*. And Hawkins, in a pinch, can also provide hair-of-hag. Why hadn't Fay thought of this before? Much earlier. Why? Because I hadn't reminded her. I can't do bloody everything, can I? I've hinted, of course. But if she misses out -- and she will -- it's her own bleedin' fault. We've heard of the fallacy of free will, haven't we, m'dears? Well it occasionally applies. I don't command the moon and stars though I'm overly familiar with Pluto. Fetch your *Golden Boughs*, m'dears, for a good read! Time is runnin' out!

"What?" says Fay, unable to direct herself towards *any* fleeting shadows at the moment -- the sun is simply too bright through her partially destroyed glass wall.

"Oh yes, dear, dreary," calls Hawkins, over the invasive roar of traffic and the whine of her high-tech vacuum cleaner. She is presently bustling by that enormous hole in Fay's unfortunate glass wall (a little additional info never hurt nobody!).

"It is far easier to say I've had a party!" shrieks Fay over the din. "How could I have said: Look. I've been robbed of a considerable amount of money and forced to submit to unspeakable acts and my flat needs tidying."

"Oh you couldn't of, dear. Couldn't of, couldn't of!"

"Do you realize that I lay here in this vertiginous rubble unconscious for hours?"

"NO!"

"I did! It was no picnic!" cries Fay, having only the most marginal experience of picnics, being, in fact, picnic-challenged – unless one includes our excursion, with cucumber sandwiches, to the Reptile House at the wondrous San Diego Zoo.

Also, m'dears, sun destroys the skin! And there wasn't time for the picnic experience. A millennium can pass in a millisecond (and did) if you're not careful.

"I should say it was no picnic!" says Hawkins, "Not one yours truly would be in the habit of attendin'! And the police?"

"Police? What police?! What do you know about the police?!"

She knows lots, actually, Fay, having been there herself, at the wrong side of the booking desk.

Hawkins stops, switches off her high-tech hoover, leers avidly at Fay. "What did they say about all them unspeakable acts, dear?"

"I did not summon the police."

"Why ever not, dear?"

"It would have been humiliating."

"You poor, dear thing."

Fay loves that remark, which securely establishes Hawkins you-know-where.

"Being forced to submit to unspeakable acts is one thing..."

Hawkins thrusts her sweat-beaded face uncomfortably close to Fay's. "Yes, yes! Oh yes!" she says.

"...Being required to relate unspeakable acts in lurid detail to a gaggle of drooling, lecherous men is quite another!"

But Fay, you've had so *much* practice at that.

"So I simply say," says Fay, eyes darting towards the ceiling for the source of my last nasty remark, "I've had a party! Why reweep old woes?"

"Good for you, dear," says Hawkins who retreats and plucks a large, firm ball of new carpet lint from the mouth of the attentive vacuum cleaner. "Uhh..." she continues, "What exactly, if you don't mind my askin', dear, what exactly was them uhhh..."

"The unspeakable acts?"

"Yeah. The very ones."

"Of an intimate sexual nature, of course."

"Oh dear, oh dear! Well they would be, wouldn't they?"

"They interfered with..." moans Fay, with pain in her eyes so intense it might as well be real. "Interfered with..."

"Your 'exotic' zones! You poor thing!"

I simply *must* master the local lingo!

Fay, recovering: "The police are hopeless in such cases. They invariably say we females are the initiators."

"The what, dear?"

"The police invariably say we asked for it."

Ach. How true, m'dears, how dismally true.

"Don't they just! And you bein' so attractive and all."

Fay loves this, a hand flies up to pat her hair, collides uncomfortably with those huge, blue plastic curlers. "Ouch," she says, and continues:

"I was a caesarian baby, plucked untimely from Mummy's womb. The bones of my head are utterly undistorted by life's first journey, that needless passage through the uterine canal."

You can say that again, sugar.

"Oh yes, now that you say so, oh yes! Your skull is quite perfect, ain't it? In its way."

"It's as though," cries Fay with much statistical justification, "It's as though just being alive and gorgeous is enough to incite some great hairy beast to intimate violence!"

"That's the price we must pay for our loveliness, dear," says Hawkins combing her fingers tenderly through her own thick, red-dyed hair.

"You've magical hair," says Fay, hair-of-hag ringing in her ears, "May I have a lock?"

"Why yes," says Hawkins, pleased to her gray roots but flinching a bit as Fay, lightning fast, whips in and shears off (with handy scissors I have provided) that small, thick hank of said she's had her eye on. Fay now has the hag's hair, to be used sparingly in an arcane but vital *rescue ritual* that has just again crossed her mind.

Her first -- but too daunting -- thought was Rita's hair. That *archetypal* hag's hair. But...

"What did they steal, dear?"

"What?"

Fay is wrenched from her contemplation of spells mislaid. Why doesn't she concentrate -- stick to the point? -- get on with it?

"With what?" says Fay, "Prithee, get on with what?"

Our task, your goal, your mission. It's nearly time.

"What mission?"

"The robbers, dear," continues Hawkins, "what did they take?"

"Besides my privacy, my self-respect, my dignity?" spits Fay.

"Uh-huh, besides that."

"Money! Sod it! Money!"

"Wouldn't they just!"

Darlings, hadn't you noticed, these days the bad guys outnumber the good guys.

Hawkins, scratching at her armpit and ponging moderately, vacuums towards a shattered picture frame, shouts over the noise, "Just like a thief, 'n' it?!

Hawkins is at the bar, was startled into giggles when Fay first buzzed it open, is still, in fits and starts, a-giggle. "You must promise not to tell them at the agency," giggles Hawkins, as mock-kittenish as Fay ever was, "These is workin' hours, dear. What a variegated selection of spirits you got here!"

Spirits?! Don't be redundant, doofus.

"A man at Harrods chose it for me. They convey everything directly to me. Everything under the sun. Whenever the mood strikes me."

Whenever the mood strikes *me*, my darling prosopopoeia.

"Aren't you the lucky one! What's your pleasure, dear?"

"I'm a whisky girl."

"What a coincidence! So am I."

Aren't we all?

"Aren't we the lucky ones!"

Well...Yes and no.

Mrs Hawkins sets the bottle on the table before Fay, squats beside her, pours a hefty one for Fay and herself. Hawkins sips, shivers, sets down her glass and pulls her dowdy orange cardigan tight around her. "Goodness, dear! You've such a draught through that great robber's hole in your wall!"

Fay breaks into tears.

"Did I say something wrong, dear?"

"I was robbed!" screams Fay, now fingering Hawkins' hairy

lock at the bottom of her own cardy pocket, "I was robbed!"

"Of course you was, Mrs Ritterhouse, dear," soothes Hawkins, patting Fay's white-knuckled fist, "Plus forced to submit to them indecent acts."

Fay stops crying as quickly as she began, glares at Hawkins who shivers again and pulls that orange cardigan even closer.

"If you don't get your glass wall-hole repaired, my duck, if I know my thieves" -- she knows several personally -- "you'll soon be robbed again!"

Hawkins pushes Fay's whisky towards her, says:

"Ain't we naughty? But it's got my vote!"

Fay snatches the whisky as fast as a salamander snaps up a fly, quaffs it then belches. Hawkins regards her with ill-concealed dismay – where did she learn her manners?! In some games arcade in Peckham? -- chalks it up to robbery and unspeakable acts, but mostly unspeakable acts, and smiles tolerantly as her imagination runs riot but is again met with a cold glare she can feel; like Jenny, like Rita before her. She yanks her dowdy cardigan yet tighter, pours another whisky for them both, shivers again, inaccurately blames it on a hole in a wall. Hair-of-hag has its disadvantages.

A sorely perplexed Mrs Mabel Hawkins frowns and picks her way down the rail-less staircase through noise and dust and partially demolished walls. Her new employer is a queer duck indeed. Queerer than Hawkins has ever known and she's known her share of oddballs. Mrs Ritterhouse'll have to pay more if she expects Hawkins to put up with this terrible untidiness every other day -- unspeakable acts or not! Of course, an occasional whisky hits the spot but...

Hawkins pauses just outside, watches a young worker (literally hand-plucked by Fay) climb in then out of Nelly's broken window, unconsciously combs her fingers through her valuable hair, fondly patting down a stiffly moussed curl and remembering 'Mrs' Ritterhouse's flattering request for a lock. Wonders if the young, handsome worker notices her becoming coiffure. But he is gone without a glance.

Grow up, Hawkins and grow old like the rest of us weary old hag-tarts.

She peers into Nelly's window. "Why, there's holes in the floor. And sand! Where did all that sand come from?" It's filthy and it's shockin' and it smells of kitty! thinks Hawkins, who will definitely ask for more money. On the sly, from Fay of course, not from the agency -- whisky-laid-on or not!

You're only here for your hair, hag. And Fay had better get serious soon or the game is forfeit – a bore. And the task, what of the *task*?! No remarks from the gallery, m'dears! I'm doing my bleedin' best. You were warned.

Rita at her window sees Hawkins waiting at the bus stop, Hawkins waves at her, flashes an exaggerated smile, mutters "Nosey Parker."

"Sweet Jesus," mutters Rita back, through the flush of a very successful hour at her novel. In spite of demolition noise, in spite of poor Nelly's... but she cannot think about that just now. "Someone get that cheeky dyed-haired hag a broomstick," she mutters, pushing (with my stringent help) the above domestic tragedy from her mind. She'll deal with the Nelly situation presently. As must I.

Rita must dress soon for her daily visit to Mrs Taylor, who hangs by a thread, doesn't recognize anyone though she mumbles every now and then. Hugh and Jenny and Ian have been for a visit as well.

Rita had a tiny contretemps with Ian. Something about smoking or drinking or foul language or all three, she can't remember which. Ian's begun to drink too. More than before. Perhaps she's a bad influence. But it doesn't matter. Because love makes the world go 'round, doesn't it, Rita? And round and round.

Don't fall off that capricious carousel just yet, ducky. You'll soon be too damned old to crawl on again.

Know the feelin', m'dears? I do.

53

Fay descends gracefully from her Rolls. It's a cinch to descend gracefully from a Rolls, 'specially if you're choking in sable (and been painstakingly coached by me). This thought has entered Fay's head but with, as usual, no mention of her game old mentor. She waves goodbye to Chauffy -- who has errands to run, about which Fay fortunately knows nothing. He's carrying on a bit of commerce on the side, needs the money. He's saving up for if Fay dumps him.

Make that *when*, sugar.

Fay winks hello to the young workman who had also caught Mrs Hawkins' eye this morning when Hawkins ran her fingers lovingly through that ruthlessly hennaed hair which will, if I can just get through to Fay, make *such* a difference for us all. We try, m'dears. We do *try*.

"Long time no see," chimes Fay at her perkiest, waving a paper bag she's just yanked from that voluminous pocket in her sable.

The young workman grins pointedly at Fay as she enters the door-less house, and grins again at Jenny as she and Hugh, on their way to visit Taylor, exit down the steps arguing about something -- having just again cut-dead Fay to whom they haven't spoken since that foetal abomination tragedy. Jenny doesn't notice the grinning young workman but Hugh does.

Me too, m'dears. I'll have a pound and a half of *that*.

Just inside the door with her eye still on the young workman, and only the tiniest bit disturbed at being snubbed again by Hugh and Jenny for whom she has immediate plans, Fay hears typing, pauses. A moment later she directs the grinning workman to remove a large section of flooring in the hallway directly opposite industrious Rita's door. She hands him a crowbar and whispers something into his ear. He grins again -- pointedly. What else? Fay-stories, amongst her workmen, are divers.

Fay is at Hugh's door. What excellent timing. She unlocks it with her master key and goes directly to the kitchen and finds their cookie tin (or biscuit tin or whatever!) and takes a box from her paper bag. She'll teach them what it means to break a blood promise to Ritterhouse Fay. She hums merrily at her little task which takes her from sitting room to kitchen to bathroom. Was it ten years ago or three months? Everything is so relative, isn't it,

Fay? Including a very old woman in hospital who might or might not be -- a relative, that is. Put that in your puns column. And remember, there is no such thing as redundancy in a saga -- leitmotivs, only.

Poor Fay. She's fuzzing a bit now too. Like Taylor. But she is only thirty at the outside. Thirty-five? She feels five hundred, sometimes (join the crowd, sugar!). Wishes she couldn't remember *anything*.

Fay locks Hugh's flat, climbs the stairs to her own, exults in the noise of building, of progress, feels at home at last. As she had years ago -- months ago?

Three, to be exact, months. Information, darlings, for the finicky who demand to know on precisely which square they only momentarily stand.

Fay pauses. "What?" she asks, (as well she should) "What was that?"

One must continuously inquire, though proper answers are sluggish, if never, forthcoming.

The sun seems preemptively to have set and a blue fog creeps round Fay's ankles as at Bill's door-less flat she spies that grinning young, shirtless workman sitting indian-style on the floor drinking from a thermos, his head and naked shoulders, somehow (don't ask!) sticking just above said fog. Fay waves again. He waves, obviously unaware he's presently bathed in that thick indigo floating moisture. Fay is feeling fuzzy so doesn't request his intimate company. She has no wish to vanish *mid-coitus* (or whatever they call it these days -- it *has* happened). She's certain something is up but not quite what.

Sometimes I wonder myself. But I usually conquer my curiosity with an appropriate incantation. Would that Fay could. Fay needs rest just now, regardless of this ripely pungent young male lurking so near her door. Rest, or she might start shattering glassware every time she blinks. That has happened too. She, as previously illustrated, routinely sets things afire. Not as often as before, mind you. But just now she has a burning desire to lounge on her white leather sofa and inhale special ciggies and think of nothing. So this is what she does.

That cat watches her from the terrace, loves the freedom of movement afforded by the hole in the wall (you'd think it would be mended by now) and in a moment this black cat is prowling yet again, daily life being *so* full of repetition, amongst that costly garbage on Fay's kitchen counter and superbly tiled floor.

"No! It's you! *You* get me into these things!"

Ho-hum, m'dears. Here we are again.

"I am simply helping you to liberate your full potential. At great cost, I might add, to myself. I'm beginning to wonder where I fit in."

"So am I."

So am I!

This is of course Jenny and Hugh as they climb the stairs through loose-hanging plaster, splintered wood, chalky dust and noise from above, below and beside -- which *doesn't* help at all.

But what of Nelly? No one seems to be discussing poor Nelly. Ach, leave that to me. We must inject a modicum of suspense here and there.

Hugh unlocks his door and they slam in. A split second later the door flies open and Jenny, screeching bloody murder, casts the cockroach filled cookie tin down the stairs into the whirling eye of demolition.

My cookie vengeance, at last! Or, if you prefer, 'biscuit' vengeance.

Hugh grabs Jenny, pulls her back, hugs her as she sobs into his shoulder. "I love you, Jenny, I love you!"

Fay, listening from her landing, timed them, heard their door crash open, saw the tin topple, scattering its wretched wrigglers from stair to stair. Why shouldn't Hugh and Jenny have cockroaches? She'd had them for breakfast, lunch and dinner. Delicacies, they assured her. Delicacies for women like her. For fallen angels trapped in infinity and forever ogling unattainable kisses 'n' hugs through bullet-proof glass. Or so it seems to Fay. *Seems* is our word for the day, m'dears.

"Perhaps they've learnt their lesson," whispers Fay, "Perhaps next time they'll be civil and keep to their blood promises and speak to me as they pass."

Perhaps not, Fay. But you're ready for them, aren't you, dearie? Prepared for any eventuality? If only you could remember.

Fay's mind clouds and a dark voice whispers "Yes, you are prepared. Yes, indeed, yes, very much indeed. Prepared like the dickens for whatever may befall thee."

Dust to dust.

Ashes to ashes.

But first, and last and first, fire.

Fay edges her door shut, drops herself once again into cool white leather, leans back, rolls another ciggie, sighs, lights it, inhales, exhales and moans "Mummy, me not so happy now. Me want to cry and cry and cry."

She would if she could but it's all beginning to close in on her, rounding her little life with ever more shadow. As planned.

"Planned?" asks Fay.

Best laid, dearie, too. We should all be so lucky.

Rita returns late from her visit to Mrs Taylor. She'd met Hugh and Jenny there, directly before their cockroach incident. They'd kept each other company, discussed the nearly unspeakable; that grim gift of the foetus. Ach! Nelly would, miraculously, be all right; a broken arm, a broken wrist, a concussion, multiple scuffs, bruises, but she'd be all right. They'd all visited her in hospital but I kept it from you, m'dears, in the interest of dramatic tension. Admittedly a bit clumsily. Ye gods! I'm only a novice at this game!

Today, poor old Mrs Taylor isn't talking, isn't improving, is worse, still has those horrible tubes stuck up her nostrils and who knows where else. She hasn't much time left. A pity she can't count her life in multiples of nine like our black cat-ami (reminds me of 'catamite' -- but there I go again, sentimental me), a resident until quite recently of that coliseum of a cat box across the hall from Rita. But after all, m'dears, let's face it, Taylor is one-hundred-going-on-five-thousand. Still...

We all feel that way occasionally, don't we? If we don't, we ought. It can be, will be, arranged. Count on it.

Rita carefully steps over the gaping hole in the floor opposite her door, lets herself in. Vandals could be tempted to break in – the place looks derelict. But vandals could hardly have done worse than your own resident vandal, could they, Rita? What is she up to now? This sorceress? This inhumane, lying creature? Jesus! What was that?! A *cockroach*?!

Rita needs a brandy, fairly leaps to the cabinet. Where is Ian? He should be here by now. Do I drink too much? Do I smoke too much? Am I vulgar? Who gives a fuck?! *He* does, dear. Ah! The price of love. The compromise. The sweet sacrifice. Put the cognac back, ducky. The weekend comes soon enough. Ian might never come again. Wheee! But here he is now, disembarking from his car! Waving! At *you*!

Love is a three-way proposition, Rita. Or, if you, my aging Francophile prefer, a ménage a' trois: You, Ian and Yours Truly, who, full of wonder peers gratefully up your Ian's pant-leg at this very moment.

Whoopee! Boxer shorts!

54

Fay is thoughtful, loiters. She's an old pro, practiced it often enough in the side-streets of King's Cross. When the chips were down.

When were the chips ever up, peaches?

Here she loiters, the portfolio under her arm in the door-less entry of Bill's old flat; remembering fondly not Bill but the young architect in the tight designer jeans who took umbrage at her innocent grope and was summarily jettisoned, forever separated from those photo-opportunities he so longed for; forever separating her, as well, from the so-called *Class* for which she momentarily pined.

Other young architects, of course, were more than happy to intercede – even his brother (What a world!). But posh, tight-designer-jeaned Archie had been terminated. His rejection of her clumsy attempt at love was a slap in her so-called *face* and was severely dealt with. Part of her hated to do it, part of her rejoiced. Never the twain shall meet? Not at all, m'dears! Not at all! Listen carefully, I can say zis only once: The twain shall indeed meet. And sizzle! Like Paris in the summer, from that sentimental song of yore.

Fay's appetites know no limit. Why has she changed so? Everything had seemed to be going for her. But she is far from perfect now. Oh, she'll think about that tomorrow, perhaps shed another ersatz/echte tear. Who cares? Ach! *I* do! Shake a splendid leg, shift your shapely arse, Ms Ritterhouse! The next square awaits your so-called *feet* (whoops!).

But obstinate Fay ignores me, sashays lazily into Bill's empty little living room, discovers two forgotten boxes beside the bedroom door, squats and pulls out a jock-strap marked "large". She chuckles and drops it back into the box. Nothing of value here, Fay, not for you. Though *I'd* adore a sniff and perhaps to try on that large jock-strap myself. If you receive my meaning.

Fay hears a noise behind her, turns. It is the young workman into whose ear she'd recently whispered soft somethings. She lays the portfolio on a long work bench and pretends to study it as he passes by, grinning crookedly, into the kitchen. She is about to follow when someone else stirs behind her. Ach! It is Bill! Frightened, she retreats behind the work bench where she finds a very large hammer, clutches it at her back.

Bill ignores her and Fay is relieved to see him merely kneel and take up the boxes. Then he turns, looks directly at her. Her grip tightens on the hammer as she produces her *helpless* smile. He stares at her for a moment, returns her smile, sets the boxes on the floor and approaches. Fay's fingers ache, the hammer is so heavy. But she might need it. Bill comes closer. Ach! What the dickens!? His lips are pursing! Golly! he is going to kiss me!

Fay spots Nelly, terribly bruised, standing just outside the door -- her arm in a sling and splinted to the shoulder -- precisely as Bill's spittle splatters dead centre on her, The Ritterhouse Fay's, upturned, kiss-expectant face.

That hammer is flung at the doorway, but her enemies have long gone, taking with them Bill's boxes and the last traces of his and Nelly's presence in Fay's House.

Fay retrieves the hammer, staggers to the wall, batters it in a frenzy of... of what, Fay? She's not sure (nor am I). Her lips were parted to receive Bill's kiss; she was prepared to forgive and forget the wrongs he, they, *all* of these sons-of-bitches had done her. They who are her Family, her only family, aren't they? That is why she has come back. Like a duckling, darlings, post-hatch, follows the first *living* thing it sees. The Fay, who could dwell in a palace has come back for Family. She had thought for a time it was vengeance but no. It was Family -- about as Italianate as one can get, darlings and not smell of garlic.

Fay remembers now, in strobe-like flashes, this house from a very long time ago. She lived in this house with her Granny a *very* long time ago but her bittersweet reminiscence is quickly shunted aside, replaced by the aching hurt of this murderous moment. "My lips were parted for a kiss of forgiveness. Billy spat on me!"

The grinning workman, ostensibly removing Bill's old kitchen sink, has listened, afraid to involve himself in Fay's fracas and too familiar with the rumours that emerge daily among his mates. Now he sticks his head out for a look-see and Fay, having retrieved her hammer, is looking right back. Ten seconds later Furious Fay and her grinning young cohort disappear behind her slamming door for a tiny afternoon's entertainment. All expenses paid, of course. But at *such* a cost.

Rita's typing erupts from two floors below. But who's listening? Besides me, my darlings?

Then, up we go, one fribbin' floor (wheeee!):

"Pulsingly pungent".

"Ah come on, Jen."

"Frothy fresh."

Yawn (that was me).

"Come on, Jenny, it's a cheap women's scent not a pint of Guinness."

"Darling, I wouldn't know a thing about cheap women."

Jenny goes back to her soy-sauce soaked sprouts, "How dare you, sirrah!"

"Come on, Jen, think *fragrance*."

"All right!" replies Jenny, throwing down her chopsticks and extending both arms to the ceiling, "Fabulous Fraggers!"

"Not bad for a start."

Says who?! A bit old hat, I say. Certain to elicit Class warfare.

Hugh scribbles on a slip of paper, sticks it in his pocket and they both take up their chopsticks and are about to poke dangling portions of things indescribable (by my lights, my dears – I am terrified of those constipating Asian pastas) into their mouths when their doorbell rings, followed almost instantly by:

"You may as well let me in, Hughie or I'll just come in whilst you're away. As Master, I have a master key."

Then, in her child's voice:

"A owner has the wight of way! A owner has his 'n' her wights!" followed by a giggle.

Honestly! As this is the very next square, a pink "attempt love" square, there is simply no place to go but here (ours is not to reason why – or is it? How often, m'dears, have we all felt compelled, for no apparent reason, to do something terribly self destructive and demeaning?). However, in this case, retreat is unthinkable. One, no matter who *one* is, simply cannot back out of ones inevitabilities. It would be a contradiction of terms. And might well fuck-up that well known Time-Continuum and elicit that proverbial Warp. Which could be a pity.

"Open the door for the monster, Hugh," says Jenny. "Get it over with."

"No."

"We has been infil-ter-ated!" cries Fay through Her keyhole.

"You're tellin' me!" mutters Jenny from the sofa bed through chopsticks quivering with anxious egg noodles.

"We is infested!" continues Fay in her best child's lisp, "Cockroaches. Zillions. I had the exterminator man over yesterday. Really, darlings! Is there something riveting here that I'm entirely missing?!

"Goodnight, Ms Ritterhouse!" says Hugh.

"This is my house!" cries Fay, peering through their keyhole, "I can burn it down if I choose!"

Jenny is now shaking, positively green. Says she needs a glass of water. Hugh races to the kitchen to fetch it.

Fay, spinning round and round outside their door, grabs what's left of a stair rail for support, hears Rita's typing from below and dashes down the stairs where she presses her mouth to Rita's door and shrieks;

"Just because you can type does not make you invincible!"

Then, as an afterthought:

"You old hag!"

Rita is startled, stops typing and abandons herself to crazy laughter. She sobers quickly as she gazes at the paper in her typewriter.

> Old Mrs Belcher lay in hospital hovering near death, unable to give any clear account of the events directly preceding her 'accident'. The poor old woman could only mutter 'the witch' and 'Mr Belcher's postcards.'
> Janet was perplexed, rested her weary but firm, middle-aged face in her cupped, baby-smooth palms. She relaxed for a moment, suddenly inexplicably longing for a shag, until the crash of another wall reminded her that unless she fought and fought hard her little flat would soon become a garage. Janet loathed the smell of axle-grease.

Rita pulls back from her typewriter, carefully inserts a cigarette into her holder, lights and puffs thoughtfully as walls under determined assault crumble in the house around her. Over the din of falling wood and plaster, though Rita is certain the walls are paper, she can just make out Fay's strident singing from on high:

> I got plans!

You got plans!
Everybody's gotta have plans!

Honestly, Fay. As though they were *your* plans.

Poor Janet…pardon me, poor *Rita* rests her weary but firm, middle-aged chin in her cupped baby-smooth hands, sighs through teeth that are her own and closes her eyes. She wonders what could be keeping Ian. She sighs again. And yet again.

Humour me, dear ones. So I digress. What of it? Grrrrr! I'm a horny old gal today. Us old gals are *so* competitive.

Fay is fully recovered by late evening and has draped herself in that exquisite red silk kimono. She hums as she hunches at her marble coffee table, munches a tart and spews crumbs over the portfolio below her strawberry-jammed chin.

And now for a bit of *fully integrated* comic-relief: Fay's call box beeps and she stuffs the last of the jam tart into her mouth, springs to answer.

"Yes?"

"Ms Ritterhouse?"

"I am and who, pray, are you?"

"The university sent me."

"The university?"

"Tutor? Philosophy?"

"Come in."

I, of course, arranged this visit via a tiny, unobtrusive ditty I thrummed into Fay's head:

Sweat of scholar,
Scholar's sweat,
Knowledge comes with ease
You bet!
Don't be greedy!
Don't be greedy!
Just a little
When you're needy!
Reach betwixt
His buttocks fair
You will find
What's needed there.
Sweat of scholar,

Scholar's sweat!
It could save your arse,
My pet!

Talk about clues, m'dears!

Fay, coached by me, is convinced that Sweat of Scholar will further her understanding of the *Nature of Things.* Honestly, it's such a hype. Why bother?

Hair-of-hag, however, seems somehow to calm her as she fingers said lock in the pocket of her horrid old cardy. Poor Fay. She has no idea that H of H might be her very salvation. But ho-hum, darlings, Fay has been inattentive for months. And her *salvation* is the very *last* thing we desire.

In any case, I simply need a pause that refreshes:

So Fay buzzes the young man into the house, opens her door and waits impatiently as he cautiously (for such an *intelligent* boy) -- picking his way through debris -- ascends the half-demolished staircase. A few moments later this bespectacled, unkempt but luminous-skinned young man in an over-large, plaster powdered, sagging-to-his-thighs, Marks and Sparks *ancient* pullover appears and our Fay leads him in.

"Drink?" she asks.

"Oh yes, please."

Fay buzzes open her remote bar.

"Help yourself. I'm a gin and tonic girl on the rocks," (you can say that again, sugar!) peeps Fay who thinks he is rather cute (such *skin*!) in a seedy way. Although his elusive equipment is buried under an acre of sagging pullover, his bobbing, throbbing, firm, young buttocks could soon supply the needful. Not an impossible task, my dears. Take it from yers truly.

The buzz and sharp thump of Fay's automatic mirrored bar door startles this cute, cautious and remarkably unkempt young scholar. But, swallowing his apprehension, he casts an intrigued glance about Fay's sumptuous flat and pours an extremely liberal gin.

For his first mistake he presses a lever labelled 'Ice cubes' but fails to hold the glass back far enough to catch the cubes and they rocket into the room as shot from a cannon, causing the walls to burst into (unheard, obviously!) hysterical laughter.

"Sorry! God! Sorry!" he exclaims from the floor on his worn corduroy knees as he grabs up several ice cubes and crams them into a glass and pours another drink (these Oxbridge types are so unhygienic). This is his second, and last, mistake.

"Those ice cubes were on the floor," intones Fay summoning her voice of steel. This is where, m'dears, *Fay* goes terribly wrong.

"W-What?" says the kneeling young scholar, "W-What?"

"The ice cubes you have just dropped into my gin have been on the floor."

"Yes?"

"Don't you follow me?"

"Sorry?"

"You may imbibe and depart."

Ach! Yet another stillborn relationship! And all you need is love (and sweat of scholar).

"What?" mumbles our helpless, humble, harbinger of elucidation.

"Do you realize that your body is a temple?"

"A what?"

"How can I learn from a fool who eats from the floor and bleats 'what'?"

Stop, Fay, in the name of love!

"I beg your pardon?" says young Seedy, too perplexed to be angry, guzzling straight gin all the same, "but your carpet is spotless."

"To the untrained eye, perhaps. However, swarming there by the quadrillions are horrid microscopic creatures that we cannot see -- an alternate world that only an unfortunate few of us are aware of."

Precisely, Fay. I've been saying that for eons. Quadrillions of angels dancing on the heads of Billions of pins.

"Hush!" says Fay and goes on: "No matter how industriously one attempts to vacuum this filth away, it will take its toll. If given half a chance."

How true! That, m'dears, is the *true* Nature of Things. Ach, metaphor -- How I adore Thee!

"Come now..." says the shy young scholar, his glass trembling, gin edging from the corner of his pink, peach-fuzz encircled lips.

"Come?" says Fay now at her opened door, "Come?! I am coming nowhere with *you*, 'Mr What?'. Set down that glass and vacate our sacred premises."

Why is it that us ladies of a certain age see themselves as shrines?

But Fay has learned her Kitchen Hygiene well. The handling of food and drink was always stressed in endless lessons that... but the thought slips away incomplete as I have grown unutterably tired of it. She stares at the boy, manipulated malevolence crackling from those soulless eyes and putting a definitive 'paid' to Sweat of Scholar. Thus casting away this additional bulwark against her personal Armageddon.

Honestly, it's not her fault. Free will has, my little chickens, damaged so many well-meaning unfortunates. But it adds zest to our game and mystery to our task.

What can he do, poor boy? Shamed, he trudges by the glowering Fay, starts down the stairs, trips on a fallen rafter and tumbles to the next landing with Fay calling after him:

"I shall send a substantial cheque to your favourite charity!"

Rita in her bathroom, has heard the tumble. She pauses, listens, and pokes her head through her door just as the unfortunate young man, directly outside and dusting plaster from his frayed corduroys, looks up. Shocked yet again, down he goes, toppling backward over a misplaced hammer, into the rubble.

Rita, in her knickers and bra but nonetheless filled with that very milk of human-kindness that Jenny so lacked for Fay, and Fay so lacked for Nelly, gazes tenderly down at the gawky, floored, bespectacled young adonis whom she immediately identifies as another of Fay's hapless victims. "She's bonkers, love. Are you all right? Come in and have a drink."

The flustered boy frantically shakes his head, pulls himself up and backs fearfully out of this house of hell. Rita shrugs and returns to her bathroom where she catches her creamed, knickered and brassiered image in the basin mirror and flops herself down on a wicker stool. Through tears of hysterical laughter, she attempts to remove her face cream.

Fay, two floors above, hears, wonders what Rita found so hilarious? Laughter is now alien to Fay. Unless it is punctuated, properly cadenced, with incantations.

Funny old world, ain't it Fay?

"What?" says Fay, "What was that?

Nothing. Bid goodbye to sweat-of-scholar, my thoughtless prosopopoeia...

"*Sweat of scholar*?"

Just get on with it, alrighty?

"Alrighty."

55

Here, m'dears, for our additional amusement, is a dainty detour de force. An example of my writhing though rapidly waning will. We must be honest about these things, n'est-ce pas? But bear in mind, m'dears, a great man once said (though his nom escapes me) that all things work together for the good. The sod, obviously, has never ventured beyond Pluto.

"How good of you to come at such short notice," murmurs Fay just above the din of her dangling bracelets – my little marmoset got the bracelet-bug from Rita on that first humiliating visit so long ago. Gibbon see, Gibbon do.

"What?" squeaks Fay.

Nothing, sugar.

"I beg your pardon?" says the man opposite.

"I thought I heard a clatter in the kitchen," replies Fay as she shakes the hand of this simply stunning person across the table of their private dining room in the small but cosy Mayfair hotel strenuously recommended by her financial adviser, Hassan Ammari. "We appreciate your cramming us into your crowded schedule at the last minute."

This puzzled man casts his definitively bedroom eyes about but sees no one to accommodate Fay's *we*.

"Ms...?"

"This little Ms," says Fay with a merry twinkle, "prefers to remain anonymous as per our conversation sur le téléphone."

"Yes. Of course."

"Refer to us simply as Madam X."

"Of course," sighs the man.

A waiter enters, hands out menus and disappears.

"Golly!" exclaims Fay tossing aside her menu, "We'd better get on with the details. You are aware of the goodly sum involved?"

Fay knows it is excellent policy to mention money as often as possible. It has been her experience that men, in particular, are impressed by it, especially *enormous* amounts of it. Especially whilst enchanting shadows dart thither and yon' amongst pricey porcelain and cutlery set upon sparkling white-on-white embroidered table clothes atop highly polished ebony wood tables duly attended by experienced, high-salaried, humpable waiters.

The *goodly* sum? The man nods, puzzled by our choice of words.

"That's no doubt why you came at such short notice? The money?"

Cooly: "It was a consideration."

"Glory! I've met an honest man! You refresh me, sirrah!"

The man is uncomfortable. No. Let's face it, m'dears, Repelled.

"Speaking of refreshment, would you like something to drink? You may as well have something. I'm paying."

There it is, money again. Although we must remember that Fay's ostensibly insulting remarks are born of naiveté, not malice. If you can swallow *that*, you'll swallow anything. No, but seriously…

The man nods and valiantly attempts a smile, says "*You're* paying? In that case, God, yes!"

"Garçon!" shrieks Fay.

The waiter is instantly at Fay's elbow and she nods to her guest, "You first, sugar."

"A double whisky (with a glance at Fay) no make it a triple"

"A Babycham, pwease," lisps Fay, "I'm a babycham girl."

The waiter nods and exits smartly.

"We're moving into pwoperty," lisps Fay with a delighted giggle (she knows men also like girlishness – but she hadn't time to prepare her tissued pout so a lisp must serve), "Luxury conversions. Quality, pwestige conversions."

Ach! All in a good cause, m'dears. Life and death. All in a good cause. Grin and share it.

"Do you follow us?"

The man nods.

"We have purchased a quite sizable mews in an exclusive quarter of our fair city (Oh, Fay, all those forties films!) and we intend to gut ('gut', it's got a ring to it) all the houses and renovate the interiors to the highest modern luxury standards, standards hitherto undreamed of. We need an image. You can provide it. Do you follow us? We wish to prematurely pique the public's palette in our project -- well before we commence."

Yes, thinks the man, women *are* from Venus – at least this one.

And *this* one too, mein herr! But *much* farther out.

The waiter enters, serves their beverages and stands by with pad and pencil. Fay looks longingly at her guest. "I recommend the Lasagne whats-its-name, the plat du jour. You order, sugar."

"Two plat de jours," says the man from the corner of his mouth, "and hold the mayo."

The waiter smiles. Fay, idiomatically at sea as ever, doesn't.

"Hold the mayo?" says Fay, "what does that mean?"

"It means 'Irish need not apply'. And wine?" he replies to the unsmiling Fay.

"Vin rose. A whole bottle. Something yummy."

"Vin rose, it is. A whole bottle. Something yummy."

"Vin rose, a whole bottle," says the waiter, looking deeply into the man's china-blue eyes, "Something yummy."

Fay grins flirtatiously at her guest. But he's eyeing the retreating buttocks of their waiter. After all, he's just 'come out'. He's got a lot of lost time to make up -- though he is reasonably certain he's fallen for our Hugh in a big way.

Fay continues to flirt simply because a Hostess sells kisses. At the moment Fay's a Hostess again -- doesn't know it, has temporarily forgotten that she's really a billionaire on what will soon be a sad safari. Stalking something -- with only a surfeit of silent squares for a guide. You try that sometime, m'dears, it ain't easy. 'Specially whilst being lashed along the way by a disapproving 'Mum'.

But now you're on your own, love.

"Huh?" says Fay.

Jim Richardson, as previously stated, finds Fay's manner repellent though she herself is a treat to behold. She might well have once held a candle to Aphrodite.

Jimmy, those incendiary allusions can be perilous.

Luncheon is served and Richardson continues to stare at Fay as she happily tilts back her head to allow the soft slide of half-chewed pasta down her swan-like throat. She is worshipping her body; appeasing it lest it turn against her yet again. Nobody but I know the trouble she's seen. In any case, m'dears, Glory hallelujah.

"Then it's settled!" exclaims Fay, my African-American spiritual (directly above) notwithstanding, "Our most generous contract to run for three years, revocable of course, at our displeasure. Goody. It is settled. We are delighted."

Richardson nods, because lacking this contract he can only nod. This must all be checked out thoroughly. 'Madam X' is obviously 'Fabulous Fragment Fay' -- he's seen her photo -- and though she's rich she's got, according to Hugh and Jenny more than one screw loose and a hatch that sorely needs battening and why did she contact him in the first place? Is it something about Hugh and

Jenny? And *him*?

Us witchy types have our ways, Jimmy.

"Goodness!" cries Fay, "I did forget! Silly old me!"

She pauses, swings a long piece of pasta to and fro on her fork, savours his steady blue eyes, is certain she spies a perky little soul therein, rejoices but mourns for a moment the loss of her own, says: "There is one condition."

Ach! Here's the catch. Jim remains attentive. He is present out of curiosity but would not turn down a sure thing if it were offered him with no strings attached -- which now, m'dears, it seems it ain't.

"You have an employee. A certain Hugh Woods?"

"Yes?"

Here it comes, thinks Jim.

Me: We would not want him involved in any way with our project.

Fay: "We would not want him involved in any way with our project."

"Oh?"

Me: We would most reluctantly be forced to call the whole thing off if he were to continue in your employ.

Fay: "We would most reluctantly be forced to call the whole thing off if he were to continue in your employ."

Angry pink suffuses from beneath the smart, loose collar of Herr Richardson's impeccable Armani shirt, climbs his neck, turns scarlet at his cheeks.

"We feel," continues Fay at my prompting, "that only *ordinary people* can develop images meant to appeal to other ordinary people. Hugh Woods' association on our project in even the most peripheral way," continues Fay, "would surely harm us."

"I am very sorry, I don't follow you."

"Mr Hughie Woods, it seems, is other-directed."

Jim's fork clangs to his dish as his mouth falls open. "Oh, Jesus!" he gasps, "You don't mean he sucks cocks?!"

"We really don't know what his sort do!"

"But it bothers you?"

Gets *me* all hot and bothered, scream I! Fuck this *ordinary people* bullshit!

"Quiet," cries Fay, who continues, "Mr Richardson, our bodies are temples."

"Have you never slipped back a silken foreskin and sucked a

sleek ...Oh! I beg your pardon, do you prefer them *cut*?"

"*Mr Richardson*!"

Oh, Jimmy, keep it up! My gorge is risen near beyond recall!

Jim Richardson rises, towers over Fay who has stopped short, frightened pasta writhing on her fork.

Here, I admit, I find myself uncommonly sorry for Fay. She knows not what she does. She's in a dark room, walls lit, as usual, by flames. And it is I who have put every politically incorrect sentence between her cunning cupid's bow lips. For effect, my dears. I'm doing my damnedest with cardboard Jimmy.

"You must try it," says Jim Richardson, whispering near Fay's ear, "I love a silken foreskin. Don't you?"

Bending, Richardson slides Fay's dish of pasta over the edge of the table into her lap "Whoops!" he cries, and is gone. Thus fulfilling our artificial though necessary cliché-retribution set-piece. Any saga worth its salt requires multitudes of the above. Or have I misread my instant-drama seminar notes? In any case, not very original, Jimmy, but under the circumstances, forgivable. Particularly because you, yourself, are such a dainty dish to set before this queen. And, most particularly, because your outré behaviour lends a hefty lift to the merciful task ever closer to hand in which you shall be, as previously intimated, peripherally though crucially, instrumental.

The waiter returns, Fay thrusts her wine glass at him, "Long time no see."

He doesn't notice the upturned pasta in her lap, nods, takes up the wine bottle and pours. What does he feel for this peculiar woman? Certainly nothing he can put his finger on – unless she *wishes* it -- the smallest of jests, m'dears, to cheer us into the very next square.

Fay quaffs the glass he's topped. He tops it again. She quaffs, absently drops the glass on the table. It rolls, bounces to the floor where the waiter retrieves it and regards Fay with some concern.

"Are you all right, Madam X?"

"We were raped."

Fay's eyes are glazed. Even if she possessed a soul you'd never see it now.

"We had a miscarriage."

"I'm so sorry, madam."

"Has Mr Jim gone?"

"The gentleman?"

"Jim was no gentleman," she murmurs and takes the waiter's hand.

Which puts me in mind of my own illustrious Mamá who judiciously maintained that a gentleman was *any* bloke who removed her douche-bag from the kitchen sink before urinating. Be that as it may…

"Our sister was murdered," moans Fay to her patient waiter, "By a woman who wore tweeds and brogues and kept hounds."

Attention! Leitmotivs, m'dears! Listen carefully as we throw a soupçon of "leit" on a major player.

The waiter, uncomfortable, moves to leave, Fay grips his hand harder. "Our mother was institutionalized. She is incommunicado."

"I'm so sorry, madam, perhaps..."

"Our father deserted us. Or did he die in my fire with the kittens? Were we interfered with?"

"Is there anything I can do, madam?" replies the waiter attempting to extricate his hand which is rapidly going numb in Fay's frantic grip.

"We were a florist-beautician-librarian-hostess. We kept a diary from the age of six. It was consumed in the conflagration when our house burned down."

True enough, darling. *Something* was consumed.

"What?" cries Fay, What did you say?!"

"I said nothing, madam," says the gentle, perplexed and dishy waiter, taking a nervy skip backward for safety.

"The fire came so close," whines Fay. "Fires must be conducted at a safe distance."

Ain't it the truth?! Is our little girl growing up at last?

Great splashing tears darken the blue tablecloth. The waiter has never seen tears so profuse, so tear-*like* – nor will he ever again. He melts and trembles as Fay whimpers and moans. He pats her hand tenderly and he admires again the magnificent sable she had insisted accompany her to her table.

"But you'll buy another house, won't you madam? You could buy a dozen."

"A dozen bleeding what?" whimpers Fay, dabbing her eyes on the tablecloth under which she has concealed the overturned pasta, whose origin is now a mystery to her.

Selective recall, m'dears. I built it in. I'm not a complete bastard.

"You could buy a dozen houses, madam," says the sympathetic waiter.

"We have, stupid! Don't you listen?!"

Fay has not meant to be abrupt with this poor young, tender -- yes, *tender*! -- waiter. Do you have any objection to that?! The woman *does* have feelings! We all have feelings! Don't be so sodding judgemental!

But poor Fay is beginning to suspect she is governed by nasty forces beyond her control.

Ach! That penny has definitely dropped. Listen for your own pennies, m'dears. I can hear them now. Billions of them clinking and clattering from another time, another place.

Nasty forces thinks Fay, racing crazily towards burnout, nasty forces linked in some sinister way with the stone walls, the flames, the serial hosings-down, the denial of bath water warm enough to bathe in. Oh! And much more.

Bitter memories fly like Taylor's shuffled postcards behind Fay's troubled brows as she is escorted from the private dining room on the arm of this concerned and tender -- yes *tender*! -- waiter who has a brother in a padded cell so is more tolerant than most.

Where *does* she dig up these helpful people? I shouldn't trust the accuracy of this up-market dining room's employee list if I were you. Curiouser and curiouser.

The kind waiter helps Fay into her limou, careful to keep her flowing sable from her pasta-stained dress which he has considerately covered with a crisp, clean tablecloth. She is either drunk or mad. He favours the latter.

So do I. Occasionally. Oops. Sorry to be so intrusive. But without me, darlings...

"Begone, you!" moans Fay, "Oh please begone!"

Chauffy, at the wheel, sees Fay's condition and correctly determines not to speak. To Fay, London is effectively still burning. Though its light is pale beside her own candle which blazes brilliantly at both ends.

Chauffy doesn't, of course, perceive it in quite this way, as he's thick. But with looks like that, who needs brains -- at any rate, for the duration. And, m'dears, I'll grant you he's no Becky Sharp.

Chauffy thanks the waiter, tips him lavishly, records an astronomical sum in his log book -- he'll pocket the difference as usual. He may be thick but he's got street-cred. Is that what they call it these days, my dears? I goose him, he yelps and starts the Rolls. He and the now stuporous Fay, couched cosily in her soft leather seat, screech luxuriously away.

Fay steps from the Rolls, still afloat in smouldering reverie. As any fool knows there's less pain there. Unassisted by Chauffy who has better things to do, she weaves up the steps of Her House, is drawn by the staccato of Rita's typewriter, pauses outside Rita's door, presses her face against it, calls pitifully:

"Riiiiiita?"

The typing from within ceases.

"Riiiiita? Forgive and forget?"

Rita freezes, listens.

"We didn't mean to be bad, Rita."

She means every word of it, m'dears. She simply couldn't help it (I mean, all those *squares*!). How often have *we* said: 'I just couldn't *help* it?'

Rita moves not a muscle.

"We weren't ourselves, Rita."

You can say that again, sugar.

"We were a little fish stranded in a dry and thirsty land where no water is."

But darling they were *constantly* hosing you down.

Tears trickle from Rita's eyes. She shivers and silently curses herself.

"Rita. Oh, Rita, dear Ritaaaaa. Circumstances beyond our control. Forgive us, Rita. Houses do burn, Rita, darling, they do. Honestly. Houses burn down all around us. Angels are cast out."

Rita is drenched in tears. Quiet as a mouse she wipes them away. She's ashamed of herself. Ashamed of her weakness. Ashamed of almost being taken in by The Ritterhouse Fay.

"Open your door, Rita. Forgive the penitent Fay. Forgive poor Fay."

Did not Lot pray nearly *endlessly* for those naughty denizens of Sodom?

Rita does not move. After a moment she hears Fay's footsteps retreat up the stairs. She takes a deep breath, wipes her eyes again and with shaking fingers, lights a now-forbidden cigarette.

Thus concludes our little 'detour' de force (which will presently prove itself wildly successful).

Tour de forces are much more common in every day life than you think, m'dears.

Honest. But then who are *you* to question *me*?

Fay pauses outside her door, searching for her keys, this time in a gold initialled, fine leather not paper, carry-bag. This contrast is not lost on her. She brightens in an instant. "Me so happy. Me so excessively happy."

She is. Until her floor-length sable floats over rubble that once, as walls, defined the hateful perimeters of Bill's flat -- not a vast area, but begging to be rebuilt according to Fay -- according to the portfolio, to become Her Very Own House. As it was in the beginning when she played on its stairs and in its closets amongst fine rugs and an odd little shrine to the dark arts. When the world was as young and loving as Fay, and as unblemished. During the days when she and her Granny were perfect. Before the exodus.

Ach, I've come all over queer, m'dears!

Fay stumbles through her door, tosses the fur at a chair and unwinds the soggy blue table cloth from her pasta-sodden lap. She strips off her dress and throws herself on the sofa thinking of what was, what could have been and what might, what *will* be. She shivers at what will be. But then, she always has. When she remembers. When I tell her.

After a moment she spots the remote and buzzes open the mirrored bar door. Nelly's plumed kewpie grins at her from beside a bottle of something-or-other. Fay grabs the bottle and pours a stiff drink, downing it as she snatches the kewpie from its glass shelf.

With kewpie, bottle and glass, she stalks (yes, m'dears, *actually stalks* like a cheap detective in a B-movie) to her bedroom, slings all at her unmade bed and crouches before the closet from which she yanks her battered cardboard suitcase. The cardboard suitcase immediately begins to complain of its neglect, whines a bit.

Honestly! But what can one expect from a cheap, definitely not biodegradable, chemical-soaked paper product.

That black cat leaps up, disturbed from its snooze on the floor amongst the folds of a discarded up-market mink and catapults from the bedroom out the ajar terrace door and very possibly through the potted trees into empty space to yet another death. I simply can no longer keep count of these little feline deaths. How they do mount!

Fay doesn't care. She is topping her brandy and, like Rita, is drinking more than she ought. With no Ian to disapprove who knows where it will lead? Fay knows. Or suspects. Witches know their fates. Just as dark angels do. When they can remember. "Why *me*?" asks Fay, not so very originally I must say, of Nelly's kewpie,

"Who am I? *What* am I?"

A work in flux, darling. And you're good fun when you do as you're told. And even when you don't.

"What?" says Fay, "What was that?"

Don't ask. Not yet. There's much to do. Not all of it frivolous. There's the task, sugar. *The task.* Arbitrary as it may appear to the Great Unwashed it is a merciful task.

So Fay sighs a giant sigh and from her tatty suitcase takes: a large ball of twine; a small box of heavy rubber-bands -- there are seven -- plus four paper carry-bags; her precious blue velvet table cloth and a blue marking pencil with which she begins to colour the lightbulb in her bed-lamp, chanting: "Darling...Honey...Sugar," accompanied (in humming thirds) by the complaining, down-market cardboard suitcase. She will soon tire, lose interest and toss these objects back into the suitcase and set Nelly's kewpie, that positively shining-with-love-and-good-will object, tenderly among them. This, of course, throws my whole bleeding balance out of whack. These valuable talismans are now suddenly worthless, couldn't shield Fay from a chocolate Easter Bunny.

How often, m'dears, do we do the wrong thing at the wrong place at the wrong time? Like a *war*? Obviously, *someone* has to suffer for it. And it may as well be *her*. As it most certainly will not be me, her maniacal manipulator (just kiddin').

Fay is about to shut the suitcase when she sees, neatly folded, Nelly's black silk scarf. She unfolds it and holds it to her cheek, chants again "Darling...Honey...Sugar."

Who knows? This scarf could be her deliverance. Could be some minor victory. She may need it again -- for something more serious. Maybe not. I haven't decided. Meanwhile, Fay, shift your arse! Get those lovely so-called *feet* into that next greedy square.

You too, m'dears. But do mind how you go.

Please.

56

Jenny is undaunted by the vaporous urban air. Backpacked with groceries she jogs beside vast queues of creeping, poison-belching cars -- far more deadly than the tinted tilting shadows of Number 13. Our papier-mâché Ms works up a good, healthy sweat -- perhaps not so effective as Sweat of Scholar but that, my dears, now seems a lost cause. Scholars, with the notable exception of manqué-me, are not, nor will be, much in evidence. My Fay had her chance and muffed it.

Jenny leaps up the front steps of our Number 13, is waved at by Rita in her window. Poor Rita, she's at that window a lot these days. Fay has inexplicably usurped her novel-muse-thingy.

Of course, Fay is watching from her window too (I alerted her), and she waits for Jenny's return, has vital things to say to her. *Vital.* Perhaps Jenny, who no longer speaks to Fay, had better listen?

Jenny makes her way through the debris and up the rubbished staircase, wishes someone would break a leg and sue Fay, wonders why she, Jenny, hasn't -- a broken leg might be worth the trouble.

Think again, Jen. We occasionally get what we wish for (now, who the fuck said that? I *must* credit my sources -- or at least provide a suitable index).

Suddenly here on a stair blocking her path is my darling prosopopoeia in a shifting cloud of plaster dust, her sable billowing, that black cat in her arms.

"Long time no see," says she.

Jenny attempts to pass, Fay moves, blocks her, the cat growls. Jenny reaches for a handrail -- there is none. She staggers backward against the commiserating wall.

"We love your jogging outfit," purrs Fay, stroking the growling cat. "We saw you from our window and simply had to comment on it. It's breathtaking. We intend to purchase one just like it."

Oh please, Jenny, *like* me, screams Fay in our respective heads, please, Jenny, *love* me!

Jenny again attempts to pass, Again, Fay blocks her.

"Please, Jen, talk a moment with Fay."

"Don't call me Jen."

"What have we ever done to you?"

"You put cockroaches in my cookie tin."

Jenny is sweating hard but now it's a cold sweat, with nothing like the previous potential of our dispatched scholar. If 'Jen' had spent a bit more time at university Fay might even have scooped said perspiration from that dark spreading spot just beneath her backpack at the small of 'Jen's' back. What might have come of that? Transformation and release?! Poor Fay, all the clues are here. But common clay, even *fired* as she is...Oh, my! Fay needs all the help she can get: Hair of hag, sweat of scholar, Class, black silk scarves, shiny kettles...properly edited incantations... and of course -- and it's a very big of course, of course: that marvellous, magical rug. But she sold out, my dears. In spite of me, your searing Sage. Oh, it's all rather catch 22, ain't it? As the great Judy once sang, compliments of the great Ira Gershwin:

"Don't know what happened
It's all a crazy gaaaaame!"

Oh I could go on! And will:

Fay continues to stroke Two-lives, "Where do you purchase your jogging clothes?" she says to Jenny, "We're ever so impressed. They're so -- we'd be a liar if we didn't say it (you'd be a liar either way, ducky) -- they're so masculine. That superior back pack. You are obviously a woman who can take care of herself, aren't you? I mean that in the nicest sense."

She does. Believe her. *I* do. Ain't I a fickle darling?

"Let me pass," replies Jenny. God! Those vibrations again!

"I'm a woman who understands precisely what a woman, any woman, needs," says Fay, "I'm...versatile, *uni*versatile. Why do you waste your time on him? He doesn't know what he wants. You can see it in his eyes. Look into my eyes, Jen, you'll see what *I* want."

It is tres difficile, m'dears, being all things to all people.

"Get out of my way or..."

"Are you threatening us?"

Fay bristles, seems to grow large and luminous. The wall and floors fearfully squinch shut their multi-faceted eyes. "Threats are subject to prosecution and, if you will forgive us," says Fay, "money talks (Ye gods! Here comes the money again!) – and one billion positively shrieks!"

You've said that before, ducky. Leave off. Give us a break. Consult your bleeding thesaurus. Sorry. *My* bleeding thesaurus.

Jenny glares at Fay. Fay smiles, continues to stroke the cat.

Jenny shudders. The vibrations mount -- no! It's only a cold she's fighting off.

"Speaking of forgiveness, that is why we are here, on this forlorn, molten sphere, all of us, to ask forgiveness. For we have all sinned and fallen short of glory."

"*All* of us?" asks Jenny, looking up the staircase for possible escape.

"All of us," replies Fay.

Darlings, I had to send her to Sunday School at least *once*.

Jenny shrugs. "You and your cockroaches. But forget it, baby, I'm just fine. I bought another tin."

Oh Jenny! You're so mundane!

"But can you buy another fellah?" says grinning Fay, "One who functions...properly?"

"I shall ask you one more time to let me pass."

Jenny shudders. She'd better do something about that cold -- and change out of these sweaty clothes.

"Hughie might as well be a woman who wants a man. Is that what you want, deep down? A woman?"

This is of course precisely what Jenny wants – sometimes -- but it's none of Fay's goddamned business.

"Ritterhouse. You're not a real human being," says Jenny more accurately than she'll ever know.

"We are as human as you are. See our fingernails?"

Fay thrusts out her hand. The cat, clutched about its neck in her other arm, struggles and growls, the staircase, ever the peace-maker, suddenly glows lavender with highlights of a refreshing pink.

Fay jabs her fingers in Jenny's face. "See how red they are? That's real blood under these nails! That's what makes them so red! They're redder than yours! They're redder than they've ever been! Do you know what that means? That means we've been given a new lease of life! New life is surging through us!"

"God! Pregnant again?"

You could be too, Jen. So lay off!

"We soon shall be! Whosoever worships in our shrine will bring forth a god!"

Or *something*, love.

The cat, choking in Fay's grasp and terrified by her shout, leaps away with a scratch and a howl and scampers up the stairs. Jenny, seizing the moment, pushes Fay aside, runs up the half-destroyed, stairs into Hugh's flat and collides with Hugh who is just exiting the kitchen with a dish of fresh-baked scones to go with their take-out Chinese.

Be assured, m'dears, neither Hugh nor Jen will ever write a cookbook.

Jenny shudders with vibrations. Struggles with wobbling walls, an undulating floor. Her feet seem clown-like, huge and clumsy, her hands, three-fingered, nails pulsating by turns mauve then orange.

Jenny hugs Hugh, the scones scatter. She kneels and attempts to gather them but stops at the sight of her clown feet and her bloated three fingered hands, slumps to the floor and screams.

"I want out of here! Hugh! Look at my hands, my feet! Get me out of here!"

Hugh, seeing nothing out of the ordinary, leads Jenny over the rippling, melon-coloured floor to the bed sofa, lays her down and sits beside her. The sofa quakes with her violent shudders.

"Okay. We're leaving. But only if you really want it."

"I want."

"I was going to tell you the minute you got here. I've been transferred to the States. A big step up. Jim's going too."

"I'm glad, Hughie! Jesus, I'm glad!"

"What about your new job? Just when you're doing so well?"

"I want out of here!"

"What's all this about?"

"I love you!"

Hugh hugs her. "I know that. I love you too."

"No you don't."

He hugs her tighter. "Yes I do."

"I love *you*! I love *you*!"

Get on with it, my little chickens!

Still holding her, Hugh backs away just the slightest bit, kisses her on the nose. "Jim loves me too, Jen. Can you deal with that?"

Jenny pulls away, Hugh grabs her hands, smiles gently. She relaxes. "I..."

Hugh plunges on. "Ritterhouse, now known as Madam X, took our Mr Richardson to lunch, offered him a contract to develop an image for a new mews project. Then demanded he fire me. She's pissed because we broke that blood-pact."

Piss and blood? How very basic. But that's me all over.

"What?!"

"Ritterhouse Fay insisted that Jim fire me or he wouldn't get the contract. He tipped a plate of pasta into her lap, told her to fuck off and promoted me."

Ach! I just knew Herr Richardson had something up his sleeve every bit as attractive as the covert contents of his knickers!

Jenny starts to cry, then laughs. Then they both laugh. Then Hugh starts to cry. "I'd never leave you, Jen, never." Then Jenny cries harder because she knows it will be all right -- Jim or no Jim -- and Hugh cries harder because it's wonderful to be loved by both Jenny and Jim and be able to return their love completely (silly boy -- my, my, the naïveté of youth!). Jenny feels the very same way (Alicia!) as they sink deep into the bed sofa and sob out their two happy bisexual hearts.

How very young of them. How very *modern*.

From her second floor aerie Fay gazes down at Rita who descends the steps to Ian's car and drives off with him to visit Mrs Taylor in hospital. Don't ask Fay how she knows they're off to see Taylor. She wouldn't tell you. Even if she knew. When angels are cast down they do retain certain advantages. Me.

57

Fay sets the portfolio on Rita's coffee table, tucks the master-key in that dowdy cardigan pocket -- she's wearing the horrid thing again, is more comfortable in it, makes her feel at home. "Ummnn, cosy," she whispers, "Me like cosy cardy."

Said belonged to her Granny. Or was it her Uncle Oscar? Was it the one he was wearing when Uncle Oscar...?

Perhaps, dear. Perhaps. Or not.

Fay begins to snoop, riffles through drawer after drawer, flinging the contents aside in a frantic search for something more interesting, more relevant, something abandoned, perhaps by Fay herself, many years before when she lived here.

Have you ever looked for something, darlings, and whilst you were looking, forgot what it was you were looking for and yet continued looking, hoping you'd remember what it was? Hoping – not necessarily desperately, like our Fay – but hoping. Just hoping. For as we all know, said springs eternal. And where there's life there's…etc. Always etc. When we want the facts only. *Always*...etc.

Was Rita's living room Fay's childhood bedroom? Fay rushes to the bathroom. She perches precariously, my dears, on Square Umpteen (I've long ago given up counting squares in my little saga, my board game). Ach! Sweet Jesus! It was here! She sheltered in this bath tub, a bath tub full of water, kept her little head down as low as she could in the water whilst flames raged and people perished!

This is too much for Fay. "Oh, my!" she cries and throws up her hands to brush away a glittering, buzzing swarm, "Golly! Me not so happy now!"

Occasionally her words fail me.

Rita's flat has burst open that ornate box again and nasty bees of memory are stinging her. Why wasn't she aware of this her first visit to Rita on that day she came back to Number 13? Months ago -- or was it years? Millenniums? In another life? Yet *another* life? God! She needs a coffee.

"Warm your coffee?" says Rita as Fay sets a kettle on, *the* kettle on.

"Yes, please," repeats Fay, "I noticed you had some excellent blends on your shelf."

"Oh. Those," rings Rita's voice, "They're ancient. I wouldn't give them to a dog."

Wouldn't give them to a dog meant *you*, Fay. She wouldn't give that lovely, expensive coffee to you! Get angry, Lassie! Get *real*! Bow-Wow!

"Damnation!" cries Fay and jumps back from the cooker. Her sleeve is on fire (but not yet, no, darling, not yet!). She sticks her wrist under the tap, douses a tiny bluish, gem-like flame, twirls to Rita's fridge and finds a large piece of cake, dispatches it in one gulp. She returns to the kettle, watches, waits. Inchoate incantations skulk nearby, vibrating the still air, tiny stones tossed into my dark, forbidding pond.

A watched kettle never boils, Fay. Didn't Granny tell you?

"Hush," says Fay, "*Please* hush."

"You're a liar, aren't you?" says Rita from somewhere.

"Of course I'm a liar. What could I have been? Under the circumstances. I'm a lot of things. You're a lot of things too. The lot of you."

"Of course we are, dear," says Nelly, "Nobody's perfect."

The images of that first party explode before her. Face after face glares at her, dismisses her, banishes her from Her Home. Where the heart is -- from paradise. From heaven. From, m'dears, whatever.

"I could have been perfect!" cries Fay at Rita's quivering cooker. I was a lovely child. Beautiful. A beautiful child. Gentle. Gentle in every way. Loving. I was a loving child. Trusting. I was trusting too. Beautiful. Gentle. Trusting...I was an angel."

Nelly's voice, clear and kind (but forever lost! -- *I* saw to that!), tinkles like a soothing bell. "It's late dear. We've all had too much..."

"Indeed we have!" cries Rita.

The kettle whistles and startles Fay from her waking nightmare. She pushes it roughly off the burner, spills steaming water on her hand, cries out, places the hand in her mouth, licks it catlike, preening.

"It's me again, dear."

Rita pats Mrs Taylor's hand. Taylor stares blankly at the ceiling. The monotonous hissing-suck of the oxygen mask is the only sound in this large, elaborately equipped private room. How could Mrs Taylor afford such a room? Ask Fay, Rita. She paid for it all. In aces. That adorable sneak!

"I aired your geraniums, love. They are flourishing. If you hear me, blink twice."

Taylor does not blink.

"Nelly and Bill have their own flat now. They bought it with Ritterhouse's chinchilla and diamond bracelet. Some consolation. I can think of easier ways of acquiring a flat. Like working the streets -- if one were young enough. Which one is decidedly not. Which is obvious. God, I go on."

You do indeed, ducky! Better to just jot it down, use it, and keep your bleedin' mouth shut. That's what writers do. Or should do. But almost never do. Take me, for instance…no, don't.

Rita plucks a cigarette, shakily sticks it in her holder. "Sorry, love. I've got to. If you don't like it, scream.

I'll scream instead. EEEEEKKKKK!

"Our house is a disaster area, Mrs Taylor, absolutely bombed out. I've ingested so much plaster dust I'm pooping little Greek columns."

Is that a smile on Taylor's face? If it was, Rita didn't see it. Rita is now thinking about Fay.

Taylor seems for a moment to float near consciousness and Rita is encouraged, takes a flamboyant puff, continues edgily. "Ian and I are getting very serious. I mean I'm getting very serious about him getting very serious about me and it had better be pronto. We're not eternal (you can say that again, ducky). I keep telling him I'm not eternal and he keeps looking at me and saying 'You're tellin' me!' Sorry, love. My nerves are shot. Anyway, I just sold another story -- part two of the 'Ritterhouse Serial', and they're commissioning hundreds of others. Guess I hit it lucky."

You hit it lucky? Honestly, Rita! Open those baggy eyes! Look at me!

"I miss you, love. Very much. I miss your damned stick on my ceiling. I wish I'd got to know you better… sooner."

Taylor's eyes flicker. "Smooch," she mumbles, "Smooch."

Rita is astonished at these first words in days, moves in close. "What, love? What did you say?"

After a very long moment, bending very close, she hears just the faintest "Hearts...arrows."

"Yes. Your postcards. What about them?"

"The witch...wants..."

Taylor's rheumy old eyes open wide for a moment then glaze over again.

"The witch wants everything," murmurs Rita.

But she's happy that Ian is just outside the door waiting for her, is happy that she can be here for Mrs Taylor. Wishes she could have done more. Life passes too fast. Too sodding fast. Before you know it, you've keeled over and you're dead as a doornail.

Fay hovers over Rita's writing table clutching with whitened knuckles her coffee in one hand and Rita's latest manuscript, in the other.

> Desiree was, Janet is reasonably sure, a witch. But how, thought Janet, could a witch be a witch and not know it?

Fay, breathing hard, reads on.

> But of course! thought Janet. Desiree was, as old Mrs Belcher was forever saying -- before Desiree pushed her down the stairs and killed her -- A curs-ed witch.

Fay squinches her forehead -- the manuscript seems out of focus. Contact lenses! She needs contact lenses, "That healthy boost into modernity," she mutters and, squinching, reads on.

> A cur-sed witch would not know she was a witch. If she knew she were a witch she could 'witch' her way out of the curse!

Oh, my! *Spells forgotten*, darling, think on spells forgotten! Rita knows. I told her. Though she doesn't know I told her. She thinks of it as inspiration. Tut-tut.

"Huh?" says Fay to Rita's typewriter. But obsolete typewriters can't speak (at the moment).

"Please!" cries Fay, "Please!"

Fay is profoundly alarmed, but reads on.

> No. Doolittle Desiree did not know she had magical powers because any curse worth its fire and brimstone would have made certain of that.

But sometimes...even a splendid curse forgets a few...details. Who is doing the cursing?

"What?" says Fay, dropping this last page of manuscript on Rita's writing table, "What was that?!"

Just now, peaches, we're denouementing, creeping across a few crucial squares ever closer our goal.

Fay snatches at her coffee, overturns it on the manuscript, cries out as the nearest wall bristles and makes a grab at her firm, shapely breasts.

"No smoking, *please*! This woman is on oxygen. Can't you read?! You'll burn us down!"

Rita takes a last puff and extinguishes her cigarette under the irate nurse's watchful eye. Rising, she throws on her coat, bends over Taylor, kisses her forehead and leaves. Just outside Mrs Taylor's room, Ian looks up from a magazine, smiles at her. Her heart jumps, she smiles back.

Ah, *aging Love*. There's really nothing like it.

Rita at her window waves goodbye to Ian. She tugs her kimono tight around her neck -- he seems to massage her neck. "Oh, Ian, stay and massage my neck, darling"-- enough of this, thinks Rita. Get a grip on yourself. Pull up your socks!

Rita wishes Ian were staying that night, feels someone is watching. They are. Not watching you, Rita, but Ian, as he drives away. Watching from above at Fay's window. Where else? Who else? *What* else?

Darlings, let's face it. It needn't necessarily always be Fay at the goddamned window. We're in this together, all of us.

Rita fidgets. She's not the fidgeting sort but tonight… she walks to and fro, picks up then throws down her French primer, primps in a mirror, files her nails, puts up her hair, checks her teeth for spinach. But she's had no spinach. Time for her cognac? Dare she? Why not? She's been awfully good lately. Best behaviour. She pours and splashes it as the telephone rings. Is she as nervous as all that? Apparently.

"Hello?"

No answer.

"Hello?" says Rita.

No answer.

"Who is this?"

Fay breathes heavily into her telephone.

The poor woman is lonely, *thinks* she is lonely. But there is pain there, m'dears, either way. Let it be.

Rita slams down the receiver, swigs a brandy, starts for the kitchen. The telephone rings again. "Bastard!" she hisses and yanks up the receiver.

Fay moans a series of extraordinarily basso-profundo moans punctuated with eerily authentic, treble orgasmic whimpers. Loneliness is a hard mistress. And love applied, but love denied, is disaster.

"Bastard bitch!" cries Rita and slams down the receiver again. Turning away, she sees her coffee-soaked manuscript askew on her writing table. "Bastard!" screams Rita, quite accurately as it happens, "You bitch-bastard!"

And she hasn't yet seen her bedroom.

Rita. Be kind. Be realistic. Fay's traceable lineage dwarfs yours, dear, by multi-millenniums.

The telephone rings again. "Merde!" she shrieks into the receiver "-- oh God, Ian! Darling! I thought it was the breather... yes...it's her. She was here in my flat tonight when we were at the hospital...Don't worry, love. I can handle her."

Can you, Rita? Bill and Nelly couldn't, Hugh and Jenny couldn't -- Jim Richardson didn't choose to. They're packing now, that latter delightful ménage à trois is departing directly for the good old U.S. of A. And *comparative* safety?

But ours is not to reason why. Ours is but to...

58

"You've ever so much more room now, dear."

Hawkins stares wide-eyed through a stuccoed arch that was originally Fay's entrance but now leads into a large, beautifully carpeted area that once contained Bill's entire flat.

"We've expanded," says Fay from the tatty chenille folds of her old bathrobe as she stretches her slender, well-formed so-called *arms* above her head and sinks into the white leather sofa. She loves the smell of old chenille, loves the look, too. Sterile Bond street boutiques are not for her. Tragically -- I adore my overblown adjectives -- *tragically,* Fay has no idea why chenille is preferable to chinchilla.

And neither do I. Although I know everything.

"I should say so, dear!" replies Hawkins to Fay's expansive renovational pronouncement, "...expanded right across your cor-ree-dor by the looks of it!" continues Hawkins, finishing this sentence brutalized by my random intrusion.

"It is our intention to redeem the whole house. To restore its former mystical glory. My builders accomplished this ..." says Fay with a wave of her hand "...in two days."

"Two days?!"

Hawkins pauses, she's polishing a mirror, leans against a genial, subtly exhaling wall of indeterminate colour and gender -- "Why that's magic!"

How perceptive, ducky. Now get back to work, you lazy slattern or I'll jettison you back to where I plucked you.

"Aren't you the lucky one?!" adds Hawkins. "Well it's a right rubbish tip downstairs and no mistake. What's your hubby do, dear?"

"We are not married," says Fay.

"It's nothing to be ashamed of, dear. Co-hab-bit-tat-in' is perfectly acceptable. Especially these days. What's your gentleman do then, dear?"

Hawkins, like a French maid, now flutters about with an outsized feathery dust mop (but don't hold your breath for the 'oui, oui, Madame!).

"We have no mate."

"*We,* dear?"

"We are single, self-sufficient and excessively rich."

Certain temperaments require constant tuning. Though I'm not always prick-perfect.

"You can say that again, dear, about 'rich'. I seen your photo in News of the World. Aren't you the lucky one -- where's kitty today?"

Fay ignores her and snatches a colourfully wrapped sweet from an ornate though anxious mauve box, unwraps it with a flourish and pops it into her mouth. She sucks dreamily as Hawkins, humming, empties a full vacuum bag into a highly-brushed-aluminium waste bin.

Had Hawkins seen the scurrilous film-show of shadows playing across the wall behind her -- those unspeakable acts touched on by Fay at their first meeting -- she might gladly have sat herself down for a few moaning though unmentionable moments. Moments unconsciously conjured by The Ritterhouse Fay (plus me) in repose. But Hawkins, ponging moderately, brow misting lightly under haggish hair, is planted as firmly in the mundane as a Mob informer's feet in concrete. No flights of fancy for her. Hawkins wouldn't know a phantom if it fucked her.

"It was ever so nice of you to ask for me special at the agency, dear. They're ever so nice to you at the agency when somebody asks for you special. Thanks ever so much, dear."

"Would you like a drink?"

At this, Fay's film-show evaporates, she's ardently thinking of *something* though I must admit I know not what. So the living room weaves a bit to the left, corrects itself (exhausting me), and is momentarily quiet, waiting for Fay to pirouette into square... whatever.

Hawkins snaps a new bag into the vacuum cleaner and leaps to Fay's side. "Shall we be naughty, dear? It *is* early."

Fay buzzes open the bar with a great thump and Hawkins squeals "Oooo! Didn't that just give me a start! Need's oiling or something, dear. You'll shake out Mabel Hawkins's choppers if you're not careful!"

"Who is Mabel Hawkins?"

"Why, me, dear! You asked for me special at the agency."

A moment later the two, heads together, are sipping delicate crystal demitasses of Drambuie.

"Aren't we naughty? You mustn't tell them at the agency, you know, that I drink on the job."

"Are you married?"

"Of course I'm married. Hubby's long gone but yours truly is still an honest woman. Don't I look married, dear?"

"You look very distinguished. You remind me of my mother. Distinguished and attractive," says Fay conjuring up some imagined model Mum.

Where *is* this going?

"Me? Distinguished?!"

Hawkins' eyes pop, "I'll give you the 'attractive', dear -- I ain't never had no problems attracting the oppeesite sex -- but distinguished?"

Fay stirs her Drambuie with a finger, her mind's eye moving longingly over happy children being impossibly kind to one another in immaculate schoolyards of various well-funded institutions of primary education (don't you *wish*?).

The immediately above: A slice of utopiana, m'dears, to balance the senses-searing dark surrreality of life at Number 13. Ironical? Perhaps. But never let it be said that I am not socially aware. Just contemplate for a moment the noble causes we've discussed along our merry way.

"Do you have children?" asks Fay, focusing in on one particular happy child looking very much as she had supposed herself in her long lost Eden.

"A daughter but don't tell no one."

"Whyever not?"

"Errr..."

"Did you love your mother?"

"That's a funny question, dear. Don't everybody? I mean she's your mum, ain't she?"

"Do you climb trees?" asks Fay.

A wondrous, vine-wrapped tree sprouts through Fay's carpet and shoots upward through the shattering ceiling. Its upper branches promptly disappear in grey wintry clouds. Its sturdy vine, whooshing by, catches Mabel Hawkins by her ginger-dyed hair and catapults her aloft. Fay, curiously unaffected, cranes her neck to watch.

Hawkins is also curiously unaffected, her gray felt-slippered feet still firm on the recently hoovered carpet as she ponders an answer to whether she does indeed climb trees.

But then (moving on!) Fay's entrance door, newly enclosed in a frosted glass cupola at the top of the stairs, chimes melodiously.

"Is Ritterhouse here?" asks Jenny almost before Hawkins, guiltily quaffing her Drambuie and hiding the bottle, can open the door.

"Why, darling," trills Fay nearly as musically as her door-chimes (which greatly appreciate my comment and vibrate affectionately), "Of course we're here! Come in! Come in! Long time, no see!"

But Jenny will not enter and Hawkins retreats under Jenny's Medusa glare to the kitchen where she begins to scour divers scorched objects, terrified that Jenny has been sent by the employment agency to spy on her..

Fay is overjoyed, exultant, sways happily at the thought of some noble, extraordinarily expensive deed in Jenny's favour.

"What is it, Jen, darling? Friend of my heart?!" cries Fay who rushes to the door, extends a hand that Jenny prefers not to take.

"We're leaving."

"Leaving? *Leaving*? I don't understand, Jenny dear. Your new open-plan kitchen is...I mean a lovely, stainless-steel top-of-the-line dish-washer is to be delivered momentarily!"

It is indeed -- I can see the delivery information now, stuffed into the butt-lovely back pocket of the lean young deliverer as his lorry lurches towards Number 13.

"Here's our lease, Ritterhouse," says Jenny, "We thought you should be the first to know. We've requested a two month rent refund due to the disturbances of building. We've been assured by our advisors..."

"Of course you'll receive the refund, Jen (and they will – *the 4th of Never* – though through no fault of Fay's). It was already in the works for both you and Rita as well as poor Granny Taylor," says Fay. "Goodness! Hughie hasn't lost his job, has he?"

"I'm afraid he has."

"How awful."

And she means it. How *could* this have happened? Hugh seems such a capable, talented man.

"We're being deported," says Jenny.

"What?! Why, darling, why?! What have you done?"

Fay is genuinely anxious in her Fay Wray way, even sans Kong (that was mean of me but I'm feeling trite – or should that be *con*trite? No. I think not),

"What *have* you done?!"

"Practically everything," replies Jenny, "We've done practically everything."

"Good for you, darlin'," mutters Hawkins who's done practically everything too, from the kitchen.

"What was that, Hawkins?"

"Nothin', Mrs Ritterhouse, I ain't said nothin'."

"We'll miss you, Jen."

"Please do not call me 'Jen'."

Jenny hands Fay a tiny box wrapped in silver paper and tied with a silver ribbon.

"Oh Jen! cries Fay, "You shouldn't have!"

"That's what Hugh said."

"What can it be? How thoughtful. Hawkins, come in at once and see what our Jen has bought us!"

"Us?" replies Jenny, "It's for *you*, Ritterhouse, and you alone."

And me too, of course. I *could* tell you what it is...

"Mrs Hawkins!" shrieks Fay, bubbling with pleasure -- it is not often Fay is given gifts, unless one wishes to include Nelly's relatively fine chest of drawers, Rita's kettle or a little jewelled fish on a chain or a kewpie doll or Number 13 itself or even a billion pound carpet. The black silk scarf doesn't count -- she stole it.

"Shut up, you!" hisses Fay who has every right to hiss at me.

"Mrs Hawkins! Attend me!"

"Here I am, Mrs Ritterhouse," cries Hawkins, rushing in as she wipes scouring-powder from her fingers to her bright orange apron.

"Got to go," says Jenny, "Our furniture left early this morning. Doesn't amount to much. We're leaving it with friends."

"Stay, Jen! Do wait whilst I open your little gift."

"No can do," calls Jenny moving quickly through Fay's glass cupola door and down the stairs, "Ian is driving us to the airport. Enjoy your house, Fay. You've earned it."

How nice of *Jen* to say Fay's earned it. Yes. Fay has worked hard to make Her Home Her Castle -- and their castle too. But they're leaving, just when everything had begun to work out so well.

Oh, darling Fay. Such staggering ignorance! But how utterly piquant!

Fay slides a stale chenille sleeve against her dampening eyes as she shifts herself sideways onto another square, "I always knew (this, directed at Hawkins)...I always knew Jenny and Hugh were my friends. Friends in need are friends indeed."

Rejoice, Fay. Leaving is precisely, at this stage of the game, what Hugh and Jenny *ought* to be doing. You're on course, lovey.

For the moment.

Fay cannot wait to open her present -- loves presents, *rare* as they may be.

"Aren't you the lucky one?!" giggles Hawkins as Fay, turbulent with gratitude, rips at the silver paper, the silver ribbon.

"They were special friends. We'd had our differences but deep down they adored us. And we, they. They've been on our gift list for donkey's years. We shall miss them but never forget them."

Not for the *duration*, anyhoo.

"Hush, you, whilst I unwrap this sublime offering!"

The silver paper comes off, revealing another wrapping of gold foil beneath. "Isn't it gorgeous wrapping paper?!" cries Fay, "She has taken such care with it!"

An enormous tear quivers then practically leaps at the grateful floor as she removes the gold foil. Inside she finds a velvet jewel box tied shut with numerous glistening, strands of gold ribbon. Fay's wet eyes gleam with gratitude. Will this tiny and obviously expensive gift be as impressive as dear Abdullah Shamaly's little jewelled fish?! Elusive fulfilment seems here at last; the love and concern of others reflected in their gifts -- to be cared about, really cared about rather than hosed against a wall, raped and cast into an eternal fire.

Or worse!

"What could be *worse*, you, you creature?!" cries Fay to the terrified ceiling.

Stick around, ducky, and you'll see.

On the street Jenny hugs Rita goodbye. Ian and Hugh are loading the last of the luggage into Ian's car as two young workers pound at a window frame of Nelly's cat box (nee flat). From above comes a scream, a heart-rending wail, the piercing shriek of a banshee, combined into a very particularly horrid, some might even say, other-worldly noise!

All heads jerk towards heaven for this terrifying screech from hell.

"Oh," says 'Jen' casually, "We gave Ritterhouse a going-away present."

"The mother of all cockroaches," says Hugh as he scoots their last suitcase into Ian's boot.

Fay is on her back on the floor, her two feet flailing the air as four. The dismayed Hawkins attempts to comfort her. "Mrs Ritterhouse!

Please, dear! You'll do yourself a injury! Mrs Ritterhouse, dear, I've just hoovered!"

"*Ms* Ritterhouse! *MS* sodding Ritterhouse!" shrieks Fay through splashing tears and spraying snot.

Snot? The genteel euphemisms of domestic life often elude me, my dears, unaccustomed as I am to domestic life.

"See you tonight?"

Ian kisses the very serious Rita who leans her head reluctantly through his car window – she'd rather he was going nowhere just now. But she nods, stands back – not enough room for her to accompany them. She waves goodbye to Jenny and Hugh. "Goodbye, my little chickens,"

Rita does not mean to imply that these two deserters are cowards, but only dear, young friends. Then, to Ian: "Hurry back, love, I'm alone now with a mad woman."

That's what *you* think, love.

59

Late that night, Rita and Ian, a cognac before the former, a lager, the latter, sit cuddling before the telly attempting to watch Rita in a terribly small part in a terribly old film. Muffled sobbing from above erupts and Ian rises, shuts the window but even then the sobbing is obtrusive, inhabits the whole house, seems even to emanate from beneath their feet.

The house is in pre-mourning, m'dears, for what's to come.

"How does Ritterhouse do it?!" snaps Rita, tearing her eyes from her intriguing young self on the telly screen, "How can she make so much noise from two floors above?"

"The walls are paper," says Ian with a smile, "and half of them are gone."

Rita is not amused, turns up the telly. The sobbing immediately doubles in volume. Rita switches off the telly. "Fancy a walk, love? It's only one A.M.."

Swathed in sable, sprawled upon smooth white leather, Fay sobs. A bottle of Johnny Walker Blue protrudes from her sumptuous, furry pocket, a lighted ciggie from her lips. Hawkins is long gone and the black cat wanders, purring, tail twitching, from the terrace through the ajar, recently repaired glass wall and stops, peers at Fay. Fay, mid-sob, reaches to pet it, "Pretty pussy, pretty pussy."

The cat hisses, scratches her hand, then rockets through the door and leaps from the terrace to it's penultimate (one assumes) death. Fay is unaware of this crazy feline waste though it is elemental to our saga, if not to our task. She remains oblivious to the rounding of shadows; pressing, crushing, squashing, diminishing this tiny, this smallest of lives. And I don't mean the bleedin' cat's, my loves. Fay is, *necessarily*, and always has been unaware of her mission. Is this *my* shortcoming? I think not. Would that I'd never started my Fay saga. It's such a bother really, stewardship. Would that she'd perished *permanently* in that fire. Though how can a fire that is not a fire, consume? Ahhhh.

Fay pointedly ignores my cogent cogitations, dabs her eyes, flicks on the kitchen lights with her remote.

Moments later, over the portfolio and three packets of delicious chocolate-covered digestive biscuits she slurps milk from a gallon carton and studies Rita's unavoidable future, in her 'garage'.

Biscuit by biscuit (or cookie by cookie, if you're fussy), slurp by slurp, page by page, Fay's orgy of ingestion becomes more frenetic. She feeds in the only way she knows. It's the devouring need of an empty heart.

Even I shed a tear in her behalf. We cannot help who or what we are, can we, my dears?

But Rita...you, Rita, beware. Your days may be as numbered as our gorging Fay's.

The workmen are early this morning. Did they bother to leave the night before? Rita attempts through the din to sleep. Defeated, demoralized, she sits up in bed, lights a cigarette and has one satisfying puff when the phone rings. She struggles into her kimono, struggles to the telephone, struggles the receiver to her ear. "Hello!"

"Gardyloo! Gardyloo!" shrieks Fay, "Slops are on the way!"

"You excrescence!" hisses Rita and bangs down the receiver, is startled by a crashing plank then struggles -- life is a struggle after fifty (make that *fifty-four*) -- to the kitchen to prepare breakfast amidst this now traditional morning cacophony.

Fay, bundled, basks nicely, thank you, on her terrace under a welcome and seldom seen sun. Hassan Ammari rang earlier to say all is well on the oil front in which he has encouraged Fay to invest heavily. There is something brewing in the Antarctic too, if things can be considered brewing in that multi-sub-zero land.

Fay gobbles newly delivered croissants and slurps premium coffee -- far fresher, far richer than Rita will ever know (It's 'flown in', m'dears). Fay is also dialling, yet again, her telephone.

"Hello?!" cries Rita from Fay's receiver.

Fay grins ear to ear, hangs up, dials again.

"Hello?" says Rita doggedly expecting a call from Ian. Fay, *driven*, breathes orgiastically through half-chewed croissant into the receiver, hangs up, rings Ammari to stick a billion more into that hot, hush-hush Antarctic drilling scheme. She yawns, stretches, allows a raven to alight before her and peck at half a croissant. She feels expansive this morning which takes her mind off her search for Granny (my whispers are incessant) -- even if she could remember what Granny looks like. She wonders why she rings Rita at all. The hag won't speak to her. Is a puzzlement. But ach! How she'd love Granny to come and live with her as in the old days, when she had lived with Granny. Before her house burned down. Had Granny set it afire herself?

"Yes," caws the raven. But he is soooo misleading. Had Granny got in over her head with those odd people?

"She had, she had!" quoths the raven, "but nevermore!"

Had Granny sold her soul (and mine) to those darling-honey-sugar people? The ones who destroyed that first hapless foetus?! Those abortionists?!

"Oui, certainement!" caws our raven who is in reality simply an overgrown crow though his colour is, as required, blue-black.

So it was those same people who had, much later, tied up Fay and hosed her down? Those same who had denied Fay hot water for a bath? A cleansing bath? A thorough scrubbing down of her temple's steps? Those awful people she'd come to wreck vengeance on? Then where were they now? Where had they been? Submerged in Rita's bath tub? Hiding under Hugh and Jenny's tatty sofa-bed? On a fridge shelf beside Bill's mayonnaise? In Nelly's closet secreted in a fuck-me shoe? No! They'd been nestled, all along, beside the rug and that little witch's shrine in Granny Taylor's chock-a-block closet. Why hadn't she seen them when she took that rug? The rug that was her destiny?

Sweet Jesus, Fay! All *that* occurred in Square Four! Forget this! We've come much too far for this retro-regret you seem so resolute to romp in.

That was cruel of me. But definitive (and deliciously alliterative). Why? Pay attention. Or figger it out fer yer selves, m'dears. There are clues simply *everywhere*!

My darling Fay begins again to sob, refuses to be comforted by my supercilious, overgrown crow.

> Janet continued to visit old Mrs Belcher in hospital faithfully three times a week. She attempted to keep the increasingly frail, semi-conscious old lady as up-to-date as she could about the steadily declining state of affairs at Number 13 which was now malignant with the tumorous presence of Doolittle Desiree nee Ritterhouse Fay, witch-in-residence...

Types Rita. Is it actionable, using Fay's real name? Could Rita be sued? Of course. But it's only cathartic mischief. That litigious proper noun will be deleted later.

Rita's telephone rings. She stops typing, lights another cigarette with the smouldering butt of the last, ignores the phone. If it is Ian he will have to wait. They'll see one another tonight. They see one another every night. Fay knows, doesn't approve -- cannot abide happiness so near and yet so far away.

Who can, m'dears? I speak from the sad experience of a millennium of moons. Misery, my darlings, cannot be over-emphasized. Misery must *never* be given short shrift. Indeed, this I have never allowed. Misery rules, m'dears! Like the dickens. And it is terribly catching. Beware! Or have you already succumbed?

Rita's telephone rings countless times before it stops. She sighs with relief but is immediately startled by the crash of metal pipes falling from a lorry just outside her window. She hurls her morning coffee at a wall. Though she left this particular type of weeping far behind in those years of mis-requited love, she begins to cry. Tears of frustration summoned by helplessness, by the fragility of life. Tears of love's lack, love's loss, love's *possible loss.*

Two floors above, Love's very personification also weeps.

Coincidence?

You betcha!

60

Hawkins' calloused fingers glide along the garish, gilt-figured balustrade as she follows Fay down the newly installed, carpeted staircase.

Carpets figure ever so prominently, don't they, in the saga of Ritterhouse Fay? Papá or was it Mamá? was a carpet sales*person*. For a time. All things are passing. Just ask St Teresa. On second thoughts, don't. We were never close.

Hugh and Jenny's flat has disappeared. What remains is thick, red carpet lapping at the edges of the absent Mrs Taylor's door. A massive floor to ceiling bookcase filled with expensive leather-bound volumes of the large-to-enormous variety rises where Hugh and Jenny once baked their numerous frozen scones and engaged in occasionally catholic liaisons. And I ain't talkin' 'bout *popish* plots – or am I?

Fay swans in her sable, One-Life-Left -- yes, m'dears, a shaggy dog hassled our cat right off the roof yet again! -- nestles ebony in her arms, growling. Fay gestures, with a nonchalance achieved only through my strenuous coaching, and proclaims: "This vast red expanse was once a flat occupied by an impious couple whose time was largely given to acts commensurate with their perversity."

Perverse?! Alas, I fear that Fay's early regimen of evangelistical tracts, though standard procedure at the time, has not been efficacious.

Hawkins, who has been idly pondering the prodigious hoovering that will be required of her by this great red desert, says:

"Zat so, dear?" her ears having previously pricked at the word 'perversity' (several sentences above, m'dears).

"It is now," continues Fay, "our philosophy room. In yonder bookcase you will find the complete works of every known philosopher from Aristotle to Zarathustra."

A swift dip into philosophy is scheduled before eternal night absorbs us one and all.

"No!" cries Hawkins, eyes still wide at the quality of this deep-piled carpeting. She'd love to run through it barefoot – intends soon to do so.

"Did you know that Zarathustra is said to have laughed on the very day of his own birth?"

"No!" repeats Hawkins as she squats and pinches up a scarlet puff of luxuriant nap between her severely nicotine-stained forefinger and fat little thumb.

"Birth is no laughing matter."

"I should say not, dear, and no mistake. I've had my fill! Four is enough!"

"Four?," says Fay, "I thought you had only one daughter."

"Four offspring, I admit, for my sins," sighs Hawkins, red as the new carpeting, "though they was all given out, you see. If you know what I mean."

Fay blinks once. No, twice -- lying in a good cause is always permitted -- continues:

"Zarathustra then lived in the wilderness and fed upon cheese and sang songs about horses."

"*Who* did, dear?"

"Zara-bleeding-thustra!"

"Yes, dear."

The sacrifices one makes for a hank of hag's hair.

Hawkins pokes yet another finger into the deep pile of this endless carpet, thinks: It's a right dust magnet!

"Z subsequently had discourse with various deities."

"Why the rotten egg!" exclaims Hawkins, now fully attentive.

"He then withdrew to live in solitude upon a mountain. Said mountain was consumed by fire but Zarathustra escaped uninjured and spoke to the multitude."

"What'd he say, then?!" cries Hawkins, eager to plumb the depths of a man who had 'discourse'.

"He founded the Zoroastrian religion, that's all!"

But what a lot of fuss, darling! When *I* need religion I just shag a priest.

"Wasn't he the lucky one?" says Hawkins, somewhat disappointed in Mr Z." You've a acre of hoovering here, dear, and no mistake. Maybe yours truly should live-in?"

Janet had now to walk through Desiree's
anteroom to reach her own flat. No more,
common ground. She dwelt in enemy territory, Doolittle's Domain.
Returning home from shopping, Janet

> passed through this ominous zone. Desiree's cursed objects lay everywhere; expensive and ugly porcelain figures, endless vases on scattered pedestals, a hideous clock at the center of a spikey star and, clinging to the walls like sleeping moths, swarms of small and sinister, framed quotations.
>
> As Janet turned the key in her door her eyes were caught by a new framed quotation, hung eye level just beside and unmissable. It read 'Do unto others.' That was all it said, 'Do unto others.'

Rita stops typing, goes to her door, listens to Fay and Hawkins who loiter directly outside.

"We gave her a chinchilla coat and she stole our boyfriend right from under our nose."

Lying cow! thinks Rita.

"Men go for women in furs, dear," says Hawkins, the very model of understanding.

The cat wriggles in Fay's arms. She's clutching it too tightly.

"But we weren't deceived!"

"Oh no, dear! Of course you wasn't!"

"We were testing the traitorous bitch."

These words, connected with the good and the generous Nelly, ring painfully in Fay's ears. Had she really uttered them herself? Nelly was special. Nelly was good. "Am I really an Antichrist?" asks Fay.

"A what?" Mrs Ritterhouse?"

"Friends must measure up, mustn't they? No. I was only testing her."

"Of course you was testing her, Mrs Ritterhouse, dear. You had every right to. Mink coats don't grow on trees."

"Chinchilla," corrects Fay and, with a wince, continues, "What's a chinchilla coat to us? The interest on our capital alone could buy a hundred chinchilla coats in the time it took us to descend our stairs."

"No!"

"Are you calling us a liar?!"

Fay's twisted face, like this marvellous new carpet, seems suddenly wall-to-wall.

"Oh no, Mrs Ritterhouse!"

The spacious room grows instantly cold. Shadows swoop up the walls and gather -- humming dirges to my cunning -- on the ceiling. Hawkins' hair has been attained. We must dispense with her. Another square emerges, swells with pride, waits. Waits.

Hawkins goes pale. Everything was proceeding so well! Mrs Ritterhouse had asked for her special at the agency and she was bearing down on an excellent live-in with drinks included day and night. Now this, this horreeble look from her employer! This frightening, bone-chilling look! Hawkins had seen it before and only narrowly avoided colliding with it. Now, it seems, the jig is up.

"We think you were calling us a liar!"

"Well you're mistaken and no mistake," squeaks Hawkins, backed into a copiously carpeted corner (!).

"You're dismissed!"

"What, dear?"

"Are you deaf?! You are dismissed! For insubordination! You've no love nor trust! You're devoid of devotion!"

"What, dear?"

"Out! Get out!"

Fay menaces Hawkins to the door. Rita is avid behind hers.

"But my bag, Mrs Ritterhouse, dear! My coat!"

"Out!"

Fay slams the door in Hawkins' face then, through the door: "We'll send them on!"

But our Fay is instantly contrite! How, now, is she to procure another lock of the hag's hair?! She was counting on another snippet of those coarse, dyed locks for...but the thought deserts her as her head reels anew.

Another lock is really unnecessary, m'love. Had you listened carefully this would not be news. But do as you will. There is zest in that. I too am mutable. How could I not be?

Fay brings a pale and extraordinarily well-formed *hand* to her forehead to ease the confusion away.

Unfortunately, the confusion has nothing to do with her.

"What?" mumbles poor Fay, "What, *please,* was that?"

But the swooping shadows have stilled and the ceiling-dirges and carpets are mute to her melancholic query and the books -- ach! all those books -- remain stubbornly between their covers.

Honestly, Fay, what did you expect? I worked so hard with you but you're a slob.

Mrs Hawkins is relieved to be outside, removed from Fay's awful wrath. She wonders how she will get home without her purse and tube-fare and clad only in this thin pullover -- Good God, it's almost Christmas! With a fearful backward glance and a mild vibration right up her spine she hurries down the street, walking briskly to keep warm. She'll borrow bus-fare from that local tobacconist with whom she is having a mild flirtation. If she's clever, it could be cab fare.

Rita, at her window, watches Hawkins' retreat into the greenhouse fumes of evening traffic, mourns yet another victim of Fragmented Fay, knows that she, Rita, is the next course. But she'll not be a dainty dish to set before the wicked queen.

More appropriate than you know, my dear. Though not entirely original. I used it myself some pages ago.

"We had a seizure. It was a seizure."

Fay brushes away, with my prompting, an excellent tear but the forgiving Hawkins, fresh from a tasty breakfast prepared by Fay's own hand, doesn't see it and Fay is not in the mood to muster more visible emotion for such an insignificant player. Insignificant indeed! She could be your very salvation, my redundant Ritterhouse, if you'd only listen to me. Ye gods! I do sound contradictory! Or *do* I?

Hawkins nods, wipes a tear from her own eye and says softly, *wisely*:

"Of course it was, Mrs Ritterhouse, dear. A seizure."

"An old war wound."

It was indeed. A serpent's bite. Or perhaps the puncture of a shining arrow loosed from the glistening bow of a demigod. Or not. So many options, so little time.

"What?" says Fay, "What was that?"

"Of course it was, dear. A war wound from some silly old war."

"A kind of mental electrical storm that makes me testy."

"Ever so testy, Mrs Ritterhouse dear, and no mistake," says Hawkins, a slow learner, treading on ever thinner ice.

Early the next morning Rita is awakened by inane humming accompanied by loud vacuuming just outside her door. She slips into a kimono, opens her door a crack and finds herself face to face with the recently reinstated Mabel Hawkins.

"You're that lady of the evening, ain't you, dear?" asks Hawkins who has been there herself, "Madam says you're to be evicted, dear, and no mistake."

"Who are you?"

"I'm Mrs Ritterhouse's live-in," says Hawkins clicking off her machine, "I'm to have me own kitchenette which is just like a kitchen -- only larger."

"Must you vacuum at this hour?"

"I'm on instructions, dear, to hoover right here, this very spot. By your door. For the whole morning, dear."

"I see."

Hawkins clicks on the shiny machine. "Keep late hours, do we, dear?"

Rita closes her door and rushes to answer her telephone:

"Listen, Ritterhouse, this number is under police surveillance! ...Ian!... I'm going mad, love. She's got some cretin hoovering her foyer who thinks I'm a prostitute!"

Rita laughs, enjoys this, in fact rather likes Hawkins. "...I'd love to, darling. The whole weekend?...You are a love. I do need to get away. I can be ready in five minutes -- strike that! Five seconds! Kiss."

Rita hangs up, claps her hands. The telephone rings again and she snatches it up. "Yes, darling?"

Down goes the telephone. Rita stands for a moment, inert, doesn't know whether to cry or simply march up the stairs and strangle Fay. But a few minutes later Rita is climbing into Ian's car and tossing her over-night case into the back seat. And, of course -- and she's harrowingly conscious of it -- being watched by Fay from above. Fay the billionaire, the monster, the witch, the fugitive from god-knows-where, the florist, the actress, the librarian, the hostess, the law secretary, the abortee -- the liar, the witch-trainee? Oh, yes, and the Fallen Angel. But who's counting?

Besides me?

Hawkins hums merrily as she hoovers, running her fingers through her newly hennaed locks, happily barefoot, as she'd promised herself, skipping from place to place over thick, nearly ankle-deep red carpet. She pauses, considers her projected small central-heated room, her tiny private bathroom and separate toilet, her kitchenette that is just like a kitchen only larger -- larger than her old kitchen anyway -- and on the *same landing*! Mrs Ritterhouse showed her the plans. It was already begun! She's so happy she could cry! But at the moment she's skipped up to one of Fay's framed homilies, reads: 'Do unto others'.

"Yes, dear, oh yes, Mrs Ritterhouse dear," she squeaks and skips away, pushing her shiny vacuum cleaner before her.

Yes, she is so happy she could cry. She will, soon enough. Her tears will be as pointless as all the others wept into their respective squares around our humble board game. Be they whopping or whoppers, they are all, to a tear, in vain fer nuthin'. Grains of sand on an endless, forgotten Sahara. Ozymandias knows *precisely* what I mean. Ask him. He'll be back soon.

61

"All furniture to the centre of the room, lads!"

Fay slams the portfolio on Mrs Taylor's postcard table as she kicks Taylor's chair aside. The red plastic carry-bag falls from its perch on the chair scattering several hearts-and-arrows postcards across the floor. One of Fay's hand-chosen -- and I do mean *hand*-chosen -- young workmen, kneels and with a crooked grin at Fay gathers the cards into the carry-bag and hangs it on the chair again. The other two men begin to shift Taylor's dark, heavily carved furniture. Crooked-grin -- not to be confused with the long discarded pointed-grin -- picks up the small table with the paraffin lamp, grins at Fay.

"Put it down, it's fragile," cautions Fay, stealing his grin on the spot, "Leave it where it is. There's a reason."

Fay knows there's a reason. She's always known the reason but she simply cannot locate it in those oft receding references just behind her stupendously smooth brow. "Why did I say that?" she asks herself, "Why did I say there's a *reason*?"

In any case, crooked-grin does as ordered and grins again, crookedly and the furniture shifting proceeds.

The furniture-shifting is complete and the young men stand erect. Is there anything more uplifting than an erect *stand* in a fine young man? But, alas, alas, they are no longer bending, ramming heavenward their muscular bottoms. Ah, well...

> So I'm going out to have a beer
> and if you're here
> when I come back
> we can talk business.
>
> (Now where did *that* come from?)

Fay flaps open the portfolio, grabs out a page and thrusts it before them, cries "The Future is upon us!"

If the Past allows it, lovey.

She snatches a large hammer from crooked-grin's carpenter apron, "Interior walls to be gutted! Get to it! We must destroy the symbols of the previous regime! Lights! Camera! Action!"

A cinematically sound statement, m'dears.

Fay skips to the kitchen wall, begins to slam holes through it as a thousand lashes from a willow rod pepper her back with every slam of the hammer. She remembers a million meals pushed through a door hatch, a billion sobbing hours spent alone, tightly harnessed, in inky darkness, a light-year beyond Pluto.

There's a disadvantage, darlings, compressing so many lives into one, so Fay's failings are pardonable. One must be cosmically aware of the Big Enchilada, that Eternal cheese-board, err...chess-board. I do wish my so-called *fingers* were capable of forming little quote signs around the 'Big Enchilada that Eternal Chessboard'. But I haven't had fingers for ages. And honestly, m'dears, without fingers life can be murder! Or indeed instigate murder. My girlish frustration could lead to anything. Perhaps has.

Crooked-grin exchanges looks with his mates at Fay's energetic attack on the absent and sadly horizontal Mrs Taylor's kitchen wall. He would wipe that smirk from his face instantly if he knew with whom he will soon be dealing; the consequences could be alarming. If I chose. But I grow semi-feeble, my delicious darlings. Life is but a daffy spark in the dark.

A light breeze ruffles Christmas lights outside the restaurant window. Rita looks at least a year younger -- this blissful weekend has washed away several stubborn frown lines. Yes, it is bracing for the both of them -- though Ian should be looking for a new job. He still hasn't told Rita. Never mind. There's so much in store for them -- and not quite what you would expect, my little loves. The game is still playing out though the chessboard analogy was unfortunate as I'm a chess illiterate I simply haven't the patience! And I'm prone to redundant but satisfyingly life-sustaining moves. Excitin', ain't it?! If you think not, just trot yourself to the nearest mirror, look into it and say: there, but for the grace of God go I. But if you do not convulse into raucous laughter immediately you've said it there is something deeply disturbing about you.

Ian reluctantly lights Rita's cigarette as a waiter serves coffee. "You smoke in bed too, love. You shouldn't."

Nag-nag-nag!

"There is *nothing* one oughtn't to do in bed, darling," replies Rita and takes Ian's hand across the table.

A little local colour here. I really like these two. Especially when they talk dirty.

"You are naughty," says Ian.

(Hey, that's my line!)

"Only to my naive old charmer," replies Rita.

They regard one another pleasantly for a moment. But Ian is worried she'll incinerate herself in bed not to mention dying of lung cancer (we must deal with *real* issues here too, m'dears) and Rita is worried that Ian is worried plus even more worried she'll never be able to live up to his expectations -- she's so used to just pleasing herself -- has for years. But why in hell should she try so hard to please him? Does he try hard to please her? Well. Yes, darling, actually. He does.

"She's mad, isn't she?" says Ian. Rita blinks and plunges back into the moment, nods.

"She wants me out, love, I'm the last."

"For a start, you can move in with me."

"I'm a stubborn old bitch. I won't budge."

"Just for the duration. Just until she quietens down."

"She's hotting up. Her deadly denouement is just beginning."

Bravo, darling. Have you been eavesdropping?

"I'm a fly in her sodding web. I can feel her fingers all over me. The kettle, Ian, remember my kettle? It's gone again. She's got it. Is it a voodoo toy? Can she stick pins into a kettle? Sometimes I think she's in my bedroom watching me -- watching us!"

"We'll get a chain latch. They have them with alarm sensors."

"Christ! She's all we speak of these days. We do have lives of our own, haven't we? Why can't she get on with her life and let us get on with ours?"

A question that *begs* to be answered!

"Because she is insane. And rich. And you live in her house."

That's not all, dearie. My woolly old will, though flagging, is still operable. If you're wondering what I'm doing following Rita and Ian about, you'll just have to hold your horses. *Everybody's* gotta have plans.

"You're in early, dear!" says Hawkins from the steps of Number 13 as she brooms away, leering all the while at Rita who has just appeared after a last longing look at Ian's car disappearing in the twilight.

"Pardon my asking," continues Hawkins, "What do you charge for a weekend, dear?"

"Why, ducky!" replies Rita, "Interested?"

Hawkins colours, runs a work-roughened hand through her garish locks, returns to her brooming -- Rita has raised one transaction that Hawkins, *to her knowledge*, has never... well, transacted.

Hardly able to contain herself, Rita throws open her door, tosses her over-night case on the floor and flings herself onto the sofa. She lies there overcome with great satisfying guffaws. A good laugh never hurt anyone. She needed that.

Outside, darkening, pulsating clouds announce -- with absolutely no prompting from me -- the arrival of a storm.

Still chuckling, Rita rises and lets herself out, doesn't bother to lock up -- Ritterhouse has a sodding key anyway.

Up the spotless, red carpeted stairs past a curious, still blushing Hawkins she goes. It's time to air Taylor's geraniums.

Rita gasps at the devastation in the old lady's flat, and cries out at a bolt of lightning so near it seems to come from the room itself.

It may have, Rita. I simply won't be pinned down here.

Thunder crashes and Rita cowers, deafened by the noise and dismayed by the room's terrible disorder; Taylor's furniture, half covered with a canvas tarpaulin, is stacked in the centre, Taylor's upturned postcard chair juts like Pisa's tower from the plaster-dusted jumble, the red plastic carry-bag swings from its back where crooked-grin hung it somewhat prior to his five furtive minutes with Fay -- this poor, furiously fuckable boy is still, no doubt, recovering. I can't keep an eye on everyone simultaneously, m'dears. Although I quite enjoy trying. Or once did. The *flamin'* end is nigh. (but then it always is) And with it…

But where are Taylor's geraniums? Ah. There they are – sweet Jesus! -- on the floor at the edge of the tarpaulin. Rita kneels, reaches for them. Then, ach! Up hurtles Fay, from beneath that tarpaulin, screaming "Villain!", her sabled arms outstretched, her hands, talons gleaming in a yet another bolt of lightning.

Rita squeals, topples backward, sprawls spread-eagled on the floor, can only shout "She's not dead yet! You cannot savage her home, you, you *creature*! You cannot!"

Fay grips her precious portfolio, scrambles from her knees so quickly she stumbles backward over Taylor's chair. The portfolio pages scatter and float eerily about the room vainly snatched at by a grieving, half-destroyed window sill and a thoroughly dispirited curtain cord. The Fay creature has awakened on Granny's cushions where crooked-grin had, possibly fearing for his life, abandoned her. She has awakened from a cosy dream of Granny and jam tarts and hot cocoa and Granny's terrifying stories -- they had to be only stories -- been rudely awakened by Rita, this hag whose hair she once coveted. This hag who lives in the garage below!

"Mrs Taylor is not dead yet!" cries Rita from the very centre of her theatrically aroused hagdom.

Fay squats, frantically attempts to gather up the proof of her future. She must have *proof.* She is now able to retain almost nothing behind those opaque mauve eyes.

I flag, m'dears (as said), I fade, I falter.

Grabbing in the air for page after swooping page of the portfolio Fay cowers from furious Rita who pulls herself up amidst the crackling lightning and deafening thunder.

"You demented bitch!" screams Rita, "You have no right here! You cannot destroy something that is not yours! This is her flat! MRS TAYLOR IS NOT DEAD YET!"

Fay leaps from terror to anger in an instant, slams the portfolio down, grabs a hammer from a work bench and beats it into what remains of the kitchen wall. "I do have the right! This house is mine! Mine! Long before it belonged to anyone it was mine!"

Sorry, my loves, I'll have to agree with her on this one, fleeting as her claim will be.

Rita the actress trembles with rage, actually throbs with loathing for this cruel creature with a hammer, this malignant monster who hacks at the heart of poor Taylor's home. Rita, enraged, is fearless. She wrests the hammer from Fay, throws her to the floor.

"Mummy! Mummy!" cries Fay, catching hold of Rita's knees, clinging. "Mummy, I'm sorry! I won't do it again! Mummy, please! MUMMY-MUMMY-MUMMY-MUMMY!"

Rita tears Fay's arms from her legs, kneels beside her, shakes her.

"MUMMY-MUMMY!" cries Fay as she embraces Rita, covers her with kisses, "MUMMY-MUMMY-MUMMY!"

Rita recoils, slaps the hysterical Fay who leaps up, cat-like and larger than she was (she *will* do this!). With a heavy thrust of her knee she drives Rita to the floor and bends, slaps her face again and again and again shrieking "WE ARE NOT AMUSED! WE ARE NOT AMUSED!"

Before Rita can retaliate, Fay careens backward out the door. Screaming, she tumbles over her new balustrade and crashes to the floor below directly into a grinning, impatient square. She lies there on the red carpeted, pedestal-ringed expanse that was once Nelly's flat.

Rita rushes down the stairs, finds Fay, still -- still as poor battered Nelly that fateful, phony-foetal day in the street. Rita kneels, feels Fay's pulse.

"Jesus," mutters Rita, this batty bitch is dead."

Lightning flashes. Thunder crashes. (Close, darlings! *Very* close! So terribly, almost eerily, appropriate for filming!) Plaster dust, shaken from every corner of Fay's house, sifts down, dusting the scarlet carpet with sinister snow.

In a blinding flash Fay is revitalized and her eyes flick open – savage and insane. Rita pulls back but not fast enough -- Fay jerks upright, claws at her, pushes her to the floor and mounts her like a raging animal, pummelling Rita with her fists. Rita is crazy with wrath, pummels back as over and over they turn in a tight, flailing embrace, bloody, lit by lightning, shaken by thunder, toppling pedestalled vases and bizarre figurines, upturning fragile furniture, shattering framed homilies, annihilating the alien order of Fay's anteroom. "You witch!" screams Rita as they roll.

"You bitch!" shrieks Fay, as they tumble, "You hag!"

Mrs Hawkins suddenly appears from her evening shopping with a half-eaten pork pie in one hand and a pint of milk in the other. "Mrs Ritterhouse, dear! You're ever so untidy!" cries Hawkins, aghast at the ruin of this ever so painstakingly tidied, gigantic room.

Fay-the-cat leaps from her wrestling perch atop Rita and stumbles punch-drunk towards Hawkins. Hawkins backs away, holding her pork pie and pint of milk defensively before her like a crusader's banner -- she's seen that crazy (soulless, m'dears, *soulless*!) light before in Fay's eyes.

Rita climbs to her feet, staggers there dazed, catching her breath. Her head rocks with the horror of what has happened. Then, the greater horror for which she might be partly responsible. She has no time to think further.

Fay snatches scissors from her furry pocket, rushes towards Hawkin with that horrid *look*, thinks Hawkins who, cornered, throws her little pork pie at Fay. Fay handily catches and pockets it. Her scissors stab the air ever closer. Hawkins flings her carton of milk. Fay catches and pockets that too.

"What are you doing, Mrs Ritterhouse, dear?!" sobs Hawkins.

"I'm a witness, Ritterhouse!" cries Rita, "don't you dare touch that woman!"

Fay ignores her, darts at Hawkins and with an expeditious snatch and snip has acquired another hefty hank of Hawkins' hair. Hawkins squeals and runs shrieking into her tiny half-finished live-in quarters at the far side of the devastated room.

"Hair-of-hag," cries Fay, breathlessly ripping open and munching Hawkins' severely squashed pork pie. "Hair-of-hag, I only wanted hair-of-hag."

Poor Fay. My poor, misunderstood darling prosopopoeia.

Know the feeling, m'dears?

Fay rams the hank into her sable pocket, takes Hawkins' pint of milk from the other, opens it with one hand and her teeth, and offers it to Rita. "Have a sip, sugar."

Rita trembles, leaning for support on the only standing vase pedestal left in the room. Her mind races. What precisely has happened here? She is perplexed, helpless. Why am I helpless? thinks Rita, swept by peculiar feelings, those odd vibrations that so recently wracked Jenny who, fortunately or not, is now standing comfortably between Hugh and Jim Richardson on the viewing platform of New York City's dependable Empire State Building.

Fay, still offering Hawkins' pint, smiles beguilingly -- as a matter of fact, smiles her *most* beguiling smile at Rita. Rita is dazed and beguiled. She shivers, accepts the milk, takes a swallow as the door to Hawkins' mini-quarters slams open and Hawkins appears; her head -- now *dually* hankless -- oddly out of balance. Her impasto lipstick askew from hasty application, her cheap suitcase -- every bit as shabby our long-lost Fay's -- in her hand.

"Look at this untidiness," she sobs, "I've had it, Mrs Ritterhouse and no mistake!"

To the door marches the disheartened, demeaned, de-coiffed and blubbing Hawkins who pauses, rakes Fay and Rita with her wet, red eyes. "TWO LOONIES!" she screams, "AND ONE OF 'EM'S A WHORE!"

Something snaps in Rita. She suddenly awakes and rounds on Fay, strikes her across the face. Bits of pork pie spew from Fay's mouth. She stares a great hurt look at Rita, a look of unutterable loneliness and pain.

Real loneliness. Real pain. Well, m'dears, as good as.

"What?" whimpers Fay, "What was that?"

But I secret myself behind a shattered homily – the one that reads, incidentally, 'Do unto others'. I'm *doing*, m'dears, my best.

Hawkins slams out the door and as Rita, still reeling, turns to enter hers, Fay, shrieks, leaps on her and throws her to the floor.

"It's your fault!" screams Fay from atop Rita's stomach, "All of it! Your fault!"

"Let me up, you mad bitch!"

"I only wanted to be friends! I tried again and again but you wouldn't let me!"

Tried again and again. I'll testify to that. Will *you*, m'dears?

"Thank you," whispers Fay to me, her invisible tormentor cum fan.

"Let me up!" hisses Rita, "Let me up or I'll kill you!"

I love a rigorous rumpus, don't you?!

Rita wrests an arm from Fay's grip, clenches her fist and punches Fay soundly on her chin. Fay sways, falls over, strikes her head on a toppled pedestal, lies there (on an unexpected square that has surreptitiously appeared!), blood trickling from the corner of her mouth.

Rita pulls herself up, sees that Fay is breathing, sees that Fay, though supine on her red carpet, is watching her through slitted eyes. "What have I become?" whispers Rita. "I'm getting out. Ritterhouse. You win."

Voila!

Rita runs into her flat, locks the door, drops to her sofa, sighs and wonders -- wonders what she *has* become -- wonders what this witch has made of her -- wonders if all the ingredients were there already, the ingredients even for murder -- wonders how culpable she, Rita, is.

You can chew on that for a while, dear. You weren't as impartial as you might have been, possibly thought you were. Who is? We're only human, ain't we, sugar? Why am I being so goddamned nice?

Rita also wonders as she has always wondered what Fay's motive was for coming back -- wonders, as a novice author of course, if Fay herself knows -- wonders why we often don't realize why we do what we do -- and finally, exhausted, dozes off pondering this positively elementary (as in school!) dilemma but is awakened by the telephone.

Fay has not moved for an hour. She's lying there precisely as Rita left her. Now her eye is caught by another framed homily, askew on the wall close by. She blinks, focuses, reads: "True nobility is exempt from fear"

"Yes, Granny," she murmurs, "Yes, Granny, my dearest old Granny."

"Ian, I'm so glad you're there," whispers Rita into the telephone. "The hospital rang about Taylor...oh, thank you, darling. I'm ready now. A bit sore, but ready....No. I'll explain all in the car. No, darling, in the car. It can wait."

Can it, Rita?

62

Fay leans heavily on her fine, shell-shaped bathroom basin, pats blood from her cut and swollen lip. She suddenly can't resent Rita. Fay was a naughty child, deserved precisely what she got from the grown-ups. "I was a naughty child. Me so unhappy," she whimpers into the mirror, squinting into those huge, soulless eyes.

I do feel a bit guilty when she goes all *ocular* on me. She's doing it more and more. Leave off with the soul-bit, peaches!

"I was a naughty child. I deserved what I got."

Debatable. Debatable.

"What?" says Fay, her two, great, mauve eyes sudden pinwheels of pain.

God! I do it to myself, don't I? The soul/eyes device.

It takes my Fay a moment to realize that her call-box is buzzing. She pats her bleeding lip again, limps from the bathroom to answer it.

"Ritterhouse Fay."

"Ted, Fay."

"Who is 'Ted Fay'?"

"'Mr Kong', Fay. Can I come in?"

"Long time, no see. Why not."

She buzzes him in, listens to his clomping progress up the stairs, opens the door then limps, humming tunelessly, back to her bedroom. Her sciatica is playing up (come to think of it, m'dears, so is mine. And I am sooo tired.)

Ted finds the door open, enters. She's an odd one, ain't she, this Ritterhouse Fay? But he's tipsy, not choosy, and she'd offered herself once, hadn't she? He's desperate himself tonight. Desperate with drink. You know how it is? We all have days errr nights like that, haven't we, m'dears? Wherein we toss 'n' turn, get horny from the horrors?

The flat is nearly dark and that violent thunderstorm which had abated, rumbles, threatening to return. Lightning flares on the terrace. There, in the driving rain, is One Life Left, scratching frantically, as though its single remaining life depended on it.

Ted slides the glass wall aside and the cat clambers through, clawing the carpet as it escapes to the bedroom and narrowly avoids Fay who now poses in the door, hair combed, freshly lipsticked, tissue-pouted, majestic in her tousled sable. She grins the grin she's nicked from crooked-grin, murmurs: "Long time no see."

"Nice weather we're havin', eh, Fay?"

Fay is motionless, her scavenged grin immobile.

"I overcharged you for my services, Fay."

No answer. Fay floats, hovers an unnoticed inch above the floor, pats at her cut lip.

"You look like you could use a refund. Who socked you in your cake hole?"

No answer. Ted takes a small bottle of whisky from his jacket, unscrews it.

"We're...pleased you came...Teddy."

Fay dabs again at her lip, her attention strays to the thudding rain against her glass wall. Ted swigs from his bottle, offers it to Fay. "I thought yer royal highness could use a little company on a stormy night."

Fay declines Ted's whisky, snatches up the remote, at the same time revealing a glimpse of nakedness beneath the sable. She buzzes open the mirrored bar door. "We prefer a glass. And ice."

"What'll it be?" asks Ted, unimpressed and moving unsteadily to the bar.

"We're a bourbon girl," murmurs Fay to the terrace.

"*Are* we?" replies Ted. He pours a large bourbon whiskey into a cut-crystal glass and shoots in a several tiny ice cubes from the spout which he deftly manoeuvres. "We're a scotch whisky boy."

"A whisky boy with a hairy back," whispers Fay to the terrace.

"You got a hairy back too, Fay. Hah hah hah!"

Ted approaches, laughing, from the bar, "That fur must have set you back some."

"Several hundred thousand, love. Prime sable. Authentic ruby buttons too."

"Coo! *Several hundred thousand!* More'n I make in a month!"

Fay says nothing.

I'm beginning, darlings, for safety's sake, to keep my distance. Time and squares are running out and that ultimate task is hard by.

"Fabulous Fragment Fay," mutters Ted and swigs a whisky.

"That's us," whispers Fay, brilliantly lighted for a thundery instant, "but that fragment has flown the coop."

And well and truly paupered you. I warned you, Ach! How I

warned you.

"Shut up!" cries Fay.

"Huh?"

"Not you, darling. Only some demon."

"Yeah, right," replies Ted, hands Fay her drink and drops into the white leather sofa, sighs "Stormy weather."

"Since my man and I ain't together," sings Fay.

"Whatever you say, darlin'"

"We had four billion pounds. Money begat money."

Had, Fay? *Had* four billion pounds?

"Well, sit down anyway, love, you make me nervy."

Fay drops herself opposite Ted, carefully arranges the immense volume of her sable and stares peculiarly at him as he takes off his wet shoes and reveals a large toe poking through his sodden sock. She studies Ted's toe for some time, takes a swallow of whisky. "Have you never had athlete's foot?"

Jovially: "I was never an athlete. Except in bed."

"Athlete's Foot is an insidious fungus."

So is humanity.

"What?" But Fay's attention has again strayed, from his toe to her terrace where lashing wind and driving rain have made rubble of her lovely outdoor furniture. Not to worry – she won't need it again. Not never, not nohow. "We were an orphan," she murmurs to potted trees bending dangerously in a savage gust.

"You wasn't no orphan, Fay."

He swigs at his whisky.

"Yes, we were."

"You're lyin'."

"I do not lie."

She doesn't. Not really. Not deliberately. I'll vouch for that.

"Thank you," says Fay.

"What?" says Ted who has been inspecting the remote control and presses a button. The bar thumps shut.

"Nothing," replies Fay.

"Damn clever those Japanese."

"It's Chinese."

"Wouldn't you know."

"Orphans are incarcerated," says Fay.

And incinerated too, love.

"What?" says Fay.

"Who're you talking to, Fay?"

"Mind yer own bee's-wax."

Ted shrugs, watches Fay with growing excitement -- as she speaks her sable falls fetchingly to one side, exposing a naked and perfect breast. But she talks such rubbish.

"Ritterhouse Fay, 1-6-4-5-2, present, Matron!"

"You wasn't no orphan, Fay."

"Then we were a florist."

"So you was a florist, eh? Ha-ha-ha."

"Did we say Florist? We meant beautician."

"Oh! So now you're a beautician!"

"Librarian! I said librarian! Don't you listen?"

Correct on all counts, my 'lying' love.

Fay turns her eyes from the terrace, peers directly at hairy Ted. "Do you climb trees?"

"Sure I climb trees!"

"Go climb a tree!"

Ted chuckles, takes another swig, moves his naked big toe across the marble coffee table, playfully touches Fay's bare knee, lately emerged from beneath its sabled fringe.

"You need a new pair of socks, Mr Kong," whispers Fay, catching her breath. She had thought he was gay. Those were her instructions. Instructions? She thinks, whose bleeding instructions? Ted fondles Fay's knee with his bare toe.

She unwraps the top of her sable, reveals the little jewelled gift of her deceased, beloved Abdullah Shamaly. "See our fish?"

Ted kneels beside her, grasps the little jewelled and golden fish, inspects it then drops his hand inside her sable and caresses Fay's breast. It is surprisingly warm. But she only stares at him with those dead eyes and toys in her sable pocket with Hawkins' hairy, hag hank.

I'm running out of steam, darlings. I falter.

Ted quickly withdraws his hand from her breast.

"We've never made friends easily," says Fay. "Though we seem, forever, to have tried."

That's true, Fay dearest. But you can't blame a gal for tryin'.

"What?" says Fay, "What was that?"

Who the hell is she talking to? Ted finds her odder than ever. But tonight he'll ignore anything for a little companionship. He does, well, have a yet odder soft spot for her.

"Do you climb trees?"

This is too much. Ted moves away, feels a bit dizzy, feels

-- what's the word? -- ah yes, 'creeped out'.

"Sure I climb trees. I just said so, didn't I? You got a short memory old girl."

"We even learned to type."

"What's all this 'we' shit, Fay?"

Ted is usually a perfect gentleman, at least very well-behaved. But he's restless with drink and Fay's silly games so "Big deal," he says, "Big fucking deal."

Can't you see she's hurting, hairy Teddy? Evening shadows are fallin' fast.

"It was easy to learn where all the typewriter keys were without looking," says Fay, "And we employed *all* our fingers. Hunting and pecking wasn't for us. We were letter-perfect. Our technique was so advanced we were asked to teach a typing class. Have you never been asked to teach typing?"

"No. And neither have you."

"Imagine! Asked to teach typing at an evening school where novels are feverishly encouraged!"

What?!

"See our fingers?"

Fay thrusts out her hand, spreads her fingers fetchingly. "Such healthy nails?! See how red they are! We've been given a new lease of life."

Not quite dear. Let me be the judge.

"Nobody puts curses on Ritterhouse Fay! Our nails were always very, very red though we never used nail paint. No one believed us. They could not believe that our nails were so naturally red, so abundantly healthy."

Ted has removed his feet from the coffee table, begun to put on his shoes. This is too much. He's tired, wants to go home to bed. Fuck a fuck tonight. Not with this loony, anyhow -- even though his soft spot has now hardened.

"What would you say to a new pair of socks, Mr Kong? It's all I can afford. I've lost my money. All of it. I'm ruined. Mr Ammari rang tonight. He is ruined too. We put it all in the South Pole."

So the money *was* cursed, wasn't it Fay? Dotty old Taylor was correct (I could have told you that). Now the money has flown like that carpet that lies snug and secure in the luxurious desert compound of some excessively wealthy individual. Or are you lying, love, about your lost lucre? My, my! I should know *without* asking but I'm so...tired. I'm weary, worn-out, fatigued, bushed, fagged, drained, done-in, whacked, dead on my so-called *feet*.

"The bedroom is this way," murmurs Fay. That phrase – again it sticks in her head. Why must she always say it? Why can't they simply follow her? They do -- when she pays them. Otherwise it is always on some sticky, beer-stained floor or in the back of a car or amongst thorny bushes in various parks or in alleys against a cold wall or in stuffy, airless cupboards -- never, well, *almost* never in a proper bedroom, some comfortably conservative coital venue. Not, that is, until she became Fabulous Fragment Fay. Poor Mabel Hawkins would have understood in spades. "The bedroom's..." repeats Fay and gestures, "the bedroom is this way."

Fay throws open her sable, lightning flashes at my beck, reveals inviting curves; those well-shaped breasts and flat tummy and creamy, full, but not *too* full thighs and, ach yes! her splendid calves. And that skin! Such skin! Her body is indeed a temple -- so why must she have been shagged everywhere but in a proper bedroom on a proper bed?! Is this some private purgatory?

I know.

"The bedroom's this way," she repeats, beseeches, entreats, implores. "The bedroom is *this* way."

Fay has Ted's attention, what's left of it after a pint of whisky and a couple of down-market joints. He rises from the sofa. "I could use another pair of socks, Fay."

Opening her sumptuous sable wider, Fay envelops the swaying, rampant Ted, the nearest she'll ever get to Love. And all she'd ever really wanted was a hug. Or a kiss. And, of course, a little lifelong devotion.

Sweet Jesus! Who must she fuck for a hug or a kiss?! She only wants to be cuddled!

Know the feeling, m'dears?

Ted's briefs fall and tangle in his dropped trousers round his ankles. He is hard and moist against her as she leads him, perforce haltingly, towards her bedroom. "Darling," she whispers, "Honey," she sighs, "Sugar. The bedroom is this way."

Hairy Tipsy Teddy is entranced. And just a bit in love.

Yeah. Sure.

63

"She says it's very important. But only a few minutes, please. And no smoking, Ms Lambert. We're very encouraged by this sudden turn for the better. It's a miracle."

Think again, sister.

"Are we alone?" rasps Taylor, ineffably frail but suspicious and sans oxygen mask. Rita sits.

"Yes, love."

"Smooch," whispers Taylor, one eye oddly askew.

"Smooch to you too, love."

"The cards, Rita, Oscar Taylor's postcards...my Oscar's postcards."

Taylor pauses, exhausted, gathers her breath, tries to move a hand for emphasis, can't, continues very slowly, "The cards I smooch, kiss. The hearts and arrows...in the red...carry-bag."

Taylor's white, furrowed face sags, merges into the pillow behind it.

"Yes, love?"

"Four stamps."

Taylor's eyes are closed now. "Four stamps," she whispers, "They always got four stamps on 'em...four stamps, two below two."

Taylor painfully gathers breath. "Hearts and arrows always got...four stamps on 'em."

"Yes, love?"

"Big money. I steam off the four stamps..."

Taylor hesitates, her eyes wander.

"Yes, love?"

"Don't interrupt..."

"Sorry, love."

"Under the four stamps...one stamp...big money... Only on the smooch cards."

Now don't tell me this surprises you, m'dears. It's as clichéd as a tropical sunset -- and I've seen my share of 'em. But it *serves*. This is only a bleedin' game, you know, though admittedly, a game of quasi-cosmic, if not comic, proportions. Square by alien square we march to our respective fates directed by we know not what. Ach!

But it is a game played by the gods. Pardon my hubris, honey.

Taylor shudders, gasps for breath, attempts to summon more. Rita snatches up the oxygen mask, offers it but Taylor waves it away, motions her closer, grips her hand. "I separate the… smooch cards," she whispers hardly audible, "They're in the red carry-bag on the back of my chair…there's five more bags, all of 'em red…in my closet where the rug was… the rug the witch took...I always use red bags for the smooch cards."

Taylor's breathing is harder, more laboured.

This is tough, m'dears, for both of us.

"Take it slowly, love."

Rita squeezes her hand.

"Can't take it slow…ain't got much time."

Taylor hasn't been so lucid in years. It's a gift of God...or something. Rita is a life-saver. Well. Perhaps not.

"Oscar Taylor sends 'em to me. Oscar Taylor, me errant husband."

Credit, at last, where credit *is* due!

"He's looked after me all these years, silly sod."

Watch it, lovey!

"But he got ahead of me, bless him. I ain't had to sell no stamps for donkey's years."

But you could have, my dear. You could have lived like a queen.

"What?" whispers Taylor and sighs, "What was that?"

"I said nothing, love," replies Rita.

Then Taylor knows. Knows it all. She shuts her eyes for a moment, conserves what little strength she's got, revels in her revelation. Remembers so many things; remembers Fay, as a small child, playing on the steps of Number 13. What a beautiful, loving child she was. Gentle. Gentle in every way. Loving. Trusting. An angel. What happened? She disappeared. Ah, yes. The gypsies carried her off. Yes. Them gypsies. But now... *Now* she is a monster! A rose decayed smells worse than a weed! Fay, the rotten rose... Then it is gone -- this spotty (*utterly inaccurate*) past is obscured by a heavy, mauve haze. Mauve was tiny Fay's favourite colour. Whatever happened to tiny Fay? Oh yes. Gypsies. Then it is all a blank. A *total* blank.

I could take it from there. But won't. The shadows grow long, ever longer, darker. The game-squares can be numbered on one so-called *hand*.

But *you* must continue, old love. The subject at hand is rare stamps.

"The smooch cards are for you, darlin'...you're slow but I like you...take my posies too...I won't be comin' back."

"Yes you will, love. You will."

"I told you, you was slow. You got my key. Take 'em now... Tonight. Before the witch gets 'em."

"Please, love, I know you'll --"

"Take them cards, damn you... the witch wants 'em. She needs 'em now. She's skint! Oscar told me! She's wiped out! Flat broke!"

Mrs Taylor attempts to pull herself up but falls back, puffing and white-faced. "Take the cards, Rita Lambert. Please...tonight.... now. Promise."

"Promise."

Taylor gropes for Rita's other hand, finds it, holds both for a moment as tight as she can while her life flies before her in a bewildering blur. "You're a good girl...like little Fay was."

Taylor's head shrinks back into her pillow, her eyes close and soon her mouth makes those familiar little flapping noises. Rita thinks of the time she's wasted, of her self-imposed exile from life. Of her bitterness. She will never waste time again. Never.

But nothing can prepare you for the sodding abyss. Ask me, Rita-writer, I *live* there.

Rita contemplates the young Fay for a moment, what Fay might have been, the innocent child Fay was. Rita feels more than a tinge of guilt and walks slowly to the door, finds Ian outside.

Fay's gift to you, m'dear, when all is said and done.

"Can I stay with you, darling?" asks Rita, "for the duration?"

Fay lies abandoned on her rumpled bed. She was simply too spooky for our lickety-split satiated Teddy to linger. Rain pounds the window. A crash of thunder wakens her. She sits up, frightened. "Mr Kong?" she cries. "Mr Kong, where are you, *darling*?"

She looks about the room, panicked. "Mr Kong?! Teddy?!

Weep for her m'dears. There, but for some happy accident of fate, go you. Or perhaps no happy accident has intervened on your behalf? In that case, weep for yourself, for I shan't. And mind the squares. Those treacherous last few squares. They can lead anywhere.

Fay sees Ted's sodden socks at the foot of her bed. "Teddy?" she whispers, struggling into her fine red kimono, "Teddy?"

She leaps from the bed, stops, squeezes both temples between her palms, attempts to squash away the screaming voices -- so many voices! But one voice rises above the rest: "She's not dead yet! She's not dead yet!"

Fay throws her sable over the kimono, steps into her highest heels, grabs her bag and slams out, down the stairs, out the door, into the driving rain. "Stop!" she screams, "Stop!" and leaps in front of a taxi that screeches to a halt only inches from her. "Christ!" shouts the driver, "What the hell do you think you're doin'?!"

"Do you know what time it is?!" asks the irate nurse, looking up from her novel, then blinking wide at Fay's magnificent though wet sable.

"She's our Granny."

"She's taken a turn for the worse, love," says the nurse, still eyeing Fay's wonderful, damp fur, "She seemed to be improving. We were quite hopeful."

"There's one! Hanging on the chair, love," whispers Rita, "She says the others are in the closet. They're red."

"Which closet? Jesus! Who turned off the electricity?"

"There's a paraffin lamp by the closet door. I've seen her use it. Matches too. Right beside it."

"Can't see a damn thing. We should have brought a torch."

"To the right I think."

A flash of lightning illuminates the room.

"Over there, darling!"

"Ah!" says Ian and strikes a match. Rita twists off the lamp's chimney and he lights the wick. In the dim light Rita makes her way to the red carry-bag hanging on Taylor's chair, fetches it.

"Here they are," says Ian from the closet, "Yes, five of 'em. Right by the door."

"Good. Look, darling, there's more on the kitchen floor." Rita gathers up the few scattered hearts-and-arrow cards, cries "Let's get the hell out of here. I'll tell Mrs Taylor tomorrow. Turn out the lamp, love."

On and on she drones. Ach! It's positively mesmerising: "Every conceivable modern convenience, Granny. Plus a splendid, glassed-in window box with vented sides so you can air your geraniums. We'll build a charming, hand-painted cupboard in your stunning, open-plan kitchen. A cupboard tailor-made for your Bovril cubes will dispense them automatically. (But where's the money coming from, liar!) We'll have toast together every morning. We'll extort milk too, from that mean old milkman. There's only us now, Granny. There's only us and we're deserted. Orphans of the storm. Nobody loves us."

Speak for yourself, darling Fay -- love's own prosopopoeia.

"Be gone!" cries Fay, "Be gone thou impious spirit!"

Rita and Ian rush through the rain down the steps of Number 13; Ian with the red carry-bags, Rita with a small suitcase. They climb into Ian's car and in a tearing screech are away through the driving rain.

"I have a confession," says Fay, "I was not pregnant by Bill."

Taylor stirs slightly in her sleep, spittle dribbles from the corner of her mouth. Fay deftly, tenderly, dabs it away with a lovely silk hanky. "I thought once I might be pregnant, dear. I wished for it, not even knowing who daddy might be. I never became a Mummy. A hostess, yes. But never a Mummy, Granny. I swear to you that all I sold was kisses and all I ever wanted was hugs. Hostesses who sell only kisses are soon discovered and forced to dispense or depart. I was a good girl so I departed. I opted for travel.

Excellent, darling, that's the script. Follow it and there's hope for you yet.

"My odyssey took me from job to job (and square to square!) and acquainted me with the ways of the world. I met many people over many years who left me as cold as a fish."

Fay unclasps her little jewelled fish and dangles it before Taylor's sightless eyes, places it around Taylor's neck. "A gift from a deceased admirer who recognized my...infinite variety, and rewarded me for it."

Huzzah!

Fay sighs heavenward from whence help *never* comes, silly cow. "I'm broke, Granny Taylor."

Taylor snorts the very tiniest of snorts. Nothing is happening under half-closed eyelids.

"I'm skint but I've already paid your hospital, Granny. And then some. This private room is yours for eternity.

Lawdy! Hardly *eternity*, Missy Fay.

"The medical world is at your feet. Paid in advance by an endowment. You have been on my gift list since time out of mind.

Wasn't I clever, Granny?"

Me too. I never neglect solemn obligations.

Mrs Taylor stirs again, moans.

"Granny? Granny?" whispers Fay who moves close, takes her hand. "Granny, do you love me?"

Taylor sighs. Fay waits expectantly. "Rita lies, Granny, don't listen to her. You're *my* Granny, not hers."

One of Taylor's eyes flutters cloudily to life. "Rita?" she mumbles, "Rita?"

"Yes."

"Rita, get the cards. Get the smoochies."

"Cards? Smoochies?" asks Fay, "Smoochies?"

"Postcards...Postcards, my darlin', my honey, my sugar…stamps under stamps…big money."

"Stamps under stamps?" asks Fay, still warming to Granny Taylor's, 'darlin', honey, sugar'. Terms of endearment so richly deserved but so seldom served up!

"Steam 'em off, Rita. They're for you…priceless stamps under stamps…big money."

Big money, *priceless*, thinks Fay, -- the ruined Fay whose flighty fortune flew. Really! How does one lose four billion pounds? Apparently quite easily in the Antarctic -- if the money's cursed. If ancient spells have been chanted. If gypsy-witches have careened around bonfires. If angels have misbehaved and been cast down. If perfect children have been abused. Just the usual things, darlings, trust me, this is not irony.

Big money! Thinks Fay, it's Fay's money. Rightfully hers! Taylor is *her* Granny, and by God she's earned it!

"Valuable stamps on all those cards?" asks Fay, taking Taylor's hand, clasping it so hard the old lady's fingers turn yet bluer.

"No, stupid," spits Taylor, suddenly animated.

"I am not *stupid*!"

"Only the… smooch cards..."

Taylor's breath comes in short stabbing gasps. "Signed with hearts and arrows...in the red bag...over the back of my chair...five more bags in the rug closet...the witch closet...big money..."

Red carry-bag?! That very bag! That red, plastic bag that swung to and fro over Fay's head as she shagged crooked-grin on the cushions in Granny's half destroyed, half remembered room. Five more red bags in the closet? Ach, yes! She had seen them stacked against her miracle rug, her cur-sed carpet, that tragically wasted resource that slipped through her so-called fingers.

But how common, m'dears, how brutally common it is to squander our advantages.

She had touched the stuffed full carry-bags, *touched* them! They had tingled under her fingers. Why hadn't she known then? Now they will save her from ruin!

A soupçon of reinvigorating melodrama, eh? Lovely stuff!

Granny is whispering something. Listen, Fay. Listen!

"What?" says Fay.

I said shut up and listen! It's your last chance! She thinks you're Rita, you idiot! Listen!

"Get the cards, Rita...before the witch gets 'em."

Fay leans in close. "The witch, Granny? The witch?"

With her last breath Mrs Taylor murmurs:

"Fay. The witch. The witch who stole my baby."

"But *I'm* your baby, Granny!" Fay, stung, draws sharply back from the old woman. Taylor's unblinking stare glazes over like *a fish out of water.*

"What?" whispers Fay, "What was that? Fish what?"

She searches in vain for the source. Not to be sidetracked by you know who, Fay cries "I shall be rich again!" to Taylor's sheet swaddled, shrunken shape.

"Rich again!" whoops Fay, "If I cannot find love, I shall have riches! Me so happy me want to cry!"

The oxygen mask beside Taylor's spittle-dribbled pillow hisses. Fay stares at Granny Taylor for a moment, feels, well, darlings, how about: 'oddly diminished'? Will that do? In any case, Fay yanks the little jewelled fish from Taylor's neck, snapping its fine gold chain. She presses the call button, hurries from the hospital room – note, m'dears: now dry-eyed. Exceedingly dry-eyed.

64

"You're the one who blubbers, ain't you?!" screams Taylor in Fay's head. "Mr LaFarge snuffed it, has he?"

"You mean the former tenant?" replies Fay to Taylor's fierce, fluttering phantom.

"Died, has he?"

"I don't know."

"He ain't still there, is he? You ain't livin' in sin?"

"Unfortunately not. There's only me. And my house burned down."

The image vanishes as Fay lights the paraffin lamp with the matches she finds (ever so conveniently) beside it -- where Ian had left them. She rips the tarpaulin from Taylor's furniture, sees a few postcards on the table but no red plastic bag. She shuffles through the cards, finds no hearts, no arrows, slumps there, stymied, her own voice ringing in her ears:

"My friends. My dear, dear friends..."

Then, suddenly, here is Rita, shimmering in the gloom of this devastated room, clear as the crystal image on a shiny new L.E.D. telly. Thoroughly modern monster, that's me, m'dears.

"…our special evening is marred by an absence," continues Fay, "That of the dear Mrs Taylor. She of the heart-shaped postcards..."

Why hadn't she known?! Fay brushes the remaining cards to the floor, screams "Where are they then?! Where are my stamps?! *My* stamps!"

Mr Abdullah Shamaly whispers into Fay's ear "My dearest Fay. I wish to marry you."

"You have a wife."

"You will be another wife."

"I'll need a house..."

Fay twists, does an about face, wild eyed, scrambling for red plastic -- like the bags Granny had carried home from Tesco's – not the ordinary bags but special promotion bags, yes those *red* bags! "Where are they?! Where are they now?!"

"You enchant me. You astonish and enchant me."

It's Shamaly again, smiling at her, waving over his shoulder as he leaves. "I'm a bit of a witch!" cries Fay after him, "The bedroom is this way!"

Her feet ache! That terrible tugging at them! That tugging towards the final square! *Need* it be so painful?

Why ever not, my lovely?

Fay fumbles through the stack of postcards, picks up one, can scarcely read it through tears. Those vain tears we discussed earlier. Those pointless tears that everyone will insist upon shedding. They've come back.

> Istanbul, April 21, 1946
> Chappie in the bazaar tried to sell me some phony coins. I said: Are they authentic? He said: Why not? I said, I'll have that nice rug instead, the shimmery one, the one that keeps wiggling off your rug rack.
> Fondly, Oscar

There is no heart, no arrow on this card. I know why. So should you if you've been paying attention!

Fay does not bother to acknowledge my multi-decibel remark, frowns and drops the heartless, arrowless and sadly *rare-stampless* card to the floor.

All the cards are heartless, Fay, depending upon how one looks at it, but more about that later.

"Where the dickens is that red plastic carry-bag?!" cries Fay, wrongly directing herself at a deformed phantom inching up a soiled wall in the kitchen. About which I could give you every detail -- from water stained, bulging floorboards under the sink to a deep Griffin's claw-scratch on the ancient fridge just to the left of the door handle, and much more -- but I shan't. Damn me, but I shan't!

"I have brought you a small token of..." whispers Shamaly into Fay's ear. She jerks her head sideways. "Abdullah!" she cries, "Darling? The bedroom is this way!"

Her hand leaps to the little jewelled fish in her furry sable pocket, caresses it. "How apt," she whispers to herself, "A little fish out of water. Like me. Stranded high and dry in a thirsty land where no water is."

If my fish motiv grows somewhat thin. It's not completely my fault. The best laid plans, you know...

Fay whirls round.

"Abdullah? Honey? Sugar?" she implores *me* though she sees

me not.

"Five more bags in the closet!" rants Taylor's ghost in Fay's head.

"What?" whimpers Fay. "What did you say, Granny?"

"Big money!" shrieks Taylor, in the closet! The witch closet!"

Fay turns so quickly she again tumbles backward over Granny's chair.

This is all quite cunningly choreographed, darlings, with clever, engraved diagrams and everything – though the light of my several moons grows dimmer by the moment.

Fay scrambles to her knees. "Granny, I'm so sorry. So sorry you're ill."

She jumps up, takes the paraffin lamp from its table, lifts the sturdy (Note, please: STURDY) hinged bolt from the closet door and enters.

"I won't be a moment, love," says Rita. "Sorry to bring you all the way back but..."

Ian takes her hand. "I know."

"I couldn't leave them alone in this house."

Rita begins to cry (more *tears*, m'dears?!). A new life is wonderful but frightening too -- what if things don't work out?

Ian hands Rita his flashlight.

I hum an old favourite, 'You Were Meant For Me' to entertain our, temporarily disengaging aging lovers.

After a moment Rita says "I love you," leaps from the car, starts up the steps of Number 13 for the last time.

The very last time, my dears upon whom I dote.

"A minute, darling, only one minute," she calls to Ian who blows her a kiss.

Thunder rumbles closer. That undecided storm has changed tack, returns at my command.

As Rita enters the house, her telephone rings. She hastily unlocks her door and answers it, half expecting, half dreading to hear Fay, the breather.

"Hello?... speaking... I'm so sorry..."

Rita's hand finds a table top for support. "She has no next of kin...I mean we don't know where he is...Yes nurse...Yes, nurse... Thank you for being so kind to her..."

And thank *you*, Rita. My mother thanks you, my father thanks you, my sister thanks you, and I thank you. Merci mille fois! Pardon my French, m'dears.

Fay is on her knees, sable soughing (love that! -- anything to do with a sable coat, that's me!), lighted lamp beside her, in the witch closet. Her fingers fly through the stacks of old newspapers. Where are the red bags?! Red plastic bags?! That stalking black cat appears from nowhere, purrs, nuzzles into damp sable. Fay stops. Listens, turns her head slowly. Her superb hearing is still intact and the walls and floors of Her House remain, where not glass, at least paper.

Reprise: And paper burns *so* brightly.

"What?" says Fay, "What was that?"

I chuckle a perfect chuckle of relief. Relief that Fay's *searing* saga, its task nearly accomplished (give us a min) surges towards solution. Then I'll rest for a time -- will it be minutes? Eons?

Fay listens. Someone is coming up the stairs. It must be Rita! Only Rita has a key now!

Moving the glowing lamp aside, Fay crouches up from the floor, softly pulls the closet door shut. That heavy, hinged bolt (much noted, admired, and feared by those who suspect it's secret – which should include you, m'dears!) drops and engages securely with a completely crucial clunk. "I'll think about that later," says Fay to One-Life, "I'm prepared for any eventuality."

Think again, ducky.

Rita pauses in Taylor's door. Does she smell burning paraffin? Yes. She and Ian had used the lamp a few minutes before. In the dark she does not note the lamp is gone (and we know where, do we not m'dears?). With Ian's flashlight Rita finds Mrs Taylor's toppled geraniums where they fell when Fay shot up, attacked her.

Strange that geraniums could mean so much to Rita. Rita who has always hated flowers -- even after performances. Could never think why. Now she's in love with them; two pots of straggly geraniums. Funny old world, ain't it Rita? First you're perched, shivering, adjacent to oblivion then you're a published writer with a lover and, well, alternatives. You're a lot nicer too, love! Not that sour, aging slag of only a few months ago. A lot has happened between and you can't begin to understand it, can you? You haven't a clue.

Well, dear, let's face it, neither do I.

"Hush" whispers Fay, "she'll hear you!"

But she hasn't. Rita departs the newly deceased Mrs Taylor's vandalized flat with one wilting geranium under each arm.

65

The moment Rita is gone, Fay's task, though she knows it not (nor do you, m'dears), is complete and she reaches for the closet latch -- Ach! There *is* no closet latch inside! She slams her shoulder against the door. One-Life hisses and cowers in the corner growling an extraordinarily menacing growl, huddled beneath that oddly glyphed, thatched shrine mounted on its knobby, ebony legs. How could Fay have missed that manqué manger when she absconded with the fabulously fragmented rug? I left clues everywhere. But Fay's clarity came and went too. Like Taylor's. The shrine itself, of course, has grown to twice its size so should I not pardon her this omission? I shall think upon it.

I have thought upon it. Nay! N-nay, n-nay, n-nay!

Fay remembers that shrine. She'd played with it during the month when Granny Taylor had fostered her, after the fire, during the time that Granny, the witch-dilettante, had taught Fay all those wonderful spells. Then they took Fay away again.

Who did? A coven? A coven under the auspices of the local authorities? They were always taking Fay away -- somebody was; taking her away, dragging her away, saying she set fires. Darlings, Fay *was* fires!

If only she'd remembered those glorious stories Granny had told her, those wondrous spells, she wouldn't be where she is now; locked in a closet with Crazy Cat who thinks it can fly -- has tried often enough, leapt between potted trees into the ether, plummeted, with lives to spare. But now that smelly cat has only one life left. Precisely like our Ritterhouse Fay who lost her other eight in hideous and indescribable ways long before you met her. But unlike One-life, Fay could fly. Did. Once. Forgot how. When angels forget how to fly, they fall. Ask Fay. Angels must fly or fall, mustn't they, Fay? You were born in fire, weren't you? You had to fly! Flee, or die.

Or so it seems to my darling prosopopoeia. So it SEEMS.

Fay slams her shoulder against the closet door again and again. For a paper house devoid (almost) of secrets, the doors at least, seem curiously intact. Fay sets the paraffin lamp on a dusty shelf, spies an ancient letter-opener on a stack of newspapers, attempts to slide it between door and frame to lift that sturdy, engaged bolt.

No luck. "When have I ever been lucky?!" she cries.

All that lucre, love! Ach! That's luck! But it's gone -- was cursed, like you and that fabulous floor mat. Now it's gone. That's *bad* luck. But luck all the same.

"No," cries Fay, "Please!" to her entrapper, the tiny, previously hesitant closet that is now alive with racing shadows that tilt the floor this way, m'dears, and that way -- tilt amongst the yellowing, tinder-dry stacks of newspapers.

Poor Fay. Poor Ritterhouse Fay. Her life is a shattering serial of loss. Lost parents, in a fire for which she may have been complicit; lost sister -- yes, she had a sister who climbed trees; a sister who was murdered (ask her!); lost friends; virginity gone before she knew what virginity was -- to Uncle Oscar. Oscar? (Titter!) That devil!

Titter! Love has many faces.

But there's more where that came from: Lost Granny; lost baby, a miscarriage, or was it two or was it three? Not Bill's babies of course but a baby is a baby is a baby, isn't it, Fay -- even a baby with two tiny horns, a tail and cloven feet?

Loss of freedom. Now there's something to conjure with. Incarceration is no picnic. Incarceration both private and public. The private came first, mother beat her (Love has *many* faces), locked her in a closet, fed her through a hatch in the door – 'God made me do it' screamed Mummy. OR SO IT SEEMS TO FAY.

And oddly, m'dears, so *very* oddly, those tinder-dry newspapers reflect specifically, nay, *confirm* the multifarious events framing this fantastical, thoroughly questionable life experience of The Ritterhouse Fay:

**TREE-CLIMBING WOMAN BRUTALLY BEATEN
BY FEMALE LOVER, HUNG IN TREE TO DIE!**

**WHOLE FAMILY DIES
IN FLAMING HOUSE!**

**CHILD EATEN ALIVE
BY KILLER-FUNGUS!**

**CHILD HELD CAPTIVE,
FED THRU SLOT IN DOOR FOR
DECADES BY MAD MOTHER!**

To quote only a few. (Love has a *multitude* of faces) N'est-ce pas, Fay? N'est-ce pas?!

"You never taught me French," moans Fay, "You never taught me!"

I never learnt myself, peaches. But who were those people, Fay?! Gypsies? Who were they who stole you away from Granny? And those fires! The hosed high-pressure water! Ach! It was firemen! Firemen come to extinguish! Oh, the cockroaches, the putrid food and the cold, grey walls! Firemen, no matter how well-intentioned, couldn't extinguish that. *That* lived in your head, darling. There was no easy access to *that*. No wonder you never knew whether you were coming or going. You were always coming, always going. Poor Fay. Poor Ritterhouse Fay. OR SO IT SEEMS TO YOU.

Have a heart, m'dears. It is not her fault. It is our fault, ain't it? Every Jack 'n' Jill of us.

I'm playing with you, my dozy dears.

Fay throws herself against the door again, the lamp shudders. One-life snarls, can't get away! Trapped like Fay! Fay the soulless, the scavenger of other people's substance: their kettles, the contents of their fridges, their furniture, their black silk scarf, their rug! Their pasts. Now we're getting there.

But are not Fay's own horrors enough to fill her emptiness, an arid plain that aches for dimpled darlings not direst demons? Who could hate a helpless and perfect child? *Who*? Apparently many could. Did. If anybody deserves Taylor's smooch-stamps and their big money, Fay does. Oscar Taylor, one among many, (some might say) owes her plenty!

For shame, Uncle Oscar! You devil!

Titter. Titter-titter-titter. Am I too, taking leave of our senses?

Why had Fay come back to Number 13? To do good? To wreck vengeance? To lord it over the others from on high? -- she *did* occupy that topmost flat. To find her granny? To find love again? What an odd place to find love, dear, in a houseful of hostile strangers -- with the exception, of course, of the good Nelly who was herself finally, irretrievably alienated.

Or was it only a sentimental journey, Fay, to the place in which you'd spent one month so many years before?

No. None of the above. NONE-OF-THE-ABOVE-NONE-OF-THE-ABOVE (shriek I)!

The paraffin lamp seems to fall from the shelf in slow motion, drenching and instantly setting afire the thatch-roofed witch's shrine -- so like a manger -- that flares up unnaturally. Fay falls back in horror. The flames explode around her, lick greedily at the yellowing piles of oh-so-combustible newspapers and cardboard boxes. And papyrus, darlings, enough papyrus to pacify a finicky pharaoh!

Alas! Fay might easily have smothered the flames with that wonderful carpet – never mind its curse. But it may as well have been in the middle east, m'dears. In fact, was. But what's this? Ach! That flamin' rug is burnin' too. How did the fire begin? Somewhere in that Midas of a sheik's palace? Or in the precious rug itself, in its shimmering peripatetic, now puling pile? Ask no questions, you'll get no lies. We've had enough already.

If you choose to label them so.

Poor Fay. If she'd had in her hand that high pressure water hose those firemen-monsters used to flatten her she might have doused these terrible flames. Or had she, just now, remembered Granny Taylor's spell -- "Darling, honey, sugar" (plus the inversion, of course).

Inversion. Such a cosy word for us cosmic queens.

Fay! Listen! A hank of Mabel Hawkins' hair-of-hag yet inhabits your singeing sable pocket. Poor Mabel was a major character in your drama. Mabel was crucial, can still serve you, save you. You never took her seriously though she was strewn with clues. I wasn't playing about. Mabel Hawkins was no lark. Nor was that innocent scholar and his perspiring, flame retardant arse. Ach! How often we neglect the curious strangers who pepper our lives! But alas for you! It is too hot to think *now*, let alone conjure. It's all your fault! No, of course it ain't. Only here and there, here and there. When fatuous free-will reared its ravenous, rattled head, upset the plans of mice and men.

The flames move closer, ever hotter. Had Fay her angel's wings she would fly from this inferno. No, love, cast-down angels cannot fly, nor can witches who have abandoned their brooms (or forgotten where they were). Nor even, us *ordinary* folks.

Poor One-Life has perished -- just now -- in a super-heated hairy puff at Fay's feet. Now Fay's shoes, fine, gold-buckled, Blahnik confections, are alight and, Ach! There goes Mabel's hank! Ach! Ach! And Ach yet again!

Oh woe is us! Here is my Ritterhouse Fay, my darling prosopopoeia, on the blazing floor of her *phoenix's nest* of a closet, not as burnt as she might be, will be, gazing at the starry now unclouded sky, as the roof and upper floor of Her House have burnt away.

Ashes and sparks dance crazily up to join those stars and from very much afar comes a voice -- no *stranger!* -- that comforts.

Me! I am that voice:

You were never a witch, Fay, nor an angel cast down. All that you are, love, is an incendiary spell. *My* spell. A game. My goodness, 'spel', in Swedish, *is* game!

My Ritterhouse Fay is a recipe of longings that weren't even her own. All the things you thought you were, Ritterhouse Fay, are false, nil, zilch, squat. You never existed before we pranced around the fire in which you were (inexorably) born, yet again. How could you have had a soul? Do you think that souls change partners like line dancers in the Virginia Reel?

Fay's fur flares into a million micro-explosions. Fay glows, blisters and melts into the burning floorboards like super-heated bacon fat. All, right at the centre, *I emphasize,* of the very last square of our game.

At the front of this burning house, this fire-storm, this whining inferno, directly below what is left of the roof, an ornate moulding twists in the searing heat, reveals engraving on a blackening bronze plate beneath: "Ritter House" it reads for an instant, then falls away into all-consuming flames.

The rain has stopped and thunder rumbles, faint, over some far side of London -- miles from Pimlico. Rita, smug, snug (dare I say it -- as a rug) in Ian's car, holds tight his big warm hand. In Rita's other hand is a postcard from a red plastic bag, one of six red plastic bags -- hers and Ian's financial future is secure.

So too would have been the financial futures of Hugh and Jenny and Nelly and Bill and Big Hairy Ted and Granny Taylor -- had she survived -- and Mabel Hawkins of all people, and Chauffy, as well as crooked-grin, pointed-grin, and that unfortunate scholar whose sweat might have been infernally handy; And the misused masseuse and miffed manicurist and the harried hairdresser and Bill's young son and his school for disadvantaged children and the kind waiter and even the mauve-uniformed young men who moved Fay's worldly goods, including that kettle, from place to place to place -- all would have profited beyond, pardon my cliché, their wildest dreams.

For my rebellious prosopopoeia had temporarily escaped me, leapt right off our game table, spoken to her solicitor, done her legal homework on an enchanting night as lucid as deluded Mrs Taylor ever experienced in extreme clarity. All of these named would have inherited several hundred millions apiece had not Fay's scheme been foiled by a maverick Antarctic iceberg – but what is an iceberg but frozen water and water douses flames (you can't fight City Hall, can you, m'dears?). Read Fay's defunct Last Will and Testament. *If you can find it!*

But all this money was cursed. These innocents are clearly better off, aren't they, without those cursed and odious pounds? Who wouldn't be? And they escaped with their lives.

You decide. Or ask them, m'dears, all of them. Just to be certain. *If you can find them.*

So here sits Rita, speeding away from the scene of the crimes -- crimes? Well, hardly. Imagine Number 13 had Fay never materialised:

Flat 1: Rita, lonely, embittered, clad in shiny-bottomed jodhpurs (jodhpurs?!), uninspired, semi-alcoholic and teetering at the edge of invisibility (her very own words) beside her ancient typewriter.

Flat 2: Nelly, cripplingly shy, *dishevelled* beyond recall, but kind, and longing, longing, positively resonating, m'dears, for love! (Like Fay). Longing. Longing. World without end, Amen.

Flat 3: Mrs *Oscar* Taylor, barmy, deserted though wealthy as Midas, plagued by terminally fractured fantasies of a plundered infant (she'd got it *all* wrong); arthritic wrists and no one to air her daisies or was it geraniums? Plus she had an imagination as big as all outdoors. Her time, in any case was exceedingly nigh (I definitely have an inside track on this one, m'dears).

Flat 4: Hugh and Jenny: together and not, vaguely discontent and grinding away at boring jobs (Now they're part of an expatriate, delicious ménage a trois soon to become a ménage a quattre -- when Jenny sends for Alicia who is an excellent illustrator). A proper fairy tale to leaven the intermittently loutish behaviour of our multi-purpose, multi-perplexed, protagonist prosopopoeia.

Flat 5: Bill, almost destroyed by a failed marriage and the heartache of his mentally challenged son, could have harmed himself. *Would* have. Trust me!

Ach! How like all of us. We fight our destinies, do we not, mercifully not knowing that it is largely futile. How much easier to just lie down and be had. Don't knock it if you ain't tried it.

Fay *tried* so hard to be good! But darlings, I, for the most part, simply wouldn't let her -- gave her too much negative baggage, too many alternate pasts (too many swappable squares on our boardgame). And, I mean, m'dears, the *crowds* that milled about in her dear, ditzy, dazzled head!

I knew. *You* didn't.

Incidentally, m'dears, I was one of that "gypsy" coven, so was Sarah Taylor -- there were seven of us (one for every coloured pen in Fay's batty rubber-banded bundle) -- who created Ritterhouse Fay, The Spell. However, my darlings, I am the chief culprit (and excessively partial to sensible shoes, tweed skirts *and* hounds).

Spells are more common than you think. Open your eyes. Look around you. Particularly if two and two do not quite equal four. In fact, they never do, m'dears. Two and two *never* equal four. Particularly here, beyond Pluto. Where we all, every mother's son and daughter of us, live.

I'm a fallen angel and a 'resident ghost' as well. I patterned The Fay very much after me. Did not the gods create mankind in their own image and for their own amusement? Mais certainement!

Of course, I couldn't give the poor cow a soul. Only The Gods can do that. But she did all right without one. Better than most of you, I daresay, considering the obstacles I placed before her, behind her, above and inside her. She even had the beginnings of a sense of humour.

We had a bit of fun with The Fay, our cyber-pet. Though my colleagues couldn't resist a bit of mischief -- I mean, darlings! -- roly-poly floors? Shifty shadows? Glyph-engraved salvers? Pulsating pornographic walls? Sudden sequoias?! *Honestly*!

In any case, here sits Rita, having not the vaguest idea of any of the above (nor should she). She is comfortably ensconced in her lover's car, reading the postcard in her hand as a clanging fire-engine, sirens blaring, charges past from the opposite direction.

Déjà vu, mes enfants?

Singapore, March 17, 1947 (reads Rita)
Honeybunch,
It is with fire that blacksmiths iron subdue
Unto fair form, the image of their thought:
Nor without fire has any artist wrought
Gold to its utmost purity of hue.
Nay, nor unmatched phoenix lives anew
Unless she burn. *Michelangelo*

(and I couldn't agree more, m'dears!)
I worship *you* from afar,
Fondly, Oscar.

This postcard is scribbled with a heart pierced by a badly drawn arrow (draftsmanship was never my métier). Rita drops this card into its red plastic bag, turns her head, smiles fondly at Ian who would *never, ever* worship *her* from afar.

Yeah, sure.

Now smiling to herself, Rita removes her other hand from her dearest Ian's, plucks another postcard from the red plastic bag. Eagerly, though obviously with a lingering sense of loss for the only lately late Mrs Oscar Taylor, Rita begins to pick off the curled and peeling outer four stamps.

This one hearts-and-arrow stamp concealed beneath the four others, m'dears, will cover the cost of a luxurious alcoholics recovery program for both Rita and Ian (Did I mention he'd begun again to tipple? -- I never promised them a rose garden).

But what a lovely funeral service Rita will purchase for Mrs Taylor -- almost as nice as the one Fay herself had planned had she not gone skint and so inconveniently but so very necessarily, perished. As phoenixes, perforce, must.

If Rita-writer, eagerly stamp-plucking, had bothered to look behind her she would have seen a sky aglow with red that was not a sunset. Had she peered closer she might have seen a wondrously coloured, fantastical bird -- with a wingspan somewhat short of a moderately sized angel's -- soaring high above still-circling cinders.

So you see, darlings, that's why Fay came back; to get everyone out of that bleedin' Number 13! This was the task of the game! I couldn't burn down a house full of people, could I? Game or no game, I'm not a monster (though if you saw me you might not agree).

As to why Number 13, that phoenix's nest, had to burn -- well, m'dears, phoenix's nests *burn*, don't they?! (see above!) That's what phoenix's nests bloody do. Ours is not to reason why.

The beams, bricks and mortar of Number 13 knew our secret, exulted in it, cowered then complied. There was not a damned (or otherwise) thing to do. If you don't believe me, consult me later. I'll get back to you when I have a min. If you've survived.

By the way, do address me as Oscar (if you *must*). Though I am partial to 'Wilhelmina'. Anyone for bridge? Wipe that soot from your posh bottoms and do sit down. That's an order!

"What? What was that?" murmurs the singed Fay, the somewhat inchoate Fay who, fresh from fiery resurrection, squats at my right so-called *elbow*. I smile my smuggest smile, extend a so-called *hand*, bend and bark: This is where *I* came in!

So, darling, back to Square One!

There it is. The Saga of The Ritterhouse Fay, in a *nut*shell (*mind* those italics). Ritterhouse Fay, who would do anything for a hug or a kiss, anything for the redemptive power of love. Fay who was, in fact, *love* itself. Love personified. "I *was*," says Fay, "I was perfect. A lovely child. A beautiful child. Gentle. Gentle in every way. Loving. I was a loving child. Trusting. I was trusting too. Beautiful. Gentle. Loving. Trusting. I was ...an angel."

M'dears, let's face it, *weren't* we all? Would that all of us, no matter what our game, had a second chance. We usually bung it up so dreadfully the first time around. The Ritterhouse Fay is actually the very luckiest of creatures. Perhaps she'll get it right *next* time?

But, consider this, the thing is, after all is said and done, she admirably performed her *task*. Our sacrificial lambie got every last one of them there super-numerical sons o' bitches out of that bleedin' house hardly a hundred heartbeats before Armageddon – hardly thirteen bated breaths before that serial phoenix's nest burnt to the ground. That's no mean accomplishment. What have *you* done lately, me lassitudinal lovelies?

To repeat!: *No mean accomplishment*, especially *these* days. When so very many houses, yours amongst them, are burning down before your very eyes! And God knows what else! *Seriously!*

66

"No! Too depressing!" cries Janet, X-ing out everything after 'especially *these* days'. She then winds in another page, types 'The End', shouts "Voilà!" as she rips this concluding page from her typewriter, and screams Parfaitement! (Rough translation: Wow! Perfect!)

Thump, thump, thump echoes from her ceiling. "Quiet down there!" shouts old Mrs Belcher from the flat above. Janet sits back from her typewriter, more than satisfied with this absolutely *final*, alteration. She sticks a cigarette into her long, ivory holder (though she *must* stop smoking!), lights it, puffs, wonders and sips – perhaps a few too many sips today -- from that marvellously oversized snifter. And alas, she'd spilt a whole snifter on a corner of her valuable carpet – must have it professionally cleaned.

But ach! What will her fellow students say -- in that evening typing class where novels are feverishly encouraged -- when she tells them she's written one, well, a bit *more* than one? It's even a secret from her dishy old David and a marvel it *ever* got written at all considering her continuing struggle to give up nicotine, not to mention alcohol. And there was that horrid noise of building from the top floor (She must find out who this mysterious new tenant *really* is – more grist)!

Of course, her subsidiary characters may have been a trifle flat. But what's a diligent dilettante to do?! And the plot might have been tighter, was often slow, circuitous and dangly when it should have surged tightly, inexorably ahead. And she was *so* hard on poor largely innocent Fay who did not come off precisely as intended -- not quite as drop-dead beautiful as she had intended. She'll work on that after the film offers begin.

But not bad. Not bad at all for a first *feverish* effort. One learns, doesn't one? Just as one learns another language – she's plugging away, not terribly effectively, at French too. French is so impressive, so uplifting, so gravitas-friendly! Janet firmly believes in self-improvement. She might even take up acting. It would be far more glamorous than being a local branch librarian (But *change* at fifty-four?).

She drops herself into her faded cretonne sofa, sticks a cigarette into her long, ivory holder, lights and puffs. Now. Where will she send this, the first happy fruit of her latterly literary exertion, her four-part saga? To a book publisher? To Pazazz Magazine?

She ponders for a moment, rises, goes to the window, gazes out. In the shadow of that appalling semi-skyscraper opposite, the choking evening traffic, including the Red Arrow bus, late yet again, inches slowly, noisily, *gristfully* through Pimlico.

Janet sniffs. "Do I smell smoke? Is that *smoke*?!" She smiles. "Yes. Smoke. But *only* from my cigarette," she laughs.

Yeah, sure.

CPSIA information can be obtained at www.ICGtesting.com
Printed in the USA
265825BV00001B/107/P